ABOUT THE AUTHOR

When *USA Today* bestselling author Alissa Callen isn't writing, she plays traffic controller to four children, three dogs, two horses and one renegade cow who believes the grass is greener on the other side of the fence. After a childhood spent chasing sheep on the family farm, Alissa has always been drawn to remote areas and small towns, even when residing overseas. She is partial to autumn colours, snowy peaks and historic homesteads and will drive hours to see an open garden. Once a teacher and a counsellor, she remains interested in the life journeys that people take. She draws inspiration from the countryside around her, whether it be the brown snake at her back door or the resilience of bush communities in times of drought or flood. Her books are characteristically heartwarming, authentic and character driven. Alissa lives on a small slice of rural Australia in central western NSW.

Also by Alissa Callen

The Bundilla Series
Snowy Mountains Cattleman

The Woodlea Series
The Long Paddock
The Red Dirt Road
The Round Yard
The Boundary Fence

Snowy Mountains Daughter

ALISSA CALLEN

mira

First Published 2021
Second Australian Paperback Edition 2022
ISBN 9781867244004

Published by
Mira
An imprint of Harlequin Enterprises (Australia) Pty Limited (ABN 47 001 180 918), a subsidiary of HarperCollins Publishers Australia Pty Limited (ABN 36 009 913 517)
Level 13, 201 Elizabeth St
SYDNEY NSW 2000
AUSTRALIA

A catalogue record for this book is available from the National Library of Australia
www.librariesaustralia.nla.gov.au

Printed and bound in Australia by McPherson's Printing Group

To Luke

CHAPTER

1

Clancy Parker didn't need to leave the rugged embrace of the high country to know who she was and where she belonged.

She smoothed a hand over the warm neck of the palomino gelding who'd needed an afternoon ride as much as she had. A crisp breeze washed over her, carrying the chill from the white caps that glistened on the jagged peaks. Earlier an eagle had soared in the air-brushed canopy overhead, but now voluminous grey clouds rolled eastwards. Only last week the sky had glowed orange and a red film coated the snow as a wall of dust had blown in from out west.

She breathed in the scent of the approaching storm and made a wish that spring rain would fall in the drought-affected areas beyond the mountain range. After a last long look at the play of shadows across the Brindabellas, she turned Ash for home.

As volatile and capricious as Mother Nature could be, she felt far safer exposed to the elements than she ever had in the shelter of a city. Her cattleman father's golden rule had been to respect the bush and the ever-changing weather. Her own was to always exercise caution. She'd leave the risk-taking to her brother, Rowan.

Ash's pace quickened and when his pale creamy ears pricked forward, she smiled. The gelding was already thinking about dinner. She glanced to her left. For a moment all she could see were her brother's Hereford cattle grazing on the green carpeted foothills. There weren't yet any calves but going off the barrel shape and full udder of the closest cow, there soon would be.

A black-and-tan kelpie dashed out from a stand of graceful white gums. The kelpie more often than not ignored any attempt to call him by name. She didn't blame him. Being called after the local town of Bundilla wasn't exactly original, even if his name had been shortened.

'Ready to go, Bundy?' Her words thinned as the wind caused leaves to shimmer and grass to ripple.

Tongue lolling, the kelpie wagged his tail and raced ahead. His glossy coat shone as dark as obsidian in the waning sunlight. If he stayed still long enough she'd take a photo. The free-spirited kelpie, who refused to be tied down to any one master, had his own social media page. Tourists drifted through town hoping for a sighting of the dog who had a following the envy of any influencer.

No one knew where Bundy would appear next or who would come out from a shop in the main street to find him waiting on the back of their ute. At least half of the district had had him visit over the past five years. In summer he'd sit in tractor cabs when the swathes of lucerne would be baled into hay, while in winter he'd be a regular inside the pub asleep near the open fire. He'd only ever stayed with her once, when he'd arrived with the local mail contractor.

Clancy urged Ash into a canter. It wasn't so much the drops of rain on her cheeks that she needed to escape but the ache of loss. Bundy's steady presence had helped her through the fog of grief when three years ago her parents' cruise on a stormy and flooded Budapest river ended in tragedy. The kelpie had slept on the rug beside her bed for a month before he'd jumped into her brother's ute and headed into town.

An icy wind lashed at her but she didn't tug the collar of her oilskin coat higher. She welcomed the cold slap of reality against her skin. Bundy hadn't been the only one to bring her comfort. While the town had rallied around her, it had been a pair of strong masculine arms that had anchored her and brought solace, even if they'd also magnified her pain. Her parents' funeral had been the only thing to bring Heath MacBride home in the past ten years. Except no sooner had he held her than he'd left again.

Even now the memory of being fitted against him retained its bittersweet power. Heath had been the only man she'd ever wanted. No matter how many dates she agreed to or how many years passed, she couldn't move on. Having such a single-minded heart wasn't practical or admirable. In the silent hours that stretched between midnight and dawn, it simply made her feel alone.

Her chin tilted. Not that she indulged such feelings in the light of day. She was grateful for all that she had and all that her life was and would be. She didn't need a partner to feel complete or fulfilled, no matter how much the well-meaning members of the quilting group played matchmaker. She had her brother, her friends and her flower farm. She looked back at the now cloud-shrouded peaks. She also had her precious high country.

Bundy stopped on a hewn slab of granite to survey the valley below. Thanks to the local journalist, Mabel, who ran his social media page, Bundy wore a blue collar with his name embroidered in large gold letters. Visitors to town had taken to mistaking any black kelpie for Bundy so he'd needed something to identify him. While he was happy to pose for a selfie, some of the other kelpies, and their taciturn owners, weren't so used to being celebrities.

White shimmered in the distance as cockatoos fluttered amongst the trees lining the Tumut River, which wound its way through the alluvial flats of the valley floor. The tension stiffening Clancy's shoulders eased. Despite the splatter of rain on the brim of her felt hat, she slowed Ash and gazed to where wisps of smoke curled from a chimney. The sight of where she'd grown up never failed to soothe her.

In the poor light, the red bricks of the historic homestead merged into a block of blurred colour. A vast silver roofline overhung the wide verandas that wrapped round the house. If she listened hard enough she could still hear the echo of her parents' laughter. Soon the daffodils would bloom and brighten the dark green void between the homestead and the coach house at the far end of the garden.

Her attention shifted to the neat rows of herbaceous peonies that ran in parallel lines across the adjacent paddock. Anticipation coursed through her, closely followed by relief. It also wouldn't be long until the peony buds burst into life. This was going to be her best year yet.

Beside her, on the rock, Bundy remained stock-still. She slipped out her phone from her coat pocket to take advantage of the rare moment of stillness. She had no idea how long the kelpie would stay but it had been three days and he'd shown no sign of wanting to leave. She took the photo, despite hair whipping into her eyes and causing them to well, and managed to send the picture to Mabel.

The raindrops intensified until all she could hear was the sound of water hitting taut oilskin. Bundy leaped to the ground and Ash shifted on his feet. It was time to go. Ignoring the vibration of her mobile phone, which she'd returned to her pocket, she headed for the shortcut through the river paddock that would lead to the stables.

A pair of shaggy highland cattle lifted their heads from where they grazed. When they realised she hadn't come bearing treats the cattle returned to eating. Her Scottish mother had made sure that wherever she could a piece of home surrounded her. The photo Clancy had taken two days ago of Bundy touching noses with the russet-coloured bull, Fergus, had been an instant social media hit. It seemed people in the cities liked highland cattle as much as footloose kelpies.

Once in the shelter of the old wooden stables, Clancy again disregarded her vibrating phone and concentrated on unsaddling Ash. Her fingers were so cold she'd more than likely drop her mobile, and the screen had just been replaced. The first of the mountain wildflowers had to be wondering at their wisdom of unfurling so early. She threw on Ash's rug. As much as she appreciated the colder months, she was looking forward to endless summer days where the sun's warmth didn't wane until late.

With Bundy loping by her side, she jogged through the rain to the back door. Water pooled on the floor of the mud room as she hung up her dripping coat and shook the water from her hat. She briefly touched the oversized sheepskin jacket draped over the end peg. There would come a time when she'd remove the last of her parents' belongings, but seeing her father's coat hanging where it had all her life still ushered in a sense of security.

An electronic beeping from within the homestead accompanied another vibration of her phone. Frowning, she kicked off her boots and raced along the wide hallway. Her socked feet didn't make a sound on the carpet runner that warmed the polished floorboards. She had her tablet and phone linked and whenever they both went off it had to be her brother calling. The time difference between here and the United Kingdom meant it would be the early hours of the morning there. Her stomach clenched.

She reached her tablet, which she left on the kitchen bench near the charger so she'd never miss Rowan's call, and tapped the green button. *Please don't let anything have happened to him.*

'Rowan?'

'Hey sis. Nice hair.'

The tightness in her chest relaxed as her brother's trademark wide grin reassured her that everything was fine.

'I could say the same thing about you.'

As windblown as her hair was, Rowan's was long enough to touch his collar and was staying that way until he came home. His ex-fiancée running off with the rural store's farm supplies sales rep may have dented his heart, but it meant he no longer had to sport the short-back-and-sides hairstyle Eloise had expected.

'I should have known when you didn't answer your phone you were out riding. Bundy still with you?'

She nodded, searching his face for a clue as to why he'd called. Despite his good humour, a faint crease indented his brow. 'Everything okay?'

'Never better.' He smothered a yawn. 'Even if those sparrows that call my roof a home don't let me sleep past dawn. Give me a cockatoo any day.'

'When are you off to Wales?'

He'd mentioned last week he was heading to Snowdonia to go hiking with a group of mates—such a trip would explain why he was awake so early. What had started out four months ago as a trip away to erase memories of his ex had morphed into a working holiday. Being a stonemason, Rowan's skills were in demand and he was currently restoring a historic house in the Cotswolds. As much as she missed him, her heart warmed at the knowledge he had moved on from snobbish Eloise.

'As soon as the lads get here.' He paused. 'Is the coach house still empty?'

'It is. But it's ready to be listed. I just need to upload the photos.'

Since losing their parents, it was only the two of them rattling around in the main homestead. One summer, as a way to assuage their grief, they'd renovated the coach house with no intention of either one of them living there. Rowan eventually planned to build a stone house on the other side of the river. Last month he'd suggested they rent out the coach house to holiday-makers and skiers. While he'd said the extra income would be handy, she had a suspicion it was to ensure she wouldn't be alone. Since he'd left he seemed intent on asking about her social life.

'Heath needs a place to stay.'

The frantic thud of her heartbeat filled her ears. There was no mistaking who Rowan meant. He and Heath had been inseparable as kids.

She didn't realise she hadn't answered until Rowan's grey eyes scanned her face. 'Did the wi-fi drop out?'

Out of view of the camera, she clenched her left hand into a small fist. Rowan had no idea how she felt about his best mate and she was keeping it that way. 'I heard you. I'm just … surprised.'

'You won't be the only one. Heath's home to paint the water tower. He'll stay in the coach house for a night but it might be more, depending.'

She didn't need a crystal ball to know Heath would be there longer. Over the past decade, Graham MacBride hadn't mellowed. Not that Heath had ever put into words that his brusque father couldn't accept his only surviving son had a creative streak. She pushed aside the hurt that lingered even after all this time. While she'd disclosed far too much, Heath had never reciprocated. Even when his blue eyes would darken as if he were about to say something personal, his jaw would bunch before he'd refocus on whatever he was painting or sketching.

A loud knocking sounded from behind Rowan on what had to be his front door. He glanced over his shoulder before speaking again. 'Heath said he can do whatever needs to be done, you don't have to make up the bed or anything, but if you could leave the keys on the kitchen bench in the next half an hour that would be great.'

Her lungs strained for air. *Half an hour.* Somehow she kept her reply steady. 'Too easy. Stay safe and don't forget the emergency number for Wales is 999.'

'I'll text once we get there.' He blew her a kiss and the screen went black.

Clancy didn't move. Her first instinct was to double check what emergency services operated in Wales. If there was another overseas accident she didn't want to feel as powerless as she had for the sixteen hours when her parents had been missing after their cruise boat capsized. But the tension that made her breaths quicken proved too much. She closed the tablet cover and dragged a hand through her tangled hair.

Half an hour.

In thirty minutes the man she'd tried so hard to forget would be back. Would he still smell of leather and sun-dried cotton? At the funeral, he'd worn some sort of expensive cologne and a slick city suit. Would the world fall away when she looked into his eyes? Most of all, would he still see her as his best mate's little sister?

A surge of nervous energy had her rush to find the large plastic storage tub that she kept in the pantry. The answers to all three questions weren't of any consequence. She was no longer young and naive, or vulnerable and blindsided by grief. Her feelings for Heath wouldn't consume her again. She was her own person and had organised her low-key, small-town life just how she liked it. She didn't need anything, or anyone, that she didn't already have.

She slowed her movements as well as her breathing as she collected eggs and bacon for a breakfast hamper and the lasagne she'd pulled out of the freezer to thaw that morning. Just as well she'd shopped yesterday. She placed the vase of wildflowers from the kitchen table that she'd picked on yesterday's ride into the tub along with the food. The pink everlasting daisies nestled between the silver-grey eucalyptus would add a homely touch to the apartment. Not that she was still stalking Heath on social media, but last week he'd been working on a mural on the side of a Stockholm building, so wherever he'd travelled from would have involved a long-haul flight.

After adding a box of matches and a folded-up newspaper, and securing the tub's lid to keep everything dry, she returned to the mud room. With Bundy by her side, and again wearing her oilskin and hat, she power-walked through the garden to the 150-year-old coach house.

She wasn't a coward, but if she was quick she could do a final once-over of the upstairs and downstairs, open the side gate and make it home before Heath arrived. When it came to Heath there was no guarantee that her emotions would be content to remain hidden let alone in the background.

A wet Bundy stayed on the small front porch while she lit a fire
in the fireplace in the loft bedroom. She looked away from the large
bed made up in crisp white linen. Thoughts about how Heath's
northern hemisphere tan would look against the sheets weren't
helpful. Nor was remembering how much muscle now packed his
once lean frame.

Satisfied the fire wouldn't die out, she went down the narrow
steps two at a time and out to the porch.

'Come on, Bundy, race you to the gate.'

Her boots kicked up water as they splashed through the puddles
collecting in the ruts on the gravel driveway. The dull chug of a car
engine and a flash of silver through the rain caused her fingers to
fumble with the gate chain. Grinding her teeth, she concentrated
on slipping the chain free then lifted her head to give the sleek
convertible that had stopped on the other side of the gate a
casual wave. Between the rain and the frantic windscreen wipers,
all she caught was a glimpse of Heath's hand as he returned her
greeting.

She walked forward, pushing the gate open. Even once his car
crawled through, the tail-lights gleaming as he drove over to the
coach house, she remained standing by the open gate. Bundy sat
beside her, his shoulder pressed against her leg. She shook as though
all warmth had been stripped from her bones. Only the knowledge
that she needed to move so the kelpie wouldn't become soaked had
her close the gate.

Her hands again proved clumsy. All it had taken was her eyes
to meet Heath's through the smudged driver's side window and
she had been stripped bare. After all these years, still she had no
defences against him. She could no more stop loving Heath than
the winter peaks could fail to be blanketed in snow.

She squared her shoulders. But with time had come a non-negotiable need for self-preservation. She'd say hello and see if he needed anything. Then she'd make herself a pot of tea, look online to see how long a mural generally took to complete and work out a bulletproof plan to make sure her heart remained in one piece. When Heath again left she refused to allow him to take another part of her with him.

Nothing rattled Heath MacBride. As a child he'd refused to look away when his father's glower found him. As a teenager he'd ridden skittish horses down steep mountain trails. As an adult he spent his days defying gravity, painting murals on multiple-storey buildings.

But as much as he tried to fight it, he was only human. He had an Achilles heel. Whenever he was around the girl, now woman, walking towards him, the ground seemed to shift beneath his feet. Clancy Parker never failed to slip beneath his skin and make him want things that were impossible.

He braced himself as he waited under the cover of the small porch roof. From long practice he knew he'd appear relaxed. His arms hung loosely by his sides and his smile would be an easy grin, even if his heart kicked like brumby hooves against his ribs.

At least Clancy was almost unrecognisable in her oversized jacket and wide-brimmed hat. He was already so far out of his depth, he didn't need to see the symmetry of her pretty features or her feminine curves. She'd always been his muse and the years away hadn't tempered the intensity of his response to her.

The kelpie beside Clancy fixed him with a steady stare. He didn't recognise the dog and the realisation added tension to the fatigue that gripped his temples. There was so much of her world he didn't know about.

Clancy stopped just underneath the roof. The rain pounding on the overhead awning was the only sound between them. The kelpie sat, water dripping from its coat. Clancy remained still and then she swept off her hat, giving him full view of her face.

His mouth dried and the drum of the rain faded. He'd subconsciously incorporated parts of the woman before him into almost every mural he'd painted. For years he hadn't realised what he'd done, then one day he'd stared into the eyes of an image he'd painted on a Polish apartment. It had been Clancy's large, expressive grey eyes staring back. As for the women he'd briefly dated when loneliness proved too much, he wasn't game to examine the suspicion that they too resembled her.

He gave what he hoped passed as a casual smile and bent towards her. Even with the distinctive smell of oilskin and rain-soaked earth around them, he caught the delicate scent of daphne. She still smelled of flowers. He kissed her cheek. Her skin felt cold beneath his lips and he wasn't sure but he thought she trembled. The shoulder-length hair falling loose over her shoulders was wet along with her boots. She had to be freezing.

He took the time while he straightened to erase all need from his face. There wasn't a day over the past ten years when he hadn't missed her. 'Good to see you, Clance. Sorry for the short notice and for dragging you out in this.'

'A little rain never hurt anyone. Long flight?'

He nodded. Against her winter-white skin, her mouth was a soft and sensual pink. He broke eye contact to look at the dog still gazing at him, its stare unwavering. 'New kelpie?'

'His name's Bundy. He's a special guest.'

Heath bent to pat the dog. His mother had mentioned a roaming kelpie who called the town home.

Bundy's tail wagged, flicking drops of water over them both.

A brief smile curved Clancy's lips. Its warmth reached a place inside him that hadn't felt alive since he'd thrown his duffle bag into the belly of a Sydney-bound bus at eighteen and jammed on headphones to silence his father's parting words. As the kelpie cocked his head to again examine him, Heath knew the dog sensed his battle to appear at ease.

He gave the kelpie's neck a last rub. Exhaustion pressed upon his shoulders like a physical weight. He'd barely slept for twenty-eight hours.

Clancy gestured towards the coach house. 'The fire's lit and there's food in the fridge. You're welcome to stay however long you need.'

'Thanks.' He passed a hand around the back of his stiff neck.

Even though no one, not even his mother, knew the exact details of his last conversation with his father, it wasn't a secret that they were estranged.

His attention lingered on the fine lines of strain around Clancy's mouth. The past three years without her parents had been tough. He slid his hands into his pockets to stop himself from reaching out to tuck the tousled hair brushing her cheek behind her ear. Any support he offered her now would be too little too late, no matter how much he'd wanted to be there for her. 'I saw Rowan a few weeks ago. He's well.'

'Rowan never said anything about seeing you.'

He weathered her scrutiny. Hiding his emotions when around her had become second nature. 'It was just a quick London catch-up.'

Rowan wouldn't have mentioned their meeting as Clancy had been the main topic of conversation. Her brother was worried about her being on her own and that her grief might be holding her back. Rowan had also talked about how the Bundilla tourism committee had been looking at projects to boost the small town's profile. It had been after their meeting that he'd made some calls and offered to paint the water tower.

She nodded before she slipped on her hat and pulled the brim low over her eyes. 'Let me know if there's anything you need.'

'Thanks. I will.'

The reality was he had no intention of being a burden, let alone creating opportunities to see her. Friendship was all that there could be between them and that had to be enough. He'd come home to help the local bush community, keep an eye on her for Rowan and find out what his mother was so reluctant to tell him, that was all.

Clancy gave him a nod and in three strides the rain and wind had closed around her and Bundy. He stared after them until all he could see was the sheets of rain falling from the heavy sky. Then he turned towards the coach house.

The warmth of the renovated red brick building embraced him as much as the flood of memories. In the white entryway hall hung a picture of a highland cow he'd painted as a birthday present for Clancy's mother. His own home might have been devoid of paintings, but Clancy's parents had filled almost every spare space with art.

His steps slowed as he took in what he'd created what felt like a lifetime ago. Edward and Isobel Parker had provided him with the use of the old shed beside the cattle yards as a studio after his father had refused to give him anywhere to work.

Once in the kitchen he flicked on the glossy black electric kettle. But instead of making a much-needed coffee, he took his phone out of his coat pocket. There was no point delaying the inevitable. The sooner his father knew he was back, the sooner he'd know where he stood.

He'd long ago accepted he'd never gain his father's approval, let alone his love. It was only his stoic mother, and the heartache she bore after losing two sons, that kept him within the family fold. He'd do anything for her. His finger hovered over her name on his contact list. Even live a lie.

He touched the screen. His mother didn't know he was home and he hoped the surprise would give her a lift. Normally she travelled to see him whenever he was at his Sydney home, which he used as a base, and it usually wasn't for longer than a weekend. The phone continued to ring. There was a chance his father would pick up but at this time of day, and in this weather, he'd either be in his farm office or watching a rerun of his favourite spaghetti western.

Heath walked to stare out of the sitting room window while he stayed on the line. The home phone was in the kitchen and his mother didn't move as fast as she once did. He hadn't missed the shadows of exhaustion under her eyes that seemed to darken with every video call over the past months.

Finally she answered. 'Darling, sorry. I was in the laundry.'

His reflection in the window captured his frown. Her words were thin and tired. 'No problem. I thought you'd be at the other end of the house?'

'This is a really clear line. Where are you?'

His mother's body might be ageing but there was nothing wrong with her razor-sharp mind. 'The coach house at Clancy's. I landed this afternoon.'

'Why have you come home?'

His frown returned. This wasn't exactly the reaction he'd been expecting. Worry, not excitement, vibrated in her tone. 'I'm painting the water tower.'

There was a beat of silence before his mother answered, her voice now steady. 'That's wonderful. The town needs some of your beautiful art.'

As much as his father saw his creativity as a curse, his mother had always been in his corner. 'Thanks. I'll be here for at least a month …'

He didn't need to finish his sentence for his mother to know he was asking if he could stay at Hawks Ridge.

Her deep sigh gave him all the answers he needed. He still wasn't welcome.

'Sweetheart … you know your father. I'll come around late tomorrow afternoon for a cuppa. Say hi to Clancy.'

The false note of cheeriness didn't fool him. Something wasn't right but now wasn't the time to press for answers.

'See you soon.'

Heath ended the call. The rain had dwindled to a drizzle and the storm-dark sky had given way to a starless night. If he looked hard enough he could make out the snow-capped peaks. So many times he'd stared at a foreign mountain range and wished he were home.

Now he was. But the knowledge didn't quieten the voice that said coming back was a huge mistake.

He and his father were still at loggerheads. He'd caused his mother concern and added to whatever was bothering her. His gaze shifted to the outline of the main homestead with its white wrought iron and multiple chimneys. And the girl he'd loved had grown into a woman who remained out of reach.

The status quo hadn't changed. Even if he'd wanted to stay, there was no place for him here. And he could never ask Clancy to leave her beloved mountains.

His jaw locked. It mightn't have been his choice to leave the first time, but as soon as he could, he'd again be gone.

CHAPTER

2

'Bundy, my arm will fall off if I hold the door open any longer.'

Clancy moved closer to the dual cab beside her to relieve the strain on her muscles. Who knew a Hilux passenger door could feel so heavy?

Still the kelpie sprawled in the patch of early morning sun on the front veranda didn't move.

'Okay then.' She shut the car door. 'I'll see you when I'm back from town.'

Bundy's tail thumped on the wide wooden floorboards before his eyes closed.

Clancy climbed into the driver's seat. She was sure Bundy would have wanted to accompany her. When her father's kelpie had passed away last winter she hadn't the heart to replace him, so Ashcroft had no other dogs. Bundy had to be bored with only having a surly cat for company. Orien had gone out of his silver-tabby-cat way to make sure Bundy remembered whose home this was, even if she did catch the two of them snuggled in front of the fire last night. Usually there was more hissing than purring whenever they were in the same room.

She glanced in her rear-view mirror to where a thin tendril of smoke curled from the back garden in the vicinity of the coach house. She could relate to having to share her space with someone who pushed her buttons.

A pair of galahs swooped in front of the windscreen and she took a second to slow. Her reflexes were sluggish, as if she too had travelled on a long-haul flight. Her only excuse was that she'd tossed and turned until the dawn birdsong warned her that if she didn't get some sleep she'd be paying a high price today. Orien wasn't the only one whose mood couldn't exactly be described as sunny when his slumber was disturbed.

She kept a close look on the sky as she drove through the avenues of bare-branched poplars that ran alongside the driveway. The backs of her eyelids felt like sandpaper but at least she'd come up with a plan to deal with Heath being home.

Her first thought had been to avoid him. Except Rowan would ask what was wrong and there was no way she could tell him. He'd only point out the obvious—Heath didn't return her feelings. Her second was that if she couldn't be with him, she at least had their friendship which she'd be a fool to ruin. So, the only practical solution was to reframe how she viewed him.

In the clear morning light, the plan didn't seem quite as foolproof, but it was the only option she had. To reduce the risk to her heart and the peaceful life she'd built for herself, she'd treat Heath like any other holiday-maker who'd come to stay. If she stuck to this strategy, she'd be able to be friendly but impersonal and her feelings would stay neatly packed away in their never-to-be-opened box.

The truth was he no longer resembled the farm boy she'd loved, even if he still wore brown dress boots. When he'd kissed her cheek last night, she'd again caught the scent of his unfamiliar high-end aftershave. As for his trendy haircut, stylish clothes and fancy car, it wasn't a stretch to see him as some city slicker here to escape the daily grind of the concrete commute.

The dual cab rattled over the cattle grid which was flanked by a dry-stone wall and she turned left towards Bundilla. Water from yesterday's storm lay in the roadside hollows and gum leaves glistened. Muddy tracks from the river turn-off, where all the loved-up teenagers went for some alone time, marked the black bitumen.

Clancy didn't usually head to town before finishing her morning jobs but Brenna had sent an SOS. Her childhood friend ran a horse trekking business and over the weekend had held her first trek for the season. It obviously hadn't gone well. So a meeting at The Book Nook Café, involving strong coffee and copious amounts of sugar, was in order. Her stomach rumbled. Scones smothered in sweet raspberry jam and thick cream definitely counted as breakfast.

When the road forked she followed the curve to the left that soon had her travelling across one of the town's many wooden bridges. The historic viaducts criss-crossed the flood plain in latticed rows of sturdy wood. Even now she loved to feel the bump of the uneven floorboards beneath her wheels. The rhythmic sound spoke of simplicity and a past slow-paced way of life when horses would have crossed over instead of cars.

Once close to town she took a back street that brought her out near the old post office with its graceful columns and arches. Twin rows of Manchurian pears lined the main street and led her into the centre of town. The ornamental trees would soon bloom to perfume the air before their white petals floated over the footpaths.

As she drew near the coffee shop tucked next to the double-storey wrought-iron pub, she peered through the windscreen at the red-bricked memorial clock tower at the far end of the street. Even after waiting to see whether Bundy would go with her, she was on time.

After a quick reverse park, Clancy traded the warmth of the dual cab for the chill of a brisk wind. She pulled her thick black coat tighter at her throat. Her usual blue floral woollen scarf was still on the hallway stand. The aroma of fresh meat pies drifted from the bakery two doors down from the café. Before she could dwell on the memory of how much Heath had loved the local pies, someone called her name.

She turned. Brenna strode towards her. Today she wore her usual boots, jeans and navy coat, the breeze lifting her long pale blonde hair. Her oldest friend was a series of contrasts. She was as fine-boned as a dancer but physically strong. A no-frills tomboy, yet her favourite colour was pink. And even though she was a twin, she'd rather do things on her own. It was the bane of her life that men always thought she needed help or rescuing, so she too was happy being independent and single.

'Perfect timing,' Brenna said with a grin before they exchanged hugs. 'So much for it being spring.'

Clancy stepped back with a smile. Out of their school year group there was only a handful who hadn't left sleepy Bundilla. Brenna's jacket might not be the height of fashion and might also smell of campfire smoke, but both of them had no regrets about staying in the mountains. 'Tell me about it.'

Together they entered The Book Nook Café. While the chairs on the footpath, draped in colourful crocheted blankets to keep customers warm, were empty, three groups of patrons filled the inside area. Clancy's steps slowed as she recognised the two elderly women seated at the far corner table. Brenna, who was behind her, collided with her back.

Clancy half turned to whisper, 'Please tell me book club wasn't on last night.'

Brenna didn't have time to answer before one of the women gave them a wave. Such a gesture may have appeared welcoming, except the woman's reserved expression failed to relax into a smile.

'It must have been,' Brenna whispered near Clancy's ear. 'I put in an apology ages ago as I knew I'd be trekking.'

Clancy silenced a groan. Thrown by Heath's appearance, she hadn't thought to call either Millicent or Beatrice Amos. Missing book club was a serious offence.

She smiled brightly and stopped at the table of the identical twin sisters. Millicent wore her silver bob a little longer, otherwise it was impossible to tell them apart.

'Morning,' Clancy said, making sure her smile touched each of them. 'I'm so sorry I didn't call to say I wouldn't be there last night.'

Millicent slowly nodded. 'Apology accepted. We're all looking forward to seeing you at our next meeting, which I'm pleased to say will be at your place. Unfortunately Ruth is no longer able to host.'

To her left, Clancy heard Brenna stifle a chuckle. Not being at book club meant she'd missed the opportunity to put forward any reason why next month's meeting couldn't be held at Ashcroft. While some members relished being hosts, Clancy and Brenna would rather take a trip on an overcrowded city train. It was ridiculous why they continued to feel so intimidated by the sisters. If it wasn't the quality and quantity of their supper they worried about, it was the social etiquette of how they arranged the chairs.

The last time Brenna hosted, not only had neither of them read the book, they'd improvised by printing off book club questions. There should be a rule about never choosing a book that shared a title with another work. Needless to say, their questions had been for the wrong book.

Clancy kept her smile in place. 'I'll look forward to it.'

With a nod to each sister, she continued towards a table nestled beside a wall full of books. She didn't know what it was about Millicent and Beatrice, but the lift of a pencilled eyebrow always made her question if she'd done something wrong.

It wasn't as if the sisters meant to be disapproving, they were just always so serious. No one really knew much about their lives or why widowed Millicent and divorced Beatrice chose to settle in Bundilla almost twenty years ago. Neither had any other family so the town assumed they could simply live wherever they wanted.

'We really should get over this,' Brenna said under her breath as she took the seat opposite Clancy. 'We're not teenagers running amuck anymore. I mean, we're successful grown women.'

'I know. I just feel like I'm always in trouble.'

Brenna's laugh was low. 'You in trouble? It was always me. You were only guilty by association or for having my back.' Brenna leaned across the table to say softly, 'Next book club remember to elbow me if I even look like I'm about to say "this book sucked" again.'

Clancy picked up the menu, which was a replica of a child's vintage picture book, to hide her amusement in case the sisters were watching. 'Sucked' wasn't exactly on the book club's approved word list. 'If you promise to refill my tea.'

Brenna laughed so hard she put a hand to her chest. They both knew Clancy only drank tea so she could take a sip and then say 'hmm' as a way of sounding intellectual.

Clancy wiped a tear from her eye. 'I must admit I do like going.'

'Me too. But a glass or two of wine does help.'

'True, and at least it is books we discuss. I swear the only thing we talked about at the last quilting meeting was finding someone for Stella now she's split with Wayne.'

Over the years, their love life—or lack of it—had also been a favourite topic, along with any disastrous dates.

'Good luck with that.' Brenna studied the menu. 'Single men are not exactly plentiful around here.'

Clancy came to her feet in case the warmth in her cheeks turned an obvious red. As of last night, the population of Bundilla bachelors had increased by one. But she'd learn what was bothering Brenna before she brought up Heath being home. 'What are you having? The usual?'

At Brenna's nod, she placed their orders and returned to her seat.

'So how did your trek go?' she asked, noting Brenna's downcast expression. 'Did you have another hen's party turn up in stilettos expecting to see The Man from Snowy River?'

'Worse. It was a group of Melbourne businessmen. I swear, if I was called little lady one more time and congratulated on my cooking skills I would have had a very unprofessional hissy fit.'

Clancy couldn't resist a smile. It was an unwise man, or woman, who didn't take Brenna seriously. 'Did Taite go?'

Taite was Brenna's twin and when he wasn't running his deer farm or making sculptures out of old farm tools he was helping his sister during the trekking season.

'He wasn't supposed to. After about five minutes, he just gave me that look, loaded an extra two cases of beer and saddled his horse.'

'He's such a good brother.'

The conversation was put on pause when they both thanked Amy, the young waitress, as she brought them their coffees.

When they were alone, Brenna answered. 'He is … but the trouble is the more beers he handed out around the campfire, the more everyone enjoyed themselves. The group have booked for a whole week next month.'

Clancy patted Brenna's hand. Not only did she lack Brenna's iconic blonde and blue-eyed beauty, she didn't share her high-spirited sass that drew men to her. When she wanted to be, she was an unassuming introvert who easily passed under any masculine radar.

'How about I come next time instead of Taite? These city boys need to learn a lesson about self-reliant country girls.'

'I'd like to see one of them call you little lady. I still can't get your don't-mess-with-me smile down pat.'

'And here I thought that was my look of serenity.'

Brenna's solemness dissolved into laughter. 'Serenity, my hat. I envy your superpower. You appear so sweet and mild but inside you are as immovable as stone.'

Silence settled between them as their scones arrived and they lathered on jam and cream. In between bites, they gave the Amos sisters a wave when they stood to leave. Once the café door closed behind Millicent and Beatrice, Clancy added more cream to her scone and relaxed into her seat. She was looking forward to the rest of the day being boring and uneventful.

Brenna lifted her coffee mug and froze. She stared over Clancy's shoulder at the main street, eyebrows lifted. 'Is that … Bundy with *Heath MacBride*?'

Clancy choked on her mouthful of scone and took her time to turn. Heath's silver convertible was parked a couple of spaces past her dual cab and he and Bundy now strolled towards the grocery store. So much for the kelpie not wanting to come to town.

She cleared her throat. 'That was my news. Heath arrived last night. He's here to paint the water tower and is staying in the coach house.'

Brenna's eyes searched hers. 'Are you okay?'

She nodded. As much as she'd hidden her feelings for Heath from her brother, Brenna had always been privy to her unrequited and all-consuming crush.

She again glanced over her shoulder. 'I mean, look at him. He dresses like a city boy and drives a car not made for country roads. I'm telling myself he isn't the same person. And the truth is neither am I.'

'It's true he does look … different.' Brenna's brow furrowed as she leaned sideways to get a better view. 'But obviously not so different that he's unrecognisable.'

The nearly deserted street now had several pedestrians all heading to where Heath had stopped to talk to salt-and-pepper-haired Dan Munroe. Bundy sat by Heath's boots as he chatted to the confirmed bachelor.

A small blue car suddenly pulled over and a tall woman dressed in yellow left the driver's seat. A four-wheel drive towing a horse float drove past, blocking Clancy's view.

'That almost looks like Cynthia but it's not her usual green car,' she said, twisting in her seat to see better.

'Because it *is* Cynthia.' Brenna pushed back her chair. 'I think now's a good time to repay MacBride that favour I owe him after he pulled my ute out of the creek that night I snuck out to celebrate winning the rugby final.'

Heath needed no further proof that small towns had long memories.

He and Bundy hadn't even made it to the grocery store before they'd bumped into Dan, one of his neighbours. They'd been exchanging the usual greetings when he sensed he was under observation and caught movement in his peripheral vision. Now he had people he knew, and didn't know, walking towards him. Against his leg he felt Bundy's warm weight as he rested against him.

He lowered his hand to touch the kelpie's head. He'd come out of the coach house to find Bundy sitting beside his car. When he'd opened the back seat door, the kelpie hadn't hesitated to jump in. He'd also shown no sign of wanting to wander off now they were in town.

As other locals approached, Dan shook Heath's hand before leaving him to chat. He'd just swapped hugs with his old primary school teacher and met her daughter and young grandson when two figures stepped out of the café. He didn't need to look twice to know that it was Clancy and Brenna. He forced himself to focus as Mrs Buchanan ran him through what his past classmates were doing.

He wasn't sure what made him glance to his left. A middle-aged woman he didn't recognise rapidly approached. By her broad smile and the zing in her step, she appeared to know him.

The next thing he knew he was pulled against an ample chest and squeezed. He breathed in the strong scent of hairspray.

'I don't believe it. You're home,' the woman gushed, voice breathless.

He eased himself away. Politeness had him smile but he still couldn't place the woman with the heavy-framed red glasses, yellow-blonde hair and vivid dress sense. Mrs Buchanan and her daughter gave him a wave as they continued on their way.

'It's great to be back,' he said, buying time.

'New car, Cynthia?' Brenna asked as she joined them. Clancy bent to pat Bundy and as her eyes met his she mouthed the word *Herbert*.

A memory clicked into place. Cynthia Herbert. Mother of the three Herbert girls. Make that a very proud mother. Her enthusiasm at the netball court sidelines and dance eisteddfods had been legendary. As was the scandal surrounding her ex-husband being caught with the local show secretary in the poultry pavilion.

Cynthia answered Brenna without looking away from Heath. 'It's Ruby's. Someone ran into the back of mine in Tumut.' She paused to draw breath and smile. 'Now, Heath ... you simply must come for dinner. It's not every day you're back and my older girls are home.'

Heath made sure his smile was pleasant but brief. It wasn't only his nomadic lifestyle that kept him single. He was a master at being non-committal. It didn't matter what country he was in, there were always matchmaking mammas.

'So ... shall we say seven o'clock tomorrow night?' Cynthia's breezy but determined tone left no room for anything but an agreement.

Before he could say thank you but he was unavailable, Clancy spoke. 'Sorry, Cynthia, Heath's in demand. The tourism committee's meeting is on late tomorrow.'

Brenna joined in. 'And the next night my barbeque's on.'

Cynthia's mouth firmed. 'Well then, how about—'

Heath gently cut her off. 'How about I take a raincheck. I hope your car's back on the road soon, Mrs Herbert.'

With a nod, he left to continue towards the grocery store. Brenna and Clancy fell into step beside him.

Brenna shot him a grin. 'Nothing says welcome home more than a dinner invitation from the Herberts.'

'Good to see you, Brenna.'

'You too, MacBride, even if you look like a city boy.'

He shrugged. 'This is me on a good day.'

'Make sure you're having a bad day when you see Taite at the barbeque. He'll think you've gone soft wearing a jacket like that.'

Heath hesitated. He hadn't misinterpreted the girls' help or assumed that there really was a barbeque. But if Brenna was having one, as much as he'd like to catch up, any get-together would involve spending time with Clancy.

Brenna stopped walking to fix him with a hard stare. 'MacBride, you are not going to blow us off just because you're some famous artist. You can either come out home or we'll come to you.'

He couldn't stop a chuckle or a rush of relief. Maybe in some small way he still had a place here. 'I'm far from famous and I wouldn't dare blow you off.'

'Perfect. See you at six thirty. Don't be late.'

'Still bossy, I see.'

'You'd better believe it.' She checked her watch before hugging Clancy. 'Thanks for the debrief and see you at six thirty, too.'

Brenna turned to give him a hug and when she pulled away she grinned. 'The city clothes can go but whatever that cologne is, it's gorgeous, so it can stay.'

With a cheery wave, she strode away.

Heath looked back at Clancy and found her watching him.

'Wise decision.' Her smile didn't quite reach her grey eyes.

'I thought so, too.' He kept his tone light to ease the strange tension between them.

Clancy's gaze slid away before she ruffled Bundy's neck. 'So you did want to come to town after all.' She briefly glanced at Heath. 'Don't worry if Bundy doesn't come home with you. If I were him, I'd have had enough of Orien's death stares days ago.'

He nodded. The fact Clancy couldn't seem to meet his eyes for long shouldn't make him feel so unsettled.

She gave Bundy a final pat and straightened. If he didn't know better he would have said her shoulders were braced beneath her black coat. But this was Clancy. They'd known each other all their lives. He was the only foolish one whose feelings had strayed outside the bounds of friendship.

'Clance.' He scraped a hand over his stubbled chin. 'I don't know how long I'll be in the coach house but if it's a problem, I'll stay with Ned.'

'Stay however long you need.' This time her gaze held his. 'No luck with your dad?'

'No. Mum's coming around later this afternoon.'

Empathy softened Clancy's mouth. 'Your studio's how you left it and Goliath's there any time you want a ride.'

'Thanks.' Rowan's unsociable blood-bay stockhorse wasn't for the faint-hearted. 'But I value my life.'

As he'd hoped, Clancy smiled. 'He'd be happy to get out of his paddock so will be on his best behaviour. Besides, he's not any worse than that chestnut gelding you had ... What was his name?'

'Tex.' He'd always been drawn to horses others couldn't handle.

'That was it. He wasn't only bad-tempered but huge.'

'He had a good heart.'

'When he wasn't trying to kick everyone to Mount Kosciuszko.'

'Tex behaved himself that day you had to ride back with me.'

He'd been helping her family move cattle and when Clancy's mare had tripped in a wombat burrow, he'd doubled Clancy home to get the horse truck. The feel of her pressed against his back, her sweet floral scent and the warm grasp of her arms around his waist had made him wish the ride wouldn't end. After that, he couldn't ignore the way he saw her as so much more than his best mate's little sister.

'I remember that ride. Tex tried to bite me when you weren't looking.'

The colour painting her cheeks had to be from indignation and not for any other reason.

'Sorry, I had no idea.'

'I told him off and he never did it again.' As if she suddenly needed to be elsewhere, she half turned. 'I'll let you keep going. You'd better get your groceries before Cynthia comes up with another date for your dinner.'

'Need anything?'

'No, I'm all good. See you.'

As she walked away, a sense of loss held him still. Something had changed between them, and not for the better. It would be unrealistic to expect ten years wouldn't alter them as people or the dynamics of their friendship. What hadn't changed was how he felt about her or the reasons why he couldn't be a part of her life. No matter how much that was all he'd ever wanted to do.

With Bundy at his heels, he headed to the grocery store. Fatigue slowed his steps and the conviction that he'd made a huge mistake settled deep into his bones.

To his relief, he didn't meet anyone he knew while he filled his trolley. When he left the store, Bundy was waiting outside. The kelpie trotted alongside him and jumped into the convertible when he opened the door. Once he was back at the coach house and had unloaded the groceries, Heath changed into old jeans and a faded blue cotton shirt.

'I know you're only feeling sorry for me, mate,' Heath said as Bundy accompanied him to the stables to saddle Goliath. 'But it's nice to have you around.'

As they approached the cluster of buildings and horse yards, Heath stared at the ridge to his right. The distinctive peaks and plateaus belonged to the place where he'd grown up. The highest point resembled a hawk in flight and was why his family farm bore the name Hawks Ridge.

The rhythm of his home, with its snowy winters and amicable summers, was as much a part of him as his art. He couldn't bear to think that one day the land would belong to someone else. His father had made it clear he'd never inherit Hawks Ridge, even if the property had been in his mother's family since her grandparents. There was a distant second cousin who owned a cattle station in Queensland and their neighbour on the left had expressed interest should they ever sell.

Heath looked away from the ridge. As difficult as his father was, at least he was as strong as the bulls he bred. The decision about the farm's future wasn't going to be one that had to be addressed soon. It was only his mother's health he needed to worry about.

After reaching the stables, he and Bundy stopped at a wire fence beyond which grazed a bay stockhorse. The gelding lifted his head to glare at them, the wind rippling through his black mane, before he snorted and resumed eating. The message was clear. Do not disturb.

Heath grinned. The strain of seeing Clancy, the continued estrangement with his father and the unknown outcome of his afternoon chat with his mother faded. He needed a challenge as well as to feel the sweep of the high-country wind across his skin. As much as his father believed he could never be both a cattleman and an artist, he knew he could, even if it was only for an afternoon ride.

To Heath's surprise, apart from the usual edgy behaviour of a horse who hadn't been worked, Goliath was caught, saddled and lunged without any major drama. But as they rode through the paddock that took them past the homestead, it was only instinct and experience that kept him in the saddle. All he'd done was look across at the front veranda and wonder where Clancy was for Goliath to become a buckjumper.

Once the gelding had finished doing his best to unseat him, Heath rubbed Goliath's hot neck and never again took his attention off him. As the foothills fell behind them and the gelding's gait became smooth and swinging, Heath relaxed. Bundy loped beside them.

A magpie warbled from a nearby scribbly gum and brush-tailed wallabies bounded through the first flush of spring growth, heading for a grove of candlebarks. Between the sunny days, cool nights and lush grass, whoever the local vet now was in town, they'd be in for a string of foundered ponies if the owners weren't careful.

A pop of colour had him ride over to tufts of yellow billy buttons and take a picture on his phone. It was a week since he'd held a paintbrush or an aerosol can and he was itching to be creative again. He took more photos.

He couldn't see a wildflower without thinking of Clancy. It was no wonder she'd started a flower farm. As a child she'd always return from a ride with bunches of wildflowers that she'd press between the pages of a heavy book. She'd then make cards or bookmarks and he was sure his mother still had some of them. She'd always had a soft spot for Clancy, as much as his father had ignored her.

At the thought of his mother the sky seemed to lose its brilliance, the clouds becoming low and sullen. He could only hope that whatever was bothering her wouldn't mean that their time together would be cut short. As it was, he was a surprise late-in-life baby and she'd always been a much older mother than those of his friends. In a world glacial with his father's disapproval, she'd always been his warmth and his anchor. Goliath sensed the return of his tension and jumped sideways as something rustled in a clump of snow grass. Heath whistled to Bundy and before long they were back in the stables and out of the wind.

He'd just flicked on the kettle in the coach house and opened his mother's favourite tea when her white sedan drove past the window. He went to meet her at the front door. As he clasped her in a tight hug, he refused to let his smile slip when he felt how thin and fragile she'd become. When she pulled away tears welled in her eyes.

'Cuppa?' he asked, keeping his tone casual. His stoic mother wasn't one for emotional displays.

'Sounds lovely.'

He waited for her to walk inside and then followed. It had only been five months since he'd last seen her in Sydney but she'd aged. Her long grey hair, which she'd styled into her usual neat bun, was now white at the temples.

'This all looks nice,' she said, gazing around before sitting on the plush creamy sofa decorated with dove-grey cushions.

He placed a plate of the caramel slice she liked from the bakery on the coffee table. 'Rowan and Clancy did a great job.'

He wasn't buying his mother's small talk. As happy as she was to see him, her face was pale and her fingers tightly clasped together in her lap. She couldn't so easily gloss over how she was or end their conversation by saying she had to go now that they were face to face.

After making their tea, he sat in the armchair to her left. There was no point skirting around his unanswered questions. Neither of them would be able to relax. 'Mum … what's going on?'

She didn't respond, just stared at the steam curling from the mug sitting on the low table in front of her.

'Are you unwell?'

Her gaze slowly lifted to his. His mother had lost two children, and for the past ten years had to walk the tense tightrope between him and his father, but he'd never seen her look so desolate, almost broken.

'Mum?' His voice was a hoarse rasp.

She swallowed. 'It's not me.'

'Dad?'

When she again didn't speak, he spoke for her. 'Has he had an accident?'

His father continued to think himself invincible by working with the bulls in the yards and riding quad bikes over steep terrain.

'He's physically as strong as an ox.' She stopped to stare out the window at the swaying branches of a cedar tree. He thought she wouldn't continue but then she whispered, 'Not long after I last saw you, he woke in the middle of the night and demanded that I leave.'

Heath's jaw clenched as he controlled his anger and kept himself silent. His mother had lost so much, she didn't now need her marriage to disintegrate.

'Your father said … he didn't know who I was but I wasn't his wife … and he only shared a bed with the woman he married.'

Heath frowned. 'He didn't know who you were?'

'No.' The single word contained the depths of despair. 'But he did the next day and everything was fine. For a little while. Then his hands started shaking and he began seeing things that weren't there. I was going to ask you to come home but you'd started a new mural. I also needed time to fully understand what was going on. We have another specialist neurologist appointment next week but there's no doubt your father has Lewy Body dementia.'

Before Heath could respond, his mother reached out to clutch his hand. 'Darling, you have to move past whatever he said the night you left. You have to put things right.' Her voice broke. 'Promise me, before it's too late.'

CHAPTER
3

Anytime you're ready ...

Clancy ignored her inner voice as she clicked from one social media page on her laptop to another. She'd started off checking the weather, had then gone to Bundy's photo feed and now had somehow ended up on Heath's page. She had work to do—she was supposed to be planning her flower farm's open day, which was six weeks away—but another few minutes and she'd have appeased her curiosity.

She stared at a recent image that caught Heath's profile as he added detail with a paintbrush to a half-completed mural on the side of a building. He wore a cap and a paint-stained grey tee that bunched over his bicep as he extended his tanned arm. She started scrolling through the comments below. Then stopped. There were almost as many red hearts as there were words.

But as gorgeous as the photo was, it was nothing compared to Heath in the flesh. The night he'd arrived, between the rain and having to hide her reaction, she hadn't allowed herself to take a good look. So yesterday in the main street, when his attention hadn't been on her, she'd taken one. And she shouldn't have. Her question as to whether the world would still fall away when she looked into his eyes had been answered.

Since he'd left, she'd been dragged on blind dates, double dates and even group dates, but never had any man affected her the way Heath did. She'd been powerless to look away. Over the years he'd filled out. The lean edge of his stubbled jaw and the easy way he moved spoke of muscles honed from an active life. His eyes were still a changeable blue and she could never really pinpoint their exact shade. Yesterday they'd reflected the navy hue of his jacket but she also knew they could reflect the deepening blue of a twilight summer sky. As for his mouth …

That was when he'd turned to look at her. From then on she only dared to make eye contact for as short a time as possible. She couldn't trust that the impact he had on her wouldn't be broadcasted all over her face. She was also supposed to be thinking of him as just another guest.

She sighed. Except limiting how much she looked at him hadn't made it feel like he'd never been a part of her life. The brief mention of when he'd doubled her home on Tex had ushered in a slideshow of memories that wouldn't fade. Her arms looped around his waist, his slow smile as he'd glanced over his shoulder and the sense of them being the only two people in the world had been things she'd never forgotten.

Realising that she was still staring at his photo, she closed the webpage. She couldn't allow her emotions to sway her off course. It was coming up to her busiest time of the year and she couldn't afford to think of anything but her peonies. If she had any hope of getting any work done, she had to prove to herself she could be around Heath and stick to her plan.

She scooped up her phone that lay next to her laptop. In keeping with treating him like a guest, she should have given him her mobile number. The practical and sensible thing to do would be to find him and exchange contact details. And this time, there'd be no going off script.

Not bothering with a coat, she headed outside. The mid-morning sun had dried the dew sparkling on the lawn and taken the chill off the wind. She also wasn't planning to see Heath for long. Orien sat on top of the dry-stone wall that surrounded the back garden, his silver tail twitching as a lizard darted in and out of the crevices.

As a boy Rowan had spent hours rebuilding the crumbling wall. The recollection of how she'd pass him the heavy and rough stones made her smile. They were the fifth generation of Parkers to be custodians of Ashcroft. Their forebears had settled in this corner of the fertile valley in the hope their descendants too would call it home. And they still did. There was nowhere else she wanted to be.

She reached the coach house and knocked on the door. All she had to do was swap numbers, act normal, and leave. How hard could it be? When there was no response, she knocked a second time. Again, only silence answered her.

Heath's car was in the carport so he was either out riding or in the studio. Her attention lingered on the sleek silver convertible. The vehicle didn't have any rental stickers so had to be his personal one he used whenever back in the country. According to Rowan, Heath had a house in Sydney. On the rare occasion she'd travelled to the city, she'd found herself looking out for him.

She turned away to retrace her steps through the garden. Heath's convertible provided tangible proof that she no longer knew who he was. The Heath she'd known would never have bought such an impractical vehicle.

Once through the small wooden gate in the dry-stone wall, she followed the path to the stables. Goliath grazed in his paddock so Heath had to be in the makeshift art studio that over the years had been left untouched. Her mother had always said with a gentle smile that one day he'd be back.

As Clancy drew near to the rusted corrugated iron shed, the only sounds were the crunch of gravel beneath her boots and the creak of wind beneath loose tin. She drew a quick breath and knocked on the door.

After a long moment Heath's voice sounded. 'Come in.'

She pushed open the door. The first thing she saw was Bundy asleep on the concrete floor beside where Heath stood with his back to her as he painted. The next thing she registered was the sombre strokes of a landscape that would have looked harsh and austere if not for the sunny yellow tufts of billy buttons.

Heath swung around and her gaze flew to his face. His art wasn't usually so dark or bleak. Neither was his expression. Exhaustion stripped a layer of colour from beneath his tan and his shoulders were rigid as though carved from mountain granite.

He gave her a brief nod and went back to painting.

She walked forward, the smell of fresh paint strengthening. Judging by the duffle bag open on the floor, Heath had brought all the essentials he'd need.

She stopped nearby, but still his hand moved across the canvas. Even to her unartistic eye she could tell the large painting would have taken hours to create.

'Heath, have you been up all night?'

She thought he hadn't heard her, then his arm lowered. The intensity in his eyes faded and his face settled into shadowed lines. Just like all those years ago, when it came to expressing his feelings he shut down. Just like then, his inability to trust or be open with her hurt.

'Not all night.' The brief lift of the corner of his mouth didn't qualify as a smile. 'Jet lag has a lot to answer for.'

'I should have brought coffee.'

He put his paintbrush into a jar of clear and pungent liquid. 'Coffee, not to mention food, sounds pretty good right now.'

'I have a spare kettle I can bring over?'

She looked away to focus on the raw beauty of the artwork. With his hair tousled, clothes creased and hands splattered with paint, Heath no longer looked like such a polished city boy.

'Thanks but it's time Bundy stretched his legs.' Heath checked the clock on his phone that sat on a nearby small table. 'I also have to get moving.'

She rubbed Bundy's belly with the toe of her boot while Heath tidied up.

When he held open the door for her, she snuck a look at his impassive face. Whatever deep emotions had compelled him to paint like he had couldn't simply be switched off. No matter how strong Heath was.

'Did you want to see me?' he asked, his gaze on the snow-crested peaks as they strolled side by side along the path to the homestead.

She slipped out her phone. 'We never swapped numbers.'

He too took out his mobile and as she relayed her number he entered it into his contacts list. Her phone whooshed as a message came in.

Her grip on her mobile firmed. So much for trying to convince herself that Heath was nothing but a stranger—he knew exactly what she loved. He'd sent her an emoji of a bunch of flowers.

When at the point where the path diverged, she used her best small-talk voice. She had to make a last-ditch effort to stick to her plan. 'Good luck with the committee. I hope it's not too hard for everyone to agree on a mural idea.'

This time his smile curved his whole mouth. 'So do I.'

She bit the inside of her cheek as she continued over to her house. Technically, her mission hadn't been a total failure. She'd exchanged numbers, treated Heath like a guest and hadn't been away too long. But she also couldn't call seeing him a success.

Brenna was right. Whatever cologne Heath now wore smelled so good it called for her to lean in close to take a deeper breath. Rumpled and paint-covered, Heath also hadn't at all looked like someone she no longer knew. As for his painting, the image of its sombre tones refused to fade.

Lost in thought as she headed through the office door, she didn't immediately register her phone ringing in her shirt pocket. When she finally pulled it free, she saw Mabel's name.

The local journalist had only been in town a year but her big heart and community spirit had endeared her to locals. She was on almost every committee, ran Bundy's social media page and never minded hosting book club. She was also at the top of the quilting group's matchmaking list. The last thing the town wanted was for her to fall in love with someone not from the area and leave. She'd been thrown together so many times with Brenna's brother, Taite, that even Brenna had thought something was going on between them.

'Hi, Mabel.'

'Sorry, you sound distracted. Is this a good time?'

'Yes, of course, I'm … just busy.' Clancy crossed her fingers at the half-truth. 'What's going on?'

'It's short notice, but I wanted to know if you had any mural ideas.'

'Does the committee need more?'

'The truth is we need less, but we want to make sure everyone's been involved so we're doing a final ring around. We'll come up with a shortlist and Heath will make the final decision. Any thoughts?'

'Probably nothing you haven't heard before. Wildflowers, the Bundilla Cup, Bundy.'

There was a pause before Mabel replied, 'Just writing these down. I don't know why I didn't think of Bundy. I'm sent photos of him every day.'

'Which keeps you busy and is why you wouldn't have.'

Mabel laughed. 'True. Thanks for these. See you tomorrow night at Brenna's.'

Clancy ended the call and left the office to make herself a coffee. The floor-to-ceiling glass of the conservatory that her mother had added to the kitchen gave her a perfect view of the section of road that wound towards Bundilla. Sunlight glinted on silver. Heath was heading into town.

Even after his convertible rounded the corner and disappeared from sight, she stared through the glass. Instead of her beloved mountains, all she could see was the desolate darkness of his painting.

This morning Heath had done the one thing guaranteed to make any attempt at detachment falter. While he might have shut her out, he couldn't completely hide what he was feeling. His picture said more than words ever could that he was in pain.

'Bundy, welcome to Home Sweet Home for the next month.'

The kelpie's tail thumped on the bare earth.

Heath tipped his head back to look at the top of his newest blank canvas. As tall as any wheat silo, the single concrete water tower featured a ladder running up its right side and a flat roof.

He'd already ordered a cherry picker from Canberra as well as lights and the other electrical items he'd need. Then, as soon as he knew what his subject matter would be, he'd order spray paint and exterior acrylic paint.

Normally before any commission he'd spend time with the locals working out the best way to reflect the community and their surroundings. But he already knew who Bundilla was. This project was a way to say thank you for the support provided to his family as well as pay tribute to the small bush town. Never before had he painted a mural that meant so much to him.

But instead of a buzz of creative enthusiasm, all he felt was flat. A flatness that didn't solely stem from physical exhaustion. He hadn't just painted last night, he'd also been on the internet researching Lewy Body dementia.

Yesterday's news had felled him as though he'd been hit by one of his father's Black Angus bulls. It was all he could do to think straight. His strong indomitable father couldn't be sick. Their time together couldn't already have an end date. There was so much that lay unresolved between them. As for what his mother had implored him to do …

If he could, he would. But even after having made a promise, it would take a miracle to repair the rift with his father. For ten years he had rebuffed any overture Heath had made. After the words '*you are never welcome in this house again*' were delivered in such a cold and precise tone, there was no room left for olive branches. Heath flinched as he blanked out the rest of what his father had said the night he'd left. Today wasn't a day to revisit how a single sentence could inflict a wound so deep that even time couldn't heal.

When Bundy whined, Heath bent to ruffle the kelpie's head. 'Sorry, mate, I'm not very good company today.'

As he straightened, he again looked at the water tower. He had a commission to complete. No good would come of wishing that when he'd seen Clancy earlier in the studio he could have discussed things with her.

Out of loyalty to her parents, he'd long ago made the decision to not darken her sunny world with the toxicity that tainted his life. Her home had been one of laughter and love and his had been one of silence and disapproval. He also hadn't ever wanted to give Clancy any reason to worry or to carry his burdens. She'd always been who everyone went to with their concerns. He could never take advantage of her perceptiveness and generosity when he knew how invested she became when solving other people's problems.

It didn't matter how many years had passed, he still felt the same way. There was no way he could bring himself to trespass on their friendship, especially with Rowan being concerned that Clancy might be lonely. He should be the one listening to her, not the one doing the talking.

Back in his car, he and Bundy drove into town and took the first right before the main street. Their destination was a small and neat weatherboard house with an old model white Hilux parked out the front. With Bundy beside him, he strode up the driveway and knocked on the back door. It swung open.

A large-framed man with snowy white hair greeted him with a broad grin. 'Well, look who the cat dragged in.'

Heath grasped Ned's outstretched hand before being pulled into a bear hug. 'It's been a while.'

'Too long,' Ned said as he released Heath to give him the once-over. 'You look like hell.'

'Thanks.'

The older man led the way into the kitchen where two mugs sat beside the sugar bowl. Ned had been expecting him. The heaviness that had descended after his mother's visit yesterday lifted.

As much as his father had failed to accept him, Ned had always had his back. He'd been so much more than a workman on their family farm. He'd been a mentor, a sounding board and a role model. Although a widower now, he'd shown the same unconditional love to Heath as he had to his own family. He'd also been, and remained, a solid and dependable friend to his mother.

'I don't need to ask if you're still drinking that instant rubbish,' Ned said as he opened a kitchen cupboard to take out a small jar.

Heath smiled as he sat at the wooden kitchen table. Bundy plonked himself on the floor beside his boots.

Unlike Ned, he didn't care about the quality of his caffeine. When in the painting zone he was lucky to remember to eat. The only hot drink he had time for was the quickest he could make.

He glanced at the red and chrome coffee machine that took up almost half of the bench and that he'd given Ned last Christmas. 'Girls still not a fan?'

'Put it this way, Fran monitors how many cups I have like a hawk but when she comes to stay I run out of milk.'

Heath chuckled. Ned's eldest daughter, Fran, was a doctor and his youngest a lawyer. Heath wasn't the only one Ned had encouraged to follow his dreams.

When the kitchen was filled with the aroma of fresh coffee, Ned joined Heath at the table.

He clasped Heath's arm. 'I'm glad you're home, son.'

'It was time.' He paused to allow his emotions to settle. 'Did you know about Dad?'

Ned stared at a spot on the wall behind Heath before replying. 'I don't know the details but I guessed something was wrong. Just like when your mother lost the boys, she's barely left the house.'

Heath took a swallow of too hot coffee as he battled his guilt. What Ned hadn't said was that there'd been another time when his mother had become a recluse. When he'd left. 'It's Lewy Body dementia.'

Ned gave a low whistle. 'That's rough.'

'It is.'

'Does he remember you?'

'I haven't seen him yet.'

'I'll come with you.'

Heath shook his head with a brief smile. 'This is between me and him. Remember the last time you stood up for me?'

'How could I not.'

Their eyes met at the shared memory. Ned was one of the few locals who'd ever dared take on his father. Heath still didn't know how Ned had put up with him and why he'd stayed and worked at Hawks Ridge for as long as he had. On the day he'd been kicked out of home, Ned had gone in to bat for him about studying visual arts at university instead of agriculture. The end result was Ned had been fired and his mother was in tears, and while Ned was checking on her, Heath had been left alone with his father.

He again took a mouthful of coffee. The rest was a history he didn't want to revisit.

From that day on, Ned refused to work for his father, even when his father realised he couldn't do without him. Ned had followed

Heath to Sydney and had only returned home after he'd made sure he had a safe place to stay. It had been Ned and his mother who'd supported him through his art degree and encouraged him to do what he loved when he'd become interested in street art and large-scale murals.

Ned's hand again clasped his arm. 'Look at you now. I couldn't be more proud.'

'Don't speak too soon.' Heath grinned to lighten the mood. They'd both already paid enough of a price for his father's belligerence. 'I haven't started the water tower yet. It could all go wrong.'

Ned gave a deep belly laugh. 'Pigs can fly. You can draw with your left hand better than the rest of us can do with our right.'

'Which I had to do after I broke mine coming off second best with that tree on the motorbike.'

Ned's expression turned solemn. It had been a similar accident that had taken the life of Kyle, the eldest brother he'd never known, at thirteen. 'You aged your mother ten years that afternoon.' Ned's attention shifted to the paint on Heath's hands. 'One of these days you'll sleep like the rest of us. At least tell me you had breakfast.'

At Heath's sheepish expression, Ned grunted. 'Two bacon and egg rolls and another coffee coming up.'

With his stomach full, and despite the amount of caffeine cycling through his veins, Heath was soon ready for a sleep.

As he stifled a yawn, Ned shook his head. 'You look like you need a nanna nap more than I do.'

'I've too much to do.'

'You know where I am if you need me.'

Heath didn't mask his love or respect for the man now standing in front of him. 'I do.'

It was only as they ambled along the driveway to his car that the subject of Clancy came up.

'So …' Ned said, with a sideways glance. 'How's Little Miss Clancy?'

Even though they'd never spoken about how he felt about Clancy, he had no doubt Ned knew. The twinkle in his faded blue gaze couldn't be mistaken for anything else.

'Rowan's worried about her being on her own.'

It was inevitable there'd come a time when Clancy would find someone. He forced back the pain that circumstances had guaranteed it could never be him.

'She doesn't look lonely to me, just busy and happy. My girls couldn't wait to leave, but Clancy belongs here.' They reached Heath's silver convertible and stopped walking. 'And so do you.'

Heath looked away to where Bundy waited beside the passenger door. 'Not anymore. I'll paint the mural, stay however long Mum needs me and go.'

'Things might change with your father now?'

Heath opened the car door for Bundy. 'Pigs really might fly. Dad made it clear Hawks Ridge will never be my home again and you know what he's like, there's no changing his mind. I'm nothing but a flaky no-good artist.'

Anger tightened Ned's mouth. Heath thought he was about to say something but he just gave him another bear hug.

'Son, that's not true and your father knows it even if he's too stubborn to admit he's wrong.'

When Ned pulled away, his creased features had relaxed. 'Now get going, you mightn't want to take a nanna nap but I do.' As he half turned, he gave Heath a wink. 'Good luck with the tourism committee. If old Dr Davis gives you any trouble and wants his portrait front and centre on the tower, just tell him Ned says what happens in bridge club doesn't always have to stay in bridge club.'

Heath chuckled. Retired Dr Davis might be an institution in Bundilla but his self-importance at having once served a term as mayor hadn't diminished with time. 'Will do.'

He drove the short distance to the centre of town and parked near the clock tower. Only a handful of cars occupied the nearby parking spaces. With the ski season having closed after the October long weekend, there would be a tourism lull until the mountain bike trails opened. So, for now, there were no four-wheel drives with ski or bike racks on their roofs, just muddy farm utes with bags of chaff or sleeping dogs on the back.

Together he and Bundy walked towards the art and craft store. Timeless aromas from The Blacksmith's Bakery and the pub further along the street drifted on the cool breeze. Across the road he could see a brightly painted yellow shelf which housed the local street library, and the bottom of the nearby shop windows were each decorated with a strip of book covers. When the summer book festival was on, real books would be piled on outdoor tables and bunting and flags would flutter over the crowd filling the main street. He ignored the tug of nostalgia and of belonging. He couldn't get used to being home.

After collecting the brushes and painting supplies that the art and craft store had ordered in for him, his next stop was the general clothing store for cotton farm shirts. Where he could, he always bought what he needed from local communities.

He grabbed a takeaway coffee and two meat pies from the bakery, one for him and one for Bundy, and ate in the park before continuing along the street to meet with the tourism committee.

When he stopped outside the heritage-listed library building, which used to be the original town hall, he gave Bundy a farewell pat.

A hushed quiet enfolded him as he walked through the front doors. His steps slowed as the years rewound. The library still possessed its familiar book smell even if the layout had changed. The main counter had been moved to the right and computers now occupied the corner where the art section used to be. As a child he'd spent hours sitting cross-legged beside the window, the weight of books heavy in his lap and their pages smooth beneath his fingers.

He headed past the half-completed community jigsaw to where the meeting rooms were located. Clancy's words wishing him good luck ran through his head. He wasn't expecting there to be any problems with the mural. He didn't mind what he painted as long as no part of the design ended up resembling her.

Heels tapped on the floor behind him and he turned to see a slim brunette wearing tailored black pants and a jacket, her arms filled with folders and a laptop. She beamed at him as he held open the door.

'Thank you.' She stopped to adjust her hold on the folders so she could offer him her hand. 'Mabel Holt.'

He grasped her fingers in his. The journalist's animated expression matched the enthusiasm that had infused her words when they'd spoken on the phone. He instantly warmed to her. 'Heath MacBride.'

A dimple flicked in her cheek. 'Nice to meet you.'

He followed her into the room. Dr Davis stood near the urn of hot water, a cup of tea in his hands. Dressed in his usual tweed jacket, pale moleskins and polished boots, he was deep in conversation with Fiona, who owned the gift shop.

Millicent and Beatrice were already seated in the chairs that had been arranged around a large table. Both had notebooks in front of them and gave him identical smiles. He'd earlier caught up with them when he'd filled up with fuel before heading to the water tower. When the sisters had seen him, they'd pulled over to welcome him home.

He took a seat to the far left as Mabel sat opposite him and Dr Davis claimed the seat at the head of the table. Fiona gave him a hug before sitting beside him.

Dr Davis welcomed everyone in his well-modulated voice. Heath tried not to fidget as the doctor's preamble reached the three-minute mark. He shouldn't have had so much coffee.

A subtle cough from Millicent had Dr Davis pause long enough for Mabel to interject brightly, 'Thank you, Dr Davis. You've summed up perfectly how thrilled we are to have Heath painting our water tower.'

When Dr Davis went to speak again, she opened the first folder and continued, 'I know everyone's busy so let's get down to business.'

After Mabel's brief explanation that the ideas for the water tower mural had fallen into three groups—notable residents, local history and the mountain landscape—Dr Davis spoke again. Heath's attention wandered. Beatrice sent him a sympathetic smile.

He wondered if Clancy and Brenna had overcome their nervousness when around the sisters. As serious and severe as Millicent and Beatrice could appear, they had fearless hearts. Without fail, at every community Christmas party they'd gifted him art supplies, even when one year his father had delivered a stony message that they had to stop. At the next Christmas party, he'd received double the supplies.

It took a second for him to register that Mabel had said Clancy's name. 'I still don't know why I didn't think of Bundy as a possible subject, so thank goodness Clancy did. Now are there any ideas on how to narrow down our categories?'

Fiona raised her hand. 'It might just be me, but tourists already come to see the mountains so perhaps we don't need the mural to be just scenery.'

Everyone nodded and Mabel typed on her laptop.

Dr Davis cleared his throat before he spoke. 'I like the idea of notable locals.'

Beatrice was quick to answer, her voice quiet but firm. 'Within reason. The mural is to draw tourists to town; it's not meant to be a personal effigy.'

Dr Davis frowned.

Millicent added her thoughts. 'I like the historical aspect, but wouldn't the picture have to be simple as it's a tower, not a silo or larger building?'

All eyes turned to Heath. 'That's correct. Whatever design is chosen, it will have to work on a singular curved surface.'

Talk then volleyed back and forth, with Dr Davis sticking to wanting to use the image of a respected local.

The brightness of Mabel's smile didn't wane, even if Dr Davis's voice now contained a touch of stubbornness. 'Okay,' she said, 'let's flip this a little. We are known as a book town but our current most famous asset seems to be Bundy. He has mass social media appeal, so in a way he is a notable local.'

This time Dr Davis's frown was a grimace.

'I agree,' Fiona said, leaning forward in her seat. 'I think Bundy should feature. But if we are really clever we can add in something from the other categories to tick as many boxes as possible.'

Millicent and Beatrice nodded.

Mabel stood and turned around her laptop so the group could view the screen. She clicked on Bundy's social media page. 'Let's see if any of these images could work?'

She scrolled through pictures of Bundy with children, Clancy's highland bull, a white horse and sitting on the back of a ute. Every so often she'd stop and when someone would comment she'd make a notation in the open folder beside her.

Heath remained silent. He'd wait until they had a shortlist before giving his two cents' worth. Three of the photos that had already been commented on would be suitable.

A flash of pink filled the laptop screen as a picture appeared of Clancy in a farm shirt, her hair in a ponytail, sitting on a rock with her arm around Bundy. Both were looking away from the camera at the river and Clancy wore a dreamy smile.

Heath's mouth dried. *No way.*

He forced himself to relax. If anyone liked the image, Mabel would make a note and keep scrolling. It would just be one of many.

Then Fiona clapped her hands. 'That has my vote. Not only is it a gorgeous picture but Clancy's family have been here for generations.'

Millicent nodded. 'Clancy loves this town and it's someone like her who will be our future.'

Beatrice smiled. 'I couldn't agree more. Clancy is our past and our future and Bundy is our present. It has my vote, too.'

Mabel looked at Dr Davis. Heath barely heard him say gruffly, 'Mine, too.'

'And mine,' Mabel said, voice excited.

He didn't comment or move. The image wouldn't have to be altered in any significant way to fit the water tower. There was no justifiable reason to say why it wouldn't work or that something else had to be used. It would have been his top pick, too.

He stared at the laptop screen. His worst nightmare had been gift-wrapped and handed to him. So much for making sure whatever he painted didn't reveal his feelings for Clancy. He'd now be spending at least three weeks pouring his heart and soul into a mural that featured the woman he loved but could never have.

CHAPTER

4

'See, I'm fine. Ten fingers and ten toes.' Rowan's face grinned out from Clancy's tablet as he held his left hand and wriggled his fingers. 'Everything's attached.'

Rowan had returned from hiking in Snowdonia and had called to say he was home.

Her laughter ended in a smothered yawn. As late as it was over there, it was early here and she was still in her pyjamas eating porridge. 'Very funny.'

The screen flickered and Rowan reached out to adjust his laptop. He used the left hand that he'd shown her. Her amusement fled. He was right-handed.

'Okay, Mr Ten Fingers and Ten Toes, let me see your other hand.'

'Are you serious?'

She gave him what Brenna called her smile of serenity.

Rowan sighed before he slowly lifted his right arm to reveal a bandaged hand. 'I can explain …'

'You said you were *fine*.'

'I am now.'

Clancy shook her head. 'What happened?'

'We were on this mad mountain bike trail—'

'I thought you were *hiking*?'

'There was a change in plans.'

'How did I know that was what you were going to say?'

Rowan's grin wasn't at all contrite. 'Because I'm your brother and you love me.'

Clancy had a sudden thought. 'You didn't just mountain bike, did you?'

Her brother's eyes narrowed. 'I already feel sorry for your future kids.'

'I'll tell them I honed my I-know-what-you've-been-up-to skills on their uncle. So what was it … abseiling, zip-lining?'

'Gorge scrambling.'

She briefly closed her eyes. 'I'm not even going to ask what that is.'

'For the record … it was a rush.'

'I bet it was.' She paused to look at his bandaged hand. 'Broken or sprained? More importantly, have you been to a doctor?'

'It's a sprain and I'm right to work.' Before she could voice her protests that he wasn't being truthful, his next words scattered her thoughts. 'Speaking of which, who'd have thought you'd end up working with Heath and being the star of one of his murals?'

Time seemed to stop. As much as she tried, she couldn't prevent herself from gaping at the screen. 'What?'

Rowan frowned. 'Hasn't anyone called you?'

Her hold on the tablet became white-knuckled. 'I haven't heard a thing. The committee meeting was late yesterday. How do you know?'

'Heath told me. Have you checked your phone?'

She was already out of her seat and rummaging around in her brown leather tote bag for her mobile. There had been a message from Heath. Fingers unsteady, she opened the text. All it said was whether he could come and see her this morning.

She picked up the tablet again. 'He wants to see me.'

'There you go.'

'I'm not doing it.'

'I know you don't like attention but you don't have to sit for him or anything. The mural's based on the picture of you and Bundy that Brenna took and sent to Mabel for his page.'

Clancy silenced her groan. She knew the photo. It had been taken early last summer when they'd gone to the river for a picnic. She'd been sitting with Bundy watching the others skim stones and remembering when she'd been there doing the same thing with Heath.

It had been on that day for a fleeting moment she'd thought he'd seen her as more than just his best mate's little sister. She'd been sixteen and he'd just finished school so hadn't long turned eighteen. The others had grown tired of skimming stones and it had been the two of them down by the river. She'd gone to skim a pebble and her foot had slipped on the wet rocks. Heath had caught her. As she'd rested against him, his eyes had darkened and his gaze had dropped to her mouth.

Even to this day she didn't know what she'd done. Maybe her lips had parted. Maybe her hands had curled into his shirt. But suddenly it was as though a shutter had descended over his face. His expression went blank and he released her as though her skin had burned.

Things had never been the same between them that summer. He'd then had the row with his father and the next thing he was gone. Without an explanation or a goodbye.

'Clance …' Rowan's quiet voice brought the world back into focus. 'If you really don't want to do it, Heath will understand.'

'I'm just a small-town girl. I did my business degree online so I wouldn't have to deal with people I don't know. I can't string coherent sentences together for book club let alone media interviews, and talking to Mabel doesn't count as she's a friend.'

'Sis, it will be okay. I promise. Talk to Heath.'

She pressed her lips closed to silence the words that talking to Heath ranked right alongside having him paint her picture and seeing the secrets that would be in her eyes. It would be obvious from the background at which part of the river the photo had been taken.

Rowan studied her. 'I'll call tomorrow.'

She forced a smile that she didn't feel. 'Be careful of your hand.'

'Of course.'

After a last glimpse of his grin, the screen went black.

Clancy pushed away her half-finished bowl of breakfast. She no longer had any appetite. Even if she didn't have to physically sit for Heath, he wouldn't be able to help but look at her through artistic eyes. Every blush, every time she grew a little tongue-tied around him, he'd notice. As for the way her pulse beat faster at the base of her throat whenever he was near … no amount of self-control would hide how much he affected her.

She ran her hands through her sleep-tangled hair. She'd saddle Ash and head into the mountains to settle her thoughts. By the time she faced Heath she'd have her wits about her to say that there had to someone else better suited for the mural.

A knock on the back door caused her to jump even before Orien uncurled in his cat bed and hissed. From the silver tabby's reaction, it had to be Heath and Bundy. She rubbed at her tight forehead.

She had two choices: ignore the knock and take a shower, or answer and get the meeting over with.

She eased herself off the stool at the kitchen island bench and looked down at the black-watch tartan pyjamas that had been a present from her mother. She'd thrown on one of Rowan's oversized rugby tops for warmth and her fluffy bed socks were mismatched. If this didn't convince Heath she wasn't model material nothing would. She headed for the back door and flung it open. Cold air engulfed her.

Heath stood in the doorway, his dark hair shower damp and hands wedged in the pockets of his stylish navy jacket. Bundy sat by him. If she'd thought Heath looked exhausted yesterday morning in the studio, today he looked even more wrecked. A rainbow of paint colours stained what she could see of his hands.

She spoke first. 'Like a jet-lag busting coffee and some breakfast?'

A brief smile shaped his lips. 'Do I look that bad?'

'Yep.'

'Just a coffee would be great.'

When he went to take off his boots, she shook her head. 'It's fine.'

'Thanks for the kettle you put in the studio,' he said as he followed her into the kitchen.

'No worries,' she said without looking at him. His heady cologne was already making her feel light-headed. As for her plan to not appear model-like, he hadn't even appeared to notice how she was dressed.

Orien greeted Bundy with another hiss and an arched back before wrapping himself around Heath's legs. Heath bent to scratch the cat's head.

Clancy took two mugs out of the cupboard and then hesitated. She had no idea how Heath took his coffee now.

'Still strong with one sugar and milk?' she asked, hoping her voice didn't come across as strained.

Not knowing the little things about Heath could only be good. It would help convince her that he was essentially a stranger. Yet the knowledge that she'd missed out on so much of his life still elicited an ache of hurt.

'Just black, thanks,' he said as he positioned himself on a stool.

Orien stalked off to his bed in the corner. His green feline eyes dared Bundy to put one paw wrong. Bundy ignored him.

Heath appeared to study her as she placed their coffees on the island bench. He glanced at her nearby tablet. 'Been talking to Rowan?'

She chose a seat on the other side of the bench. The expanse of pale grey marble provided a welcome space between them. 'He just called.'

Heath reached for his coffee without taking his attention off her. 'You're not happy with the committee's decision, are you?'

Her sigh turned into more of an exasperated huff. 'Look at me. I'm no mural model.'

For a brief second his eyes flickered over her face and then the old blue-and-red Bundilla Brumbies rugby top she wore. An expression she couldn't decipher tightened his features. 'You are far more of a model than you think.'

'Rubbish. I know it's for a good cause and I'm really honoured … but as I said to Rowan, I'm a small-town girl who likes going under the radar and living a quiet life. The publicity will do my head in.'

'There will be some promo involved as that's what this is all about, bringing people to town. But you don't have to do any interviews. I'll handle it.' He paused to give her a slow smile. 'I've no doubt Dr Davis would be more than happy to share the limelight.'

She stared into her coffee. Dr Davis would relish the attention. But while Heath had understood her reluctance, he hadn't given her an out. She looked up. She simply wasn't doing it. She couldn't be thrown into contact with him, even in small doses. She couldn't have him discovering her secrets. 'What was plan B?'

Heath didn't immediately answer. When he did, his tone was low. 'I know that's your I'm-not-giving-in voice but ... I need you to be my model.'

'Why?'

The single word hung between them.

She held her breath. Would Heath open up, even just a little?

He rubbed at his jaw and the rasp of his whiskers filled the silence. 'I thought I had more time for the project, but I need to get it done as soon as possible.'

'So you can leave?'

'Yes and no.'

She shook her head against the disappointment. He still couldn't trust her. The coffee she sipped was as bitter as her thoughts. She'd known he'd leave again but to hear him say it so casually was like he'd left without saying farewell all over again. As for the way he was using their friendship to make his life easier, this was more proof he wasn't the man she'd known.

Her gaze locked with his. 'There would be a ton of photos of Bundy with other locals. Pick one.'

In his eyes she thought she'd see a will as implacable as the marble their coffee mugs rested on. Instead she saw sadness.

'Clance … I have family stuff to sort out. I've known you all my life, I could paint you blindfolded.' He reached into his jacket pocket and took out a piece of paper on which the photo of her and Bundy had been printed. Heath had folded the edges so there was no background, just her and Bundy. The day of the photo she hadn't worn a hat but Heath had now drawn one in and the brim shaded her eyes.

She didn't know if it was his intense stillness, the rawness of his tone or her relief at her face partially being concealed by the hat brim, but her resolve wavered.

For a second she thought he would reach out and touch her hand but instead he cleared his throat. 'Can I please use your photo? I wouldn't ask if it wasn't important.'

She looked at the hat Heath had drawn, which he'd only briefly seen the night he'd arrived. He'd captured every battered detail, even the small hole at the crown. She needed no further proof that he noticed details about her that no one else did. But he'd come as close as he ever had to asking her for anything.

She replied before self-preservation could stop her. 'I'm not being paraded around town like a celebrity. I'd do more harm to Bundilla's image than good. And you have to get at least eight hours' sleep every night.'

Relief didn't lighten his expression. If anything the grooves bracketing his mouth deepened. 'Thank you.'

As he folded away the picture she spoke again. 'And …'

'And?'

'If you need any help with your … family stuff … let me know.'

'Sure.'

But as he slipped the mural design into his shirt pocket, she didn't miss the flicker of a muscle in his jaw.

Orien chose that moment to spring from his bed, hiss and swipe his paw in front of Bundy's nose as the kelpie rolled onto his side and stretched. Bundy opened one eye and then shut it again.

The distraction eased the tension in the room.

'You weren't wrong about Orien's death stares,' Heath said, tone again casual before he took a mouthful of coffee.

'Give them another five minutes and they will be best buddies. Are you sure you don't want anything to eat?'

Heath shook his head, his attention settling on the rugby top she wore. 'Does that belong to anyone I know?'

She frowned, not immediately understanding what he asked. When she did, the images she'd seen of Heath with different women flipped through her head. He'd had far more opportunities to swap clothes than she'd ever had. 'Yes. Rowan. I don't make a practice of wearing exes' clothes.'

'Fair enough.'

She continued to frown. Heath didn't need to know there hadn't been any significant exes or that her relationships rarely made it past the three-date mark. After all, he was the reason why she couldn't connect with anyone else, let alone feel anything resembling a spark. 'That jacket ... was it chosen by an ex or were you jet-lagged and it seemed like a good idea at the time?'

The corner of his mouth lifted. 'Neither. Mum chose it.'

Clancy hoped her expression conveyed amusement and not relief. When it came to the women on his social media pages, she'd never been sure which had been fans, girlfriends or just friends. 'No way. Your mother's always had such good taste. You still better not wear it to Brenna's tonight, though.'

'Taite's already told me not to turn up looking like a soft city boy.' Heath stood to collect their empty mugs to take over to the sink. 'Would you like a lift? No point taking two cars.'

Still processing the fact that his citified jacket wasn't from an ex, Clancy took a moment to reply. She'd always counted on Rowan to spill any of Heath's dating news but her brother had never divulged any specifics about Heath's love life. But no information hadn't meant that he didn't have one.

'Thanks. Brenna said six thirty. I'll come over about six.'

'I know, mate,' Heath said under his breath as Bundy looked across at him as they walked back to the coach house.

What had he been thinking offering Clancy a lift to the barbeque? His only excuse was sleep deprivation and that he'd wanted to make sure she really was okay about the mural. Her expression had still been pensive when he'd left. Once at Brenna's there wouldn't be much chance of a quiet chat, let alone one that didn't take place before an audience.

He opened the front door with a heavy sigh. He should have known Clancy would have been in contact with Rowan. He'd planned to call her last night to tell her about the committee's decision. But after a long talk with his mother about her day with his father, time had gotten away. Knowing Rowan would be awake, as it was only morning in the United Kingdom, he'd instead spoken to him.

Heath headed to where his laptop was set up on the small kitchen table. In order to help his mother, and his father if he'd ever let him, he needed to complete the mural as soon as possible. For this to happen he had to bury his fears about having Clancy as his model. He passed a hand around the base of his neck. He just hoped he hadn't revealed too much when he said he could paint her blindfolded.

He took a seat and reached into his pocket for the mural picture before smoothing it out on the table. Most of his designs were monochrome but this time he'd use colour. This way he could capture the striking contrast between Clancy's pale skin and the lustre of her red-brown hair. Bundy, with his intelligent amber eyes and glossy black coat, also wouldn't be done justice in neutral tones.

His attention lingered on Clancy's image. How could she think of herself as not model material? This morning her long hair might have been tousled, her face makeup free and her curves hidden beneath oversized clothes, but his heart had hammered just like it always did. Despite all the times she'd appeared in his art, he'd never been able to capture the true essence of who she was. The light in her grey gaze, her innate warmth and her quiet intensity were all things that set her apart. Her beauty went beyond the physical.

The tick of the kitchen clock reminded him he had lots to do. He opened his laptop. Now that the mural composition had been finalised, the next thing on his to-do list was to work out how much paint he'd need. Once his calculations were done and the order placed, he headed into town to the water tower. After borrowing Ned's pressure washer he cleaned what dust and dirt he could reach off the concrete without the cherry picker. Just like on previous visits, Bundy showed no sign of wanting to leave. The kelpie wasn't the only one to keep him company.

Curious locals as well as out-of-towners slowed as they drove past or stopped for a yarn. While he appreciated the interest, once he started painting he'd have a tunnel vision mindset where he wouldn't want to stop until he was done. It was even more important than usual that he finish this mural as soon as possible. Last night he'd pushed back his next project in Toronto to buy himself more time with his parents.

He packed away the air compressor in the lockable shipping container he'd had delivered overnight and had driven past the last of the wooden bridges when his mobile rang. Expecting it to be his mother, as he'd mentioned yesterday he wanted to see his father, he answered via bluetooth. It was only when he'd accepted the call he registered it was Clancy's name on the screen. 'Hi, Clance.'

'Hi. You must be in the car—there's a bit of an echo.'

The muscles across his shoulders tightened. Having Clancy's voice fill the space around him triggered memories of her sitting on a box in the studio while he painted, her stories making him smile. The sun had always shone a little brighter when he'd been with her.

'Yep, I've just left town.'

'Bundy with you?'

'He is. We seem to share a love for meat pies.'

Her soft laughter charmed his senses and made him long to make her laugh again. 'Thanks for the offer of a lift tonight but Brenna wants me to head out early.'

'No problem.' He worked hard to keep a sudden sense of loss from rasping his reply. 'See you there.'

'Okay.'

The call ended and he tapped the music playlist on his mobile to fill the silence and emptiness within him with a country tune. No good would come of revisiting the past or wishing things could be different. He could only be thankful that however many exes Clancy may have had none were who she had been looking for. He turned up the song's volume. It was only a matter of time before someone did come along, and when they did he wouldn't again be able to set foot in Bundilla.

He kept the music playing until he parked outside the coach house.

After a ride on Goliath and a shower, he dressed in the blue farm shirt he'd bought yesterday, his oldest jeans and a navy woollen jumper with a half zip. It was the best he could do to look casual without wearing clothes covered in paint. Just to make sure he didn't appear too citified, he ran a hand through his too short hair. Even though he'd last seen Taite when they'd caught up at a Sydney rugby game two seasons ago, he was sure Brenna's brother still didn't own a brush.

With Bundy asleep in the upstairs bedroom in front of the fire, he left the back door ajar so the kelpie could get some fresh air and Orien could sneak inside. Despite all the hissing and hackle-raising that morning, the two of them had indeed been best buddies when they'd searched for lizards in the dry-stone wall.

Clancy's dual cab wasn't in the car port as he drove out. At least tonight they'd be surrounded by people and it would be easy to hide his feelings for her. It was when they were alone that the walls he'd been so vigilant at keeping in place seemed to crack. Giving in to the need to know who the men's rugby top had belonged to was a wake-up call. His emotions couldn't again seep through his self-control.

At the end of the poplar tree–lined drive he turned right to follow the road that skirted the valley floor. This time he was content with silence as he took in the natural beauty. Even as he watched, late-afternoon shadows settled over the tall peaks. The white gleam of snow dulled and a blush of rose-pink spread across the sky. Despite all the spectacular scenery he'd seen overseas, there was no place like home.

He took the next turn and followed the narrow road until it became gravel. All colour had now faded from the horizon and against the muted backdrop the hulking mountains formed dark and jagged voids. If it wasn't so important to get the mural finished as soon as possible, he'd have tied a swag to Goliath's saddle and headed into the high country to paint.

A huge iron archway loomed on his right. He slowed to pass beneath the entryway constructed out of farm machinery and rusted tools. When Taite wasn't working, he spent his downtime welding in his shed.

The beam of Heath's headlights illuminated two deer on the side of the driveway, except their eyes didn't blink. Made out of recycled scrap metal, the two life-sized sculptures appeared almost real. Further along, Heath stopped to examine the skill and detail on a brumby mare and her foal. While Taite only ever called his creations a hobby, he was proof that art and running a farm could co-exist.

Heath continued on to the single-storey farmhouse set in front of a cluster of outbuildings. Brenna occupied the original homestead while Taite lived in a stone cottage closer to the creek. His argument had been that he was the unsociable one and would spend more time in his custom-built workshop than wherever he lived. But Heath suspected Taite knew that the target on his bachelor back would be reduced if he lived in a smaller and more rustic dwelling.

As Heath pulled up alongside a mud-splattered Hilux, the scent of wood smoke filtered into the car along with the aroma of onion and steak. His mouth watered. Too busy using the pressure washer earlier, he'd skipped lunch. In the nearby paddock a sizable group of locals were congregated around a fire pit flickering with orange flames. In true sociable Brenna style her barbeque wasn't a low-key gathering.

He unclipped his seatbelt and gave the group a quick scan. There was no sign of Clancy. As he strolled through the parked vehicles he noticed a difference from ten years ago. Before there would have been utes tricked up with sky-high aerials, bull bars and light bars. Now there were family friendly four-wheel drives with baby seats.

He looked away from a car that had a tiny pink bike on the back. He had to be careful that the yearnings for a family and a home with the woman he loved didn't drown out his need to create. For if he didn't have art to fill his life, he'd be left with nothing.

A broad-shouldered figure dressed in jeans and an oilskin strode over to the gate to greet him.

'Well, well, look who's here.' Taite's smile flashed in the gloom.

Heath returned his hug. There was a reason why Taite created havoc every rugby season. The deer farmer was nothing but muscle.

Taite held him at arm's length. 'I don't know what Brenna was going on about. You look the same …' Taite frowned. 'Except for your hair.'

'Blame Rowan. He told the London barber I needed a going-home-to-see-my-mother haircut.'

Taite chuckled. 'Enough said. Meanwhile he's looking like one of his highland cows.'

Childish laughter came from over near the fire pit. Heath turned to see three small girls in jeans and cowgirl boots chasing each other.

Taite too looked across at the children. 'I'm guessing some things have changed?'

He nodded, taking in the number of prams parked amongst the crowd. 'You could say that.'

'There's not many of our vintage left.' Taite dipped his head towards a cluster of male guests who all had stubbies in their hands. 'As for those young fellas, they mightn't look old enough to shave but when it comes to punching above their weight, they have all the moves.' He grinned before clasping Heath's shoulder. 'Just as well us oldies can still teach them a thing or two. Beer?'

'Speak for yourself—my moves are long gone. I'd love one.'

'If we're quick we can head to the workshop. Brenna's inside with Clancy and Mabel doing secret book club business.' Taite waved at a man cooking on a barbeque illuminated by the light spilling from what had once been the original stables. Inside the wooden building, chairs and hay bales were arranged around a food-laden table. 'Matt's got the barbeque sorted. His little bloke's hungry.'

Heath followed Taite to a gator and they drove the short distance to a large steel shed. Overhead the first of the stars gleamed and the breeze carried a hint of winter's chill. As soon as he walked through the wide doors, Heath knew this wouldn't be a quick visit. A half-completed horse dominated the floor space, while scattered piles of scrap metal indicated Taite had a backlog of new projects.

Taite handed him a stubby from the beer fridge and set about giving him the grand tour. They'd only just finished their beers and hadn't started to discuss Taite's current sculpture when Brenna called. Taite didn't have to have his phone on speaker for Heath to hear Brenna say they'd better get their butts back there otherwise they'd be eating peanut butter sandwiches for dinner.

By the time they returned, the area around the fire pit was empty. The clink of cutlery sounded from within the stables and the chairs and hay bales were almost all occupied. Over near the barbeque Clancy stood with Brenna and Mabel. All three wore jeans, boots and dark coats. One of the men who Taite had said was part of the younger crowd piled steaks on their plates with a confident grin.

Brenna turned to shoot him and Taite a look from beneath an arched brow. 'About time. Heath will pass out from hunger.'

Heath gave an apologetic smile, his attention only half on Brenna as the guy behind the barbeque gave Clancy a wink.

Beside him he heard Taite placate his sister. 'I gave him a beer.'

Brenna shook her head and handed them both a plate.

When Heath again looked at Clancy she was inside the shed with Mabel choosing from the assortment of salads. When their plates were full, they moved to a corner to sit on a spare hay bale.

It wasn't a coincidence that instead of adding steaks to Taite's plate, the young fellow behind the barbeque handed the tongs to him. 'There you go, big guy, they're all yours.'

After sliding a beer out of an esky filled with ice, he sauntered over to join Clancy, Mabel and now Brenna.

Taite sighed. 'They have all the moves.'

Heath only nodded. When he'd glanced over at the group, Clancy's eyes had met his and she'd given him a smile.

But as people went back for seconds and then enjoyed a dessert of pavlova and fruit salad, Clancy no longer appeared to notice him. In fact, whenever their paths crossed she'd introduce him to the closest person as though he was a guest and she felt obliged to make sure he had someone to talk to. Meanwhile, it wasn't only the younger man with the confident grin who had attached himself to Clancy, Mabel and Brenna—his mates had as well.

As the temperature dropped and the wind picked up, parents carried tired and sleepy children to their cars. The crowd filling the stables dwindled. He and Taite joined the girls around the fire pit as they laughed and toasted marshmallows. Their wet-behind-the-ears admirers had gone to raid the esky for more beer. In the glow of the firelight he caught Clancy give him a glance before she took another marshmallow from out of the packet.

Brenna handed him a stick. 'Here you go, MacBride. You look like you need more sugar.'

Beside him Taite groaned. 'More sugar? You've already given us two pieces of pavlova. I'm going to have to double my run tomorrow.'

After the group laughed, Brenna took orders for coffee and with Mabel returned to the main house. Taite stoked the fire and then disappeared into the darkness, Heath guessed to collect more wood.

Clancy offered Heath a marshmallow before gazing into the flames. Mr Confident Grin strode over but when Heath's eyes met his, the younger man hesitated before turning on his boot heels to return to the shed. He mightn't have the moves the young fellas did but his do-you-really-want-to-be-here stare still worked just fine. It was important he talked to Clancy alone.

Heath rotated his stick so as to not burn his marshmallow. 'Clance,' he said, voice low, 'are you really okay about the mural?'

She sent him another quick look. 'I'm fine. Really.'

His phone vibrated in his pocket and he slipped it free to check the short message. He thought he'd concealed his reaction until Clancy asked softly, 'Bad news?'

'It was just from Mum.'

Clancy broke eye contact as her marshmallow burst into flames. She stared at it before tossing the stick and charred marshmallow into the fire.

'If it was bad news, you know you can tell me. That's what friends do … they support each other.'

He stilled. There was a new note in her voice he hadn't heard before, a note he would have labelled as hurt.

'Clance …'

'It's all good.' Chin lifted, she went to turn away. 'Forget I said anything.'

He reached for her arm. Big mistake. He never touched her. He simply didn't trust that his self-control would hold. Even beneath the layer of her coat he could feel her slender strength that on that long-ago ride had been wrapped around him. All he could breathe in was her floral scent that never failed to weaken his resolve. And all he could feel was the deep need to kiss her that hadn't diminished over the years.

Jaw tight, he lowered his arm. 'I was going to say … Mum agreed it was time to see Dad. I'm going tomorrow.'

For a moment Clancy didn't move and then her fingers curled over his. Before he could react, her hand lifted and cold air replaced the warmth of her touch.

Then she was gone, leaving him with a soft 'good luck' and a smile that would stay with him long after the last of the starlight had faded into the grey palette of dawn.

Nowhere did spring like the high country.

Clancy straightened from pulling out weeds from a peony bed and let the slight breeze lift her hair and cool her forehead. The winter world around her was coming back to life. The poplars along the driveway sported a tinge of green and a cluster of yellow daffodils bloomed between the coach house and main homestead. She shrugged off her heavy coat and draped it over the wheelbarrow beside her.

The call of a mother cow drifted to her. It wasn't only her peonies she checked every day. This morning's early ride around Rowan's cattle had revealed two overnight calves. Her gaze traced the granite ridges at the valley edge bathed in sunlight. Somewhere up there, brumby foals would also be standing on their wobbly newborn legs. She just hoped they'd stay protected and safe. Wild dogs wouldn't usually take on a brumby mare, but there'd been recent reports about an aggressive pack.

A gust of wind made the plants beside her dance. The crisp winter temperatures and heavy frosts had produced an abundance of lush foliage and buds. Herbaceous peonies usually didn't like being disturbed but even the tubers she'd divided and moved in the autumn would flower. All she needed now was some more warm spring days and she would be in peony-picking heaven for the next month.

Well, she hoped she would. Last year a cold early November had been followed by a heatwave and the season had been over in three weeks. Until the marble-sized peony buds were bigger they remained vulnerable to a late frost. She really needed the weather gods to cooperate. The cattle markets weren't what they used to be and the upkeep on the historic property remained high. The flower farm she'd started four years ago had to pull its weight financially.

She grasped the handles of the wheelbarrow and headed for the row of compost bins. Which was why she had no time to obsess over Heath. The breeze carried away her long sigh. Something easier said than done.

Last night might have been the closest he'd come to letting her in but her regret over their conversation around the fire pit deepened. Instead of being cautious and curbing what she said, she'd allowed emotion to blindside her. She should have ignored her hurt that he hadn't confided in her and not acted on either her worry or her need to help him.

She dumped the weeds into the closest compost bin. She'd been going so well, too, for once sticking to her plan to treat him like any other guest. But between Heath's casual country clothes and the firelight flickering over his face, it had been impossible to not see him as anything but the man she knew.

A man who had enough things to contend with without the little sister of his best mate changing the rules of their friendship.

She had to accept that her relationship with him didn't include the acceptance of emotional support. She also had to forget how his light clasp of her arm made her skin heat, heart race and senses fixate on the masculine beauty of his mouth.

She pushed the empty wheelbarrow over to the large packing shed. So, today had to be all about damage control. She'd find an excuse to see Heath and when she did she'd be bright and breezy to prove nothing had changed between them.

With her jobs completed, she returned inside without glancing at the coach house. A photo on Bundy's social media page had shown the kelpie and Heath beside a cherry picker. With Heath already at the water tower, it was likely he'd be seeing his father that afternoon. Technically she didn't need to go to town this morning but last night at Brenna's they'd planned the book club supper menu and she needed baking ingredients.

She glanced over to Orien who lay sleeping on the floor in a stream of sunlight. 'I'm sure you need cat food, too, don't you?'

Without opening his eyes, the silver tabby gave a wave of his tail.

Clancy grabbed her leather tote bag before she could change her mind. Being impulsive had already gotten her into trouble. But the sooner she made things right with Heath, the sooner she could focus on making sure she had everything ready for when the peony season started. She also had her quilt to finish for the drought relief drive plus needed to read the book that had been chosen for book club.

Once in town, she parked a block away from the grocery store. The walk would help expend her restlessness at soon seeing Heath again.

She'd only made it as far as the pub when a woman called her name. She slowly turned to see Cynthia speeding towards her.

Today Cynthia wore a fire-engine red dress to match the frames of her glasses and her yellow-blonde hair was piled into a bun secured with a red scrunchie. In her hands was a large white cake box.

'Morning,' Cynthia said, her smile as bright as her outfit.

Clancy nodded at the box. 'Someone's birthday?'

Cynthia's laughter was a little too self-satisfied. 'Morning smoko for Heath.'

Clancy resisted looking past Cynthia to check if any, or all, of her lookalike daughters were in town. If they were, Heath might need a heads up. She instead asked, 'The girls with you?'

'Yes, but only Larissa and Hannah.' Cynthia paused while she looked Clancy up and down. 'I think you'll make a very good mural model.'

Clancy smothered her groan. She'd been so caught up in thinking about Heath she'd forgotten she'd be the favourite topic of conversation for at least the next two days. 'Bundy's being painted, too.'

'So he is. It's such perfect spring weather I think I'll take a photo of him with Larissa and Hannah. Just in case your photo turns out to be not quite … suitable.'

Clancy kept a straight face. Heath definitely needed a heads up. 'Don't forget to send any photos to Mabel.'

She may as well have not spoken as Cynthia had left to go over to where her car was parked nearby. Larissa, who was in the front passenger seat, gave her a wave. Her younger sister, Hannah, who had taken to dressing in black, simply stared.

Not making it too obvious, Clancy texted Heath as she walked away.

Cynthia and co. about to do a smoko delivery.

Before she could return her phone to her tote bag a reply whooshed in.

In cherry picker. Not down for another hour.

Her fingers hovered over the screen. As much as she wanted to ask when he'd be seeing his father she couldn't again overstep the mark. If Heath was in the cherry picker there was no way she'd be able to see him to show that things were okay between them.

She typed a quick reply. *Glad you don't have a fear of heights.*

Only of matchmaking mothers. Leaving soon?

What do you need? Coffee? Pies?

Flowers, if it's not too much trouble.

She glanced at the florist shop at the end of the block. Her throat ached with the knowledge that Heath's kind and caring side still existed. He wasn't just visiting his father.

Will drop some on my way past.

Thanks.

She went to reply but then deleted it. It would be wise to end the conversation there. She'd buy her groceries and visit Rebecca in the flower shop. By then Heath would be out of the cherry picker.

She'd only just reached the sliding glass doors of the grocery store when she again heard her name. She looked over her shoulder to see Dr Davis making his way across the street towards her. Despite the spring warmth the doctor wore his customary tweed jacket, moleskins and highly polished brown boots. She couldn't tell from his expression whether he was happy or disappointed that she would be the one featured on the water tower.

'Just the person I wanted to see,' he said as he joined her on the footpath. 'Now, about the mural … I've already prepared a press release and have organised publicity shots.'

She suddenly shared Heath's need to get the water tower project completed as soon as possible. Dr Davis must have missed the memo that she wanted to stay out of the spotlight. 'Dr Davis, that's very kind but—'

He cut her off with an indulgent smile. 'It was no trouble, it's the least I can do. We make a great team. You and Bundy will be the faces on the mural and I'll be the public face in the press.'

'Sounds wonderful.' Heath had more than handled keeping her out of the limelight.

Dr Davis nodded as he half turned, eager to leave. 'I've an appointment with Joe for a haircut. I can't be looking dishevelled for my new photos.'

He power-walked in the direction of the barber shop.

Smiling, Clancy stepped inside the grocery store and looked around for anyone else she might know. At this rate Heath would have finished the entire mural by the time she made it to the water tower.

Her trolley was a quarter full when she spied the trim forms of Millicent and Beatrice dressed in their usual sensible pants and plain-coloured jumpers in aisle three. Conscious that most of her grocery items were for the book club supper, she ducked into aisle five.

When discussing the menu with Brenna and Mabel, she'd come up with a way to prove that she was far more than a book club member who drank copious cups of tea and usually said the wrong thing. She was someone who listened, especially when the sisters ever made a brief mention of their past, and someone who also thought of others. She couldn't now have the sisters see anything in the trolley that might ruin her secret weapon.

She grabbed the last item she needed and made a beeline for the checkout. To her relief the teenage boy manning the counter didn't make small talk as he scanned her items. She was soon back in the sunshine and when she checked the clock tower it had only been forty-five minutes since she'd messaged Heath.

After a quick stop at Rebecca's for flowers and to let her know the peonies were not quite ready, and the café for a takeaway black coffee, Clancy was on her way to the edge of town.

As she drew near to the water tower she caught sight of Heath high up in the cherry picker as he blasted off dust and dirt with the pressure washer. At the tower base was a shipping container with a fold-out table and chairs out the front.

Her phone whooshed with a text.

Coming down now.

She quelled a rush of happiness that Heath had been watching out for her and settled her sunglasses more firmly in place. The next five minutes would be all about appearing normal.

By the time she'd parked and opened her car door, Bundy had raced over. Heath followed close behind. She bent to pat the kelpie, thankful her sunglasses concealed the worry she knew would be in her eyes. So much for Heath getting eight hours of sleep. He didn't only look dusty and windblown but bone-weary.

She handed him his coffee. 'Thought you might need this.'

His grin kickstarted a fluttering in her midriff. 'You read my mind.'

To hide the warmth in her cheeks, she dipped her head towards the nearby small table that didn't only just hold Cynthia's white cake container, which now had her phone number scrawled across the top, but an assortment of other smoko deliveries. 'You won't be going hungry.'

'Another week of eating like this and the cherry picker will be flat out holding me.'

Their shared laughter eased her concerns there'd be any awkwardness after Brenna's barbecue. She was right to have made sure things were back to how they should be between them.

Heath's expression sobered as he looked at the bunch of daisies, carnations and sprigs of silver eucalyptus she'd placed on the table. 'Thanks for these.'

'You're welcome.'

They both knew these flowers represented more than a bouquet of pretty spring blooms.

'I'd forgotten how it's not always easy to duck in and out of a small town.'

'Tell me about it.'

Heath took a swallow of coffee before speaking again. 'I owe you an apology, Clance.'

She fought a frown. This wasn't how she'd envisioned that their meeting would go.

He continued without waiting for a reply. 'My father might have disowned me but growing up I was surrounded by people who cared and that included your mum and dad.' He paused as emotion darkened his eyes. 'We are friends, Clance, and I'm sorry I wasn't there for you when you lost them.'

She blinked to suppress the hot well of tears as her grief surged. Things were not back to normal. This grave and intense Heath looking at her as though he could see through the shield of her sunglasses at everything she had to hide scared her. He'd break her heart all over again and then be gone without any goodbye.

She forced her voice to remain steady. 'You don't need to apologise. You supported Rowan whenever I struggled to, and you came back when you needed to.' She attempted a smile. 'I hope your dad sees reason, but if he doesn't, even if my mum and dad are no longer here, you'll always have a home with us.'

Before she could say anything more or let her emotions break free, she turned and left.

Coffee cup cooling in his hand, Heath stared at the road Clancy had taken long after her dual cab had disappeared. Her words didn't fool him. Their conversation couldn't have gone any more wrong than if Bundy had chased a black cat across his path.

The last thing he'd ever wanted to do was cause Clancy pain, and in the space of twenty-four hours, he'd upset her twice.

The hurt in her words last night had made sleeping impossible. So, after the barbeque, he'd painted in the studio and as soon as it was light he'd come to the water tower to finish cleaning. If the spotlight he'd ordered had arrived, he would have come earlier. All the while he'd worked, he'd thought through what to say to Clancy to make amends.

Still he gazed at the empty road. But his apology hadn't gone as planned. While Clancy had smiled before she'd left, it had been a weary gesture that spoke of anguish and loss. In all the years he'd known her, she'd always been buoyant and resilient. Even when pets had died, or she'd injured herself, her optimism had shone through her sadness and pain. It crushed him to see the light of her joy dimmed.

Heart heavy, he went into the shipping container to dump his undrunk coffee in the garbage can. He'd lost count of the times he'd gone to call or email after her parents' accident. But a part of him had always been unable to follow through. He didn't know if it was his father's words that Clancy was better off without him or the fear that beneath his support she'd sense his true feelings, but days turned into weeks, months and then years.

Rowan had worked out a long time ago how he felt about his sister and had kept him updated. Whenever he'd said she'd been doing it tough, he'd always ended by reassuring him how much better she was now doing. If he hadn't, Heath would have dropped everything to come home. The only time Rowan had ever said he was worried about her was at their recent meeting in London.

He scrubbed a hand over his face. So much for keeping an eye on her for Rowan. From here on in it was a priority to ensure that his friendship with Clancy found its way back to the uncomplicated and easy relationship it once was. He couldn't cause her any more hurt.

Needing to keep busy, Heath carried the smoko deliveries and flowers to his car. He put the table, chairs and water compressor into the shipping container and locked the door.

Once at his convertible, he didn't immediately reach for the door handle.

Bundy cocked his head to the side as he looked at him.

'Are you sure you want to tag along? It's going to be a rough afternoon.'

Bundy's tail wagged and Heath opened the door to the back seat.

Their first stop wasn't far out of town. Gravel crunched beneath his tyres as he drove through the iron gates of the local cemetery. To his left, a stone wall surrounded the pioneer graves with their weathered sandstone headstones, while to his right the sun glinted on modern black granite. He parked in the shade of a scribbly gum and then, with Bundy beside him, made his way through the plots to a row of neatly tended graves.

He stopped at the first two graves, taking in the fresh flowers and dust-free headstones. Despite all the stress his mother had been under caring for his father, she still kept the family plots pristine. He placed some carnations and daisies in the vases on his maternal grandparents' graves. Just like the brothers he'd never known, he also had no memory of his pop or the uncle who was buried next to them. His memories of his grandma were few but precious. He added flowers to his uncle's grave before standing in front of his oldest brother Kyle's resting place.

Even though he'd been born twenty-two years after Kyle, he felt like he knew him. His mother had shared stories of his sense of humour and his love of the bush and had shown him photographs of his too short thirteen-year life. Heath added flowers to the ones already filling Kyle's vase and moved to Andrew's grave.

While it had been a farm motorbike accident that had robbed them of Kyle, it had been a car accident on a wet winter highway that had taken Andrew. He'd been heading back to Sydney University, where he'd been studying for an agriculture degree, when he lost control around a bend. Just like Kyle's memory, his mother had made sure Heath knew all about the brother who was twenty years older than him. It was his father who refused to talk about either Kyle or Andrew.

He placed flowers on Andrew's grave and after a quiet moment went in search of two other headstones. When he found the graves of Clancy's parents, he added the last of the flowers to their vases. Just like his own family plots, Edward and Isobel Parker's graves, and those in the rest of the row, were tidy. Clancy too was a frequent visitor.

After another moment of silence, Heath made his way to his car. As he and Bundy left he looked through the side window at the mountains that watched over the cemetery like silent sentinels. However the next hour went, and however unwelcome he was made to feel, the high country was still home and the blood of his ancestors who'd also called it home flowed through his veins.

The drive around the valley edge seemed to take longer than usual. When he rounded the corner and saw the front gate of Hawks Ridge, his heart pounded. Next summer it would be ten years since he'd had words with his father. In all that time he'd never been back.

He drove over the cattle grid, taking in the changes. Rust now showed through the white of the railway sleepers that had been assembled into a fence to flank the gateway. The mailbox sat at a tilt and the farm sign on the top right sleeper also showed signs of age and neglect.

He continued forward at a crawl, not because of sentiment, but because of the potholes gouged in the road. The driveway was long overdue needing to be levelled with the tractor blade. The further he drove, the more tension constricted his chest.

The hay shed had tin missing from the roof and the tractor beside the machinery shed hadn't been moved for so long grass had grown around its flat back tyres. Blackberries chocked gullies and briar boxthorns grew thick and vigorous beneath trees. A nearby fence was crushed by the weight of a fallen branch and only a handful of Angus cattle grazed in the paddock.

No wonder his mother had kept him away. She'd always insisted on meeting at his home in Sydney. He'd always thought it was so he wouldn't encounter his father, but now he could see another reason. The disrepair surrounding him wasn't a recent occurrence.

It would have taken years for the once well-kept farm to become so derelict.

He pulled up beneath the ancient fir tree. The original farmhouse had burned down in a bushfire when his mother had been a child, so compared to Clancy's homestead, this one wasn't old. But with the flaking paint and rusted roof and gutters it looked like it too had survived for over a century. The only things that looked well cared for were the neat garden beds and the mown lawn. His mother had always enjoyed working in her garden. At times of loss, it had been her therapy and her solace.

He glanced over his shoulder at Bundy. 'There's a shady spot on the front veranda perfect for sleeping through family drama.'

There wouldn't be any pet dogs to take offence at Bundy's presence. When he'd been young he'd had a Jack Russell called Minnie who had been his constant companion. Otherwise there'd only ever been working dogs. His father hadn't seen the value in having an animal who didn't serve a purpose. Heath unclipped his seatbelt with a sigh. Much like how his father viewed a son with a career in visual arts.

The small wrought-iron garden gate creaked as he and Bundy walked through. They'd only taken a few steps on the stone pavers when the front door swung open. Heath didn't expect to see anyone but his mother. When they'd spoken earlier she'd told him she wouldn't be telling his father that he was visiting. She'd been worried he'd refuse to see him. So she'd asked Heath to come at lunch when usually his father was in a good mood and clear-headed.

'Hi, darling, how lovely you brought Bundy with you.' Delight shone in his mother's smile and her tiredness appeared to lift as she bent to hug the kelpie. 'I'll fill up his water bowl.'

Heath couldn't stop his brows lifting. 'Bundy's been here before?'

His mother nodded as they walked towards the house. 'He came for a couple of weeks last summer.'

'How was Dad with him?'

'He ignored him but that's no surprise. We haven't even had working dogs for a while now.'

They climbed the front steps and Heath waited for his mother and Bundy to go through the door first before following them into the cool of the house. Just like the garden, the inside was immaculate and in as good repair as could be expected. The scent of the beeswax polish from the dining room furniture gave way to the smell of freshly baked bread as they entered the kitchen.

A green salad and platter of cold meats sat on the bench along with a plate of his favourite jam slice. Emotions unravelling, he could only watch as his mother collected a stainless steel dog's bowl from under the sink. With the small but functional kitchen appearing unchanged and the aromas of his mother's homemade cooking, it was as though time had rewound and he was eighteen again.

He placed a plate of the deliveries he'd received that morning next to the jam slice while his mother poured water into Bundy's bowl from a large glass jug sitting beside the kitchen sink.

Heath noticed a second jug full of water. 'The house tank empty?'

She didn't look at him as she replied, 'The pump's out.'

'When did it stop working?'

His mother appeared to not hear him.

'Mum?'

'Last week.'

He stepped forward to give her a hug. Her voice had sounded defeated. 'I'd have come home ...'

He felt the shake of her head against his chest.

When she pulled away her expression was imploring. 'I don't need things fixed. I can make do. I just need you and your father to put the past behind you.'

He silenced the words that any reconciliation would be up to his father. He'd made a promise to the woman before him, plus he too wanted the past to be the past. 'Is there still a toolbox in the laundry?'

'There is, but …'

He'd already left. Seeing as very little had changed he was sure he'd know how to bleed air from the pump that serviced this end of the house and get it working again. But when he went to the small shed which housed the aged pump, the water around the base made it clear no tricks or replacement parts would get it functional again.

He returned to the kitchen. 'The pump's had it,' he said as he walked through the door.

A tall man stood by the fridge. His work shirt and jeans hung off what had once been a solid frame. But there was nothing frail about the look he shot Heath from beneath the bristles of thick grey brows. Lines of discontent turned his scowl into a glower.

'Of course it's had it. Call yourself a handyman? You came all the way from town to tell me that?'

Heath froze. He didn't know what was worse—seeing his once strong father a shell of his former self or that he didn't recognise him, even though Heath had known this was a possibility.

His mother too appeared immobile, her only movement being her hand lowering to rest on Bundy's head as the kelpie sat close beside her.

Heath took another step into the kitchen. But before he could say 'Hi, Dad', his father's expression changed.

If he hadn't seen it for himself, he would never have thought his father could appear vulnerable. Raw emotion slackened his mouth and softened his features. Then familiar anger fired in his eyes and blotted his complexion.

Heath held his glare. He had no doubt his father recognised him.

As much as his mother had seen him as a surprise gift after losing two sons, his father had never wanted him.

'Hi, Dad.'

His steady and measured words reverberated in the tension like a hammer hitting iron.

'I thought I made it clear.' His father's gnarled hands clenched and unclenched by his side. 'You are a disappointment and are never welcome in this house again.'

His mother stepped forward, face white. 'Is that what you said to make him leave?'

Heath didn't look away from his father. Just for a second an unfamiliar emotion flickered across his weathered features. Then his father barked, 'Yes.'

'That's all you said?'

The uncertainty and anguish in his mother's face kept Heath quiet. His father had lied. But he had no option but to conceal the truth as well as what his father had gone on to say. For if he didn't, the person whose world would be forever changed would be the mother he loved.

As his father nodded, Bundy walked over to him and thrust his nose into his fisted hand. His father didn't look down or acknowledge the kelpie but Heath didn't miss the way his father's fingers relaxed or the tremors that shook his hand.

Bundy padded back to his mother and lay on the floor at her feet. Just having Bundy near seemed to provide her with reassurance. The hunched line of her shoulders lowered.

He again met his father's hard stare. 'Dad, I'm in town to paint the water tower and you will be seeing more of me.' When his father went to interrupt Heath arched a brow. He was now as tall as his father and could look him in the eye. He also wasn't a powerless eighteen-year-old anymore.

His father's mouth compressed into a thin line, but he didn't speak.

'This is Mum's home just as much as it's yours. I will be back this afternoon with a new pump.' He glanced at Bundy. 'And tomorrow with a dog.'

CHAPTER
6

'Let me get this straight,' Brenna said as she slowed Lulu, her black stockhorse mare, so that she rode alongside Clancy as they checked Rowan's cattle. 'Heath doesn't talk about anything personal or ask for help, so you remind him that friends look out for each other. Then yesterday he apologises for not being there for you, which in my book is opening up, and you want to run a mile?'

Clancy answered with a sigh. 'Yes.'

Brenna's pale blue gaze studied her. 'I get it.'

'You do? Because I don't.'

Instead of feeling happy that Heath had lowered his guard, she felt more on edge than ever.

'You're worried Heath might leave again.'

'Might? He *is*. He said so.'

'People don't always do what they say.'

'He has to. He works all over the world. It's not as if I can go with him. My life's here.'

'Rowan's away overseas.'

'Only for the short-term.'

'It's still spending time away from the farm.'

Clancy didn't answer. A cow standing away from the others caught her attention. She appeared to have recently calved but there was no cute cream-and-red baby in sight. She walked Ash closer before stopping. A sweet-faced calf lay curled up asleep in a hollow. She headed back to Brenna and Lulu with a smile. So far there were three new additions to tell Rowan about when she called to check on his hand later.

Brenna cast her a long look. 'You're one of the most tenacious people I know. You can't give up on how you feel about Heath.'

'I'm not. Even if Heath does share more of himself, at the end of the day I'm still Rowan's little sister and that's the basis of our friendship.'

'Trust me … the way he looked at you at the barbeque when he thought no one was looking was not how a best mate looks at his friend's little sister.'

'You're joking.'

'You know I'd never lie.' Brenna's teasing tone turned serious. 'As good as Heath is at hiding how he feels, he did not like Nathan Wilcox hanging around you.'

Clancy stayed silent. Nathan was a shameless flirt. Sure, he seemed to be singling her out this past month but it didn't mean anything. The young stock and station agent had a string of local conquests and he knew there wasn't even a remote possibility she'd become his latest one. He simply liked a challenge.

Brenna continued, her tone gentle. 'Between his father and losing his brothers, Heath's had a tough run.'

Clancy nodded as she guided Ash around a rabbit warren. 'I still wish I'd kept my mouth shut. It goes without saying I'll be there if Heath needs me, but now I'm the one who has to keep their distance.'

'You sound like you've made up your mind.'

'I have. You know I'm not a risk-taker.'

'For the record ...' Brenna's grin turned mischievous as she glanced past Clancy. 'If I had a man who rode a horse like Heath, I'd be taking every risk I could to make sure he stayed in town.'

Clancy shook her head with a laugh. Brenna's top criteria when it came to potential suitors was their horsemanship. Clancy pitied any man who couldn't ride; they didn't stand a chance.

The click of horse hooves on granite had her turning in her saddle. Her amusement fled. It hadn't been a kangaroo or fox that had caught Brenna's eye, just an irritable blood-bay gelding, his rider and the kelpie running by their side.

There was no denying Heath looked at home on a horse. Broad-shouldered and long-legged, he rode with a relaxed masculine grace that wasn't for show. His skills had been honed taking cattle to and from the Hawks Ridge high country. There wasn't a horse he couldn't ride. The year before he left town he'd won the coveted Bundilla Cup, where he'd competed in the mountain race against stockmen twice his age.

Heath gave them a wave and headed their way.

'Brenna ...' Clancy said, voice low. 'Don't even think about suddenly having something urgent to do and dashing off.'

Brenna's expression was all innocence. 'I wouldn't dream of doing such a thing, even if three's a crowd.'

Heath gave them a nod as Goliath fell into step beside Brenna's mare. The gelding's flattened ears made it known he didn't like not setting the pace.

'I see Goliath's his usual charming self,' Brenna said.

'This is him in a good mood. I'm lucky I didn't see stars when we went past Fergus.'

Clancy couldn't hide her grin. The highland bull and Goliath were a little like Orien and Bundy—they had a love-hate relationship. 'Not mentioning names but a certain brother of mine was bucked off and did see stars at that exact spot.'

Brenna and Heath laughed. Despite the amusement relaxing Heath's features, fatigue still hollowed his cheeks. As much as it had been on her mind about how his visit with his father had gone, she'd resisted contacting him. She wasn't again overstepping the unspoken rules of their friendship.

Brenna smirked. 'Just as well you still know how to ride, MacBride.'

Clancy hoped Heath didn't pick up on the pointed glance Brenna threw her way.

'It's good to be back in the saddle.'

Brenna nodded. 'Well, anytime you want to head into the hills or go to the hut, let me know. I could do with a couple of days away for fun and not work. Taite would be keen, too.'

'I will.'

While Heath was talking to Brenna, Clancy snuck a sideways look. He'd swapped his usual brown dress boots for a scuffed cowboy pair and wore faded jeans with a paint-covered long-sleeved black Henley. Thanks to the morning's warmth, she and Brenna had also left their coats behind.

'Clance, you in?' Brenna asked as she rode ahead, leaving a clear line of sight between Clancy and Heath.

'I'll be busy picking.'

She kept her smile in place even when Brenna looked over her shoulder, eyes narrowed. If she wasn't flat out cutting and sorting peonies, she'd find another reason not to go. The last thing she needed was to spend time with Heath. Especially if she was having trouble looking away from where the thin material of his shirt outlined the toned muscles beneath.

Heath rode up alongside Brenna. Whatever Brenna thought she'd seen at the barbeque couldn't be right. Heath almost seemed to be going out of his way to not look at her. She allowed Ash's pace to quicken until she caught up with them both.

In front of them a pair of calves chased each other, their tails in the air.

'Too adorable,' Brenna said. 'Even if they do grow up to be cranky cows.' Brenna pulled a face. She had always been a horse girl.

When Heath chuckled, Clancy relaxed into the saddle. It was like old times with the three of them riding together.

Heath whistled Bundy to his side as the kelpie, nose down, set off along a trail. The kelpie must have caught scent of a rabbit. Since he'd been at the coach house, he'd kept the hares that had nibbled on her peonies away. Now all she had to worry about were the cockatoos.

Conscious she hadn't said much, she glanced across at Heath. 'More pressure washing today?'

His gaze didn't hold hers for long. 'Should be done by lunch.' He paused as Goliath leaped sideways as a rabbit that had been hiding in the snow grass darted away. When the gelding settled, he continued. 'Don't suppose either of you have an hour to spare this afternoon?'

Before Clancy could even think of an excuse, Brenna replied, 'Sorry, my next lot of trekkers are arriving, but I'm sure Clancy will be free. Why?' She ignored the look Clancy threw her.

Heath stared at a point between Goliath's ears. 'I'm going to the animal shelter to choose a dog for Mum and Dad. I'm far from a pet expert so could do with some advice.'

Goliath again spooked, this time at a galah fluttering its pink and grey wings as it landed on the nearby water trough.

Even before Heath had quietened the bay gelding, Clancy knew she would offer to go with him. It was no coincidence that Goliath, who had been walking sedately, now acted up. The horse was reacting to Heath's tension.

The visit to the animal shelter would give her a chance to gauge how the meeting with his father had gone. If getting his parents a dog was any indication, it had gone well. She swallowed. If so, Heath might no longer need to stay in the coach house. Once he left she'd be lucky to have any one-on-one time with him.

She spoke before she could think through what a bad idea it was. There were bound to be puppies involved and seeing Heath's tender side was not going to help keep her heart safe. 'I could meet you after lunch.'

This time his attention rested on her for longer. Brenna had slowed Lulu, allowing Clancy and Heath to look directly at each other.

'It shouldn't take long.'

'MacBride,' Brenna chided. 'You'll be lucky to leave in under an hour and with only one pet. If I had my way I'd adopt them all.'

Heath smoothed a hand over Goliath's neck as the bay pranced. 'I'll head back before Goliath decides to become a buckjumper. There's another calf past the yellow box trees. He's fine, so no need to check on him and his mum.'

Clancy thought Heath took a last look at her before he rode away, but she was sure she would be the only one overthinking meeting up again. Her gaze followed him as he cantered Goliath along the ridge. She'd grown up surrounded by horsemen but had never before appreciated the way a man rode. Heath really did look good on a horse.

Beside her Brenna cleared her throat.

Clancy turned to see Brenna smiling at her before she said, tone smug, 'I'm not saying a word, other than if we don't head back now we'll be late for quilting.'

It took an hour to ride home, unsaddle the horses, turn Lulu out with Ash so Brenna could collect the mare later and get on the road to town. Once they'd arrived at the small community hall and set themselves up at a sewing machine, it only took ten minutes for the subject of Heath to come up.

Brenna stopped sewing her pink half-square triangles to lean over to Clancy and whisper, 'It's my bet Norma mentions Heath first.'

Clancy kept her voice low as she picked up a rotary cutter. They might be the youngest of the quilters but they'd soon learned that while elderly Vernette might have trouble hearing, at their quilting meetings she didn't miss a thing. 'He'd be old news. Sandra's daughter's baby is due tomorrow. Everyone will be busy guessing gender, weight and name.'

To their left Sandra's sewing machine sounded like it was on overdrive as the former nurse finished a tiny quilt in pink, blue, yellow and green.

Brenna merely kinked a brow.

Clancy forced herself to concentrate on lining up her green floral fabric on the cutting board. She had no time to think about

Heath or what matchmaking plans the quilting group might hatch. The quilts many of them were working on were going to drought-affected communities out west and she had a lot to do on hers. At least the large log cabin quilt that was a joint group effort was completed and now being raffled off to raise drought relief funds.

She'd spent last Saturday morning rugged up against the wind with Brenna outside the post office selling tickets. Dan, despite having no woman in his life he could give the quilt to, had been kind enough to buy a whole book of raffle tickets. His generosity had then extended to returning with two hot chocolates to warm them up. If anyone needed matchmaking, it was reserved loner Dan.

She glanced around at the close-knit group of ladies, many of whom had been her mother's friends. Today it was a full house with almost every seat and table occupied. The bench beside the kitchen sink was laden with an assortment of baked goods for morning tea. It was when the group stopped for a cuppa and the noise of the sewing machines quietened that advice was sought and swapped and many a town problem solved.

It had been her mother's unfinished quilt that had first brought Clancy to the group. She'd wanted to complete it in memory of her craft-loving mother, and Brenna had come for moral support. Even now, years later, whenever she was there Clancy still felt her mother wasn't far away. Someone would comment that Isobel Parker had always liked that pattern, or a certain colour combination had been her favourite. The quilting group missed her mother almost as much as she did.

Realising she'd stopped cutting and that Mrs Moore on her left was studying her, Clancy smiled and placed her cut triangles into a neat pile.

Sandra finished sewing and after snipping the threads on her baby quilt glanced around the hall. 'Before I forget, Mabel asked me to remind everyone that the drop-off deadline for formal outfits is this Friday.'

Mabel was collecting dresses and suits to send to an organisation that distributed formalwear to drought-affected towns so local school-leavers could attend their graduation balls.

Mrs Moore nodded. 'My granddaughter has given me three dresses so I must remember to bring them in.'

Clancy exchanged a glance with Brenna as she thought back to their own long-ago formal. While Clancy had a few gowns to sort through and donate, tomboy Brenna wouldn't have a single one. She'd shocked the school mothers by coming in a pantsuit long before they'd become fashionable. She'd refused to wear a dress, let alone be sprayed in fake tan or have her hair and nails done.

Sadness dimmed the smile in Brenna's eyes. While Clancy mightn't have had her mother with her for the past three years, Brenna's mother hadn't been in her or Taite's life since their final year of high school. It had been just after their formal that their mother was diagnosed with a brain tumour.

Clancy leaned over to squeeze Brenna's hand.

The front door swung open before sensible heels clacked on the floorboards. 'Sorry I'm late,' Norma gushed. 'I was chatting to that lovely young man painting the water tower.' She looked around the group, her round cheeks rosy and her expression animated. 'Why didn't anyone tell me he was such a sweetheart? He's nothing like his father.'

Clancy silenced a groan even as Brenna gave her a told-you-so smirk. Norma had arrived in town after Heath left and had never met him.

Edith, on Clancy's left, put down the quilting square she'd been sewing by hand. 'According to Cynthia he's not seeing anyone.'

The energy in the room seemed to vibrate.

Norma took a seat but made no move to open the cloth bag containing her quilting. 'Well then, this is going to be fun. We can't let any single man go to waste … especially one as nice as Heath. Let's start a list of matches … there's Stella …'

'Let's not.' Clancy hadn't realised she was going to speak until her words sounded. She softened her serious tone. 'Heath's only in town for a few weeks. That's hardly enough time to start a proper relationship.'

Norma's eyes twinkled. 'I'd only known my James for two weeks before I knew he was the one.'

Edith nodded. 'My parents were engaged after a week and while it might seem hasty, they were together sixty years.'

Clancy refused to give ground. The last thing Heath needed, even if things were better with his father, was to be a marked man. Not only would it slow down the mural if Norma wasn't the only local dropping by, but the idea of Heath finding someone made her stomach pitch.

'I'm all for love at first sight but let's leave Heath to do what he came here to do. Stella's already had her heart broken. I'd hate to see her hurt again.'

As the heads around her bobbed and the conversation turned to popular baby names, Clancy busied herself with cutting more triangles. No matter how heartwarming it would be to see Heath surrounded by adorable dogs this afternoon, she needed to heed her own advice.

'Step one done,' Heath said as the cherry picker reached ground level.

Bundy's tail wagged. The kelpie had grown used to how the telescopic boom operated and as soon as Heath began his descent, he'd be at the bottom waiting for him. But today, instead of sleeping in the shipping container, Bundy had headed off in the direction of town. He'd spent the morning there before making his way back to the water tower at lunch.

Heath shrugged off his safety harness. In the midday sunshine the concrete beside him gleamed a pale matte grey. His muse had returned and he couldn't wait to get started on the mural.

Bundy sidled closer for a pat and he tickled behind the kelpie's ears. 'I missed you. Hope you had fun wherever you were.'

He packed away the pressure washer. Before he could lose himself in his art he had to visit the animal shelter with Clancy. Then he had to make sure his father let whatever dog they chose stay. The new addition to his family was as much for his father as it was for his mother. He'd spent hours last night researching the benefits of pet therapy with dementia patients.

When he'd returned yesterday afternoon with a new pump, his father had been noticeably absent, but he'd seen him scowling through the kitchen window as he spoke to jack-of-all-trades Taite on the phone about installing the pump. When he'd returned inside and water flowed through the kitchen tap, the relief on his mother's face made the earlier gut-wrenching encounter with his father worth it.

He'd collected the old wooden kennel from the back of the shed and, after dusting it off, put it in the spot his mother had chosen on the veranda. She'd then given him a list of items the new dog would need. Today, she'd already texted twice reminding him to message as soon as he and Clancy had made a decision.

He checked the time on his phone before heading for his car. He would grab some pies for lunch before meeting Clancy.

The knowledge that he'd hurt her still cut him up inside. Spending time together while they chose a dog wasn't going to make up for that or for her belief that he didn't value their friendship, but it was a start.

He knew when he'd asked Brenna and Clancy if they had a spare hour this afternoon that Brenna wouldn't be free. Taite had told him when he'd helped with the pump that the next lot of trekkers were arriving today. He'd still included Brenna as he hadn't wanted her to feel left out or to put Clancy under any pressure about accompanying him. He hadn't missed how quiet she'd been on their ride.

He glanced to where his phone lay on the front passenger seat. Clancy had messaged earlier to set up a time to meet and to say she'd brought Orien's pet carrier in case he chose a small dog. She'd also offered him her dual cab with the dog chain on the back if he needed it. While her texts had been friendly, he couldn't shake his unease that things weren't back to normal between them.

After buying the pies, he drove to a quiet spot near one of the historic wooden bridges that crossed the Tumut River. He and Bundy settled on a bench beside the riverbank track to enjoy their lunch. As a child he and his mother had often walked along the path that was popular with joggers.

In the distance, clouds hovered low over the mountain peaks and the breeze carried the sweet scent of spring blossoms. Somewhere close by a tree would be in bloom. He lowered his shoulders and let his tension ebb. A kookaburra perched on the nearby bridge kept them company while they enjoyed their pies.

Once they were done, Heath drove the short distance to the animal shelter. He slowed as he passed the drop-off pens for stray dogs and cats. Clancy's white dual cab was already in the car park. As he drew closer he could see her in the driver's seat talking on her phone.

He parked beside her and turned to look at Bundy. Beyond the car windows a cacophony of dogs barked, but Bundy appeared more interested in sleeping. Whatever he'd done in town had tired him out. Heath made sure the back windows were open so the kelpie would have fresh air.

As he left his car, Clancy greeted him with a smile. She still wore the same jeans, boots and navy jacket from their ride earlier, but her red-brown hair was now pulled into a high ponytail. The hairstyle was the same as what she'd worn in the mural photo and just like then it revealed the beauty of her bone structure.

He could blame staring at her high cheekbones and the delicate line of her jaw on a professional need for accuracy—she was, after all, his mural subject. But the truth was he couldn't stop looking at her. She made his senses burn in a way no other woman had.

'Thanks for meeting me.' He looked over at the pens to their left which were full of excited dogs. 'I think Brenna's right. This might take a while.'

'It's such a lovely idea to get your mum and dad a dog.' Clancy peered through the window at the snoozing Bundy. 'Not that Bundy seems at all interested.' She straightened to face him. 'I take it going home went well?'

Distracted by the way the sun teased out the red in her hair, he wasn't quick enough to hide his reaction to her question. When her eyes widened, he knew just how much his expression had revealed.

After their conversation at the barbeque, he couldn't brush off her query. He also couldn't tell her the whole truth. His mother wasn't ready for people to know his father wasn't the man he once was. As for his father's animosity, nothing had changed; he still wasn't free to reveal the true reason behind their estrangement.

He chose his words with care. 'The only thing that has changed is that I'll be visiting Mum as much as I can, whether Dad likes it or not.'

Sympathy softened Clancy's eyes and for a moment he thought she'd touch his arm. Instead she reached up to adjust her ponytail. 'I'm so sorry he still hasn't come round.'

A middle-aged woman approached to nod at Clancy before holding out her hand to Heath. 'I'm Alice.'

He clasped her hand. 'Heath.'

'You might resemble your mother but I can still see your father in you. He mightn't smile much, but after his visit here I always knew he wasn't as tough as he looked.'

Heath hid his shock. 'My father was here?'

'Yes, he adopted a Jack Russell many years ago. I'd just started working here. I can't remember her name ... but she was deaf and we didn't think she'd ever find a home.'

Heath pushed back the memories of being told as a young child that his four-legged best mate had died. While his mother had held him and wiped his tears as he'd held the small cross he'd made for her creekside grave, his father's words had been to grow up. 'Her name was Minnie.'

'That was it. Such a sweet little thing. So what type are you looking for today?'

'An easygoing companion.'

'Perfect. Follow me.'

Clancy fell into step beside him. 'I never knew you had a dog.'

'It was before I went to school. Rowan helped me teach Minnie to play fetch.'

The conversation lapsed as the closer they walked to the kennels, the more the barking gained volume. They hadn't even made it to the path that ran between the parallel rows of enclosures when Clancy veered to the left.

She stopped at the end pen in which a small white dog with oversized black ears wagged his tail and yipped. 'This one's so sweet,' she said above the din.

Next to the small white dog were three fluffy border collie puppies. He went to pat the wriggling bodies pushed against the wire. He chuckled as the larger puppy tugged at his shirtsleeve.

Clancy came to his side. 'This is just a cuteness overload.'

As she leaned in close to pat the pups, her ponytail slid over her shoulder to touch his jacket. She was so near that all he could smell was flowers and all he could focus on was her smiling mouth being within kissing distance.

Shoulders locked, he moved away to where Alice had stopped midway along the two rows.

Alice gestured towards a group of pens. 'These are our older dogs who won't have as much puppy energy.'

Heath gazed at the expectant faces and wished he could take every one of them with him. 'I'm guessing these guys have been here a while.'

'They have. The puppies never stay long but these fellows often do.'

Heath focused on a larger dog. While his body was a sandy brown, his face was almost white with age.

'What's his name?'

'Jasper. We're not sure of his breed, but we think he's part red heeler. He's only ever had the one owner who passed away and the man's children couldn't take him. He would be the oldest dog we have and with his arthritis will need special care.'

Jasper's big brown eyes stared at him and while the dogs around all barked, this fellow stayed silent. When Heath moved closer, his tail wagged. Heath had brought Clancy along for advice, but as the dog continued to gaze at him he knew he was exactly what he was looking for.

'We'd love to give Jasper a new home.'

'Like father, like son,' Alice said with a grateful smile.

Heath turned to look for Clancy who had moved along several more pens. When he pointed to the dog in front of him, she gave a thumbs up before bending to gaze into a pen that contained a golden retriever and her puppy.

When he and Alice joined her, Clancy straightened. 'What's the story with these two?'

Alice answered. 'They're a mother and daughter who were surrendered. Iris has diabetes and the cost of her insulin proved too much for her family.'

Clancy didn't reply. Instead she stared as the puppy yawned before flopping on the ground and resting her head on her tiny honey-coloured paws.

Heath watched as Clancy's expression turned serious. 'Clance?'

She glanced at him, her eyes a soft grey. 'It's time I had a dog again.' She gave a carefree smile he hadn't seen since he'd arrived. 'Make that dogs, plural.'

Alice's face beamed. 'I'm so pleased.'

Clancy snapped a photo of Iris and the puppy on her phone before they all went into the building to complete the paperwork. Once everything was in order he and Clancy returned to the car park. Both needed to visit the veterinary surgery as well as the rural store to obtain the items they'd need. They'd then return to collect Jasper, Iris and her puppy.

'I can drive if you'd like?' he said as they crossed the car park.

There was only a slight hesitation before she nodded.

But as Clancy settled into the passenger seat and turned to give Bundy a pat while Heath texted his mother, he realised he'd made a grave error in judgement. The close confines of the convertible magnified his awareness of how beautiful Clancy was and how he'd do anything to return the joy that he'd glimpsed in her smile back into her life. Even at the expense of his own happiness. Hands tight on the steering wheel, he made small talk until they reached the rural store.

Once his boot was packed full with dog beds, toys and other items, their next stop was the local veterinary practice. There a blonde vet nurse helped them stock up on medical requirements and special-diet dog food. By the time they left, he'd crossed everything off his mother's list.

'Just as well I have lots of room,' Clancy said as she transferred her purchases into her ute. When she was done, there was just enough space inside to fit the pet carrier that would keep the puppy safe. Iris would ride in the trayback.

The dual cab had a second dog chain in case Jasper needed to travel with Clancy. But when Jasper was introduced to Bundy, the two dogs showed no signs of aggression and were soon secured in the back seat of Heath's car.

With a wave, Clancy left the car park. Heath followed. Iris wore a doggy-grin as the wind rushed over her where she rode on the back of the dual cab. Clancy waved again before she took the road that would lead to Ashcroft. Heath continued around the valley edge.

Once at Hawks Ridge, he parked in the shade of the fir tree. A curtain in the front living room window quickly fell back into place. His mother had been waiting. She sped down the steps and over to the convertible as Heath let both dogs out.

'What a distinguished fellow you are,' she said as she stroked Jasper's nose. The old dog pressed against her legs, wanting more pats. His mother's happy laughter erased what seemed like years from her features.

By the time Heath had carried in the two loads of dog items, Bundy and Jasper were in the kitchen being fed an early dinner. The murmur of a television beyond the open lounge room door let him know where his father was.

As he walked towards the doorway, he heard his mother's quiet voice. 'Darling … he's not himself today.'

A western played on the television screen but his father appeared asleep in his upright leather recliner. As Heath stepped into the room, his father's eyes opened. But instead of the usual chill or heated rage, their expression was empty. He had no idea who Heath was.

His father frowned slightly. 'The broken pump's out the back. Lydia will show you the way.'

Heath caught movement in his peripheral vision before Jasper padded on silent paws over to his father. The old dog rested his head on his father's knee. His father was immobile for a moment and then his shaking hand moved to rest on Jasper's head.

Heath left the room. Long after he'd returned to the coach house, the image of his father and Jasper stayed with him. Even after he'd replicated it on canvas and moonlight filtered in through the studio window, the tightness in his chest refused to leave.

He stared at the picture he'd painted. On a distant ridge, a wild dog howled. If his father couldn't retain his memories, he'd capture them for him.

CHAPTER

7

'I knew I should have called you Trouble,' Clancy said to the energetic puppy burrowing beneath her bedcovers.

She'd already been up once to let Primrose and Iris outside. But the cold morning air and exercise did little to wear the puppy out. It wasn't even breakfast and Primrose had bounced onto her bed. Now that the pup had worked out the sliding laundry door could be opened by the push of a curious nose, tonight she'd be locking it.

As Primrose's head popped out of the covers and the soft puppy snuggled into the crook of her neck, Clancy couldn't help but laugh. Iris and Primrose hadn't been in her life a day and she already couldn't imagine not having them around.

She carefully turned her head to check on Iris where she slept curled up on the rug beside the bed. There had just been something about the light-coloured golden retriever that had tugged at her heartstrings. The lost expression in her eyes had echoed her own sense of displacement. Even though the walls around her were those of her home, without her parents, and now Rowan for a short while, she felt adrift.

The bundle of warmth cuddled against her wriggled before trying to chew on her hair. Clancy flipped the covers off her legs. 'Okay, I get the message. It's play time.'

Primrose wasn't listening. The puppy had leaped off the bed and launched herself at her mother.

Clancy threw Rowan's rugby top over her pyjamas and headed into the laundry to see what damage Primrose's sharp little teeth had done. Last night she'd puppy-proofed the room but had left a handtowel hanging beside the sink. When she'd later checked on the mother and daughter she'd found half of it over near the washing machine and the other in Primrose's bed.

For Orien's sanity she'd made sure the kitchen door had remained closed. When she'd introduced the dogs to him he'd merely flicked his fluffy silver tail before jumping onto the kitchen windowsill to clean his paws.

As they walked along the hallway, Primrose sped ahead, her feet skidding on the polished wooden floorboards. Clancy's cheeks ached from smiling. Not only was Primrose going to be more efficient than an alarm clock, she was going to be a great time waster. All Clancy wanted to do was to watch what she did next.

She stopped to pat Iris's head. 'Don't worry, gorgeous girl, I haven't forgotten about you.'

Iris's tail brushed against Clancy's legs. Iris had already proved to be a gentle soul and hadn't fussed when Clancy injected her after-dinner insulin.

Once at the back door, Clancy pulled on her long gumboots covered in a peony pattern that had been a present from Brenna. She could only hope Jasper was settling into his forever home. Heath's mother would be thrilled to have him. As for Heath's father, if he wasn't, at least being a workaholic meant he'd be out in the paddocks.

It had been as much of a surprise that Heath's father had been to the animal shelter as it was learning Heath had once had a pet. Growing up, he'd always spent time with their animals as he'd never had any of his own.

Before the back door was fully open, Primrose bounded outside. Clancy and Iris followed. Despite the sunshine of the past few days, this morning the sky appeared sullen and the wind blew with urgent intent. Heavy dew glistened on the cobwebs strung between strappy agapanthus leaves.

Heath's car wasn't next to the coach house, signalling that he and Bundy had already headed to the water tower. She had no doubt Heath wouldn't be getting close to eight hours of sleep. The studio light had been on until late.

Primrose wriggled through the gap in the wooden garden gate and bolted towards the packing shed. Whatever the pup had seen, most likely a hare, it had triggered her instincts to chase. Clancy and Iris again set off after her. When Clancy stopped at the shed and slid the door open, Primrose spun around to race over.

Both dogs accompanied her inside. Galvanised iron display buckets gleamed in the corner and piles of white plastic buckets stood in neat towers. Behind the heavy closed door to her left was the cool room, while to her right stretched her long sorting table. Above the table on a corkboard hung all her gardening implements.

She bent to rescue an extension power cord from Primrose's mouth. As tidy as the shed appeared, it would soon be filled with mess and the fragrance of handpicked blooms. Once the frantic picking season started, it wouldn't be long until she'd have peony-brain and be seeing peonies even in her dreams.

She collected the wheelbarrow and slipped on her gardening gloves. She'd do some weeding and her daily bud check before breakfast. While Primrose hindered more than helped, Iris retrieved any weeds that missed the wheelbarrow. With the barrow half full, Clancy made the trek to the compost pile.

After she'd tipped the leaves into the end wooden box, she scooped out a handful of the maturing compost in the middle box. Too dry, it crumbled in her hand. She uncurled the nearby hose, turned it on low and draped it over the box edge.

She returned the wheelbarrow to the shed and when Primrose made a dash towards the back garden, Clancy set off after her. According to the complaints of her stomach, breakfast was long overdue.

Once the house was quiet and Primrose was passed out in her dog bed, Clancy finished her morning cuppa and went for a shower. With her morning jobs completed, she had a little time before she needed to check the cattle. She still needed to pick out dresses for the drought formalwear charity to drop off to Mabel tomorrow.

After sorting through a section of her walk-in robe, she placed a floor-length black gown on her bed along with a shorter emerald green dress she'd worn to a local wedding. Both would be appreciated by someone else. Her hand stilled on a dark crimson dress. With a full skirt of multiple layers of chiffon and a fitted, wrapped bodice, the gown had been her own high school formal dress. She'd again worn it when she'd attended a ball at the completion of her online business degree. The gown had come to represent the end of significant chapters in her life.

She took the dress off the hanger and held it against herself, the delicate chiffon cool and smooth beneath her fingertips. She'd always thought the colour too rich for her skin tone but her mother had talked her into trying it on and once she had, no other dress compared. The question was, would she ever wear it again? She examined the narrow waist. Would it still even fit?

After shrugging off her long-sleeved cotton shirt and yanking down her jeans, she pulled the dress over her hips. It was going to be a tight fit. When the dress reached her chest, it refused to move any higher. Since the gown was strapless, she peeled off her last layer, leaving nothing but bare skin, and breathed in. The side zip took some tugging but it finally slid into place.

She frowned at the walk-in robe door mirror. As a kid she'd been pretty much straight up and down but there was no doubt she'd filled out as a teenager. If she wasn't careful how she breathed, she'd burst a seam. She unzipped the top of the dress and drew a welcome breath. When she tried to keep sliding the zipper down, it refused to move. Even after using force, the zip wouldn't lower any further.

She wasn't sure what triggered the memory of her turning on the hose in the compost bin, but the realisation she'd left the tap on caused her to forget about the zip and spin towards the doorway. Beyond the mountains, communities struggled through another year of drought and she couldn't waste the water she was lucky enough to have. Not to mention she'd soon have a mini flood.

Fabric swished as she went to the back door to pull on her gumboots. Iris trotted behind. Once outside, the wind gathered in the layers of the full skirt, causing chiffon to float around her. She bunched the skirt into her left hand as she made her way through the back garden gate to turn off the tap behind the packing shed. With the water supply now cut, the brown waterfall over the bottom paling of the compost bin would soon stop.

Busy keeping her hem off the ground and her hair out of her eyes, she retraced her steps. Too late she realised that Iris wasn't the only dog by her side. Bundy was too. Her hold on the skirt of her dress tightened. The coach house car port was no longer empty. Iris and Bundy raced towards Heath as he walked over.

Her chin tilted. Heath had seen her in far worse outfits than a ball gown hiked up around her knees and peony-decorated gumboots. One weekend when camping she'd worn pyjamas with cowgirl boots the entire time after the bag with her clothes had fallen off the ute.

'Morning,' she said, as though she were simply wearing her usual farm clothes.

'Morning.' To Heath's credit his expression remained deadpan. After a fleeting glance at her dress, his attention returned to her face.

'Wind too gusty for the cherry picker?'

'Mechanical problems. I've come home to make some calls.'

Part of her skirt slid free from her grasp and ballooned between them. A muscle seemed to work in Heath's jaw as the chiffon brushed his arm before her hair again made it difficult to see.

She brushed the tangled strands from her face and regained control of her skirt. 'I can see why Brenna doesn't wear dresses.'

'Off somewhere?'

'Not in this gown. Mabel's collecting formalwear for school-leavers affected by the drought. I made the mistake of trying this on before remembering I hadn't turned the shed tap off.'

'Wasn't that your year twelve formal dress?'

She stilled. Heath had left before her school graduation. It also had been eight years ago.

Her surprise must have shown on her face because Heath spoke again, his voice quiet. 'Rowan had a photo of the two of you in his wallet.'

'That's right, he did. Before he replaced it with one of him and Eloise.'

At her wry tone, Heath smiled, even if it didn't quite meet his eyes. 'So I wasn't the only one glad to see the back of Eloise?'

'Not by a long shot.'

Despite the chill of the wind, the longer she stayed talking to Heath the warmer she felt. No longer did he resemble a city boy. With his tousled hair and paint-covered blue shirt and jeans, it was as though he'd just rolled out of a swag.

She curled her fingers deeper into the crimson fabric to curb the urge to trace the stubbled line of his jaw. 'I'd best get this thing off before Primrose wakes up and destroys the house.'

'Primrose … I like it.'

'Trouble would have been much more fitting.'

Heath's deep chuckle caused goosebumps to ripple over her bare arms and her grip on her skirt to loosen. The chiffon again fluttered and drifted upwards as if reaching out to him.

'Are you keeping the dress?' he asked, the breeze thinning his words and making them sound almost strained.

'I think so … if I can get it off. Mum was with me when I bought it. Actually, while you're here …' Without thought she lifted her arm to reveal the snagged side zip.

There was no way she would be able to get out of the gown by herself. Besides, over the years Heath had untangled fishing lures from her hair, plucked burrs from her clothes and pulled off her too tight riding boots, so asking him to help with the zip wasn't anything unusual.

Then his eyes appeared to darken as he stepped closer and the scent of his woody cologne replaced the sweet fragrance of the jonquils lining the drystone wall and she knew she'd made a massive mistake.

When he ducked his head to examine her dress, she held her breath to make herself smaller so his fingers would have room to easily manoeuvre the zipper and she then could move away. If she'd felt flushed standing an arm's length apart, now she felt as though she'd stayed too long by a winter fire. His barest touch against her skin left her feeling light-headed. Needing air, she breathed in, and the expansion of her chest caught his fingers between her skin and the dress.

'Almost got it,' he said, his tone calm as if he were untangling Rowan's misaimed trout lure.

She breathed in again and didn't dare look down a second time to where his hand appeared a dark tan against her pale skin.

Heath tugged at the zip and the graze of his fingers across her ribs caused her heart to pound with such force he had to hear it. She willed it into silence.

With another tug, the zip gave way.

Air flooded her lungs. Her right hand lifted to hold the bodice in place, but as hair whipped across her eyes, she let go of the dress to clear her vision. The chill that slid over her bare side made her realise just how much the top of her dress gaped. She clamped a hand on her chest to prevent Heath getting a side flash of the reason why her gown had become such a snug fit. To her relief, he'd half turned.

'Keep the dress,' he said over his shoulder. 'I'll find my old black dinner suit to drop around to Mabel.' Still not looking at her, he whistled to Bundy. 'I'd best make these calls.'

As he strode through the garden, she stayed still. The speed at which she was again alone left her stunned. The intensity of her reaction to him left her breathless. But however overwhelming her reaction was to his touch, he appeared unmoved. Just like all those years ago at the river when she'd slipped on the rocks and he'd caught her, he couldn't wait to get away.

Shaking from the cold and her steps leaden, she returned inside. Her plan to treat Heath like any other guest had officially failed. As for deluding herself that Heath was someone she didn't know, no matter what her head said, her heart knew who he was as much as her body just had. She kicked off her gumboots.

She was now left with no options other than running a mile or making sure she kept her distance. The first was physically impossible, so she'd just have to make do with the second. She stripped off the ball gown and it fell in a cloud of crimson chiffon across her bed. The dress no longer represented the end of a chapter, just the dashing of her hopes. She threw on her work clothes and headed to the back door to pull on her boots. Iris and Primrose could enjoy the garden sunshine while she took a long ride.

On the way to the stables she looked at the mountains standing resolute and tall and squared her shoulders. She was not going to allow herself to tumble headlong into loving Heath again. She had to hold a part of herself back. Even with grown-up curves spilling out of a too tight dress, she was still just the little sister of his best mate.

He should have known that the cherry picker having mechanical issues wasn't going to be the only thing to go wrong today.

Heath entered the coach house and even before he'd walked past the picture of the highland cow in the entryway, he raked both hands through his hair. His jaw ached and tension rendered his body as wired as if he were about to attempt eight seconds on a bull at the Bundilla rodeo.

Helping Clancy with her ball gown had pushed his self-control to its limits. Even now he had to stop himself from turning to go after her. Having her so near and yet so far out of reach had shredded his defences. It had been bad enough that he'd let on that he recognised the dress from her formal, which he hadn't even attended. He'd then been a heartbeat away from fitting her against him and kissing her in a way that would break every bond of friendship.

The delicate contours of her collarbones, the fall of her chestnut hair down her pale back and the soft swell of her curves against the crimson gown were all scored on his senses. When she'd breathed in and his fingers had been trapped against her satin-smooth skin, he hadn't dared look at her. How he felt, and how much he wanted her, would have burned in his eyes.

He'd never been more thankful than when the zip finally shifted. Another few seconds and the last layer of his control would have disintegrated. Even after he'd turned so Clancy couldn't see his face, he'd still breathed in the fragrance of daphne and could still feel her warmth. Somehow he'd kept his voice steady and put one foot in front of the other to walk away.

Bundy's whine brought him back to the present. He stood in the middle of the kitchen facing the window that overlooked the main homestead.

'I know, mate,' he said with a sigh as he ruffled Bundy's neck. 'Helping Clancy with her dress was an even worse idea than offering to take her to Brenna's barbeque.'

He had to get busy. It was the only way to distract his testosterone. When he next saw Clancy he had to have his emotions buried so deep they'd never resurface. Should Clancy ever know of his feelings, things could never be the same between them. She needed a friend, not someone who would only complicate her already disrupted life.

Half an hour later, he'd gulped down a coffee, organised for someone to take a look at the cherry picker and had called his mother to offer to drive them to Canberra tomorrow to see the neurologist. Except the only way she'd convinced his father to see the specialist was by saying that the appointment was for both of them. Heath had agreed that if he went too, he'd only make a volatile situation worse. His last call was to organise the local tyre place to send someone to replace the rear tractor tyres while his parents were away.

His to-do list completed, he and Bundy returned to the water tower. With no working cherry picker, Heath busied himself with prepping for when he'd apply the exterior paint. The acrylic layer would seal the concrete and act as a base for the spray paint. He'd just opened a box of aerosol cans when gravel crunched beneath car tyres. Through the container door he saw a smiling Cynthia leave an apple-green sedan.

'Well, hello there.' Cynthia's lively greeting was matched by the brightness of her purple coat paired with an orange skirt. As much as Heath appreciated colour, the jarring combination made him wish for sunglasses.

An equally colourful younger version of Cynthia walked behind her, wearing red jeans and a candy-pink top, while a second daughter trailed several paces behind. She too had yellow-blonde hair but was dressed all in black. The compressed line of her mouth communicated that she wasn't thrilled about having to leave the car.

When Cynthia stopped before him, Heath thought she'd throw her arms around him, as she had in town, but instead she thrust a plate of lamingtons into his hands. 'Special delivery from Larissa, our prize-winning show baker.'

Heath didn't need to know which daughter was Larissa. The taller blonde's face lit up, while the other daughter rolled her eyes.

He smiled. 'Thank you.'

Larissa seemed to blush but Health became distracted by the younger sister taking a sideways step to peer into the shipping container. Interest flittered across her face when she noticed the box filled with small clear nozzle caps before she again appeared bored.

'If you're wondering,' he said, 'they're fat caps.'

This time the younger sister couldn't hide her excitement. 'Oh, cool.'

'Take a look if you like.' He moved aside and nodded at the black ink smudged on the fingers of her right hand. 'I'd be interested in seeing some of your artwork next time you're passing by.'

Where he could, he always paid help forward as well as supported fellow artists. He slipped his wallet from his back jeans pocket and took out a business card. 'Shoot me a text if I'm up in the cherry picker.'

As he passed her his card, she gave him a shy smile. 'Thanks … I'm Hannah. I want to study art at uni next year and I'm not sure if my portfolio's up to scratch.' With another smile, she walked into the shipping container.

Heath glanced at Cynthia. Her mouth hung slightly open and relief shone in her eyes. He wasn't sure if it was because he'd connected with one of her daughters or because Hannah no longer resembled a moody teenager as she inspected the aerosol cans.

Behind Cynthia, expression wistful, Larissa checked her phone. After a quick look to make sure her mother wasn't watching, she tapped off a message. Heath hid a grin. As determined as Cynthia was to play matchmaker, Heath suspected her daughters, at least these two, had their own plans.

He went to join Hannah and twisted plastic nozzles onto several cans of paint before handing them to her. 'There should be something around here to use these on.'

While Hannah and Larissa sprayed their names on an oversized cardboard box, Heath made small talk with Cynthia. Careful to avoid any topic that might lead to a dinner invitation, Heath limited their conversation to what had happened when someone had run into the back of her car. It wasn't his imagination that when Hannah and Larissa finished decorating the box, they swapped looks.

Larissa approached Cynthia with a sweet smile. 'Mum, we need to go. We've taken up enough of Heath's time. Don't forget Tim's coming to look at the broken dishwasher.'

Before Cynthia could do more than say 'Now girls', both daughters had taken hold of her arms to usher her away. Hannah looked back over her shoulder to give Heath a grin.

After he'd waved them off, he settled into a camping chair to share one, and then another, lamington with Bundy. Cynthia hadn't exaggerated. Larissa could bake. He was contemplating a third when tyres again sounded on the gravel. This time his visitor was Ned, who was dropping off a chainsaw.

The older man's eyes twinkled as he sat in the spare chair and Heath passed him the plate of lamingtons. 'I heard the grocery store sold out of flour.'

Heath groaned. 'At this rate, I'm never going to get this mural started, let alone finished. Bundy and I'll either be eating or jogging with Taite to make sure I don't have to let my belt out.'

Ned chuckled before his expression turned serious. 'How's your father?'

'Some days are better than others.'

'Your mother must be exhausted. He's never been a good patient.'

'Jasper seems to have already calmed him down.' Heath offered Ned the last lamington. 'He sits with him and comes into the kitchen to let Mum know if anything's wrong. Last night Dad was sure there were spiders on the television cabinet.'

Ned stared outside at a point midway up the water tower. 'Your mother's a good woman.'

'She is. Thanks for the chainsaw. I dropped Dad's off in town. Hopefully they can get it working.'

'Let me know if you need any help with that tree.'

'Will do.'

Ned chewed slowly before he spoke. 'Clancy's peonies must be ready soon?'

Heath fought a quickening in his blood at the vivid memory of Clancy in her crimson ball gown. 'I'm no flower expert but the buds still look green.'

'Tell her to let me know if she wants a hand. There's only so many times I can mow the lawn.'

Ned's small garden was immaculate and his house and tool shed spotless. In his spare time he restored rocking horses in readiness for when he'd finally be a grandfather. Last week he'd sent Heath a picture of the dapple-grey horse he'd just completed. 'If this cherry picker isn't fixed soon I may need that scaffolding you have behind the shed.'

'I can drop it around. That flashy car of yours isn't much use out here in the bush. It can't carry anything.'

This was familiar banter. Despite Ned's words, the only reason Heath owned such a vehicle was because car enthusiast Ned had been with him when he'd gone shopping. He'd taken one look at the luxury convertible and said Heath had to have it. 'I'm happy to swap.'

Ned's grin grew as he dipped his hand into his pocket for his keys. He tossed them to Heath. 'Now there's an idea.'

Heath chuckled. 'I do need it back in one piece.'

Ned gave him a wink. 'You'd better come and supervise. The sun's out, I think I'll put the roof down and take it for a spin out on Overflow Road.'

'I've already lived dangerously enough for today.'

At Ned's curious look, Heath gave a brief smile and handed him his car keys.

He shook his head when Ned sat behind the wheel, turned on the ignition and revved the engine. Gravel spun beneath the convertible's tyres as he then left.

Heath locked up the container before clipping Bundy onto the chain on the back of Ned's Hilux. Once he'd removed the fallen tree from off the fence at Hawks Ridge he'd at least have a way of transporting the cut wood to the house. He hadn't yet seen the winter wood pile but he had no doubt it needed replenishing.

After a quick stop at the grocery store to pick up some items for his mother, he headed out of town. The chug of the diesel engine provided the only sound as he followed the edge of the lowland valley around to Hawks Ridge.

When he drove through the front gate, he noticed with satisfaction that the mailbox no longer leaned at a tilt. The railroad sleepers were a freshly painted white and the large sign rust-free. His plan had been to start there and work his way back to the house.

The driveway potholes and the worn-out suspension in the old Hilux caused Heath to bounce on his seat. Once the tractor tyres were fixed, he'd grade the road. As he had no hope of getting his convertible back anytime soon, while he had Ned's Hilux he'd also book it in to get the suspension replaced.

He slowed as he passed the fallen tree to assess the fence damage. By late afternoon he should have the wire upright. His next job would be to muster the cattle who had free run of the front paddocks. From yesterday's head count, he suspected the farm was only carrying a quarter of the stock it used to. But all the cattle were in good condition. Somehow his mother had been keeping up with the cattle work.

He parked in his usual spot near the old fir. The wind whistled through the needle-like leaves. His mother straightened from where she was digging in a rose bed. Jasper left his sheltered spot in the sun beside the veranda. His brown eyes were bright and he moved across the lawn with an ease Heath hadn't seen yesterday. Last night his mother had sent a photo of Jasper asleep in the memory foam bed that would support his joints.

Heath patted his sandy-coloured coat before Jasper and Bundy chased each other into the garden. He continued over to his mother. Jasper wasn't the only one to appear years younger. Colour warmed her cheeks and a smile relaxed her mouth.

'Hi, darling. No luck with the cherry picker?'

He shook his head. 'Dad sleep well?'

'He did. He's in the living room. Lunch?'

'Bundy and I ate our body weight in lamingtons for morning smoko, so we'll move the tree first.'

His mother's laughter was something he hadn't heard in quite a while.

After he'd unpacked the groceries in the kitchen, he made his way to where the noise of a western movie filtered from out of the living room. His steps didn't slow as he headed through the doorway. After what the day had thrown at him so far, his father's temper would be the least of his worries.

His father glanced at him, no recognition on his craggy face. His hand shook where it rested on the armrest. 'The broken pump's out the back.'

Heath nodded, taking note of where the remote control was and if there was anything his father might need. After a last look, he quit the room to head to his childhood bedroom. Once inside he collected the dinner suit he'd worn over a decade ago that hung in his wardrobe. With it draped over his arm, he looked around the room.

It was just as he'd left it. A red, white and green quilt blanketed the bed and an array of framed family photos stood on the corner of his empty desk. His attention lingered on a photograph of his father with his arms around Kyle and Andrew when they were boys. His father's smile was as foreign as the affection in his gesture.

Heath's gaze flicked to the only two photos that were of him. One was with his mother as a baby and the other, again with his mother, was when he'd graduated from school. His father had cut him out of his life long before their infamous conversation.

Needing air, he headed for the back door off the laundry. The wooden door opened but when he went to push the screen door it didn't budge. He placed his suit on the washing machine and reached up to check that the ancient door closer hadn't rusted or jammed.

Steps shuffled behind him. He turned to see his father looming in the laundry doorway. His voice growled, 'What are you doing?'

At first Heath thought his father still believed he was there to fix the pump. Then he met his gaze. There was no mistaking the hostility. His father knew exactly who he was.

'Hi, Dad.'

'I asked you a question.'

He kept his words calm. 'I'm fixing the screen door.'

A grunt was all he received in reply.

His father's moments of lucidity would become rare. He needed to try to understand him as well as find a way to broker peace between them. He'd start with the little Jack Russell who they'd both cared about.

'Dad, what happened to Minnie? No one ever told me why she never came home.'

The skin of his father's face seemed to tighten. 'That's none of your business.'

Heath didn't immediately reply. An unfamiliar expression had swept across his father's eyes. An expression that in anyone else he'd have described as anguish. Except he'd never seen his father show any emotion other than disgust, anger and disapproval.

'Dad, I loved her too.'

Fury mottled his father's cheeks. 'Enough.' His narrow gaze shifted to the screen door and then back to Heath. 'Fixing things and bringing your mother a dog isn't going to change what I think of you. You'll never get Hawks Ridge, and it won't make you worthy of Clancy Parker. You'll only ruin her life.'

'Leave Clancy out of this. I don't have an agenda and you know it.'

'Do you remember what I said the day you left?'

A chill that wasn't from the wind howling beneath the roof eaves gripped him.

'In case you need a reminder, I'll say it again.' His father's eyes blazed with a rage that was as cold as it was cutting. 'You are no son of mine. Never have been, never will be.' He swung away as if the sight of Heath caused him physical pain. 'If you don't believe me, ask your mother.'

Clancy's prediction that Primrose would be both a time waster and trouble had proved to be an understatement. She stopped typing and looked away from her computer screen to listen. Beyond her office windows the mountains stretched into the blue serenity of the morning sky while inside there was an unusual silence.

Primrose and Iris had been with her for only four days and yet it was hard to imagine life without them. After ignoring the golden retrievers the first afternoon, Orien had become their best buddy. If they weren't wrestling or chasing each other, they were jumping on lounges or hiding under tables. Just as well they were adorable.

A sudden crash sounded. Clancy looked to where Iris lay on the floor beside her office desk. 'Here we go again.'

They left the office. Clancy had puppy-proofed everything but she'd obviously missed something. And that something was in the kitchen. Orien had jumped onto the island bench and even as Clancy watched, the silver tabby used his paw to knock her car keys off the edge. Primrose waited below, pouncing on them as they landed. Clancy's metal water bottle had already been a casualty and had rolled beneath a chair. When Orien walked across the bench towards an empty glass, Clancy scooped him up and put him on the floor.

'I think it's time you both went outside.'

A low bark from Iris as she stared out the kitchen window towards the driveway had Clancy turn. The Amos sisters' small white car drove through the twin avenues of poplars. Too late she looked back at Orien who had leaped onto the side bench and used his head to push the wire fruit bowl off the side. Primrose yipped with excitement as bananas, pears and apples cascaded onto the ground. The puppy tore off after an apple as it rolled across the room.

Clancy only had time to rescue the bananas and two apples before the doorbell chimed. After putting the fruit in the refrigerator, she scanned the kitchen benches to check there was nothing else movable and that the cookbooks she'd been searching through weren't on display. She wasn't yet sure quite how to pull off her book club secret weapon and if the sisters came inside she didn't want any clues that she was planning more than the usual supper.

At the front door, she brushed off her black puffer vest. Knowing her luck she would be covered in dirt from her morning jobs. With a glance over her shoulder to check that Orien and Primrose weren't about to bolt past, she opened the door and slipped outside. Millicent and Beatrice stood on the top step. Today they each wore a grey jumper with their neat black pants. Thankfully Millicent's longer silver bob provided a clue as to which twin was which.

Clancy smiled and made a silent plea that any further crashes from inside wouldn't be heard on the veranda. The serious sisters rarely visited and when they did she made sure she looked like she had her life in order. Orien and Primrose running amuck wouldn't exactly contribute to such an impression. 'This is a nice surprise.'

'Morning,' Beatrice said with a brief smile. 'We were passing and thought we'd drop by.'

Millicent's attention seemed to be on her hair and Clancy resisted the urge to check if a leaf was caught there.

'Would you like a cuppa?' With any luck the apples under the table wouldn't be noticeable if she took the sisters into the conservatory.

Instead of answering, both Millicent and Beatrice stared at the bottom of the nearby window. While no sound could be heard, Orien had jumped onto the window ledge and Primrose was tangling herself in the lace curtain trying to reach him. Every so often Orien would pat Primrose on the head with his paw.

Clancy suppressed a sigh.

Millicent frowned. 'I didn't know you had a puppy.'

Clancy moved to open the door and Iris padded out. 'Make that a puppy and her mother.'

She wasn't sure what to expect from the sisters, but her first guess was that they'd have been concerned about the implications for book club. A couple of members had pet allergies. But instead, as Millicent gazed to where Iris stood in front of her wagging her fluffy cream tail, her frown dissolved into delight. 'A golden retriever. I had one as a child.'

As happy as Millicent was to see Iris, Clancy didn't miss the sadness that turned Beatrice's expression even more sombre. The sisters were notoriously private but over the past twenty years whispers about their past had established that the sisters as children had not always been together. There were locals who knew the true story, and she was sure her mother had as she'd once said the sisters didn't have a lot to smile about growing up.

Millicent glanced at Beatrice and her eyes softened. 'Thanks, we'd love a cuppa.'

When the sisters walked through the doorway, Primrose skidded around the dining room corner to see who had arrived. This time Beatrice smiled.

Between puppy licks, Orien bolting past at full speed and Iris's tail wagging, the wide hallway no longer felt spacious.

Once they'd managed to reach the kitchen, Clancy directed the sisters into the conservatory. She then went to open the back door to let the dogs and Orien outside, and on her way to the kettle scooped up the remaining apples and pears.

Thanks to knowing exactly how Millicent and Beatrice took their tea, it wasn't long until she was seated across from them. Both sisters sat with their hands folded on the table in front of them. The lemon aroma of the slice she'd baked last night filled the sun-drenched conservatory and steam curled in delicate spirals from their mugs.

Clancy offered each woman a piece of slice and waited. She hadn't bought the just-driving-past line.

Millicent spoke first. 'Are you really okay about being on the mural?'

Clancy blinked. Not only did the personal question take her by surprise but Millicent no longer looked severe but genuinely concerned. She nodded. 'I am.'

'We just wanted to make sure,' Beatrice said.

'Thank you but Heath has also double-checked.' She made sure her voice sounded normal. The sisters would register any change in her tone. No matter how much she'd battened down her heart, Heath asking for her help to finish the mural early still made her feel warm inside.

Millicent's attention remained on Clancy. 'How is Heath?'

'Fine, I think. I haven't seen him for a couple of days.'

She didn't miss the beat of silence before each sister raised their mug to their lips.

The conversation turned to the unpredictable spring weather. After they'd finished their tea, Clancy walked Millicent and Beatrice to their car. She stayed on the veranda to wave them off. As soon as their white sedan disappeared over the crest of the driveway, she took her phone out of her vest pocket and dialled.

Brenna answered almost straight away. 'Hi, Clance. What's up?'

'You wouldn't believe who just visited.'

'Clancy of the Overflow.'

She laughed at the familiar joke and turned to sit on the old church pew that gave her a perfect view of the mountains. 'Millicent and Beatrice. They wanted to know if I was okay about the mural. They also asked about Heath, which wasn't all that strange, but something was up.'

'You know … I have a theory.'

Clancy smiled. Brenna always had lots of theories. It wasn't movies she watched, but people. 'About who?'

'Millicent, Beatrice and Heath.'

'The sisters and Heath?'

'Yes. They seemed to know exactly what we were all up to as teenagers but they especially kept an eye on Heath.'

'I didn't notice them treating anyone differently.'

'Think about it. Book club and the book festival have always been their thing. They weren't even on the tourism committee until Heath offered to paint the water tower. I heard from Fiona that they personally asked Dr Davis if they could be involved.'

Clancy barely registered Brenna's words. 'Did you say Heath *offered* to paint the tower?'

'Yes. Why?'

Clancy thought hard. 'I have a theory, too ... but not about the sisters and Heath. He needed to come home and that's why he has to finish the mural asap.'

'Couldn't he have come home anytime?'

'Technically ... but he never has. Why now? I always thought he'd been asked to paint the mural.'

'Maybe he's had enough of travelling? Maybe he's lonely?'

'Going off the number of women draped off him on social media, I doubt that.'

Brenna laughed softly. 'I thought you'd stopped stalking him.'

'I have. I'm just ... looking ... occasionally.'

'Uh-huh. Don't worry, you've nothing to worry about—they're only fans.'

This time Clancy laughed. 'I thought you'd stopped stalking him too.'

'Not a chance.'

Clancy's amusement ebbed. 'It's family stuff that has brought him home ... stuff that has to be about more than just his father being difficult.'

'Does this mean you're still going to keep him at arm's length?'

She hesitated. Her heart said she'd never deny Heath any help but her self-preservation urged caution. 'He'll never open up to me, so I'll never have to answer such a question.'

A loud horse whinny drowned out the last of Clancy's words before Brenna's voice sounded. 'Sorry, I'm in the stables. Off topic, do you want to come to the hut tomorrow night? Taite's coming.'

'I'd love to but I couldn't leave Iris and Primrose.'

'I'm sure Ned would house-sit like he did when we went skiing.'

'Heath might be able to as well.'

'True but he's coming too. He's had more mechanical issues so Taite talked him into having a night off as the cherry picker part won't arrive for another day.'

Clancy bit the inside of her cheek. When Brenna first mentioned camping out at the hut she'd been determined not to go, but things had changed. Ash would enjoy the ride and over winter she'd missed not rolling out her swag and sleeping under the stars. She also enjoyed seeing the secret waterfalls that only flowed in spring. Once peony season hit she wouldn't be going anywhere.

As for Heath, now that she knew he'd come home for a reason, she wanted to keep tabs on how he was doing. After the way she'd reacted to him while in her gumboots and ball gown, this would also be a perfect opportunity to prove to herself she could be around him and keep herself in check.

'I need to talk to Ned, but count me in.'

'Great. See you about ten.'

Clancy ended the call and headed through the front door. The trouble with Brenna's theories was that once she voiced them, they tended to create a life of their own.

After she'd let Iris, Primrose and Orien inside and saddled Ash for their morning cattle check, her brain refused to stop whirring. *Were* the sisters more invested in Heath than anyone else? She swung into the saddle. If they were, how could she not have known? When it came to Heath, her radar had always been finely attuned.

The sisters had always bought Heath art supplies for the town Christmas party but they'd been very good at knowing what presents to buy all the local kids. The book about silver brumbies they'd gifted her still had pride of place on her bookshelf.

Her thoughts stayed with her as she rode past where Fergus and Fenella grazed, their shaggy highland coats rippling in the breeze, and continued as she and Ash made their way into the foothills. But once amongst Rowan's cattle, she concentrated on making sure the herd were in good health.

She stopped Ash to watch a mother cow who appeared to be on designated babysitting duty. While she chewed her cud in the shade of a gum tree, a trio of calves chased each other through the gully. The larger two stopped to butt heads.

When she caught sight of a cow and calf away from the main herd, she headed Ash in their direction. She was sure this was the pair she'd taken a closer look at yesterday. The bull calf didn't seem to have as much energy as the others. As she drew near she could see the indents in his hollowed-out sides.

She rode closer. Milk dripped from a front quarter of the cow's swollen udder. When the calf moved towards his mother, wanting a feed, she shifted away.

'You poor mamma. We need Trent to take a look at you.'

Clancy turned Ash towards the other cows. She'd bring in a small mob so as not to stress either the cow with mastitis or her calf.

Working quietly, she mustered a group of cows and their calves and soon had them heading towards home. The track to the cattle yards was a familiar one and the cattle were content to amble. The mid-morning sun warm on her shoulders, Clancy relaxed into the saddle. Clouds drifted across the mountain peaks and the lyrical notes of a currawong carried on the breeze.

But when the cattle yards and then the shed housing Heath's art studio came into sight, thoughts about Heath left her troubled. The more she pondered on Brenna's theory, the more she knew the sisters did have a special interest in Heath.

When he'd been in hospital after a rugby concussion, they'd arrived before Clancy and her mother. When he and Rowan had gone away to their Sydney boarding school, Millicent and Beatrice had been frequent visitors. As for the sisters' motives, Clancy could only assume they looked out for Heath because of the way his father treated him. They weren't the only locals to do so; Ned particularly had his back.

Clancy frowned at the corrugated iron art studio that continued to be Heath's sanctuary. The question was, what else had she missed about the man who meant so much to her?

Heath took a step back to look at the canvas he'd been working on since early morning. The painting had been inspired by the previous day's memory of seeing his father rest his forearms on the gate and stare at the mountains. What Heath hadn't included was the shake in his father's hands or his confused expression as he'd shuffled back to the house. The trip to the Canberra specialist the day before had left him disorientated.

Chest tight, Heath went back to painting. The neurologist visit hadn't delivered any surprises. With his father's hallucinations, fluctuating periods of lucidity and tremors, all that had resulted was an official confirmation of Lewy Body dementia. It had also led to some tough discussions with his mother. She'd eventually need help caring for his father and there would come a time when his needs couldn't be met at home and he'd have to go into care.

The tears in his mother's eyes had broken Heath's heart and reaffirmed his decision to not do as his father had said and ask her about the past. He refused to cause her any more distress.

She'd already lost two sons, and he wouldn't have her fear that she might lose him as well. If it was true that he wasn't his father's son, then he could understand why his mother had perhaps needed to seek comfort elsewhere. The memories he had of his father were that he'd always been a cold and difficult man.

As well as completing the mural, his immediate priority was making sure his mother would be okay. He'd pushed back another overseas project to buy more time before he had to leave. His mother continued to want to keep his father's condition private, so he'd compiled a checklist of online and face-to-face support groups and professional agencies for when she was ready.

As for his own sadness and sense of powerlessness, he too had to keep that hidden, especially from Clancy. He couldn't take advantage of her kind heart and empathy. He hadn't been there when she'd needed him and he couldn't now be selfish by expecting her to be there for him. He also couldn't bring any more shadows to her life.

The low moo of a cow calling her calf had Heath look up. Rowan's cattle shouldn't be this close. Paintbrush in hand, he crossed the shed to look through the open door. Bundy was already outside and watching as a small herd of cattle approached. Behind them Heath could see the purple of Clancy's shirt and the gold gleam of Ash's palomino coat.

He wiped his brush on a rag before adding it to the assortment of brushes soaking in a glass jar. He'd make sure the cattle yard gates were open.

As he went outside and over to the circular yards, Bundy ran to Clancy's side to help her walk the cattle along the fence line. Heath swung the closest gate open and then made sure the gates into the second yard were closed. Clancy gave him a wave which he returned as he went to stand outside the studio so he wouldn't be in the way. The cattle filed past and he soon saw the slow-moving cow with the tender udder.

Once the herd was inside the yards, he made his way over to Clancy. She was already off Ash and slipping the metal gate latch in place. Her hair spilled from beneath the brim of her hat and glinted red across her shoulders. He filed away the image for a future painting.

Ash nudged him and he stroked the gelding's nose.

'Thanks for getting the gates,' Clancy said as she gave Bundy a pat.

'No dramas.'

Her gaze sharpened as she straightened and took in the paint on his hands. 'Are you getting any sleep?'

'I am.' He grinned to erase the worry in her expression. 'My stipulated eight hours.'

Clancy looked at Bundy. 'Has he?'

The kelpie wagged his tail.

'Just as well.'

'I can be here for the vet if you have other things to do?'

'Thanks. Trent's on his way. He's been seeing a horse at the Joneses'. Brenna said you were having more mechanical issues.'

Heath didn't immediately answer. Clancy's eyes were the muted grey of a winter dawn. Something bothered her more than having a sick cow. But before he could ask if everything was okay, a diesel engine chugged as a white ute with a canopy crested the hill.

Clancy left to lead Ash over to the shade of a grey box tree while Heath went to open the gate. The driver of the mud-splattered ute gave him a nod as he drove through.

There was no mistaking this new vet for old Max Crossing who'd been the local veterinarian for decades. Trent had a head full of dark-blond hair. When he left the vehicle, Heath also saw that he was broad-shouldered and tall and that he and Clancy greeted each other with an easy camaraderie. Bundy was also pleased to see him and rolled over on his back to have his stomach rubbed.

As Heath approached, the vet held out his hand. 'Trent Windsor.'

The vet's open expression and the humour in his brown eyes made him instantly likable. Heath shook his hand. 'Heath MacBride.'

'I've heard all about you and the water tower project. Mabel's my flatmate.'

He nodded, racking his brain for anything Rowan might have mentioned about the man standing before him. Trent Windsor with his country boy affability and his obvious love of animals could be considered Clancy's perfect match.

Heath stayed still while Trent and Clancy fell into step beside each other as they walked towards the yards sharing a laugh. They weren't just casual acquaintances but appeared to be good friends.

Shoulders braced, he strode over to the cattle. All he'd ever wanted was for Clancy to be happy and to have a reason to smile like she had when she'd chosen Iris and Primrose. Clancy deserved to have a decent man who'd made the high country his home by her side and a family to grow old with. The sooner it happened the better. Even if such a prospect caused a little more of him to wither inside.

While Trent gathered what he needed from his ute and Clancy made sure the end gate on the cattle race was shut, Heath went into the yards. Using low stress handling techniques, he cut out the cow and her calf. When they walked up the race he closed the gate behind them. Once Clancy had carefully caught the mother cow's head in the head bail, Heath opened a side gate to let the calf out so he wouldn't be kicked.

Trent busied himself with examining the cow. When he went to strip out the milk from the infected quarter, the cow's back leg lashed out, but she settled as the pressure in her udder was relieved.

Clancy's phone rang and she moved away to take the call.

Her conversation carried to Heath. 'Hi, Ned, I do … but I've a cow with mastitis who'll need antibiotics so I'll stay … Are you sure? … Thank you. Will do.'

Clancy returned to give Heath a smile. Her earlier gravity appeared to have disappeared. 'Ned says he's happy to keep your car until you're back from the hut.'

'I bet he is. That Hilux of his has no suspension.'

Trent looked up at him from where he cleaned the cow's udder. 'That's not the silver convertible I saw in town this morning?'

'Was it still in one piece?'

Trent grinned. 'I couldn't tell from all the mud.'

'I knew there was a reason why Ned wanted me to get an all-wheel drive.' Heath pulled a face. 'In another life he must have been a rally driver.'

He didn't miss Clancy's quick look before she joined in with Trent's laughter.

After the vet had administered a dose of intermammary antibiotics and handed Clancy two spare tubes, the mother and calf were reunited. This time when the calf went to feed, the mother remained still. White bubbles of froth formed at the corners of his mouth as he filled his empty belly from the three mastitis-free quarters.

Heath went to again get the gate so Trent could head off to treat a foundered pony. The vet and Clancy shared a few quiet words before he slid into the driver's seat. He nodded to Heath as he drove by.

By the time Heath returned, Clancy had let the mother and calf out into a small adjacent paddock where it would be easy for them to be returned to the yards for the next round of antibiotics.

'Goliath and I can take the others back if you'd like?' he said as the remaining cattle congregated at the yard gate.

'Do you have time?'

'I'm not meeting Hannah until after lunch.'

'She'll love chatting to you about her art. She's had a tough time since her parents' divorce.'

'I'm looking forward to seeing her portfolio.' He followed Clancy's gaze to where Trent's vehicle was still visible on the road leaving Ashcroft. 'Trent been here long?'

'Maybe two years? It doesn't seem that long ago though since Max retired.'

'Is Trent on Cynthia's hit list?'

'He is single but when he came to town he was engaged. He lost his fiancée eighteen months ago in a freak snowboarding accident. Everyone understands he's still grieving.'

Heath stared at where Trent's ute was now a white speck in the distance. The vet had suffered a deep loss and yet he had kept the wheels of his life turning. Trent's strength was yet another reason why he and Clancy could be compatible. Heath looked away from the road only to find Clancy studying him, a slight crease in her brow.

He swung away before she could read every secret he held. 'I'll clean the studio then catch grumpy Goliath.'

'Heath …'

He half turned.

'The family stuff you need to finish the mural for … Is everything fine?'

He chose his words carefully. 'Everything's … as expected.'

Her eyes narrowed but she didn't say anything other than 'Okay' before she changed the subject. 'Are you right for a swag for tomorrow night?'

'I'll grab one and an oilskin when I'm home this afternoon.'

'Thanks for doing the cattle.'

'Anytime.'

But she was already on her way over to Ash.

The memory of Clancy watching him with such intensity refused to fade while he moved the cattle. It then lingered even after he'd met Hannah at the café. Clancy had never looked at him in such an intent way before; it was as though he were a stranger. He'd always counted on their familiarity insulating him from her perceptiveness. She already knew who he was and wouldn't look any deeper.

When Hannah closed the cover on her portfolio and looked up as the café door opened, he forced his thoughts off Clancy.

What could only be Cynthia's middle daughter sashayed towards him. Just like her sisters she had the same yellow-blonde hair, but whereas Larissa's good nature warmed her blue eyes and Hannah's interest was only in art, this sister's confident smile said it all. He had his answer as to whether or not Cynthia's second daughter would be on board with her mother's matchmaking. She was in no need of any help.

The older teen slid into the spare seat. 'Hi, I'm Ruby.'

Beside him he heard Hannah sigh. 'Rubes, we're not finished yet.'

'You've been in here for ages. I've got things to do.'

Heath didn't miss Ruby's almost secretive smile as she glanced out the door. He casually glanced sideways and saw a red ute with aerials and a five-post bull bar cruising along the main street.

He looked back at Hannah. 'Maybe we can have coffee again next week?'

'I'd like that. I can bring my sketchbook.'

Ruby ignored the conversation while she texted on her phone.

This time Hannah noticed the red ute that again cruised past.

She turned to her sister. 'I thought you and John had broken up. You told Mum you wanted to go to the library.'

Ruby flicked back her long blonde hair. 'We're on a break and I did go.' She frowned. 'Then Millicent and Beatrice saw us in the park.'

Heath hid his grin as he went to pay the bill. While many things had changed around town, some things hadn't. The sisters were still keeping an eye on Bundilla's next generation.

After they'd left the cosy café with its walls full of books, he walked Hannah and Ruby to Ruby's small blue car. Bundy came over from where he'd been keeping an elderly woman company while she sat on a bench in the sunshine. After taking a drink from one of the nearby dog water bowls that could be found up and down the main street, the kelpie jumped onto the Hilux trayback.

They'd only cleared the town limits when Heath's mobile rang. He answered using Bluetooth.

Rowan's voice filled the cabin. 'Afternoon.'

Heath chuckled. 'Which means it's late over there and you've just got back from the pub.'

'Guilty as charged but I've been home for a while. I've been talking to Clance.'

Heath's amusement fled. 'Is she okay?'

'She's fine. Just a heads up, she suspects you came home because something's going on with your parents. It might be an idea to talk to her about what's happening with your dad.'

As quiet and unassuming as Clancy could be, she was also one of the most single-minded people he knew. She wouldn't pry but at the same time she'd be determined to help. But there was something else he wanted to talk to Rowan about. 'The new vet ... you haven't mentioned him before.'

'I wondered when you'd meet Trent. There's nothing to say except if you're asking if I think he'd make Clance happy, the truth is I reckon he would.'

Heath took his time answering. 'I think so, too.'

Rowan sighed. 'I'm not saying this because you're my best mate, but the person who'd make Clance the happiest is you. You've always just been able to get each other. But the window's closing. You either have to tell her how you feel or let her go.'

'I can't ask her to leave the mountains ... and I can't stay.'

'I understand, but if being with Eloise has taught me anything it's that while we think we know where our lives are headed, we don't. Just think about what I've said.' Rowan stifled a yawn. 'Now I need to get some shut-eye before my resident sparrows wake up.'

Long after their call ended, Heath stared at the road sweeping before him. He could no more tell Clancy what was happening with his father than he could tell her he loved her. After how close he'd come to kissing her when he'd helped her with her ball gown, he'd be a fool to stretch his self-control any further. Any personal disclosure, however small, and he couldn't guarantee all the other emotions he had to hide wouldn't break free. For if they did, there wouldn't only be no going back, there'd be no way forward.

CHAPTER
9

'Come on, Goliath, it's not that bad.'

Clancy couldn't help but smile at the stockhorse's sour expression as Heath led him towards the horse float. It was as though the gelding was being asked to dress up as a unicorn and parade through town.

Ash had simply walked on, eyes bright and ears forward, and was waiting inside.

Beside Clancy, Ned chuckled. 'Goliath has the look of a horse who will make it known as soon as he can that he isn't happy.'

'Just as well it's Heath riding him and not me.'

Clancy watched as Heath spoke softly to Goliath, and despite his ill humour the gelding followed him into the float.

Today Heath was paint free and dressed in faded jeans and a navy half-zip sweater. He hadn't only collected his swag and oilskin from home but a well-used hat that she recognised. The angle at which he'd pulled the brim over his face caused a familiar ache. It was as though she were again looking at a young Heath and just like then she found it impossible to look away.

The nip of sharp puppy teeth on her finger reminded her she held Primrose. Now that Goliath was loaded she put the restless pup on the ground. Primrose immediately took off after a magpie perched on the nearby wooden fence.

Clancy glanced at Ned. 'Are you sure you want to do this?'

Ned chuckled again. 'My bag's already in your spare room.' He bent to pat Iris who had followed him around since he'd arrived. 'You and Heath go and have some fun. We'll be fine.'

Clancy nodded as she ran through a mental list. The mother cow was already much improved and only had one more lot of antibiotics to go. There was cake and cookies in the pantry for Ned and a list on the fridge of what the dogs and Orien were fed for dinner and when Iris had to have her medication. When Heath had left Hawks Ridge yesterday, Bundy hadn't jumped into the Hilux but instead had chosen to stay with Jasper, otherwise he'd be hanging out with Ned too.

Heath walked over. 'Mr Grumpy's on board. We're all good to go.'

After a hug to Ned and a last pat to the dogs, Clancy slipped behind the wheel of her dual cab. As she clipped in her seatbelt, Heath settled into the passenger seat. She tried to ignore the way the cabin suddenly felt small and all she could breathe in was the scent of wool, leather and whatever cologne it was Heath wore that still made her want to lean in far too close.

As she drove away, she let out a silent breath to try and relax. They weren't even five minutes into their trip and her awareness of Heath made her stomach flutter. She'd always been acutely conscious of him but it was as though she now looked at him through new eyes. She didn't want to miss anything else.

While he appeared at ease as he gazed at the mountain peaks, the clenched hand on his thigh let her know he was just as tense as he'd been yesterday at the cattle yards. She didn't know what had happened in the days since they'd visited the animal shelter but if she'd thought Heath had been on edge when he'd come home to Bundilla, his tension had only increased. Whatever the family stuff he was dealing with, it was serious.

When she'd asked him about it yesterday, he'd again avoided her question. But she'd learned her lesson from Brenna's barbeque and so she'd changed the subject. While still hurt by Heath continuing to shut her out, at least now her plan to keep her emotional distance wouldn't be under threat. It was for the best things stayed as they were; she'd not survive should their connection deepen. Heath had already indicated that as soon as he could he'd return to the world he'd left.

Once the cherry picker part arrived tomorrow all he'd be doing was working, so today she'd do what she could to make sure he had the fun Ned said they should have. She felt Heath look at her before he broke the silence. 'Clance, this might seem a strange question, but … are you lonely?'

She didn't try to hide her surprise at either his serious tone or his words. The having fun part was obviously going to have to wait. 'Maybe a little without Rowan around but now with Primrose and Iris, the house doesn't seem so empty.'

His lips briefly twitched. 'So Rowan's been replaced.'

'Does it sound shallow if I still miss his Sunday roasts?'

Heath's deep chuckle made her smile. 'Not at all. But what about partner lonely?'

They'd never lied to each other, even if Heath was either silent or economical with the details about what was going on in his life. 'I'd like to settle down and have a family but there's no rush. Besides, I want what my parents had and I won't settle for anything less so no … I'm not lonely on my own. What about you?'

From the corner of her eye she saw his fist clench tighter. 'Travel's hard on any relationship.'

'I'm sorry.'

'Don't be. The only serious relationship I've had is with work.'

She kept her voice steady to hide her relief. 'That actually does sound lonely, especially if you move around a lot. Maybe one day you'll stay in one place?'

'It's not likely.'

'Why?'

'Why?'

'Yes, why?' She cast him an assessing look and found him staring at her, dark brows lifted. 'You can't be a rolling stone forever. What about Hawks Ridge?'

Heath looked away. 'Dad's made it clear it will never be mine.'

'You're not serious? Hawks Ridge has been in your mother's family for generations.'

'I don't want to come between them.'

Anger replaced her shock. Locals often excused Graham MacBride's belligerence because of how he lost his sons, but what type of man would disinherit the son he still had?

'Heath, Hawks Ridge is your home, these mountains are part of who you are. And don't say they aren't because I know you.' She took a breath to slow her words. 'Wait until I see your father next. He is lucky to have you as his son.'

It was as though a light suddenly switched off behind Heath's eyes. His features settled into an unreadable mask. 'Promise me you won't say anything. This is between him and me. His fuse isn't exactly long at the moment.'

'It never has been. Don't forget his glower doesn't work on me.'

A smile returned some life to Heath's eyes. 'How could I? You telling him off for not congratulating me on the Bundilla Cup is the only time I've seen him lost for words. But promise me, Clance.'

'Okay. I won't take on your father.' She glanced at Heath. 'Until his fuse is longer.'

She thought Heath was about to say something before he gave a single nod.

A sudden thought struck her. 'Why did you ask if I was lonely? Has Rowan said something?'

Heath replied without meeting her gaze. 'It was on my mind.'

Her grip firmed on the steering wheel. He hadn't answered her second question. 'Heath MacBride, did Rowan ask you to keep an eye on me?'

An unfamiliar emotion flittered across his face. 'Clance ...'

'Don't *Clance* me. Is that why you're in the coach house?'

'No, but Rowan is concerned about you, and yes, as I'm here and he isn't ...'

She had no words that she could voice. The man she loved was keeping a *brotherly* watch over her.

Heath continued, his words low. 'It really has been on my mind ... especially after I met Trent. He's a good guy and you deserve to be happy.'

Clancy stared at the road and ground her teeth. If Brenna could see her now there would be no look of serenity on her face. Her frustration was underpinned by a new sense of desperation that triggered a need to fight. She wasn't a risk-taker but in that moment she wanted to disregard all common sense and tell Heath he was the only one who would ever make her happy.

Instead she fought for calm. He was already under enough stress and if she was going to act out of character she needed to think things through a little more. Was revealing her feelings worth the price of losing their friendship?

When she was sure her emotions weren't about to go rogue, she spoke. 'One, nobody needs to keep an eye on me. Ever. Two, I don't need anyone in my life to be happy.'

Heath's reply was a quiet rasp. 'Both points noted.'

She shot him a look. She didn't know what she expected to see in his expression but there was a bleakness in his eyes she'd never glimpsed before.

Then his hand lifted and he smoothed the loose hair from her ponytail off her cheek and behind her ear. 'I'm sorry, Clance. I … we both were … out of line.'

She could only nod. The slow sweep of his fingers over her skin caused an ache in her throat that would only make her voice husky.

The turn-off to Glenwood Station appeared and she slowed to leave the bitumen road.

For the rest of the drive they stuck to small talk about Taite's deer and brumby sculptures. Once at Glenwood Station they were too busy unloading the horses and saddling up to talk again.

As she tightened Ash's girth, Brenna came over. 'What's going on between you and Heath?'

'Nothing. We cleared the air.'

'Interesting.' Brenna glanced over Clancy's shoulder. 'When MacBride looks so stony-faced there's a whole lot of thinking going on.'

Clancy lowered the saddle flap and attached her lightweight swag behind the saddle. 'Trust me, the only thing he'd be thinking is that good guy Trent would be a perfect match for the apparently very lonely sister of his best mate who he promised to keep an eye on.'

'Ahh … I can see why the air needed to be cleared. Heath and Trent have met?'

'Yesterday.'

'It's about time. MacBride's had it too easy for too long. A little competition is just what he needs.'

Clancy didn't answer as Heath and Taite rode over. Both had swags behind their saddles and oilskin coats rolled up on the front. Goliath appeared his usual surly self, sidestepping instead of walking forward, while Taite's young buckskin startled as Brenna shut the door of Clancy's dual cab.

She smoothed Ash's neck as the gelding stood quietly. At this rate she'd be the only one who would have an uneventful ride. Like Taite, Brenna was riding a green broke horse she hoped to one day use on their treks.

Clancy swung into the saddle. Heath's eyes locked with hers. She didn't know if it was because she was seeing him through a different lens or if it was just wishful thinking but the intense way he stared at her wasn't exactly brotherly. Then Taite said something and the moment was lost when Heath looked away.

Brenna joined them on a chestnut sporting a large white blaze. Just like Goliath, the mare had trouble walking in a straight line. Her glossy coat was already slick with sweat.

'Let's get this party started,' Taite said with a grin as he led the way along the creek flats and up into the hills. The track they followed wasn't well used as they travelled the long way round to the high country hut. For the professional treks, Brenna used a less taxing route that explored the far side of the station.

Clancy kept away from the other three until their horses settled. It wasn't long until Brenna rode alongside her. Ash's placid nature would calm the nervous chestnut. Taite and Heath continued ahead and were soon out of sight.

After Clancy and Brenna descended into a valley, they found Heath waiting at the river. The ride already had been good for him. He sat relaxed in the saddle, his shoulders loose and his expression almost boyish. The white gleam of his smile caused Clancy's breath to catch. Finally she was seeing Heath with all of his tension stripped away. She needed no further proof that the mountains were as much a part of him as they were of her.

He dipped his head to the left. 'Taite's gone to check that a deer we saw wasn't one of his.'

Even Heath's voice seemed different. Less taut. More carefree.

Crashing sounded in the undergrowth before Taite and his buckskin reappeared.

'It was a feral deer, but ...' Taite stopped his gelding at a section of the riverbank and studied the ground. 'I saw a wallaby carcass and wild dog tracks ... not a lone dog, but a pack.'

Brenna rode over to also look along the creek bank for tracks. 'There has been some stock losses further along the valley but we don't usually have any problems.'

Taite's expression turned grim. 'Let's hope they're long gone.'

The clatter of hard hooves on water-smoothed rocks filled the quiet as they followed each other across the river. The terrain grew steeper and they stopped at a clearing to give the horses a breather. Brenna pointed to a distant ridge—part of the national park—that through the haze appeared blue. A herd of brumbies, led by a black stallion, galloped across the open grassland. The horses' manes and tails rippled in the wind before they disappeared into the snow gums.

Lunch was a cold camp at a large glade that provided yet more sweeping mountain views of the western side of the Snowies. When Heath shared his salad roll with Goliath, Clancy took a photo to send to Rowan. For once the irritable gelding looked as though he was enjoying himself. She then busied herself with snapping pictures of the purple eyebright wildflowers to stop herself from taking more of a laughing Heath.

As the daylight faded they climbed the last leg of the track to the historic hut. Built of corrugated iron, rock and alpine ash timber, the rustic structure had provided shelter to many a weary rider. After the horses were unsaddled, fed and watered in the yards, it wasn't long until the scent of wood smoke drifted on the cold evening air. The hut had an internal fireplace but tonight they would sleep around the campfire.

Between the fresh ingredients Brenna had brought in her saddle bags and the non-perishable staples she kept in the hut, soon a lamb stew was underway and the aromas reminded Clancy of how hungry she was.

When Heath's fingers brushed hers as he passed her an empty plate, she was glad of the darkness that hid the heat in her cheeks. She was supposed to be proving to herself she could be near him and keep herself together. She wasn't supposed to be blushing like a teenager.

But after the fire died down and they sat in its warm glow enjoying their golden syrup dumplings, she made the mistake of looking across at him. When their gazes met, she couldn't repress a rush of longing or glance away. As the seconds passed, hope flickered into life deep inside her. Heath also didn't look away. This time she had no doubt that he stared at her in a way he never had before.

At this rate he'd be lucky to get eight minutes of sleep, let alone eight hours.

Canvas rustled as Heath rolled onto his side and rested his head on his elbow. While warm in his swag, the night's chill crept over whatever bare skin it could reach.

In the flickers of the firelight he could make out Taite stretched out to his left. Brenna lay past him, while Clancy slept across from him. Even with the distance between them, all he could hear was her gentle rhythmic breaths.

It had been a rollercoaster of a day. He might have vowed to not cause her further hurt but a fat lot of good that had done him. Now he'd made her angry. And she had every right to be. He and Rowan were in the wrong for not giving her the space to live her life. While things now appeared to be back to normal between them, the damage was irreparable. Another layer of his control had disintegrated. There'd soon be nothing left.

He'd been a fool to have ever thought he could come home and things wouldn't have changed. Maybe it was youth, maybe naivety, but despite all the years he'd loved her, before he'd left he'd never had any trouble containing his emotions whenever around her. Now, all he did was feel and all they seemed to do was hit sparks off each other. He refused to believe that his father was right when he'd said he was no good for her.

As for Clancy's belief that he needed to stay in one place, he only wished he could. But unless it was with her, he couldn't again make Bundilla his home. Even then, without Hawks Ridge he wasn't sure what his staying would look like. He'd still have to travel for his art, and as for being a cattleman, land holdings like Hawks Ridge didn't come on the market often and when they did they had a hefty price tag. As much as he knew his father was wrong, there remained a sliver of doubt that being an artist and running a property would work. Both required a substantial investment of time.

His swag rustled as he rolled onto his back to stare at the scattering of stars across the night sky. Even though Trent wasn't looking for a relationship, the local vet had become the face of the future he'd always wanted for Clancy. A future that ensured she'd never have to leave her beloved home and high country. While he wished Clancy happiness, he'd be lying if he said that the thought of her loving someone else didn't leave him feeling jealous and displaced. It had been hard enough seeing the young local pay her attention at Brenna's barbeque.

He scraped a hand over his face. The cherry picker part couldn't arrive soon enough. He had to expend his feelings in his mural before he did or said something they'd both regret.

He hadn't realised he'd drifted off to sleep until the sound of a restless horse caused his eyes to open. By now the eastern horizon had lightened to the grey of a new day and a heavy dew intensified the earthy smell of wet earth. The darkened valleys would be blanketed in mist and the wallabies and kangaroos would be stirring for their dawn breakfast.

A horse hoof again stamped while others shuffled. Heath flipped back his swag and slipped on his jacket and nearby long oilskin. He went over to the horses and after finding nothing amiss, went to stoke the fire and put on the billy. Footsteps sounded before Clancy appeared shrugging on her own oilskin. She sat next to him on the tree stump that had long ago been cut for a seat.

As she yawned, she ran a hand through her hair. The scent of daphne wrapped around him. He leaned forward to put more wood on the fire. It was either that or tangle his hands in her tousled hair and kiss her.

'Please tell me you haven't been up all night,' she said, voice husky from sleep.

He took his time with the fire. 'No. Goliath was restless. Cuppa?'

'Thanks but it's more sleep I need, not caffeine.' She rubbed her hands in front of the fire's warmth. 'It's freezing, why don't you go back to bed, too?'

He shook his head as he stared into the flames and took his time to answer. 'I never thanked you that day of the Bundilla Cup … for what you said to Dad.'

'You didn't have to. It's what friends—'

He cut her off with a smile that he hoped didn't reflect his strain. The word 'friends' was becoming one he never wanted to hear again. 'I know. But my father is an intimidating man and there wouldn't be many adults let alone teenagers who would have said what you did to him.'

She shrugged. 'He needed to be told it wasn't acceptable to snub you in front of the town when you won.'

'I believe your exact words were … "Mr MacBride, if your heart was any colder everything you touched would turn to ice. Now, go and congratulate Heath."'

'I was sixteen and did love being dramatic.'

Heath kept his laughter quiet so as to not wake the others. 'And he did, it's the only time he's ever said well done.'

Clancy didn't smile. 'I stand by my words.'

'It's all good. Ned and your father both said well done plenty of times.'

Silence settled between them as they gazed at the fire. When Clancy smothered another yawn he stood and, even though he knew he shouldn't, held out his hand. 'Come on, back to your swag you go.'

Her fingers curled into his and he pulled her to her feet. In the narrow space between the seats and the fire their oilskin coats brushed. The firelight bathed her fine-boned features in a soft glow. She stared at him, eyes sleepy. His gaze dropped to the curve of her mouth and the sweet fullness of her bottom lip. When he realised, he let go of her hand and went to turn away.

A canine shadow flittered in his peripheral vision and his hand shot out to again clasp hers. From over in the yards a horse snorted and hooves shuffled. Clancy appeared oblivious. Half asleep, she looked down to where their fingers were entwined.

He bent his head to whisper in her ear, 'Wake Taite and Brenna. We're not alone.'

When she didn't move, he touched her cold cheek. 'Look to your left.'

She slowly did so and then stiffened as though she'd suddenly become fully awake. He released her hand and moved to pass her a solid stick from the pile of wood near the campfire. Without a word, she disappeared into the gloom. Heath turned to add wood to the fire to fuel the flames and create more light before resting the ends of three other sticks in the coals.

The one shadow had become at least three. Then a black void to his right emitted a low snarl. Even though wild dogs were known to stalk humans, they usually stayed away. But in this case, being in a pack had emboldened them.

Taite strode over to the fire, his expression serious. 'The girls are with the horses.' He picked up one of the sticks that had caught alight. Orange flames danced on the end. 'They mightn't be afraid of us, but let's see how they like this.'

He waved the wood through the air and the shadows slunk away only to reappear in different locations.

Heath went to take a second stick from out of the fire when a shrill horse whinny was followed by the drum of agitated hooves. He was already on his way to the horse yards even before Brenna's urgent voice called out, '*Heath.*'

In the dim light Brenna's pale hair gleamed from where she held on to two horses that were milling in the yard corner. Goliath's dark shape charged around the circular perimeter, his snorts reverberating in the silence, while Ash stood rock-still in the middle, as though on guard.

Fear slammed into Heath's chest. On the ground at Ash's front feet lay a sprawled figure. He couldn't remember scaling the wooden fence. When he reached Clancy's side he touched her shoulder. Time seemed to stop, then she stirred. Air rushed back into his lungs. Mud flicked his cheek as Goliath careered too close and he moved closer to Clancy to shield her.

He helped her into a sitting position and pointed to outside the yard. When she nodded, he scooped her into his arms and carried her through the gate that Taite held open.

As if from a long distance away he heard Brenna say, 'Dogs are gone.'

Taite had lit a lantern in the hut and once inside Heath carefully settled Clancy onto a chair. Brenna's boots clattered as she entered and went to a cupboard to take out a first-aid kit.

All the while Heath stared at Clancy, his hands holding hers. She stared back. He'd never seen her eyes so wide and large. He'd also never seen her skin so white it was almost translucent. She blinked as though suddenly realising where she was.

'Will everyone please stop looking at me like that? I'm fine.' She eased her hands away from Heath's. 'Nothing's broken.' She lifted her right leg. Her oilskin coat fell away to reveal her muddy cowgirl boot. 'But if someone could get this off I'll have a nice sprain.'

Brenna's quiet laughter broke the tension. 'I forgot how bossy you are when you're supposed to be helpless.'

'Helpless.' Taite smirked. 'I remember the time you socked me when I jumped out of the stables to scare you.'

Heath remained quiet. He hadn't missed the wash of colour filling Clancy's cheeks. Something else was going on besides her not liking being the centre of attention, even amongst friends. Her eyes met his and then slid away. To give her some space, he went to collect a box to prop up her foot with.

She glanced across at Brenna as he eased the wooden box beneath her right foot. 'Are the horses okay? That dog had a real go at Goliath.'

'He's fine. Goliath landed a good kick before he sent you flying.'

When no one else moved to take off Clancy's boot, Heath knelt to grasp the heel. 'Ready?'

She nodded. Other than a grimace when he first started to slide off the boot, she didn't react. But when his fingers skimmed over the curve of her lower calf as he eased off her navy sock, she trembled. He stopped.

'Keep going,' she said through gritted teeth.

With her boot and sock removed, the injury was obvious. A swollen lump obscured her ankle bone. He carefully cupped her foot in his hand to check if the alignment was out and if they were dealing with a fracture. But everything appeared normal.

Clancy threw Brenna a look and she stepped forward, holding a roll of crepe bandage. 'I don't know about anyone else but a strong coffee sounds pretty good right now.'

'I'll put the billy on.' Taite turned towards the door. 'I'll also start packing.'

'We can't leave now,' Clancy said, tone determined as she looked around at their faces. 'I don't want to spoil everything.'

'You haven't spoiled anything.' Heath crossed his arms. Even though he knew Clancy was fine, the urge to touch her to reassure himself that she was okay hadn't faded.

Clancy's chin lifted. 'It isn't even light and there'll be fog. Besides, I'm hungry.'

When no one said anything, Clancy sighed. 'Okay, if we stay I'll take pain relief.'

Taite grinned. 'Coffee and breakfast it is.'

After a last look at Clancy, Heath went to help Taite. By the time bacon and eggs were sizzling on the cast-iron plate over the fire, and the mauve of sunrise streaked the sky, Clancy was back around the campfire. Heath had moved a tree stump so she could elevate her injured foot. Every so often she shifted on her seat. It seemed as though her right shoulder was also sore.

Once breakfast was finished, swags were rolled up and the hut readied for the next visit. Every time Clancy went to move, Brenna threw her a stern glance. When Taite headed to the horse yards and Brenna had her back turned, Clancy quickly stood. Heath moved to offer her his arm.

Her cheeks were still colourless but her grip on his forearm was firm. 'What I really need is a crutch.' She looked over at the wood that had been collected for the next campfire.

Brenna spoke from the hut doorway, 'Clancy Parker, don't you dare sweet-talk Heath into getting you something to lean on. Stay right where you are until we're ready to go.'

Clancy pulled a face. 'How else am I going to get on Ash?'

'You're not,' Taite said as he led Goliath towards them.

'No way.' Clancy took her hand off Heath's arm and rested her knee on the tree stump for balance. 'I'm not riding back on any horse other than Ash and I certainly am not going with Heath on grumpy Goliath.'

If Heath didn't know her better he'd say there was almost a note of panic in her words.

'Clance,' he said quietly. 'He'll be fine. I won't let anything happen to you. He'll carry our weight easier than Ash.'

Her forehead furrowed as she looked over at the yards. Heath knew she didn't need anyone to tell her that the other horses were too young and inexperienced to deal with two riders.

Brenna joined them. 'Here, I'll take this so it will be easier to double. Heath's will fit you both.' As she reached for Clancy's oilskin and slid the bulky coat off her shoulders, Brenna leaned in to murmur in her ear.

Clancy's lips pressed together. 'All right. But we're going the short way home.'

Brenna nodded as she rolled the coat into a bundle to be attached to Ash's saddle.

Taite led Goliath over and Heath gave Clancy a careful leg-up. After unbuttoning his oilskin, he swung on behind. Stiff and rigid, she held herself away from him. Not making any comment he made sure the sides of his coat covered her before taking hold of the reins. Despite the now blue sky, it would take time for the wan streams of sunlight to provide any real warmth. As his arms settled around her, he felt her flinch. Her shoulder had to be giving her grief.

'Clance?'

She shivered. 'Let's just get home.' Her voice emerged tired and muffled.

He nodded and blanked out the floral scent of her hair and the way its silken softness brushed his jaw. 'Okay.'

Conscious of Taite and Brenna riding nearby, he stripped all emotion from his face. This time Brenna rode Ash and led her mare to make sure they could return home as fast as possible.

After the first twenty minutes, Clancy's shaking had subsided and she'd seemed to relax. Over the next twenty minutes, it was as though she'd melted against him. He rested his chin on the top of her head as she burrowed into his coat and he guessed his warmth. He tightened his hold to pull her close.

For a bittersweet time he held the woman he loved in his arms. But once they arrived at Glenwood Station he'd have to let her go.

Rowan didn't frown much but when he did Clancy was reminded of the storm clouds that could eclipse the high-country peaks without warning.

'You could have been seriously hurt.'

'I wasn't. See …' Clancy moved the camera to show him her bandaged ankle resting on the lounge ottoman. She hadn't wanted to tug on jeans over her injured ankle so wore black leggings. 'Dr Clark said nothing's broken, unlike a certain someone's arm.'

His frown deepened. 'I never said it was broken.'

'No, you said it feels like a sprain which in Rowan-speak means you never saw a doctor. Then when you did it must have been broken. Otherwise why have you kept it out of sight every time I've spoken to you?'

'Have I mentioned how much I pity your future teenagers?'

'Many times. Show me your hand.'

Rowan held up a royal blue plaster cast.

Clancy held the tablet closer to take a better look. For a cast that could have only been on a week it was looking rather dilapidated. 'Are there holes in there?'

'Who knew a screwdriver could dig through rock-hard plaster?'

He lifted his arm to show a huge indent. 'Plaster apparently also doesn't like being rubbed along the edge of a brick wall.'

Clancy closed her eyes. 'You wonder why I worry so much.' Her eyes flew open. 'Speaking of worrying … I have a bone to pick with you.'

'I know and I'm sorry. Don't be mad at Heath. I asked him to look out for you.'

'That's just what I need. Two brothers watching over me.'

Rowan's gaze seemed to sharpen. 'Two brothers? Is that how you think of Heath?'

Clancy's mouth dried. She'd never told Rowan how she felt about his best mate because he'd never asked and she wasn't sure how he'd take the news. It also was embarrassing to hold on to such unrequited feelings for as long as she had. She couldn't bring herself to lie, so she settled for flippancy.

'I'm lucky enough to have you for a brother. I don't need Heath, too.'

As she'd hoped, Rowan grinned but not before she caught a flash of what looked like relief pass over his face. 'One day I'll have to share you with someone, I can handle that if it's the right person, but no, you don't need any other brother but me.'

Clancy kept her tone bright despite the mistiness his words brought to her eyes. 'Trust me, when it comes to broken bones, one brother is definitely enough.'

Rowan chuckled. 'So, how long will Ned help out?'

'He's in no rush to head home so probably until I can drive.'

'He's a braver man than I am for taking on Primrose and Orien. Heath sent me a video last night when they visited the coach house. Nothing's safe.'

She had no idea what was happening on the other side of the lounge room door but whatever the ruckus was, she heard Ned's voice saying, 'Okay, you two rascals, outside you go.'

'I can't wait for you to see them.'

'Me too, but it will still be a while yet. Clance ... once your peonies are done and dusted, if you find yourself at a loose end, why don't you come over for Christmas? Ned would be fine to look after everything and you already have your passport.'

She searched Rowan's face. He knew she was never at a loose end; she was always busy no matter what time of year it was.

'I'll keep that in mind.' Even as she said the words, certainty filled her that she'd never have the desire or need to leave Bundilla. 'But I didn't get my passport to travel, it was just in case a certain brother took one risk too many and I needed to fly over.'

Rowan's grin was unrepentant. 'It's getting late, talk to you tomorrow. Make sure you keep off your foot.'

'Will do, if you go easy on your hand.'

After the screen went black, she reached for her crutches but didn't leave the lounge. She needed a moment before she went into the kitchen to see Ned. They were going into town for groceries and she had no doubt Ned would call in to check how the mural was going, as with the cherry picker now operational Heath had spent most of yesterday painting. Before she saw Heath again, she needed to be ready.

Even now, the memory of being in his arms yesterday proved overwhelming. Her nerves were as tightly strung as baling twine on a hay bale and her emotions remained raw. She didn't have to be a rocket scientist to know that sharing Heath's oilskin, let alone doubling with him, was a very bad idea. It had only been Brenna's promise that she'd be the one to drive her home via the hospital that convinced her to ride with Heath. Otherwise she would have saddled Ash herself.

But the knowledge that it would be a short journey and that she then wouldn't have to deal with him provided scant comfort. His warmth, his strength and his care all cocooned her far more than the coat that sheltered them both. At first she'd tried to stop herself from leaning against him, but resistance had proved futile. With every step Goliath took, the momentum caused their bodies to touch and it just became too hard, and too cold, not to give in.

She ran a hand through her hair. If she thought Heath smelled good when she was standing next to him, it was nothing compared to being so near her lips could brush the tanned skin at his throat. She'd somehow twisted sideways so she was half on his lap, his arm around her waist anchoring her in place. When they'd reached Glenwood Station she'd heard Heath tell Brenna that she'd fallen asleep. While her eyes might have been closed, they only were so she could savour being pressed against the steady beat of his heart.

Even now the swirls in her stomach hadn't subsided. More had happened on their trek than her injuring herself. For the first time, she was certain Heath had looked at her in a way she'd never believed possible. And when he'd helped her to her feet around the campfire, even half asleep she'd registered that for once he hadn't been reluctant to touch her, and more importantly his attention had centred on her mouth.

Taking hold of the crutches, she pushed herself to her feet. Except she didn't want to cling too hard to whatever shift there may have been in their relationship. If anything, now was the time to make sure she protected her heart. Until she knew for sure what this was between them, she had to physically and emotionally keep her distance. Once the mural was done and his family stuff was sorted, Heath would be gone.

Ned greeted her with a grin as she hobbled through the kitchen doorway. 'Primrose is busy destroying what's left of the back door mat so now might be a good time to make a break for it.'

By the time she was seated in the passenger seat of Heath's convertible and Ned had slid behind the wheel, she was grateful she didn't have to drive. She didn't know what caused her the most pain, her arms from the crutches or her ankle. As she clipped on the seatbelt she tried to ignore the lingering fragrance of Heath's cologne.

'What a car,' Ned said as the engine roared to life.

She laughed. Now that she knew Ned had chosen the convertible, Heath's out-of-character car choice made sense. 'You will have to give it back sometime.'

Ned winked. 'Not while you're on your crutches. It's lower and easier for you to get into.'

Ned turned on the local radio station and Clancy sat back in the leather seat to enjoy the ride. Creamy jonquils and sunny daffodils waved at her from beneath the driveway poplars which were now almost completely covered in a light and leafy green. Every so often there would be a missing splash of colour from where the cockatoos had chewed the flowers off at the base. Thankfully they'd so far stayed away from her peonies.

Once they reached town there were more signs that spring had arrived. The bare branches of the Manchurian pear trees that lined the main street were covered in delicate white puffs. Unlike her last town visit, the main street also had a traffic jam. Thanks to a brown duck and her fluffy ducklings, who were crossing the road, there was a three-car hold-up. When the mother and babies safely reached the footpath, the first car crawled forward, the windows down as the passengers took photos.

Clancy watched as the ducks waddled into the park heading for the pond. 'Only in Bundilla.'

After a stop at the grocery store, a visit to the library and then the café for books and a coffee, just as she'd predicted, Ned suggested they call in to see Heath on the way home.

When the water tower came into sight, Clancy bit her lip. The concrete now sported splotches of colour. Heath was high up in the cherry picker. The telescopic boom seemed so flimsy when compared to the solidity of the concrete.

Ned glanced at her. 'Heath always wears a safety harness.'

'He'd better.'

Heath had either seen his car or Ned had texted, as the cherry picker started to lower.

The closer they drove the more she could distinguish blocks of pink, black and a pale colour that was in the right position to be her face. She hoped her colouring wasn't that shade in real life. She knew she'd inherited her mother's fair Scottish complexion but the paint on the water tower was almost white.

When she saw Bundy leave the spot where he'd been asleep in front of the shipping container, it reminded her of what she had to tell Heath. But as the cherry picker arrived at ground level and he unclipped his harness to walk over, the thought was replaced by another one. She wasn't anywhere near ready to see him.

When they'd ridden together, he couldn't see her face. Now he'd be privy to every micro expression. The hammering of her pulse and the dryness of her throat warned her that her feelings weren't exactly under control. She took her time levering herself out of the passenger seat and after Ned passed her the crutches, getting them into the right position.

Heath approached with a smile. 'Anyone for sponge cake? I've had a recent delivery.'

'If that's from Nancy,' Ned said, 'I won't say no.'

Clancy raised a brow. Ned was supposed to be watching his sugar as his doctor daughter, Fran, was worried about pre-diabetes. He'd just had two vanilla and custard slices at the café.

When Heath glanced at her she answered quickly. 'I'm fine, thanks.'

He nodded as he looked at her crutches and then her injured foot. If he was experiencing any discomfiture at seeing her again it didn't show. The only thing she could read in his expression was concern.

When her palms prickled with fresh nerves, she nodded at the mural. 'You've done so much.'

'It's a start.'

Ned waved a hand towards the cherry picker. 'Why don't you go up and take a closer look?'

She was shaking her head before Ned had finished. 'I'll be right.'

The last thing she needed was to get up close and personal with Heath in a metal box that couldn't exactly be described as big.

'We don't have to go up very high,' Heath said, his gaze never leaving hers.

She didn't know what it was, an odd note in his voice, a flicker of wariness or something else in his eyes, but she realised that he wasn't as comfortable being around her as he appeared. And the notion unsettled her. Their friendship had been a steady constant in her life, she couldn't bear it if it unravelled. She had to prove to him, and herself, that at a fundamental level nothing had changed. If he wanted to show her the mural she couldn't refuse.

'Okay. But if there's even a breath of wind, I'm back on solid ground.'

A smile crinkled the corners of Heath's blue eyes. 'Deal.'

Getting into a rectangular box on crutches was easier said than done. But eventually she was inside and standing away from the rollers, brushes and paint buckets that were on board. Heath handed her a harness and she bit the inside of her cheek. Even with holding on to the side guard rails for support, she was going to need help slipping the loops over her arms and legs.

When Heath moved in close she could see the darker flecks of blue in his irises and a smudge of paint on the lean curve of his jaw. She gripped the side rail to stop herself from tracing the thin streak of paint. On autopilot she lifted each arm and shifted her weight, until the harness was in place. Every brush of Heath's hand on her leggings and rugby top was as though his hand had slid over her bare skin.

She hadn't realised that she'd held her breath until he turned away to activate the controls. As the hydraulics propelled them upwards, she forced herself to focus on the water tower looming in front of her and not on the man within arm's reach. Once they were in the middle of the mural, Heath stopped the cherry picker.

She reached out to touch the cold, hard concrete. 'Is this really my skin tone?'

Even as she asked, she knew the answer. Her hand was a perfect match to the paint shade. She glanced at Heath, feeling vulnerable. He noticed so much about her. How could he not see the way he affected her?

Instead of looking at her outstretched hand, he was studying her hair. She again took hold of the safety rail. Her dizziness had nothing to do with how high they were. In that moment, the intensity with which he gazed at her felt intimate and awoke every longing she'd ever hidden.

She wanted him to stare at her like that when he wasn't working out how to paint her hair. She wanted him to look at her like that before he cupped her face and kissed her. She wanted him to gaze at her like that as they watched their children play and grew old together.

She dragged her attention back to the mural. Even when back on the ground, despite all her plans and best intentions, her heart would never be safe. Keeping any sort of distance between them was impossible. From the moment she'd slid her arms around his waist when he'd doubled her home on Tex all those years ago she'd known who and what she wanted. She didn't care if she didn't take risks, had no new plan and hadn't thought things through. She wasn't letting Heath go without a fight.

Heath took a swallow of breakfast coffee and stared down the main street. The aroma of his plate loaded with The Book Nook Café's speciality bacon and eggs failed to entice him to eat.

Bundy had only been gone minutes and Heath already felt like something was missing. As hard as he stared, he could no longer see any flash of black and tan amongst the strolling locals rugged up against the morning chill. He'd always known Bundy would eventually have somewhere else to be but he'd become used to having the free-spirited kelpie around.

They'd been awake early and instead of painting in the studio they'd gone to Hawks Ridge to drench the cattle. Once they were done Bundy seemed restless and instead of coming inside the homestead to see his mother or Jasper, the kelpie had jumped onto the back of the Hilux. Heath had taken the cue that it was time to head to town for breakfast. But no sooner had he taken a seat outside the café than Bundy had licked his hand and loped away. Now here he sat with no Bundy to share his food with.

He again gazed at the empty street. It wasn't only Bundy he was missing but also Clancy. His need to feel her softness and warmth against him had only intensified after their ride back from the hut. A lifetime of having her in his arms would never be enough. Yesterday in the cherry picker when the sun had picked out the copper highlights in her hair, he'd had to fist his hand against the urge to slide his fingers through the silken strands. It had been his lucky day that she'd been focused on the mural and not on him.

But as hard as it was, he had to remember all the reasons he'd come home. He hadn't come back to Bundilla for her to discover his feelings or to disrupt her life. He was here to paint the mural and now help his parents.

He flipped up the collar of his coat against the brisk breeze before starting to eat. No wonder there were crocheted blankets on some chairs for patrons brave enough to sit outside before the sun radiated its warmth.

The vibration in his shirt pocket had him reach for his mobile. Clancy's name illuminated the screen. Brow furrowed, he took the call. She usually only texted.

'Hi Clance, everything okay?'

'Yes, are you in town and is Bundy with you?'

The soft cadence of her voice washed across his senses. 'As soon as we arrived he took off somewhere.'

'Sorry, I meant to tell you yesterday. Every Thursday morning he's a story dog.'

'Story dog?'

'He's gone to school. He sits with the kids while they read. Everyone knows Thursday is Bundy's day so they make sure he's in town.'

'Poor Bundy … no wonder he wanted to hurry up and get here. He disappeared this time last week, too.'

'He'll be fine. Hope you get lots done today.'

Now was the perfect place to end the conservation but in the not so distant future chatting like this with Clancy would be nothing but a memory. 'That's the plan. How's the ankle?'

'It's not the problem, my arms are. The sooner I can weight-bear the better.'

He chuckled at the ire in her voice. Unlike Rowan, Clancy was a cooperative patient and would use the crutches for the proper length of time, no matter how inconvenient they were. 'It won't take long. If it makes you feel better Rowan had to get another cast and was told that if it too was damaged it would be wrapped in pink animal-print tape.'

Her laughter made him wish he was there with her to see her face. The grey in her eyes turned silver whenever she was amused. 'I spoke to him last night and he didn't mention a word.'

'I'm sure he didn't.'

'I'd better go. Have a good day.' He hoped he hadn't imagined the reluctance in her words.

'I will.'

He set about finishing his breakfast so he could make sure Bundy had made it to where he needed to go. It wasn't long until he was driving along the familiar route that would take him to the small school where he'd spent the first half of his childhood. On the opposite side of town to the water tower, the historic school—which would be soon celebrating its sesquicentenary—enjoyed panoramic views of the mountains. So much so that in winter he hadn't been the only student who stared out the windows wishing they were skiing.

He parked at the front gate and surveyed the cluster of school buildings. Little appeared to have changed. The original stone schoolhouse with its honey-coloured walls looked like it was still in use. Back in his day it had been the library. The large concrete area at the front was now covered by a pitched roof that would provide shade in the summer and shelter when it turned cold. From the rectangular patches of green he could see beyond the buildings, the school still had its herb and vegetable gardens.

His footsteps echoed in the quiet as he walked through the gate and along the path to the front office. Come recess time, the playground would be filled with noise, colour and energy. From the number of backpacks sitting on the bench outside the nearby classroom, the school's enrolment had doubled since he had been there.

A wide blank wall caught his attention. If he ever spent time in Bundilla again, he'd volunteer to help the school paint a mural.

As he stepped up onto the veranda, a familiar voice called his name.

He turned to see Mrs Buchanan, his old teacher, walking out the door of a classroom. 'Heath, how lovely to see you again.'

He returned her hug. 'I didn't realise you were still teaching.'

'I've been principal for five years now. I hope you don't mind me asking but while you're here, as we're lucky enough to have some budding artists, would you be open to having classes come to see you work?'

'Of course. Anytime.' He gave her a card from out of his wallet.

Despite her now grey hair, the smile Mrs Buchanan gave him was exactly as he remembered.

'Did Bundy arrive okay?' Heath glanced over at the classrooms. 'I'm sorry if he was late. I didn't realise he came here every Thursday.'

'He did. Why don't you come and see what he does?' She led the way to the end classroom. 'A few years ago Mrs King had him accredited. She has since left but he still turns up every week and a trained teacher's aide sits with him and the kids.'

Mrs Buchanan opened the door and Heath looked in to where Bundy, who wore an orange story dog vest, sat with a young woman on a mat on the floor. A small blond boy, his expression earnest, read to the kelpie. Bundy's tail wagged when he saw Heath but otherwise he didn't move.

Heath edged away from the doorway with a smile. 'I can see why he keeps coming back.'

'He's much loved and has made a huge difference to the confidence and literacy of so many children.'

Heath walked alongside Mrs Buchanan as they retraced their steps along the veranda.

When they were outside the office, she spoke again. 'Before I forget, please thank your mother for the drawings she sent in for the sesquicentenary celebrations.'

'Drawings?'

His mother had mentioned the school's 150th birthday celebrations but nothing about contributing anything.

'Yes, we put a call out for any memorabilia that might be of interest for the display and she sent in pictures that all three of you had drawn while in kindergarten. Would you like to see them?'

'I would.'

He had no idea his mother had saved anything of his from school, let alone artwork of his brothers. While his mother had kept Kyle's and Andrew's memory alive, there was still so much he didn't know about them.

He accompanied Mrs Buchanan into her office where she took out three folded pieces of paper from an oversized envelope. 'This is yours.'

The years rewound. He was again in his blue shirt, grey shorts and new black boots trying to listen to the teacher when all he wanted to do was draw. Finally, he'd had a coloured pencil in his hand and a piece of paper in front of him. After he'd written his name in large letters across the top, he'd filled the page with a picture of him and Minnie digging in the garden.

Mrs Buchanan handed him the next drawing. Kyle's name had been written by an adult in black marker above a drawing of a large and a small stick figure in lead pencil beside what looked like a tractor.

He opened the third drawing. Again an adult had written Andrew's name but instead of a basic stick figure Andrew's picture was as detailed and colourful as Heath's. But it wasn't the realisation that perhaps his brother had also liked to draw that kept his attention on the picture but the composition. Andrew's image was of their father on a brown horse. Heath simply didn't recognise him. His father's smile was so wide it filled the lower half of his face.

He carefully folded the pictures and handed them to Mrs Buchanan. Relief slid through him that Kyle and Andrew hadn't appeared to share his lonely childhood.

Mrs Buchanan returned his brothers' drawings to the envelope but kept his out. 'Maybe you could sign yours for the display?'

The request touched him. His father mightn't be proud of what he'd achieved but Mrs Buchanan was. 'Sure.'

He signed his name on the top corner and wrote a note to wish the school a happy birthday.

After wishing Mrs Buchanan farewell, Heath returned to the water tower.

Once in the cherry picker he concentrated on finishing the base blocks of mural colour. When he stopped to swap the paint sprayer for a roller brush, he realised Bundy was back. He went down to see him and give him a long belly rub.

'Sorry, mate. Next Thursday I'll get you to school on time.'

For the rest of the day Heath made the most of the warm and still weather. When Cynthia arrived with Larissa for a mid-afternoon smoko drop-off, he gave them a wave.

By the time the early evening shadows arrived, the wind had picked up, making working in the cherry picker impossible.

He and Bundy arrived back at the coach house to the sight of Ned carrying a carton of beer through the garden. 'I thought we might need a few cold ones.'

Ned's words were code for one of his daughters would soon be visiting and he didn't want to be caught with beer in his house. Last time Fran had been home Ned had sent him a picture of the zucchini spaghetti she'd made for him. An hour later he'd sent a photo of himself at the pub eating a huge chicken schnitzel and chips.

While Ned put the beer in the fridge, Heath went to give Bundy his dinner. When he joined Ned on the lounge, he passed him a beer. Heath clinked the bottle against Ned's before taking a long swallow.

Beyond the kitchen window the cedar tree swayed and the last of the apricot glow of sunset leached from the sky. The mountain peaks appeared shadowed and stark. Just like his thoughts.

He couldn't ask his mother about what his father had said but there was someone who he could ask. Someone who called him 'son' and who had been, and still was, close to his mother. Someone who was now a widower, unlike ten years ago when any questions would have only caused immense heartache.

'Ned … are you my father?'

Ned stiffened, his beer bottle halfway to his lips. His hand slowly lowered and his weathered face seemed to age. 'No … but I know why you're asking. Your father's said something, hasn't he?'

'Twice now.'

Ned's knuckles whitened where his hand gripped his beer. 'So that's what he said to make you leave.'

'The thing is, it explains everything. My hair's dark and my brothers were blond.'

'You looked the same as kids. Your hair only turned darker when you were older.'

'What are you saying? That he is my father?'

'The truth is … I don't know.'

'Dad has no doubts.'

Ned shrugged. 'Some would say you take after your father with your height and build. I also think you have the same jaw.'

'And others?'

'Others only see a resemblance to your mother but that could be down to you having the same hair and eye colour.'

Heath stared at the mountains that were now almost indistinguishable against the night sky. He'd trust Ned with his life. The older man would always tell him the truth, no matter how painful it might be. 'So why don't you know for sure I'm his son?'

Ned's voice deepened. 'I don't need to tell you that your mum's life with your father hasn't always been easy … especially after they lost the boys.'

'Was it ever?'

'When he wants to be, your father can be very charming. You know he was a city boy?'

'You're kidding. All I know is that he's an only child and his parents died when he was in his mid-twenties.'

'His family was from Sydney and when he came here looking for work, I opened my big mouth in the pub and said your grandfather needed help at Hawks Ridge.'

'You were there already?'

He nodded. 'So your father turned up the next day, wet behind the ears, and I taught him everything he knows.'

Heath didn't say the obvious that his father had then married their boss's daughter. He knew Ned had loved his wife but an edge of bitterness had rasped in his words.

He took a swig of beer before speaking again. 'You know … I've never seen my birth certificate, and I never thought it strange that I had a passport for ID even though we never travelled. Mum's always insisted that she do the paperwork for anything official. Even now she makes a joke about not being ready to retire from being my PA.'

'Your mother's a smart woman …'

A sombre silence settled between them.

Ned cast him an assessing look. 'Will you talk to her?'

'I couldn't. She has enough going on with Dad and bringing up the past will only cause more hurt.'

'If it's true, don't you want to know who your father is?'

Heath didn't hesitate. The man sitting beside him was the only father he'd ever need. 'No. Unless Mum wants to tell me.'

Ned didn't immediately answer. Instead he rubbed at his eyes as if tired. 'One day ... not now ... ask her about your brothers. There are things you haven't been told.'

At Heath's frown, Ned shook his head. 'I've already said too much. What I can say is that when Kyle died your mother withdrew into herself, but when they lost Andrew she left town for a long while ... and when she came back it was with you.'

CHAPTER

11

'I have a new theory,' Brenna said, her amplified voice filling the kitchen thanks to Clancy having put her on speakerphone.

Clancy took her time to reply as she juggled holding her mobile and a bottle of orange juice while also trying to shut the fridge door and keep her crutch in place. It required a great deal of multitasking to make herself breakfast.

'Please don't tell me it involves Heath. I can't stop thinking about your other theory.'

The heavy bottle of juice thumped as she sat it on the marble island bench. She readjusted the crutch beneath her arm. It was day three of crutches and even though she was now only using one, she couldn't wait to walk on her own two feet again.

'No, this isn't about Heath and the sisters but Rowan.' Clancy could almost hear the smile in Brenna's voice. 'You know how he trashed his first plaster cast? I bet there was a hot nurse or doctor he had to go back to see.'

Clancy laughed as she left the phone by the bottle of juice and went over to the cupboard that contained glasses. 'Let's hope you're right but I don't want him to get too settled over there. I want him to come home.'

She placed a tall glass on the island bench beside a plate. With Ned on the tractor slashing between the peony beds, Iris, Primrose and Orien were outside. For a short while the kitchen was an oasis of calm and her conversation with Brenna could continue uninterrupted.

'True, and the last thing he needs to do is come back after Eloise's news.'

Clancy turned from where she was putting bread in the toaster to look at her mobile on the island bench. 'News?'

'That's why I'm calling. Eloise is pregnant.'

Instead of moving closer to the bench, which would take extra time because of her crutch, Clancy leaned over as far as she could to swoop up her phone. Except in the process her elbow caught the top of the empty glass, knocking it sideways. When she tried to catch it with her free hand, she lost hold of her crutch. As if in slow motion, it fell forward, the handle knocking her plate to the floor. The shatter of glass on polished wood was only matched by the explosion of white china.

She froze. As if from a distance she heard Brenna say, 'What was that? Are you okay?'

'I'm fine. Hold on a sec …' She bent to stretch her arm out to reach her crutch. With her bare feet and all the shards scattered around her she couldn't otherwise move. Dragging her crutch over, she took hold of it and as she straightened slipped it under her arm so it could take her weight. She took her phone off speaker and held it to her ear to hear Brenna better. 'Are you serious?'

'Fiona from the gift shop told me last night at the pub. I tried to call but you didn't pick up.'

Clancy mentally did a quick calculation. Rowan had been away for four months and had left almost straight after Eloise ran off with the farm supplies sales rep.

'How far along is she?'

'Fiona said about four months.'

Clancy groaned. 'The baby could be Rowan's. He mustn't know she's pregnant or he would have told me. Heath mustn't know either.'

'This can't be good.'

'Tell me about it.' She gazed around at all the pieces of glass and china surrounding her. 'I have to go. I need to talk to Rowan before it's too late over there.'

'Tell him hi from me.'

As soon as she ended the call with Brenna, she video-called Rowan. Usually she did so on her tablet which had a bigger screen but as it was on the side bench near the window and out of reach, her phone would have to do.

After a few beeps, Rowan answered, his voice sleepy as he pushed himself to a sitting position in bed. 'Hey, Clance.'

'Sorry I woke you. Brenna says hi.'

'You called me to tell me your best friend, who I still haven't got even with for short-sheeting my swag at pony camp, says hi?' Amusement softened his words as he rubbed at his chest with a hand covered in still pristine plaster.

'She also said Eloise is pregnant.'

Rowan came fully awake. His smile died as his arm lowered and his eyes sharpened. 'How long?'

'Four months.'

The tension firming his jaw eased. 'The baby isn't mine.'

Clancy searched his face. There was no sadness there, just a deep weariness.

'You're sure?'

'Clance.' The corner of Rowan's mouth kicked into a half smile. 'As much as I love you I'm not about to discuss my love life, or lack of it, with you.'

'Good, because that would be just a little too much information.'

His expression grew serious. 'We've never really talked much about Eloise and why you didn't tell me that you didn't like her.'

'You were so happy and … everything happened so quickly.'

Rowan had always been there for her. The only time there'd been distance between them was when he was with Eloise.

'If I ever look like I'm not thinking with my head again, promise you'll tell me … or get Heath to.'

'I promise.'

Rowan smothered a yawn. 'So what else is happening? How's the foot?'

'I'm down to one crutch and will ditch that hopefully tomorrow.'

He looked past her as if checking out what was in the background. 'Why are you in the middle of the kitchen?'

She used the camera to show him her bare feet and the surrounding shards of glass and china. 'Let's just say I'm not exactly free to move at the moment.'

'However that happened, you did a good job.'

'Believe it or not, it's just one glass and a plate which I need to get cleaned up. Sleep tight.'

But as she ended the call and took a closer look at the destruction she realised there was no way she could even start to get rid of the mess. If she was closer to the island bench she could have levered herself up and slid over the top to get off the other side. At least then she would have been able to get to the mud room to put on shoes.

She texted Brenna an update and then frowned at the phone in her hand. Ned was old school and wouldn't have his mobile with him in the tractor. He wouldn't have wanted any distractions. Which left … She dialled Heath's number. There was a chance he'd already left to work on the mural.

When his phone went to voicemail she didn't leave a message. Instead she looked around. If she had to do this by herself she would. She just needed one clear place to put her good foot before she made it to the island bench. The phone in her hand burst into a country music song. As she answered, she caught Heath's name on the screen.

'Hi. Thanks for calling back. Are you in town?'

'I'm just out of the shower.'

She blanked out images of a lean and tanned Heath wet from swimming in the river. Imagining how he'd look all grown up and slicked in water wasn't going to keep her voice steady. 'If you've got five minutes I need help with … something.'

'I'll come over now.'

'I'm in the kitchen … make sure you've got boots on.'

For a fleeting moment Clancy thought about smoothing her bed hair and straightening Rowan's old rugby top that she'd again worn over her pyjamas. Except unlike when Heath last saw her in the kitchen, this time she didn't have long pants on, just an oversized T-shirt that she suspected didn't hang much lower than the rugby top's hem.

As for how she was going to go about fighting for him, she was yet to think of a plan that didn't involve making a fool of herself. Before she could come up with anything sensible that wouldn't prove a threat to their friendship, she needed to be able to move.

She heard the back door open. Heath must have jogged over. She willed herself to relax as his boots sounded on the hallway floorboards. But when he filled the kitchen doorway, her tense fingers dug into the foam of the crutch handle. As much as every man she'd ever gone on a date with had left her unmoved, when it came to Heath it was impossible to remain unaffected.

In the two weeks since he'd arrived, his dark hair had grown, and it was now shower damp and tousled. His jaw was clean-shaven and he wore no jacket, just paint-splattered jeans and an emerald green work shirt.

He frowned as he stopped to stare at the floor. She didn't know how but broken pieces had shot across the room. 'Please tell me you have shoes on.'

She shook her head.

Glass and china crunched as Heath rounded the bench. His face serious, he didn't slow as he approached and in one movement grasped her waist and lifted her. Her lungs filled with his fresh clean scent and his strength made her long to run her hands over his shirt to feel the corded muscles below.

But before she could do anything but breathe and blink, she found herself on the smooth cold marble of the island bench. She didn't miss the way his hands didn't linger on her waist or how when he laid the crutch on the bench beside her, he kept hold of it for longer than he had her.

His gaze swept over her bare legs and feet. His mouth settled into a grim line as he focused on her sprained ankle on which she now wore a fabric brace instead of a bandage. Where the brace left the area above her heel exposed, a dark bruise faded into yellow.

'Heath, why are you so angry?'

'I'm not.'

His crossed arms contradicted his words.

'You are. My ankle and this'—she waved a hand around—'were accidents and could happen to anyone, especially if they're a klutz like me.'

'You're not a klutz.' He sighed as he unfolded his arms. 'What did happen?'

'I was a little distracted when Brenna called and told me Eloise is pregnant.' As Heath's expression darkened, she quickly added, 'I spoke to Rowan and the baby isn't his.'

'That's a relief.'

'You're telling me.'

Heath again stared at her ankle. 'I don't like seeing you … hurt.'

The admission surprised her. 'I don't like seeing you hurt either but I can look after myself, remember.'

A too brief smile shaped his mouth. 'I remember. Now let's get this cleaned up. Where's the vacuum cleaner?'

'Over in the—' As she spoke she went to slide along the island bench to the far side so she could get off, find some shoes and help. Except she'd barely moved before the warm weight of Heath's hand settled above her knee. His fingers curled around her leg to hold her in place.

Their eyes met and held. The raw intensity in his gaze now wasn't from anger. He almost seemed as stunned as he was that he'd touched her.

He slowly lifted his hand. 'How about you stay where you are?'

His words were hoarse and low before he turned away to collect the vacuum cleaner.

She managed a nod. There was no way she could speak and sound anything but breathless. Her skin burned as though the shape of his hand had been imprinted and beneath the rugby top goosebumps tingled over her arms.

The realisation that Heath had looked at her the same way as when they'd sat around the campfire kept her still and quiet. And the relief, even if he only felt a slight attraction, made her hope unfurl and her stomach flutter.

Perhaps the way to fight for him was simple. All they had to do was be together. Whenever they were, there was a tension, a pull, that hadn't existed before. A pull that might do what she couldn't, and that was scale the wall he'd encased himself in.

The shadows of exhaustion beneath his eyes and the hollows in his cheeks all confirmed that whatever the family matter was that he wouldn't talk about, it continued to hold him in its grip. He was hurting and she hadn't lied when she'd said she didn't like to see him in pain either.

She hadn't noticed her hands had twisted together in her lap until Heath stopped vacuuming. Without the hum of the vacuum cleaner and the rattle of glass against hard plastic, the kitchen fell silent. 'You're very quiet.'

'Just thinking …' She paused as the wariness she'd seen the other day at the water tower flashed across his eyes. 'About my to-do list.' For her new plan to work she had to act like nothing had changed between them. Otherwise spending time with her would be the last thing he'd be wanting to do. 'Before I get busy with my peonies I have to complete my quilt and finish our book-club book.' She pulled a face. 'It's already hard going.'

The tension stiffening his shoulders appeared to ease.

She kept her tone chatty. 'You've shaved?'

'I've a few media interviews this morning. Dr Davis is holding a press conference at the park.'

'Has Bundilla ever actually had a press conference?'

Heath smiled as he looked away to scan the floor. 'Not until now.'

'Can I come with you? Ned will be in after lunch and can take me home.'

'Sure.' He rubbed at his jaw. 'There'll be reporters around, though.'

'I'll stay out of their way.'

Noise again filled the room as Heath finished the vacuuming. He emptied the vacuum cleaner into the garbage and returned it to the cupboard.

'Okay,' he said, as he came over to the bench, face expressionless. 'Now you're good to get down.'

Just like before, once he'd lifted her and she was where she needed to be, his touch didn't linger. But this time she'd been prepared. She'd placed her hands on his shoulders to feel the toned flex and bunch beneath his shirt. Her arms only lowered when he placed her crutch under her arm.

'I'll be in the studio. Text me when you're ready,' he said, already on his way to the door.

Clancy wasted no time having breakfast and a shower. Instead of her usual jeans, cotton shirt and black coat, she slipped on her favourite vintage green frock which she paired with a cropped denim jacket. It was too difficult to wear anything that needed to be pulled over her ankle.

She rummaged around in her walk-in wardrobe for the left boot of her good cowgirl boots. They were tan in colour with white and green flowers embroidered across the top and toes. Not having a hope of fitting into the right one, she slid on a navy sock to keep her toes warm. She then messaged Heath while sitting on her bed. There'd be no more multitasking when balanced on a single crutch.

Other than a muscle working in his jaw when he held the convertible door open for her, Heath didn't appear to notice how she was dressed. Even before they'd passed the main house he'd put on the local radio. Content with small talk, she sat back and relaxed. Just like the mountain wildflowers that lay dormant beneath the snow during winter, she was going to have to be patient to reach Heath.

When they arrived, there was no doubt the media were also there. The parking spots were all occupied with cars bearing television station logos. Beneath the shade trees in the park, rows of white chairs were set up along a wooden dais. The press conference had to be starting soon.

Heath found a spare parking spot outside the pub which wouldn't leave her too far to walk wherever she needed to go. She made sure she was out of his car by the time he came to help. Already, curious glances were being sent their way.

Heath's convertible never failed to draw stares and the local grapevine didn't need much content before it went into broadcasting mode. While it wasn't unusual for her to wear a dress, being seen in one with Heath might be enough to start a rumour they were on a date. There was no way she could face the quilting group if even a whisper of such a thing went around town.

'Have fun,' she said with a smile as Dr Davis waved to Heath from over in the park. He obviously wanted to get things started.

Heath sighed. 'I'd rather be painting.' He looked at her foot. 'Message me if you need to go home before Ned comes in.'

'Will do.'

With a cheery wave, she hobbled away. Instead of following Heath, Bundy stayed with her. Their first stop would be to see Rebecca in the florist shop to give her a peony update. With her single crutch the pace was slow, but the sun was warm on her shoulders and the breeze gentle in her hair. They stopped to rest as white petal blossoms from the trees lining the main street swirled through the air like snowflakes.

Feeling someone looking at her, she glanced across the street. A man on the footpath near the park stared at her and Bundy. He headed towards them, his stride long. With his camera-ready blond hair, white shirt, tailored navy trousers and pale blue tie, he looked out of place in the quaint streetscape.

His grin flashed as he approached and held out his hand. 'Hello, I'm Mitch Holden.'

From his expectant expression he clearly assumed she'd know who he was. She had no idea. She shook his hand. 'Clancy Parker.'

'The mural model herself.'

She pulled her hand free. 'Trust me, there was no modelling involved.'

Mitch laughed, a deep and attractive sound. His practised charm was wasted on her. She gripped her crutch, ready to continue walking. 'Enjoy your time in Bundilla, Mitch.'

'I couldn't possibly ask you some questions?'

'No, thank you.'

'They won't take long.'

She might be a small-town girl but she wasn't letting any smooth-talking city reporter press her into doing anything she didn't want to do. 'Of course they wouldn't.' She gave her serene smile. 'My only comment is we are very fortunate to have a world-renowned street artist painting our mural and that people need to visit Bundilla to see the finished product.'

She sensed Heath nearby, even before his boots rang on the footpath and he stopped beside her. The brush of his arm against hers was no accident. He was letting her know he was there if she needed him.

Mitch's grin was suddenly a whole lot less charming.

'Heath, we were just talking about you. Heath MacBride, meet Mitch Holden.' She didn't wait for the two men to acknowledge each other before she spoke again. 'Now if you'll excuse me, Bundy and I have somewhere else to be.'

She walked away, head high and inwardly smiling. Her copious-drinking-of-tea days could be over. There was hope for her at the next book club meeting, after all. Who knew it was so easy to string a coherent sentence together?

Somehow Heath survived the myriad of morning media questions, the numerous photos and the visit to the water tower where a drone filmed him painting. While Dr Davis was in his element promoting Bundilla and talking about his time as mayor, Heath couldn't wait for it to be over.

Now back in the park, he masked a frown as he shifted in the plastic chair he'd moved into the shade of a jacaranda tree while he waited for the last journalist to talk to him. Publicity was part of what he did, and it benefited whichever community he was working with, but never before had he been so distracted.

He continually kept a watch out for Clancy. He'd told her she wouldn't need to be involved in any promotion and he couldn't now have her again bailed up by a reporter. He looked over to where Mitch Holden was interviewing Dr Davis near the rotunda. Especially if they were of the hot-blooded male variety.

Mitch's questions all seemed to be about Clancy, and Heath noted he'd looked around the crowd almost as much as he had. He didn't blame him. Usually quiet and content to be in the background, today Clancy didn't have a hope of being overlooked, even if she hadn't been wearing one cowgirl boot and using a crutch.

Her dress clung to curves that thanks to the crimson ball gown haunted his dreams, while the above-knee hemline showcased the shapely length of her legs that he'd been all too aware of in the kitchen that morning. Her chestnut hair fell in glossy waves around her shoulders and whatever she wore on her lips only drew attention to the perfection of her mouth. It was no wonder he was having trouble paying attention to the questions he'd been asked.

He flexed his tight shoulders. Rowan may have asked him to keep an eye on her, but all his life he'd been looking out for Clancy. Initially because she was his best mate's little sister and because her parents had provided him with a haven of warmth and acceptance. It had felt like the right thing to do to return their kindness by making sure their daughter was okay. Then, it was because he loved her.

But the reality was, she'd never needed watching over. He had no doubt she would have dealt with the kitchen mess had he not been there. And as for dealing with Mitch Holden, she hadn't needed any assistance. As serene as her smile had been, it had been underpinned by steel. Summer snow would fall in the mountains before she'd answer the reporter's questions.

The knowledge that Clancy didn't need protecting threw him. He'd remained silent about the ugly parts of his life to shield her. Now it seemed there was no longer a need to keep their worlds separate. But as his father's words, that he'd only ruin her life, replayed in his head, Heath knew there was still something he had to protect Clancy from. Himself.

She had to feel the current that ran between them when their eyes met. She had to know that things had changed. But the cold hard truth was that their lives ran along different courses, with no obvious way to intersect. He couldn't live with himself if he ever proved his father's words true. As a woman walked towards him with a notebook in her hand, he erased all tension from his face and stood to shake her hand.

The newspaper interview proved to be quick and after another photo snap he was free to leave. But instead of returning to his car, he walked out of the park and across the main street in search of Clancy and Bundy. Ned had texted to say he'd been held up in case Clancy wanted to go home.

Heath heard Clancy's laughter before he saw her. She was sitting outside The Book Nook Café. Bundy lay at her feet and Trent sat beside her. From their empty plates and the way they faced each other, they'd had a long lunch. Clancy again laughed at something Trent said. Neither appeared to notice him.

Bundy wagged his tail as Heath stepped up onto the footpath.

Clancy turned before offering him a quick smile. 'Are you all done? Like a coffee? Lunch?'

He gave Trent a nod before he answered. 'I am but have to get back to work. Ned's not in town yet, so if you wanted to head home I can take you?'

'I'm in no rush and can wait. If I run out of things to do I'll hang out with you and Bundy.'

Trent touched Clancy's hand. 'I can drive you home.'

Heath looked away from the sweetness of Clancy's smile as she shook her head. 'It's your day off.'

'I'd enjoy the trip.'

'Thanks, but I'd feel bad taking up so much of your time.'

'Okay but if you change your mind give me a call. I really don't mind.'

Clancy looked at Heath, seeming to miss the earnest edge to Trent's words. Heath didn't. The local vet appeared a genuine guy and while there might only be friendship between him and Clancy, he knew firsthand how easy it was for such feelings to deepen.

Clancy studied him for a moment. 'Did all the interviews go okay?'

'As far as I know they did. Dr Davis has lined up another media conference for the opening.' Heath moved off the footpath. 'I'd better make sure there's a mural to talk about.' His eyes briefly met Clancy's. 'See you later?'

It must have been a trick of the light, but her eyes turned serious. 'You will.'

As it was, when he did see Clancy again it was from the top of the water tower as she and Ned dropped off afternoon smoko. Ned had texted to say not to come down as the evening's forecast was for strong winds. So he'd stayed in the cherry picker to make up for the morning's lost painting time.

When he'd returned to the coach house, he cooked a barbeque before he and Bundy went into the studio. Ned usually joined them for dinner or for a beer afterwards, but tonight he was in town as his daughter Fran had arrived from Melbourne.

With the heater on against the chill and Bundy asleep in his customary place on the rug, Heath busied himself with finishing the latest picture of his father. In this painting, his father rode a chestnut horse behind a mob of black cattle.

The first indication that he had visitors was the creak of the steel door, followed by a blast of frigid air over his forearms left bare by the pushed-up sleeves of his hoodie. Then Primrose bounded in, her fluffy puppy body quivering with excitement. After racing over to Heath for a quick hello she made a beeline for Bundy. Iris followed more sedately and then Clancy appeared. Dressed in boots, jeans and her black coat, she walked with a slight limp, no crutch in sight.

Heath gave Iris a pat and then raised a brow at Clancy's footwear.

She grinned as she stopped in front of him. 'I should have worn boots days ago. They support my ankle fine and I could have ditched those hideous crutches earlier.'

From over on the mat, Primrose made mock growling sounds as she wrestled with Bundy. Iris padded over to join them as if needing to supervise.

Clancy sighed as Primrose's growls grew louder. 'No surprises why we're out walking. Somebody doesn't think it's bedtime.' She paused to stare at where his half-zippered hoodie gaped. 'I saw your light.'

He resisted the urge to lift his hand and rub at his chest. After showering he hadn't bothered with a shirt; when in the creative zone he didn't feel the cold. No doubt he'd have paint somewhere over his skin. 'Bundy will soon tire her out.'

Clancy didn't appear to hear him as she hobbled over to where the pictures he'd painted of his father lay stacked against the wall. If he'd known she was capable of walking to the studio again he would have covered them with a drop sheet. The works still felt too personal and raw to be seen. He also couldn't have Clancy asking questions. Her perceptive brain was always ticking over.

His shoulders stiffened as she looked across to a second lot of paintings. In the middle of the stack was a half-finished portrait of her wearing the crimson ball gown. He hadn't been able to complete it as the exact expression in her eyes continued to elude him. Otherwise the canvas would have been locked away in the back cupboard.

To his relief she bent to look at the first pile. 'Can I?' she asked, glancing at him.

He nodded and, jaw tight, went back to painting. He heard the sound of the pictures being moved as Clancy examined each one.

'Heath,' she said, her voice quiet as she came to stand beside him. 'The pictures of your father ... they're beautiful.'

'Thanks.'

'Has he seen any of them?'

Heath shook his head.

'Because he still doesn't want anything to do with you or your art?'

He made the mistake of looking at her. 'Both.'

Her eyes searched his. 'It's almost like ... you're saying goodbye.'

He didn't answer as he focused on the half-filled canvas in front of him. As he'd feared, Clancy saw far too much.

She spoke into the strain. 'Are you? Is this family stuff to do with your dad ... is he unwell?'

Heath stopped, wiped his brush on a rag and added it to the others in the glass jar beside him. As much as he wanted to tell her what was going on with his father, he couldn't. His mother didn't want anyone local to know apart from Ned. He also needed to keep a wall between them. Any degree of emotional closeness would only threaten the tenuous grip he held on his self-control. Clancy could never have the life she wanted and deserved with him.

He folded his arms and faced her. 'Both Dad and Mum aren't getting any younger.'

'Heath MacBride, do I need to give you the what-friends-do talk again because if your jaw was set any harder it would crack like winter ice.'

'No.'

'At least tell me if Rowan knows. You need to talk to someone.'

He couldn't give her a straight answer. If he admitted that Rowan knew, it might send the message that he valued Rowan's friendship more than hers, and that simply wasn't true.

She saved him a reply by speaking again. 'Okay then.' As mild as her words were, there was a new fierceness to her gaze. She took a step forward. 'Let's see if this will be three from three …'

She lifted her arm and ran her fingertips along his cheek. His reaction was instinctive. Her touch had the power to expose everything that he fought to hide. He turned his head and caught her hand in his.

'For once …' Her words were husky. 'Give me a straight answer. Why do you do that? When we were at the river the summer before you left and I slipped? When you lifted me onto the bench this morning? Or is not wanting to be near me just another thing you can't talk about?'

Even though he knew he shouldn't, he kept hold of her hand. He'd never seen her eyes filled with such hurt or heard her voice echo with such sadness. He'd again caused her pain and the realisation ripped through him, shattering the last of his defences.

'Because I'm human.'

The truth slipped out low and rough.

Her eyes widened and when her gaze flew to his mouth he fought a groan. The intensity of her stare was like a physical caress.

'Clance … we can't cross that line.' Even as his voice rasped, his head lowered. 'There's no going back.'

'It's already too la—'

He didn't let her finish. His hands were in her hair and his mouth was on hers.

Just like her smile, she was sweetness mixed with strength. Her hands slipped into his jacket and brushed over his collarbones. Soft and pliant, she moulded herself against him and wound her arms around his neck as though she would never let him go.

He deepened their kiss. It was as though all the parts of him that had remained alone and displaced had been waiting for Clancy to fill them. And he never wanted to feel empty again.

When they separated, he kept a hand on her waist and the other in her hair. Her eyes were still wide but this time with delight. Her cheeks were flushed and her smile was so beautiful it made his heart ache.

'*Finally*. Sparks,' she said, voice breathless.

He couldn't help but match her smile. Her joy was contagious. Crossing the line between them shouldn't make him feel so light.

He savoured the feel of her palm lying flat on his bare chest over his heart. 'Now's not the time to tell me how many times there weren't any.'

She wasn't listening, just kissing him again.

This time when they drew apart, he rested his forehead on hers. He hadn't forgotten her original question. 'Dad has Lewy Body dementia and it's likely he'll be in full care within months.'

She drew back to see his face, her fingers brushing through his hair. 'I'm so sorry.'

'That's why I need to finish the mural ... to help Mum and to spend time with him.'

'Does he still know who you are?'

'A couple of times ... it wasn't pretty.'

'How's your mum?'

'Devastated.'

He didn't add she was also still wanting him to make peace with his father. The reason why he couldn't wasn't a conversation he'd be free to have until he knew the truth. And he might never know what that was.

Something about what he was feeling must have shown on his face as Clancy pressed her lips to his jaw. 'I'm here anytime you need me.'

He nodded as she eased herself away.

At the loss of her warmth, his conscience stirred and he cupped her cheek. 'Are we good?'

'We are. But you're exhausted and need sleep, eight hours to be exact.' She smiled over to where Primrose was curled up beside Bundy before stretching to brush her mouth over Heath's. 'And I'm taking a certain puppy home before she gets a second wind.'

CHAPTER

12

When the dawn glow slipped beneath the blind in Clancy's bedroom, she was already awake. Light crept across her room.

After she'd lost her parents she'd been uncertain about what each day would deliver. But after last night in Heath's studio, she couldn't wait to see what the day would bring. She still couldn't believe Heath had feelings for her that went beyond friendship, and that he'd had them for possibly as long as she had. The memory of the need and possessiveness in his touch caused her happiness to soar.

As for the way the smooth tanned skin of his torso had heated her hands, she couldn't get enough of him. Describing what had surged between them as sparks had been an understatement. It felt like she'd waited forever to feel Heath's mouth on hers. And she'd wait forever again if she had to.

Her joy ebbed. While there had been a victory, she was yet to win the war. Until she was by Heath's side and a future together was assured, she'd not stop fighting for him. She hadn't missed the way regret had clouded the clear blue of his eyes when she'd left his arms. Rowan might have not been thinking straight when he'd been with Eloise, but Heath had always been a deep thinker and would now be doing nothing but that.

With his father not well, he already had a lot on his mind. She'd known whatever had been going on with his family was serious. If things now moved too fast between them, the added layer of emotional intensity could prove problematic. She knew how overloaded she'd felt by her grief and how she'd struggled to see things clearly. So she'd trusted her instincts that had said after their kiss to keep everything upbeat.

A wet puppy nose on her hand warned her Primrose was awake before a cream fur-ball launched itself at her face to deliver good-morning puppy licks. Primrose had been asleep on one side and Orien on her other, while Iris lay on the floor rug.

In under two minutes, everyone was awake and out of the bedroom. Unlike the past three days, the kitchen didn't smell like Ned's bacon and egg breakfast. While his daughter visited he'd stay in town but he would soon return to help pick peonies.

After Orien and the dogs went outside, Clancy checked her messages. She'd sent a quick one to Brenna last night after she'd returned from the studio. As she was away on a trek phone reception would be patchy and she didn't expect a reply. But waiting on her mobile was a text from Brenna saying it was about time with a string of red heart emojis.

Barking erupted from within the back garden and Clancy moved to look through the kitchen window. Bundy had joined the golden retrievers, which meant Heath was still in the coach house. It was important that she saw him as soon as possible. While she wasn't having any doubts this morning, he could be. She needed to reinforce the message that while they had crossed into uncharted territory, their kiss was nothing to have second thoughts about. She glanced at her tablet. But first, she had to talk to Rowan before he went to bed.

When she opened the tablet cover she saw she had a missed call from him. Surprisingly nervous, she hit the dial button. As much as Rowan regarded Heath as a brother, perhaps he wouldn't like them being more than friends. It would break her heart having to choose between them, let alone if she strained their friendship.

Rowan answered straight away, his expression grave. Fully dressed, he sat in a lounge chair as if waiting for her call. Her hopes sank.

'Hey, Clance.'

'Hi. You look serious.'

'Heath called last night.'

'And … you're not happy?'

His brows lifted. 'Happy? I'm over the moon you're finally being honest with each other.'

'You *knew* how I felt?'

'For years, Clance, but don't worry, I never let on to Heath.'

'Please tell me it wasn't that obvious … that the whole town doesn't know.'

'No, they wouldn't, but Mum and Dad did. That's why they kept the studio, it was their way of saying they thought of Heath as family.'

Clancy couldn't answer. Knowing that Heath had had her parents' blessing made her eyes mist.

Rowan spoke again. 'But with the two of you being in different places they also knew that if you were to find your way back to each other it would take time.'

Clancy groaned. 'I thought the quilting club's matchmaking was bad. If you offered Heath the coach house so we would see each other I'm not sending you more Tim-Tams.'

'It wasn't the reason, Heath needed a place to stay, but it did cross my mind you being in close proximity might be a good idea. I also could have told Heath the tourism committee would like the idea of a mural.'

She examined his face. 'So, if you already knew, why did you look so serious when you answered?'

'We've never talked about this before and I wasn't sure how you were going to take me knowing. I'm also no relationship expert, but Heath has a lot going on, so the timing isn't great.'

'That's been on my mind, too. Don't worry, you know I'm not a risk-taker. I'll make sure we take it slow.' High-pitched puppy barking erupted outside from over near the water tank. 'I need to go. Primrose must have found the green tree frog again.'

'Night, and Clance … as fearless as Heath is when it comes to you he isn't a risk-taker either … but there might come a time when one of you will have to take one.'

Rowan's words lingered and she shook her head to dispel them as she went outside in her pyjamas and gumboots to make sure the green frog was out of Primrose's reach on the tank wall. She probably had another day and then the peony season would start. Between her picking and Heath finishing the mural, for at least the next two weeks they'd be lucky to steal more than an hour together. As for what happened when the mural was finished, that was a question she didn't yet want to think about. Heath's priority had to be his parents. All she knew was that she refused to lose him only when she'd just found him.

She returned inside for a shower. Even though Heath had seen her enough times in her pyjamas and it had never mattered before, it somehow mattered now. Their relationship had been reset and she didn't want to take anything for granted. Once dressed in jeans and a cherry-red shirt she made her way to the back door where she pulled on her cowgirl boots that provided support to her ankle. Then, zipping up her black puffer vest, she left the warmth of the homestead.

As she walked through the garden, she slowed to breathe in the perfume of the white jasmine spilling from a nearby trellis. Riding was still out of the question, but with Ned in town she'd need to check the cattle so would take the gator. While in the foothills she could also see what wildflowers had bloomed. The mauve burr-daisies hadn't been out on her last visit.

When she reached the coach house she saw Primrose, Bundy and Iris stretched out in the sun on the pavers in the sheltered barbeque area. Orien had no doubt returned inside the main house via his cat flap to enjoy some peace and quiet.

Once at the front door, she didn't have a chance to knock or collect herself before it swung open. Heath stood in the doorway, his feet bare, wearing jeans and an open-necked blue shirt, his expression solemn. 'Morning.'

She gave him a bright smile. 'Morning.'

'Like a coffee?'

She nodded and looked past him in a silent question. Whatever the delicious aroma was coming from the kitchen, it made her mouth water. Breakfast hadn't been on her to-do list.

'It's cinnamon and blueberry pancakes.'

A rush of emotion held her quiet. Heath hadn't forgotten that this was her favourite breakfast and one that her mother had always cooked for special occasions.

'Clance?'

He tucked her loose hair behind her ear, his fingers lingering on her cheek. The care in his touch was almost too much.

She fought a wave of panic. It wasn't only for Heath's sake that they had to take small steps. He had the power to destroy her. She'd loved him for so long she almost couldn't let herself truly believe that he felt something for her. She couldn't give her hope wings, only to find that he'd never been hers in the first place.

There was no chance that she could have hidden her thoughts; Heath knew her too well. So when he dropped a kiss onto her temple and pulled her close, she relaxed against him.

His deep voice rumbled. 'We'll be okay.'

She turned her face to his and the tenderness in his kiss silenced the fears that even being in his arms was a risk in itself.

When his head lifted, the vivid blue of his gaze made her smile. This was the colour his eyes had been when he'd studied her hair so intently on the cherry picker.

'We will.' She made a conscious effort to lighten the intensity between them. 'I hope you made lots of batter because I'm starving.'

After she'd had seconds and the dogs each had their own pancake, Heath made two coffees and joined Clancy on the lounge. When he sat beside her and lifted his arm, she moved in close. His fingers threaded through her hair.

'Guess what I'm painting today?' he said, as he allowed the long strands to slide over his hand.

'Hope the wind cooperates because if it's like my real hair it'll blow everywhere.'

He chuckled. 'Luckily for me it's in a ponytail.' His thumb traced the line of her bottom lip. 'Clance … in your photo you have such a Mona Lisa smile. What were you thinking?'

She drew away a little to look at him. 'Is this a trying-to-understand-your-mural-subject question?'

'It's me asking for me. The photo was taken at the river where we used to skip stones.'

She settled back beside him. She hadn't been mistaken in thinking he'd recognise the picture's setting. 'Lots of things, I guess ... but mainly about what life would have been like if things had been different.'

'With us?'

'Yes.'

'When you slipped at the river ... you have no idea how many times I've thought about that moment or how much I wanted to kiss you.'

The pain she'd felt for all those years was mirrored in his face.

'We were young, and you left that summer.'

'I'm sorry I never said goodbye.'

She silenced her questions about why he'd gone so quickly. The answers would involve his father.

'Apology accepted. And I'm sorry I didn't get in my farm ute and come after you.'

'You didn't have your licence and as for your ute, it wasn't even roadworthy. You wouldn't have made it over the front cattle grid without things falling off.' The smile left his eyes. 'Once things with Dad settle, I can't stay. I've projects to complete and communities who are depending on me.'

'I know.' She trailed her fingers over his collarbone where last night he'd had a streak of green paint. 'But there's no reason why you can't come back. And it's not like you're leaving tomorrow ... we have time to take things day by day, week by week.'

His eyes searched hers. 'Are you okay with that?'

'I am.'

Going slow was what she needed and what she'd expected he needed, too. From the way he'd been touching her she was also certain that whatever wall had fallen between them had been replaced by another.

A suspicion confirmed when his mouth covered hers. Their kiss had the power to steal her breath, and his, but she could feel his restraint. The urgency and hunger he'd revealed last night was now carefully reined in. But for now, she was content. Small steps came with small risks.

When their kiss ended, Heath smiled and again slid his fingers through her hair. 'With Ned not here, is there anything you need help with? I've got a school group coming in so I don't have to be at the water tower until later.'

'I'm checking the peonies and taking the gator to see the cattle.'

Even though Heath's attention had barely left her mouth he didn't kiss her again. 'Like some company?'

She couldn't hide her delight even if she tried. It was the simple things she'd always wanted to share with Heath. 'I'd love some. We could take the dogs.'

After they'd all piled into the gator, Clancy realised her suggestion hadn't been such a good idea. Bundy and Iris were fine where they rode on the flat tray of the gator—Clancy had no concerns that either dog would race off after the cattle or kangaroos. As for the puppy wriggling on her lap, she wasn't so sure.

Once they'd driven around a group of cattle and checked that the cow who'd had mastitis was going well, they headed past the snow gums on the track that wound through the grass tussocks towards another cluster of cattle.

Heath glanced at Primrose as she tried to chew on Clancy's fingers. 'No wonder my boot had so many holes.'

'Oops, sorry.'

'I have a feeling a certain kelpie took it outside for her.'

Clancy couldn't stop laughing. It felt so good to have the fresh air filling her lungs, wildflowers bright against the snowy peaks and the man she loved by her side.

Just like when Heath had ridden into the high country to go to the hut, the rugged mountain beauty also clearly spoke to him. He gazed around, expression at ease, as if trying to absorb everything.

The seep of dark shadows across the range and the momentary loss of warmth when clouds obscured the sun caused her to shiver and her mood to shift. She looked away from the deteriorating weather at a patch of still blue sky and cuddled Primrose's puppy softness closer.

The stars seemed to have finally aligned for her and Heath. She didn't now need any more storms to extinguish the light in her life.

The crunch of tyres on gravel sounded like any other vehicle that visited the water tower. However, when childish voices grew in volume outside the shipping container, Heath knew exactly who his visitors were. Fifteen excited six-year-olds.

'Wish me luck,' he said to Bundy as he twisted the last of the fat caps on his new box of aerosol cans before they went outside.

The small sea of expectant faces broke into wide smiles as Bundy appeared. The dark-haired teacher's aide who worked with the kelpie for story time walked forward and patted him before clipping on a red leash. Mrs Smith, the kindergarten teacher, had mentioned that whenever he was on school grounds and around students he had to be on a lead.

For the next hour, Heath did what he could to make the class laugh and to hold their attention. He showed them the different painting equipment he used and then each child had a turn shaking an aerosol can until the small ball inside rattled. They then all sprayed a line on some cardboard. When they moved over to the cherry picker, interest brightened the eyes of the students familiar with farm machinery. He put on the harness and talked about safety and when he raised and lowered the cherry picker to show how it operated, the oohs and aahs made him smile.

He looked out over the tiny faces and blanked out the yearnings for a family that surfaced whenever he had contact with infants or children. He and Clancy were only just starting to navigate their way through being more than friends. They were a long way from having their own little people.

A girl with blonde pigtails pointed to the water tower where he'd outlined Clancy's face. 'That's Clance.'

'It is.'

He left the cherry picker and took a copy of the mural picture from out of his jacket pocket for the students to pass around.

'She's so pretty,' a girl with brown hair said before handing the picture to the boy beside her.

Once the picture had done the rounds, he slipped it back into his pocket.

'Does anyone have any questions?'

After reassuring the girl with pigtails that when it rained the paint wouldn't wash off and talking about the cherry picker hydraulics with a boy wearing farm boots, it was time for the class to pile back into their minibus.

Heath waved until the small white bus reached the bitumen. Tomorrow he'd have the older kids to visit and they'd be a tougher audience.

He readied himself for several hours of work. Now that Clancy's pink shirt was finished, he had to get as much of her hair done as he could today. But after he'd elevated the cherry picker platform, he didn't make a start. Instead, he stared at the outline of her face. It was as though he could feel the smooth texture of her cheek, feel the slide of her hair through his fingers and smell the scent of daphne that clung to her skin.

They hadn't even spent twenty-four hours being more than friends and he was just as overwhelmed as she was. It felt so right being with her, he couldn't now imagine not having her in his life. He'd given his word to Rowan he'd be upfront with Clancy, so that morning he'd been honest when he said he couldn't stay. He'd braced himself for her answer, ready to accept if she said things had to stop there. Except she hadn't.

And while his leaving hadn't appeared to bother her, it concerned him. The reality of being away for months, of coming home for weeks and then going again would test even the strongest of relationships. He'd already committed to at least two years' worth of commissions. His father's words that he and his art would only ruin Clancy's life never seemed to be far from his thoughts.

He slipped a mask over his face and using an aerosol can applied a brown-hued base paint to the drape of Clancy's ponytail. There was no going back. All he could do now was implement as much damage control as he could to protect her. As hard as it was when she was in his arms, he had to show self-restraint. Somehow he had to make sure the intensity that consumed them last night, and had undone him, didn't again.

That way when things with his father were more certain, when Clancy's peony season was over and they were able to discuss the future, if she wanted to walk away she could do so with as much of her heart intact as possible. The rattle of the aerosol can deafened his ears as he gave the paint a vigorous shake. As for his own heart, it was already far too late.

He'd swapped to using a paintbrush when his phone vibrated in his pocket. He used his clean hand to check the caller ID. It was his mother.

He took the call but didn't have a chance to speak before her words rushed out, urgent and unsteady. 'Your father ... he's not here.'

'Where's Jasper?' Even as Heath spoke, he lowered the cherry picker to the ground.

'With him. I went to have a shower and was as quick as I could ...'

Heath briefly closed his eyes. It was almost the middle of the day and his mother had only just had a chance to have a shower. Now wasn't the time to talk about him coming over to help in the mornings or getting in help for when he couldn't be there. 'Where have you looked?'

'*Everywhere.*'

He stripped off his harness. 'He could have taken Jasper for a walk.' But as he said the words, he knew they weren't true. If his father had wandered off it was because he was disoriented and confused. 'Mum, how about you make him lunch for when he turns up. You know how he likes his routine. I'm on my way.'

'Good idea.'

As he'd hoped, the practical suggestion would give his mother something to do until he arrived. 'See you soon.'

He carted his equipment over to the shipping container before jogging to Ned's ute that he was again using. Bundy followed.

The trip around the valley perimeter seemed to take forever. Whenever he glanced at the horizon the clouds clinging to the peaks appeared heavier and darker. He just hoped his father wasn't anywhere in the hills. At least if he and Jasper were on foot they couldn't have gone far. With any luck he could be sitting in the tractor or have fallen asleep in a shed. The fact that Jasper was with him gave him hope that they'd be able to find him as the dog would bark when called. He also felt reassured that wise old Jasper would look after his father.

As soon as the Hilux passed through Hawks Ridge's front gate, he slowed to scan the paddocks on either side of the driveway. His father could have decided to walk to the mailbox to collect the mail. He wouldn't have known it was Sunday. Heath also kept a watch on Bundy in the rear-vision mirror in case the kelpie picked up his father's or Jasper's scent.

But when he reached the house and parked beneath the fir tree, there'd been no sign. His mother raced down the front steps. Her long grey hair wasn't in its usual bun and her gardening clothes were crumpled. 'See anything?'

He shook his head and took her hands in his to stop her from wringing them. 'Mum, we'll find him.'

Her fingers clasped his, their hold desperate. 'I've already looked in the stables, the machinery shed and the workshop.'

'We'll find him,' Heath again said softly, squeezing her hands.

She stared at him for a moment and then her grasp relaxed. 'We will. Thank you for coming out so quickly.'

He kissed the thin skin of her cold cheek. 'I'll call if I've any news.'

While there was a UHF radio in Ned's ute, Heath didn't want to broadcast on the public channel that his father was missing. No one, apart from Ned and now Clancy, knew he was unwell. Thanks to the town being used to not seeing his anti-social father, there hadn't been any enquiries about his whereabouts.

He returned to the Hilux with Bundy. A check of the feed shed, the hay shed, the cattle yards, and a double-check of the stables, workshop and machinery shed all came up empty. But there was something he realised that wasn't in the machinery shed where it should be.

His mother answered after the first ring. 'Have you found him?'

'Not yet but the old farm ute ... where are the keys?'

Jingling sounded as his mother went to the key rack in the kitchen cupboard to check. 'They're here. The ute also has a flat tyre.'

'Not now. I fixed it yesterday. Check Dad's secret key stash in his office.'

'Secret stash?'

'Yes, in the small right drawer of his desk.'

He'd had to resort to using the hidden keys whenever he wanted to take the farm ute into the paddocks and paint.

The office door creaked before his mother spoke again. 'The drawer's open ...' Metal again jingled. 'It has all the keys I thought your father had ever lost ... but no ute key.'

Heath examined the tracks in the wet mud. At first glance they looked like they could be from him driving the ute around yesterday, but he had a bad feeling about what he'd find if he took the dirt road that led to the hills.

He kept his words casual. 'Maybe Dad's taken Jasper in the ute to check the cattle. He watched me drench them the other day.'

'Yes, that would be it.' Hope brightened his mother's voice. 'He's been asking about the one with the sore leg.'

'Bundy and I'll take a look.'

'I'll have the kettle on for when you all come back. The weather's closing in.'

'Thanks.'

His cheery tone didn't match the tension that ached in his jaw. Now past the machinery shed he could see a single set of tracks imprinted in the mud. While his father could have taken this route to check the cattle, the road also led to the dam. A deep and large dam in which he'd caught yabbies as a kid and swum his horse after a hot day of cattle work.

He'd spoken to his mother yesterday about how his father was coping. She'd reassured him that he was handling not being able to do the things that he used to do. He could be angry and frustrated, but it wasn't anything to be worried about.

When the tracks didn't turn left towards the paddock gate, beyond which black cattle grazed, a wedge of fear lodged against his ribs. He wasn't convinced his uncommunicative father had been entirely honest with his mother. A belief confirmed when he topped a rise to see a battered white ute parked on the steep slope of the dam wall. The ute's nose was close to the water's edge and both doors were open.

Mud spun and gravel flicked the underside of the Hilux as Heath sped up the hill. From when he'd swum in the dam he knew the ute was positioned in front of the deepest section. Should the ute roll forward, the dark and still water would close over it, dragging the vehicle under and out of sight.

When he reached the ute, the intense silence told him the engine wasn't running. His father sat straight-backed in the driver's seat, staring straight ahead. Heath had his door open even before the last rumble of the Hilux diesel engine died.

Jasper sat in the passenger seat and when he saw Heath and Bundy he whined before wagging his tail. His father didn't move or respond. Heath's hands itched to take the keys out of the ignition and pull on the handbrake but he knew the situation had to be approached the right way. If he angered or frightened his father he could take his foot off the brake which was the only thing keeping the in-gear ute stationary.

'Dad,' he said, voice calm and low.

His father's expression appeared to crumple and his throat moved as he swallowed. 'Andrew ... I'm so sorry. I didn't mean the things I said.'

Shock held Heath silent. He'd never seen his father so vulnerable or heard his voice sound so broken. He'd also always had the impression that his father's relationship with his older brothers had been harmonious.

'Dad ... it's Heath.'

Even when his father glanced at him, recognition didn't harden his eyes or temper the anguish making his craggy features haggard. 'I never got to say goodbye.' His voice cracked. 'Why do I never get to say goodbye?'

His father's foot shifted on the brake. Heath was poised to spin the steering wheel to turn the wheels away from the dam and to wrench on the parking brake.

His father's stare narrowed and it was as though Heath was looking at another person. Contempt curled his father's lip.

'It's you.' Anger thickened his voice. He jerked his head towards Jasper. 'Get this dog out. I can't do what I came here to do with him staring at me.'

Heath didn't pretend to misunderstand what his father was saying. The fact he didn't want to send the ute into the dam with Jasper in it was telling. Somewhere inside the man he'd become was the man who'd chosen to give a forever home to a deaf Jack Russell.

'Dad … this isn't the way.'

'There is no other way.' His father's voice exploded not just with rage, but also fear. 'I'm not wearing an adult nappy. I'm not being trapped in a body I can't control.' As his father went to push Jasper out the open door, Heath leaned into the ute to grab his arm and to pull on the handbrake.

'Let me go.' His father fought against his hold. 'Do what you've been told for once in your life.' His chest heaved. 'Just let me die. *Please.*'

'I can't.' Heath didn't recognise the hoarse rasp that was his voice. 'For you and for Mum.'

At the mention of his mother, his father stopped struggling.

Heath continued, his words gentle. 'You haven't said goodbye. You need to, for both your sakes.'

He thought his father wouldn't answer, and then he sagged, all fight leaving him.

Heath held him. It didn't matter if the man who'd hate him even more after this wasn't his real father. He still loved him.

His father stiffened before he tore himself away from Heath and shot him a look of cold contempt.

Heath slowly straightened and took out his phone. He wasn't surprised to find his hands shaking.

Just like earlier, his mother answered after the first ring.

'I've found him.' She needed to know the truth however distressing it was, but he'd spare her the details. 'He's fine and wasn't quite where we thought he would be. You know what Grandma used to say … cattlemen don't really get lost, they just don't know where they are … Well, Dad lost his way for a short while. He's ready to come home now.'

'It's too soon to lose him. Is he really okay?' Tears muffled his mother's thin voice. 'Are you okay?'

He looked to where his father glowered at him. 'He is but I'll need something stronger than a cuppa when we get back.'

CHAPTER

13

Clancy was officially in peony heaven.

She glanced over her shoulder at the buckets of hand-picked peonies that filled the back seat of her dual cab. Yesterday she'd finally seen the stripes of petal colour on the ball-shaped buds that she'd been waiting for. No longer firm to the touch, the large buds were now marshmallow soft.

Up before her alarm, her breaths had blown small white clouds as she'd picked the cold climate blooms. She didn't mind how chilly it was, what she didn't need was a heatwave like last year or a major storm for at least the next month. Herbaceous peonies took years to flower and she was yet to break even money-wise. Once picking was over and her flower farm open day was finished, Mother Nature could make it rain, hail or shine as much as she wanted.

Clancy slowed as she passed the WELCOME TO BUNDILLA sign. This peony delivery was to Rebecca at the florist shop, plus there was a small cluster of blooms that she'd place on her parents' graves on the way home. Every year the first flowers she picked were always for her mum and dad. She then replaced them every week until the season ended.

She hadn't planned to come to town this morning but Ned insisted she deliver the peonies as it would give her a chance to keep off her injured ankle. Mabel had then called to ask if she could swing by her office for a quick interview. The journalist was a keen supporter of local business and a peony article in the weekly local paper would benefit Clancy as well as Rebecca. Also, she didn't classify interviews with Mabel as media promotion; it was a chat between friends.

So she'd see Rebecca and Mabel and then head home to continue picking. She'd also make sure to set some flowers aside for Heath to take to his mother tomorrow. He too had been up early to go to Hawks Ridge to help out before the second school group came to see the mural. She wasn't sure exactly what had happened with his father yesterday but when Heath had come around last night he'd been subdued and weary.

His brief explanation that his father had had a bad day didn't contain specifics but she was content for now that he was letting her partway into his world. She didn't want to pressure him into telling her more. It would be difficult seeing his once strong father confused and needing help. It also had been enough that after she'd kissed Heath a smile had returned to his eyes.

When the water tower came into sight she leaned forward to peer through the windscreen to take in the changes. She wasn't the only one intrigued. Two cars and a caravan were parked at the base of the tower and grey nomads chatted to each other as they walked around taking photos. The media coverage had spread the word and Heath's mural was already proving a drawcard.

In the bright sunshine, the pink of her skirt shone and her completed ponytail fell from beneath her battered hat. While her face wasn't yet finished, Bundy's was starting to take shape. It was no wonder Heath was in worldwide demand. His talent in creating large-scale lifelike images was unmistakable. Even from the little done on Bundy's image, Heath had captured the sheen of his black coat and the intelligent glint in his amber eyes.

Even though she knew Heath wouldn't be there yet, she checked the cherry picker to make sure. She'd message him when she left town to see if he wanted a coffee.

The thought of seeing him caused a flurry of happiness in her stomach, which she did her best to ignore. She wasn't becoming complacent or taking for granted that Heath was finally hers. The feeling of unease that had gripped her yesterday when they'd checked the cattle refused to leave.

She reached the main street and when she drove past the columns and arches of the post office she waved. Norma and Gladys from the quilting group were sitting behind a small table on which the log cabin quilt was displayed. The duo were taking their turn at selling raffle tickets to raise drought relief funds. Both women waved in return.

After another block, Clancy parked outside a stylish storefront on which the green painted timber had been sanded back to reveal the honey-coloured wood beneath. The shop's name, THE FLOWER MEADOW, was scrolled in a flowing white script across the glass. Rebecca had brought a little touch of elegance to sleepy Bundilla.

With her arms full of peonies, Clancy pushed open the door.

She breathed in the intoxicating cocktail of floral scents. 'Have I said how much I love this place?'

Rebecca laughed. 'Maybe once or twice. The fragrance of flowers never gets old.' The florist moved to help Clancy with the peony buckets. 'And now I'll have peonies to add to the mix.'

'These are pink doubles, too.'

The pink varieties were universally popular and possessed a stronger perfume than the darker maroon shade which she'd also brought.

'Perfect. You have no idea how much I've been looking forward to these being ready.'

Clancy grinned. Rebecca had a wedding she was doing the flowers for this weekend.

She went to collect the other two buckets of peonies. She might be biased but there was something special about the old-fashioned flowers that unfurled into ruffled blooms the size of her hand. Once valued for their medicinal properties to alleviate headaches, asthma and pain during childbirth, they were now considered a symbol of good fortune and were sought after for bridal bouquets.

After the peonies were safely inside Rebecca's cool room, Clancy headed back out to the main street. Pedestrians, a mixture of boot-wearing locals and out-of-towners, ambled along carrying shopping bags and peering into shop windows. Amongst the usual muddy four-wheel drives a blue ute with a mountain bike on the back was parked outside the bakery. The next seasonal wave of visitors had begun.

She collected an empty mason jar and a small bunch of pale pink peonies from the bucket left in her dual cab. But before she could continue along the street to the local newspaper office, Millicent and Beatrice approached.

'Morning, Clancy,' Millicent said with a reserved smile. 'Lovely flowers.'

'Thank you. They're for Mabel.'

'We're looking forward to seeing you both at next week's book club,' Beatrice said, her words solemn. 'How are you going with *Banks of the Seine*? It's one of our favourite books.'

Clancy silenced her groan. 'That's great to hear. I hope … to finish it soon.'

She wasn't the only one finding the heavy duty historical set in Paris hard going. Brenna had so far sent three texts saying how much she loathed the hero and that he'd never look good on a horse.

'It's so nice to see Heath welcome at Hawks Ridge again,' Millicent said, looking along the street as if hoping she'd catch sight of him.

Clancy nodded. It was no surprise that his distinctive silver convertible had been spotted turning into his front gate. But it wasn't for her to say that nothing had changed between Heath and his father, let alone the reason why he was at Hawks Ridge.

Beatrice continued. 'It will do Graham and Lydia good to have company. It's been months since we've seen either of them in town.'

Clancy also wasn't surprised that the sisters had sensed something was amiss. Now would be the perfect time for a conversation change. 'It will. Did you know Heath got them a rescue dog?'

Both sisters smiled. Clancy blinked. It wasn't the instant softening in their expressions that caught her off guard but a fleeting realisation that on the rare occasion their faces were relaxed, they didn't only resemble each other but someone else she knew. The impression slipped away before she could fully grasp it.

'Yes,' Beatrice said, her smile lingering. 'It was such a lovely thing to do.'

Millicent touched her sister's arm in a silent signal. 'We've taken up enough of your time, Clancy. Enjoy the rest of your day.'

When the sisters continued walking, Clancy strolled in the opposite direction. At the corner she turned left to where a two-storey Victorian building stood. If she remembered her local history correctly, the building trimmed in green wrought iron had initially been a bank but for almost 130 years had been home to the *Bundilla Times*.

When she reached the cream cast iron posts, she headed beneath the overhead veranda to push open the front door. Beyond the wooden counter, desks and filing cabinets were arranged into cubicles and along the side wall, shelves were filled with past volumes of the paper.

Mabel gave her a smile from where she sat at the far end of the room and motioned for Clancy to come through. She didn't know how Mabel did it but she always looked as though she'd stepped out of one of the glossy magazines she wrote freelance articles for. Today Mabel's shoulder-length brown hair was in its usual straight style and her tailored black jacket and pants were immaculate.

Clancy tugged at the collar of her faded blue work shirt that hadn't seen an iron in years. Just as well Mabel said she had photos to use from the previous year when she'd come to Ashcroft with a young newspaper photographer. Most of the photos taken had been of the peony beds but there'd been a couple of Clancy holding a bucket of blooms.

Mabel gave her a hug. 'Thanks so much for dropping round.'

'No worries.' Clancy handed Mabel the jar of peonies.

Mabel touched the delicate pink petals that were showing through the caps of green. 'These are so beautiful. If I had my way it would be peony season all year round.'

Clancy smiled as she took a seat in the spare chair beside Mabel's desk while the journalist went to fill the mason jar with water.

When she returned she sat the flowers beside a photo in a white frame that looked to be of Mabel and her sister. Mabel hadn't talked much about her family. All Clancy knew was that her parents lived on a farm in Armidale. She looked away in case the photograph was something Mabel mightn't want to discuss.

But the journalist picked it up and turned the frame so Clancy could see the photo. 'That's Soph, my older sister.'

'You could almost pass as twins.'

Mabel laughed but the sound was hollow. 'We could when we were young. She moved to Perth after she was married. Her husband isn't exactly big on family get-togethers so I haven't seen her for two years.'

'That doesn't sound good.'

'It's not. Nick's as controlling as he is charming but I know my sister and there will come a time when she's ready to come home.'

Clancy thought back to how Eloise had kept Rowan away from both her and his friends. 'If you ever need to see Soph, Brenna and I can come with you.'

'Thank you. That means a lot.' Mabel took a last look at the picture before placing the frame beside the peonies. She slid open her top drawer to take out a book. 'Did you end up finding a copy of this? I'm finished if you want to read it.'

Clancy grimaced as she saw the familiar grey-toned cover of *Banks of the Seine*. 'I did and I wish I was done. How did you even get through it?'

This time Mabel's laughter contained its usual lightness. 'Chocolate and red wine.'

'It's one of Millicent and Beatrice's favourite books.'

Mabel glanced at the photo of her sister. 'I can see why. It's about the unbreakable bonds of siblings.'

'I obviously need to get past the first chapter.'

Mabel grinned. 'That might be an idea. If it helps, you're ahead of Brenna. She's only read the first four pages.' Mabel reached for her pen and notebook. 'Now, I had a couple of questions …'

Ten minutes later, Clancy was back in the sunshine and making her way to the café. Heath hadn't answered her text but she'd grab him a coffee anyway.

When she arrived at the water tower she could understand why she hadn't had any reply; the small white school bus was only just leaving.

Heath gave the bus a wave before he and Bundy came over to where she'd parked.

'Perfect timing,' he said as he opened her car door.

She didn't care if her heart would be in her smile. While it was only early days, she no longer had to hide how much she cared about the man before her. 'Are you happy to see me or the coffee?'

He stole a quick kiss. 'After that group … both.'

She left her seat to pat Bundy. 'Were they that bad?'

Heath took a mouthful of coffee. 'Put it this way … Primrose would have a longer attention span.'

When the wind ruffled the front of his dark hair she resisted the urge to step in close and smooth it back into place. Even though they were alone, now she was out of the dual cab they were visible to anyone driving past. She hadn't needed to talk to Heath about keeping what was between them under wraps. He knew as well as she did the stretch of the Bundilla bush telegraph and the speed at which it operated.

She settled for reaching out and lacing her fingers with his. No one would notice from the road. 'I think the sisters know something's up with your parents. They mentioned how they haven't seen them for a long time.'

'Mum hasn't been returning their calls so they'd have to know something's wrong.' A crease furrowed Heath's brow. 'The trouble is, Mum's adamant she doesn't want anyone to know about Dad. She's also refusing any help.'

'I thought she was close to the sisters?'

'She is. They used to come to Hawks Ridge when I was young.' Heath finished his coffee. 'I'm hoping Mum will feel comfortable telling them about Dad soon because she needs her friends around her.'

'Maybe she feels that everything's out of control and this is one thing she can control? She could also be worried that people won't understand about your father's illness, but they will. It's not like she needs to hide anything.'

Heath's only reply was a nod before his thumb brushed across the back of her hand. He slipped his fingers free as he turned to head over to the shipping container.

Clancy didn't immediately follow. She slid her clenched hands into her coat pockets. It didn't matter that they'd crossed the friendship line, Heath was still keeping secrets. An unmistakable bleakness had just dulled his eyes. There was something more he wasn't telling her, and this time it was about his mother.

'I think that's a fair swap,' Taite said with a broad grin. 'A paddock ornament for plough discs.'

Heath looked at the so-called paddock ornament in the horse yards in front of them. The grey mare was making the most of the grass that had grown within the unused round yard. The old stockhorse had retired from trekking and spent her days living the good life in Brenna's river paddock. She now had come to Hawks Ridge to be pampered and fussed over. After the interest his father had shown in the cattle, and the joy his mother received from having Jasper around, he was hoping the gentle grey mare would be good for both of his parents.

He glanced at the horse float he and Taite had filled with plough discs. 'I thought Brenna said your shed was full.'

'It is. Brenna doesn't know I'm using the back one as well. You can never have enough rusted old bits of machinery.'

Heath shook his head. 'I'd like to be a fly on the wall if she ever finds out. How big is it?'

'Big. Why?' Taite looked around at the nearby sheds. 'You've got more things to get rid of?'

'Yeah. Dad's … getting old.'

He hadn't realised his voice revealed something of the sadness and loss inside him until sympathy washed over Taite's face.

As good as a mate Taite was, he had to respect his mother's wish for privacy, so he couldn't say any more. But Taite understood. His and Brenna's father had passed away five years ago and although he wasn't a hoarder, he'd liked to collect things. They'd inherited everything from milk cans to tools and old cars which was why Brenna now liked empty sheds. While some items had gone into the local museum or to collectors, it had taken years to sort through everything and they were still not finished.

'Anytime you need a hand, or your mother does, let me know. I know how hard it is to go through a life's worth of things.'

'Thanks.'

Taite clasped his shoulder. 'I'll make you a fire pit out of these discs and just say the word if you ever want anything bigger.'

'I'll start a collection of Dad's old tools … there might be a time when one of those benches you make would be good for Mum.'

'Too easy.'

When the roar of Taite's V8 ute engine faded, Heath walked the short distance to the garden to collect an outdoor bench. He carried it over to the yards and positioned it in the shade of a cedar tree before braving the tack shed.

Despite the dust, cobwebs and the clay wasp nests, the bridles, saddles and horse gear weren't in too poor a condition. Another use would have to be found for the woollen saddlecloths the moths had chewed through, otherwise everything just needed a good clean. He found a curry comb and body brush along with a red head collar and lead that still had the tags attached.

He came outside to the sight of his father sitting on the bench, Jasper lying at his feet. Heath stopped. He'd hoped that having a horse again at Hawks Ridge would bring his father comfort and give him a tangible connection to his past. He just hadn't thought his father would respond so quickly.

His relief faded. Even with his wide-brimmed hat and boots, his father failed to resemble the man he'd once been. Instead of a work shirt and jeans, he wore a grey polar fleece jacket with elasticised tracksuit pants and his once strong shoulders were stooped.

Heath forced himself to walk forward.

'Morning, Graham.'

He'd taken to not calling him Dad to help with his confusion and to defuse any potential antagonism. While sometimes, like now, his father appeared to accept him, on other occasions his presence still angered him. There would come a time when he'd have to move back home to help more, but for now he'd continue to do all that he could from the coach house.

'Morning. What's her name?'

Heath sat on the bench. 'Shadow.'

'She's new.'

'She is. Would you like to pat her?'

His father pushed himself to his feet and shuffled over to the steel fence. Shadow ambled close to sniff his hand.

Behind him, Heath heard his mother approach. He turned to find her wiping the corners of her eyes with a white handkerchief. She gave him a watery smile before sitting on the bench and opening the cloth bag she carried to take out her knitting needles and wool.

When Heath went into the round yard, his father came with him. Together they brushed the placid mare. At the first sign of his father's hands shaking, Heath helped him back to the bench where he took a seat beside his mother.

Heath spoke to her softly. 'I can sit with Dad if you like.'

'It's fine, darling. I'll knit a few more rows.' She touched his arm. 'Thank you. It's just what he needed.'

His father gazed at the grey mare, his expression peaceful as though he were in another time and place.

His mother spoke again. 'I finally finished the digital scrapbooks of when you all were young. They're on my laptop if you want to take a look now you don't have to head into town so soon?'

The forecast was for the wind to pick up this morning, which meant that even if he was at the water tower he wouldn't be able to use the cherry picker. So he'd planned, wind permitting, to work late that night using the spotlight that had finally arrived.

Once inside he texted Clancy to see how her second day of picking was going and made himself a coffee. A padlock secured the key cupboard shut, which now contained all the keys from his father's secret stash. Since his father's adventure yesterday his mother now locked the external doors whenever she wasn't with him. Heath had then ordered an infrared door alarm that would let her know whenever his father left the house.

He sat at the kitchen table and opened the laptop he'd bought for his mother's last birthday. It wasn't password protected and he clicked through to Kyle's scrapbook.

He sipped his coffee as he took his time looking at the images of his smiling and adventurous oldest brother. All too soon they finished. At thirteen, his brother's life had barely begun. He opened Andrew's scrapbook. Like Kyle's, Andrew's contained photographs from his birth but this time they went through to his teenage years and into his second year of university.

Coffee forgotten, he clicked on his own scrapbook. He wasn't sure what he was looking for, and if there even would be anything to either disprove or prove his father's words. He studied the first photograph, which was of his mother holding him while seated in a chair. He couldn't have been more than a few days old and was swaddled in a white blanket.

Unlike Kyle and Andrew's opening photos, which had also been of his mother holding them, this time his father wasn't standing beside her. He took a closer look at his mother. In the other two pictures the background had been white and sterile as though in a hospital room, whereas this one looked to be in a living room he didn't recognise. She was also dressed in proper clothes unlike the dressing gown she'd worn in Kyle and Andrew's pictures.

He gazed out the window into the neat garden where a willie wagtail perched on the stone bird bath. There could be a simple explanation. His photo had been taken when his mother was already out of hospital. His father had simply been in the paddock. Not that she'd ever talked about any of their births, but perhaps she also hadn't been well. She had been an older mother by the time he was born.

The willie wagtail flew away but still he stared at the bird bath. The whispers inside his head that wanted to know the truth were growing louder. He'd meant what he'd said to Ned; he didn't need to know who his biological father was for himself. If he did talk to his mother it would be to free her from whatever secret she was keeping.

This had to be the reason why she'd isolated herself and his father since he'd become unwell. She was worried that with his confusion his father would say something damaging or incriminating. He looked back at the computer screen. Now wasn't the time to bring up what his dad had said, but perhaps, if there was an opportunity, he would.

Footsteps sounded as his mother walked in holding his father's arm. Heath shut down the laptop. He'd check the pantry for what groceries were needed, make lunch and then prepare an easy dinner before getting back to the mural.

Thanks to the wind cooperating and the bright spotlight, Heath had been able to work late and complete Bundy's face. Fingers chilled and body tired, he and Bundy headed back to Ashcroft. Beyond the Hilux windows the mountains were moody and dark and the night sky almost starless.

When he arrived at the coach house, light glowed from the packing shed. It had to be Clancy working late. Now that picking had started, Ned was again staying with her and he'd texted earlier to say he was cooking dinner and to ask if Heath would be home to eat. He left the Hilux and hesitated. Common sense said to leave Clancy be as she would be tired. But the part of him that missed her said he should see how her day had been.

The corrugated iron shed door creaked as he opened it, the sound lost under the blare of country music. As cold as he'd been up on the cherry picker, it was nothing compared to the packing shed.

Clancy wore fingerless gloves, a beanie, a long navy coat and her peony gumboots. As she moved along the bench on which cut plants were grouped, she walked with a slight limp. It was only when Bundy ran to her side that she realised she had visitors.

She swung around, her instant smile banishing the shadows of his long day. 'This is a nice surprise.'

Heath didn't answer; he just kissed her. He'd more than missed her.

When he lifted his head, her cheeks were pink and her grey eyes almost silver.

'Need a hand?' he asked, voice husky.

'Have you eaten?'

'Hannah brought dinner around. She knew I was working late.'

'She's a good kid.'

'She is. It's also thanks to her there's been no more dinner invitations from Cynthia. She told her mother that as I'm now her friend, I'm off limits to her sisters.'

Clancy's fingers touched his cheek. 'Did your dad have a better day?'

'He did. Shadow's already a big hit.'

'And your mum?'

'She's had a better day, too.' He dropped a kiss on her cold nose. 'So what can I do to get you out of here before you get frostbite?'

'I'm almost done ... but if you could help me sort through the last of these that would be great. I have the markets this Saturday and I'll also be putting my flower cart out at the front gate this weekend.' She flicked him a glance. 'Are you warm enough?'

Her thoughtfulness made him want to kiss her again. But he'd already tested his self-restraint enough for tonight. He moved to the bench where what looked like a scalpel sat beside a bunch of peonies. A nearby large garbage bin was filled with leaves. 'Am I stripping the stem?'

She placed an already done peony beside the scalpel to show him how far along the stem the leaves had to be removed. He soon had the bunch completed and reached for more.

Clancy looked over from where she was sizing peonies using a small piece of flat wood that had two holes cut in it. 'That was quick. I'm still lucky not to lose a finger using a scalpel.'

He grinned. It felt good to even be doing mundane tasks with Clancy. 'Don't worry, I came off second best in the art rooms at uni many times.'

When he was done, he went over to a bunch of yellow peonies that Clancy had sorted and were at the end of the long table.

She nodded at the box of cellophane bouquet sleeves. 'Bunches of five and then off to the cool room they can go.'

When the yellow peonies were sitting in the cool room buckets, he packaged up the white, pale pink and finally the deeper pink blooms.

As he put the last five into cellophane, Clancy came over from where she'd cleaned the now empty table.

Her brow creased as she leaned in close to touch the closest peony. 'It's late, so I hope I'm seeing things, but that's not an ant, is it?'

He inspected the small black dot before brushing it away. 'Just a speck of dirt.'

'Phew. Ants love peony nectar.'

Her gaze went from the peonies to his mouth and then met his.

When her lips parted, he couldn't remember putting the peonies on the table. All he knew was that when his hands framed her face, Clancy was already flush against him, her fingers sliding through his hair.

The battle to keep their kiss safe and contained was already lost. Heat and need again flared between them. He fought her heavy jacket to gain access to the curves beneath while Clancy's palms slid under his shirt.

It was only the shock of icy air on the bare skin of his lower back that acted as a reality check. Another few moments and he would have lifted Clancy onto the table and another line between them would have been crossed.

He raised his head and knew the moment she too realised just how close they'd come to doing the opposite of taking things day by day. Her eyes widened. Breathing ragged, they stared at each other.

He spoke first. 'Clance …' Her beanie was on the floor somewhere and he ran his hand through her tousled hair to cup the back of her head. 'We need to slow down.'

'I know … but I missed you.'

'I missed you, too.'

Her smile was sunrise bright. She trailed her fingertips along the line of his jaw. 'Okay, let's start again. We'll go back to taking small steps.'

He nodded before he bent to collect her beanie. As he slipped it over her hair, he gave her a careful and gentle kiss.

'See,' she said, eyes soft as they drew apart. 'No problems.'

But after they'd left the shed, their fingers entwined as they strolled through the darkness, the hammering of his heart and the grumblings of his testosterone didn't share her optimism. When it came to the woman beside him, there would come a time when no amount of self-restraint would be a match for how much he wanted her or for the way she made him feel.

CHAPTER
14

Bundilla might be known as a book town but every second Saturday it became a market town.

Clancy stepped back from her stall set up in the green expanse of the park to check everything was in place. The square gazebo was wonky but she'd hammered the pins into the ground with such determination even gale-force winds couldn't move it. She'd covered plastic boxes in grey material and they now formed neat platforms on which her galvanised steel buckets filled with peonies would sit.

Her banner hung perfectly straight above where she'd sat two camp chairs. She always added an extra one as at past markets locals would sit with her to chat. In her ute were handwritten signs, plus anything else she might possibly need, from tape and safety pins to emergency chocolate.

Two stalls down, Rosie had set up her homemade candle display and the scents drifting on the breeze were divine. Further around past the duck pond was the food corner and already the waft of bacon and eggs made her stomach rumble. She'd make a quick stop to pick up some breakfast for herself and Rosie before the food vans got busy and it was time to put out her peonies. There was still twenty minutes before the markets opened.

As the bacon and egg aroma intensified, she turned to see Rosie approaching with two rolls. 'I thought I'd get in before the queues.'

'Great minds …' Clancy said with a grin.

They headed for Clancy's camp chairs to eat and catch up. She'd last seen Rosie at Brenna's barbeque. Rosie lived on the other side of the valley and in between raising her young family and farm work she made candles. Her dream was to one day open a candle shop in town.

When they'd finished their rolls, Clancy made a coffee run to the nearby coffee van and then they both busied themselves with their last-minute preparations.

The morning passed in a flurry of customers, talking and stripping off layers as the clouds gave way to sunshine. By late morning Clancy only had one bucket of peonies left and was down to her pink cotton shirt which sported the peony farm logo over the right pocket. She drank deeply from her water bottle. She wasn't the only one feeling the spring warmth. To her left a water bowl positioned under a tap had been popular with the local dogs as they strolled past with their owners.

Hannah now occupied the spare chair beside her. She'd come to draw Clancy's peonies. Although she was dressed in her usual black clothes, Clancy had caught a glimpse of bright pink and orange socks. Whereas before her customary expression had been moody and disinterested, her smile now made a regular appearance. Between school finally being finished and her art portfolio having been submitted to a Canberra university, it seemed the stressors in her life had diminished. Clancy suspected that Heath's friendship and interest in Hannah's art had also helped lift her spirits.

When Hannah again scanned the crowd, Clancy tried to hide her concern. Hannah had made sure Heath was off her mother's matchmaking hit list, so she only hoped she didn't have a crush on him herself. She knew how easy it was at eighteen to think about nothing but Heath. Except when Hannah looked at the people ambling past and her expression brightened, it wasn't Heath her gaze had latched on to, but Dan.

This time Clancy didn't hide her frown. Dan was a single man of few words who just seemed to have never found the right person, but he was also old enough to be Hannah's father.

'Hannah?'

Hannah glanced at her, making no effort to hide how she'd stopped sketching now she'd seen Dan. 'Dan's here.'

'He has been for a while. Don't you think he's a bit old for you?'

Hannah's eyes rounded before she laughed. 'Of course he is … but not for my mother.'

'Your *mother*?'

'I know she's always playing matchmaker but she's the person who really needs someone in her life.'

If the bush telegraph was to be believed, Hannah's father and his poultry pavilion girlfriend were now in Dubbo expecting their first child. For all of Cynthia's energy and colourful zest for life, the past years would have been difficult raising three daughters on her own.

She glanced at Hannah's half-completed peony picture that she didn't appear too interested in finishing. 'You're up to something, aren't you?'

Hannah's youthful face looked innocent. 'Me? Never. I just might have bought one of those really heavy pots for Mum's birthday and she'll need a hand to load it into her car.' She came to her feet. 'Dan's so nice, and after he and Mum chatted for so long outside the library the other day, I'm sure he won't mind helping.'

Clancy shook her head as Hannah practically skipped through the crowd towards where Dan was talking to the local honey stall holder. Clancy made a mental note. It wasn't Cynthia's matchmaking zeal that the town needed to be wary of but her youngest daughter's ingenuity.

It wasn't long until Hannah returned. She settled back into the camp chair with an air of satisfaction.

'Mission accomplished?' Clancy asked.

'Two missions accomplished.'

Clancy raised her eyebrows.

'Mum's going to buy him a coffee to say thank you.'

Clancy laughed. 'Remind me to never talk to anyone too long outside the library.'

Hannah joined in with her laughter but her knowing smile had Clancy suddenly checking the time on her phone to conceal her expression. Not that Hannah had seen her and Heath together, but she must have picked up on something. Either that of there were other rumours flying around about her that she didn't know.

'Anyone for a cupcake?'

Clancy looked up to see Brenna standing in front of the stall holding a plate of cupcakes decorated in white icing and tiny butterflies. When it came to market day stall shopping, Brenna always visited the food area first. 'As if we'd say no.'

Brenna walked into the gazebo and Clancy left her camping chair to give her a seat. She flipped over a nearby plastic crate to sit on. Brenna passed around the plate of cupcakes before she reached into the canvas bag that she'd placed at her feet. 'I struck gold at the book stall.'

Clancy eyed the pile of books Brenna produced. All three had bright and cheerful covers, and the authors were also ones she and Brenna had previously enjoyed.

Brenna reached into the bag again. 'You'll never believe what else was there.'

She pulled out another book with a flourish.

Clancy grimaced as she recognised the dreaded *Banks of the Seine*. 'No way.'

'I thought if I read it in hard copy instead of eBook I could get into it more.'

'The only reason it was at the second-hand stall was because reading it in paperback doesn't make it any less heavy going.'

'I liked it,' Hannah said in between mouthfuls of cake.

Clancy and Brenna stared at her.

'What? It's not that bad if you skip the politics. One of the sisters is a Parisian artist.' Hannah's eyes turned dreamy. 'One day I'll go there. Heath says the art museums are amazing.'

This time Clancy and Brenna looked at each other before they again gazed at Hannah.

'So,' Brenna said, 'if you had to talk about it at book club, what would you say?'

For the next five minutes they picked Hannah's brain. When they were done the book didn't sound as bad and Clancy vowed to give it a second go as well as skip the politics.

When Dan and an animated Cynthia ambled past, each holding a coffee, Hannah packed away her sketchbook into her black backpack. 'My work here is done.'

At Brenna's questioning glance, Clancy said, 'Don't let Hannah catch you talking to anyone on the main street unless he looks good on a horse.'

'Trust me. I won't. My last group of male trekkers called me princess. I don't know if that's a step up or down from little lady.'

After Brenna and Hannah left, Clancy spent the final half an hour of the market on her own even though she always seemed to be waving to people she knew. She'd had a successful morning and only had three bouquets of peonies left in the final bucket. After selling another bunch, she sat in her camp chair and sent Heath a text to see how his morning was going. He'd had a slow start with an influx of locals and out-of-towners stopping by to see where the mural was up to.

As busy as she'd been since her alarm had woken her that morning, he hadn't been far from her mind. The chemistry that had burned between them last night in the packing shed still simmered. So much for not being a risk-taker. Apparently she was when she was so close to Heath she didn't know where her breath ended and his began.

She still couldn't believe the speed at which she'd lost control. It was only thanks to Heath retaining a semblance of common sense that things didn't get more out of hand. He was right. They were supposed to be taking things at a snail's pace. She'd just have to remember that the next time she slid her hands over the smooth heated skin of his lower back.

She glanced at her phone. Usually Heath would text back straight away. He had to be talking again. She stared at the blank phone screen. As much as their physical connection ignored what pace they were supposed to be going at, their emotional connection was playing by the rules. Well, Heath's was.

It shouldn't bother her so much that he hadn't mentioned whatever was going on with his mother. She could only hope that when they did know what the future held for them, and there was no more need to go slow, the wall that remained between them would come down. Because if it didn't, no matter how much she loved him and would fight for him, if she was the only one to share the deepest parts of herself, it wouldn't be enough to sustain a relationship.

Something made her look up. Even though the crowds had dwindled there were still plenty of people milling around, full bags hanging from their arms. A man walked past the book stall with a black kelpie by his side. She smiled. Even without the paint on his jeans, she'd know Heath's stride anywhere. He moved as though he had something he had to paint or somewhere he needed to be. She was careful to keep her smile casual. Small towns might be short on population but they were big on curiosity.

Heath's grin was brief, but his smile stayed in his eyes as he handed her a coffee. 'Thought you might need some caffeine.'

'Thanks.'

Their fingers brushed as he passed her the coffee and she fought to stop herself from stepping into his arms.

He picked up the last two bunches of peonies before slipping his wallet out of his back jeans pocket.

She shook her head. 'You don't have to buy them. You know you can have as many as you like for your mum.'

'Thanks, but …' He handed her the correct money. Their fingers again touched. 'You're running a business.'

'You sound like Rowan. Are you rushing back to the mural?'

This time his grin lasted for longer. 'Not while you have a coffee to drink.'

She carried the bucket with Heath's peonies over to the camp chairs. No one would take a second look at them sitting next to each other. It was well known around town they were friends. They took a seat and when their knees connected, she didn't move away. The display of now empty buckets concealed them from any inquisitive glances.

Heath chuckled. 'Bundy's quite the celebrity.'

At the front of the stall the kelpie was having a selfie taken with each member of a four-person family. From their loud exclamations Clancy worked out they were from Queensland and were followers of his social media page. An older couple approached, also wanting pictures.

Bundy's tail wagged a third time as Trent appeared. It was just a subtle change but, where her knee touched Heath's, she sensed him stiffen. She gave him a sideways look. While his expression was relaxed, there was a new tightness around his mouth.

As the vet and Bundy walked over, Heath stood.

Trent smiled at Clancy. 'It looks like you had a good morning.'

She left her chair. 'I think almost everyone was in town today.'

Heath and Trent exchanged nods.

'You're just the person I need to see,' Trent said as he glanced to where Bundy sat by Heath's boots. 'Bundy's due for his annual needles. I can come to the water tower sometime next week or you could bring him to the clinic?'

'We'll come to you.'

'I'll look forward to the visit.'

On the surface Heath and Trent's conversation appeared normal but there was a subtle undercurrent of unexpected strain. Bundy's head turned and he too looked between the two men as they spoke.

Clancy bent to put her coffee cup in the garbage to hide her thoughts. She'd almost forgotten about Heath's comment that Trent was someone who he believed could make her happy. As much as she'd had to do with Trent since his fiancée died, they'd only ever been friends. Except the smile he'd just given her had been filled with a warmth she hadn't remembered before.

As she straightened, Heath's unreadable gaze met hers. In his hands were the two bouquets he'd bought for his mother. 'Thanks for the flowers.'

'No worries.'

Heath glanced at Trent. 'See you Monday.'

Then he was walking away, Bundy by his side.

She didn't have a chance to turn to watch him leave before Trent reached for the closest empty bucket. 'How about I give you a hand to pack up?'

'I hear you, mate,' Heath said, rubbing Bundy's neck as the kelpie rested against his legs. 'I can think of better places to be.'

It was five minutes to ten on Monday morning and they sat in the corner of the veterinary clinic's waiting room. They'd arrived ten minutes earlier but two of the vet nurses had come out to have their picture snapped with Bundy so they'd only just taken their seats.

While the kelpie sat quietly beside Heath, what sounded like several kittens meowed unhappily in a cardboard box to their right. The teenager who sat next to her mother every so often stuck her hand through the top of the box to reassure a kitten as its tiny tabby head popped out.

Along from them a small white dog sat on its owner's lap, its attention fixed on the kittens. From the dog's quivering, Heath was left in no doubt that if a kitten escaped the highland terrier would leap off its owner's lap and give chase. Thankfully, like Bundy, the white dog was on a lead. Across the room sat an elderly man with a cat carrier at his feet. Except inside wasn't a cat but a Rhode Island Red hen. As the kitten meowing grew louder, Heath exchanged glances with the older man. The vets were in for a busy day.

Heath gave Bundy another pat and looked at the clock on the waiting room wall. Two days might have passed since Trent had come to Clancy's market stall but his unease at seeing them together hadn't decreased. He had no doubt Clancy only saw Trent as a friend but he suspected the town's assumption that Trent wasn't yet ready for another relationship was out of date.

He may have read too much into the way Trent looked at Clancy, but if he hadn't, she could have the perfect future within reach. A future with a decent man that ensured she raised a family in the high country she loved. He passed a hand around the back of his neck. A future he wasn't certain he could give her.

The door of the first consulting room swung open. Trent strode out and called Bundy's name. It was no coincidence that every female in the waiting room smiled. With his clean-cut country boy looks and likeability, Trent put people at ease. Heath left his seat, his muscles feeling every minute of the hours he'd stayed awake to finish his latest painting; this one of his father had also featured Minnie.

He and Bundy followed Trent into the room. Without being asked, Bundy jumped onto the consulting table.

Trent laughed. 'Anyone would think you were a frequent flyer.' The vet continued to smile as he checked Bundy over. 'Thankfully you're not here often, as no one would get any work done. You're our most popular patient.'

Heath stayed silent. The receptionist had mentioned that Bundy's vaccinations came with a health check. This also wasn't a social visit and he didn't want to take up Trent's time with a waiting room full of clients.

But after Trent administered the first of Bundy's needles, the vet spoke again, his tone conversational. 'Bundy's been with you for a while now, hasn't he?'

'Three weeks. I'm sure he'll get sick of hanging out with me soon.'

Trent gave Bundy another needle. 'The mural looks almost done.'

'The plan is to finish by the end of the week.'

'And then?'

Heath knew they were no longer talking about Bundy or the mural. Trent's good-humoured expression had disappeared.

'I'll spend time with my parents before heading overseas for my next commission.'

'And Clancy?'

'Clancy's life is her own business.' Heath held Trent's hard stare with one of his own. 'Trust me ... she doesn't appreciate people taking an interest in what she does.'

Trent didn't break eye contact. 'She's already been through enough.'

Heath nodded. Trent was only speaking the truth. 'The last thing I'd do is hurt her.'

Something in his voice must have given Trent the answer he'd been looking for because he moved away to type on the computer. 'I hope so because then I can count on you to do the right thing.'

Heath didn't say the words that when it came to Clancy, that was a given.

As if knowing that the conversation was over, Bundy jumped onto the floor.

Trent gave the kelpie a final pat. 'That's you done for another year.' He straightened to look at Heath, his manner again professional. 'I keep Bundy's paperwork on file and cover his medical costs, so you're right to go.'

Once outside, Heath let Bundy off his lead and rolled his tense shoulders. He didn't know what was worse: having his suspicions confirmed that Trent's feelings for Clancy ran deep or Trent's assumption that Heath's return to his normal world was going to hurt her. Just like his father, the vet didn't believe there could be any common ground between Clancy's small-town life and his nomadic one. The breeze carried away his sigh as he headed for Ned's Hilux. The trouble was, part of him shared the same belief.

He'd never been so glad to strap on the cherry picker harness and get back to work. He needed his creative focus to clear his head of all whispers about whether or not he and Clancy could have a future. But as he waited for the jolt as the cherry picker platform lifted, nothing happened. He tunnelled a hand through his hair. His mechanical issues weren't over.

He returned to the shipping container. Bundy half opened a sleepy eye as if to say stop making so much noise. After a call to the cherry picker mechanics, where he was assured that someone would be there first thing tomorrow, Heath made himself a coffee from the generator-run kettle.

While he dialled the landline at Hawks Ridge, he helped himself to the brownies the sisters had dropped around yesterday.

His mother didn't take very long to answer. 'Hi, darling, how did Bundy go with Trent?'

'Good. Need anything from the grocery store as the cherry picker's not working again.'

'Will it be right by this afternoon?'

'No. Why?'

'I was thinking I might come in. I'd like to see the mural and we could have a coffee.'

'Sounds great.' This was the first time his mother had shown any desire to leave his father. 'I could call Ned. He could sit with Dad for an hour.'

'I spoke to him yesterday and he said he could drop by anytime. Clancy wouldn't mind if he took some time off picking.'

'We could walk along the river, too.'

It had been their thing when he was young to look at the historic wooden bridges that crossed the flood plain. He'd been fascinated by all the angles and lines.

'I'd like that.'

'Do you want me to come and get you?'

'Thanks but I need to drive. After your father ... wandering the other day I need to feel normal again.'

'I understand. Shall I meet you at the café around three?' That was the time when his father was usually asleep.

'Yes, I can be there by then.'

Heath ended the call. In the months before he'd come home his mother had done her grocery shopping in the evening before closing time when the town was empty. It was an encouraging sign that she now wanted to visit during the day. It was also a relief that she'd been in touch with Ned as well as been more open about his father's illness.

The next person he called was Clancy.

'Hi, Heath.'

The husky notes of her voice made him wish there was no need to take things slow. All he'd ever wanted was to wake up with her warm and soft in his arms and hear her saying his name.

'Like an extra helper? Thanks to the cherry picker, I have the morning off and Mum doesn't need me at home.'

'Don't take this the wrong way, but no. You were up late last night, I saw the studio light, plus you've been working hard to get the mural finished. Take some time off to relax.'

'I'm fine.'

'Seriously, go for a counter lunch at the pub, take Goliath for a ride or just sleep.'

'Really?'

'Yes, really. I'd best go. Primrose has run off with my glove. Let me know what you decide.'

Heath slowly lowered the phone. Then he lifted it again to dial Taite's number.

He took a while to answer and when he did machinery clanked in the background. 'What's up?'

'Need a hand? I've got mechanical problems and have the morning free.'

'All morning?'

'Yes, until three.'

'Fancy a ride in The Beast?'

The Beast was an antiquated four-wheel drive Taite had added modifications to. 'Surely it's not still around?'

'Technically this is The Beast version three. We could go up to the ridge track?'

'I like your thinking. Need anything from town?'

'No, just a passenger that doesn't tell me how to drive.'

Heath chuckled. Even though they were twins, Brenna and Taite couldn't co-exist in the same space for very long. 'See you soon.'

As he headed for the Hilux, he whistled to Bundy. 'Road trip.'

He turned on the radio and relaxed in the driver's seat for the journey around the valley to Glenwood Station. Going four-wheel driving with Taite was the perfect antidote to stop himself from thinking about Clancy and how much time he was wasting not being at the water tower.

When they pulled up in front of Taite's stone cottage, a black vehicle was parked outside. Once a regular four-wheel drive, the raised body now sported a bull bar, rock sliders and brush bars, and that was only the modifications he could see. Beneath the bonnet there would be more.

Taite strode out of the cottage with a huge smile and carrying a backpack. When they were settled in the four-wheel drive and Bundy was on the back seat, Taite revved the engine, sending a pair of galahs fluttering from a nearby tree. Heath shook his head. Whatever exhaust system Taite had put on The Beast, it was far from quiet.

Taite followed a dirt trail leading into the foothills that overlooked where his deer grazed within their high wire fences. Soon the gentle hills steepened and the gullies plunged as they reached a granite ridge. Taite stopped at the crest of a sharp descent before edging the four-wheel drive forward. Using low range, he carefully navigated his way over the jutting rocks and through the crevices gouged by running water. The more the ute tipped and swayed the more he and Taite grinned at each other.

They reached the bottom to the sight of black cockatoos perched in the red stringybarks. This time Taite didn't rev The Beast but the birds still took to the sky, the yellow of their tail feathers flashing.

Taite headed for a nearby incline and they crawled their way up to the ridge top. Once there, Taite continued until he took a track that sloped down to where a creek flowed through a narrow gorge. Thanks to yesterday's storm, the clay soil remained slick and the tyres struggled to gain traction as they followed the creek downstream.

When the valley opened up into a grassy plain, Taite pulled up alongside a circle of blackened stones. Heath knew the place well. He, Rowan, Taite and other school mates would meet here in the school holidays. It might have been a girl-free zone but it hadn't always been a beer-free zone.

'Ah, the memories,' Taite said as he turned to reach for his backpack tucked behind the driver's seat.

Heath smiled. 'We're lucky Beatrice and Millicent never knew about this place.'

They found some dry wood and soon the aroma of barbequed sausages wafted on the breeze. Heath sat back in the camp chair Taite had packed and let himself absorb the colours and textures of the bush landscape around him. It didn't matter where he was in the world, whenever he was homesick, he'd always paint a high-country scene.

When there were no longer any sausages left to smother in sauce, wrap in bread or share with Bundy, they extinguished the fire.

Instead of driving back the way they came, after checking the clock on the dashboard, Taite took the shortcut home. Soon the deer fences came into sight and then the large silver roofline of his workshop.

'Home with time to spare,' Taite said, tone satisfied as he parked beside the Hilux. 'Next trip, let's test that all-wheel drive system in your fancy car.'

'I'll have to get it back from Ned first.'

Taite laughed. 'Good luck with that.'

After a quick look in the shed at Taite's latest sculpture, Heath helped load the fire pit Taite had welded out of the plough discs onto the Hilux. Before he left Glenwood Station he messaged his mother to say he was on his way.

When he arrived at The Book Nook Café his mother's white car was already parked outside. He entered the cosy book-lined café in which about half of the tables and chairs were occupied. He scanned the crowd and didn't see anyone he knew except for his mother, who sat in the far corner with a teapot beside her while she read. Next to her teacup sat a pile of books. Her grey hair was coiled into a neat bun and instead of the gardening clothes he'd become used to, she wore a lightweight cream jacket with a navy skirt.

She looked up from her book and smiled. He forced his own smile to stay in place. The contentment in her expression reminded him how little he'd seen her relax since he'd been home.

He kissed her cheek as she stood to greet him. 'Darling, like a coffee?'

He shook his head. Her teacup was empty and so too would be the teapot. He didn't want her to waste any of her short visit to town sitting with him while he finished a coffee. 'It's nice outside, let's walk.'

She collected her books and with a smile at the young waitress led the way out to the main street. Bundy was waiting for them beside the door.

By the time they'd walked one block his mother had waved at three of the four cars that had passed. With every called out hello, her shoulders seemed to straighten and the colour returned to her cheeks.

As they passed the gift shop, Fiona rushed outside to give his mother a warm embrace. 'Lydia, it's so good to see you.'

'You too.'

'I haven't seen you for a while.'

'Life's been busy.'

Fiona gave his mother another hug. 'Next time you're in town let me know and we can have a cuppa.'

Heath and his mother kept strolling. At the next corner they turned to amble towards the river. When they reached the bench overlooking the water and the first of the historic wooden viaducts they took a seat.

His mother looked at the ground at their feet. 'Do you remember using a stick to draw the bridge in the dirt?'

'I do.' Drawing had always been part of who he was. 'Where do you think Andrew and I got our artistic side from? Grandma?'

She took a moment to answer. 'Andrew?'

'Mrs Buchanan showed me the drawing he did in kindergarten.'

His mother studied the ripples in the river with a half smile. 'Andrew did draw but not as much as you. All I know is it isn't from my side ... none of us had an artistic bone in our body, even Grandma.'

He wasn't sure if it was the memories of Andrew that accounted for his mother's tranquillity or her deep attachment to her parents, but all he knew was that he wanted her to be free to enjoy many more such moments. He couldn't change his father's illness but he could do what he could to lift another weight she carried. There never would be a right time to ask her what he felt like he now had to, for her sake. There only was ... now.

'Mum ... is Dad my father?'

The transformation was instant. Sadness, hurt and despair flashed across her face, leaving her features pinched and white. What he didn't see was surprise.

'So that's what it was.' Her voice was barely more than a whisper. 'Your father *promised* me … The night you left he said you weren't his son, didn't he?'

Heath slowly nodded. 'I'm only asking for you … not me. You also don't need to give an answer. I just don't want the past to cause you any more pain.'

Tears filled her eyes and while she continued to look at him, she didn't appear to really see him or to have heard anything he'd said.

'Your father changed after he lost Kyle and then Andrew. He stopped letting in the people who should be in his life, especially you.' She gripped his hand with almost a desperate strength. 'Beneath all the grief and anger, he loves you. That's why you have to make peace with each other.' She pushed herself to her feet, her movements slow and weary. 'I'd like to see your mural and go home.'

He stood to hug her. Always a tall and strong woman, she felt frail and fragile as she clung to him. While he didn't hear the sound of her sobs, he felt them as they racked her thin shoulders.

When she was ready to walk, he took her arm and matched his steps to hers.

Unless his mother was to reopen the door to the past, he would be leaving it firmly closed. Whatever the truth was, it might never lose the power to hurt her.

CHAPTER
15

The day of book club had arrived.

Clancy straightened from where she was cutting white peonies in the late-afternoon sun and looked around. Normally she was the only one working but having Ned help this season had made a huge difference. In the ten days since the peonies were ready they'd picked almost half of the beds. For the past few afternoons the clouds had gathered over the peaks before rolling across the valley and delivering a late-afternoon storm. But so far the rain had only been brief squalls and her peonies had suffered minimal damage.

She rubbed at the ache in her lower back. After last season ended early with the heatwave, she needed things to go smoothly this year. She also needed things to go well for book club tonight. She'd prepared her secret weapon, cleaned the house and finally finished *Banks of the Seine*. Brenna was coming around early to help set up.

Ned drove over in the gator from where he'd been in the yellow peony bed. Together they loaded her flowers and headed for the packing shed.

Once the peonies were on the table ready to be sorted, Ned gave her a grin. 'Do we need a code word for tonight?'

Clancy shook her head with a laugh, seriously hoping she wouldn't. 'Thanks again for taking Primrose and Iris over to the coach house.'

Ned had also offered to come to book club and act as a diversion if needed.

'I haven't yet told Heath we're on Primrose-sitting duty.'

'That will be a noisy surprise for when he gets home.' Since his mechanical issues two days ago, she'd hardly seen him. 'That's if he's back in time.'

'He has been working late but he's hoping to have the mural finished in the next few days.'

'I wonder how long he'll then stay?'

As much as she tried she couldn't strip the concern out of her voice. She hadn't needed to tell Ned that there was something more than friendship going on between her and Heath. There was no mistaking the way Heath greeted her with a kiss whenever he saw her. But even with them taking small steps, the future didn't seem any clearer. The only thing she was certain of was that living a life without Heath just wasn't an option.

'As long as his mother needs him.' Ned's solemn words matched his now serious expression. 'Clance ... it's not my place to stick my nose into other people's business but Heath's never been one to share his emotions. It just isn't something he's ever had a chance to do. Every anniversary of his brothers' deaths, every birthday and every Christmas, he's shouldered his parents' grief and made sure they got through. Just because he keeps everything on the inside doesn't mean he doesn't care.'

'I hope so. I know Heath's always been a closed book plus he's going through a difficult time with his father not being well ... I don't want to lose him.'

'You won't. Just hang in there.' Ned patted her arm. 'Now, off you go. You've got better things to do than listen to an old man's ramblings.'

Clancy hesitated. She'd been planning to work for another hour but if she went now she'd have time to give Heath a call as well as do a final sweep of the front path and veranda. 'Are you sure?'

'Yes.' Ned winked. 'And our book club code word is Primrose.'

Before she left, she kissed Ned's weathered cheek. 'Thank you ... for all of your help and especially for your ramblings.'

As it turned out, the extra hour was much needed. After leaving a voicemail for Heath when he didn't pick up—he'd be covered in paint or talking with another visitor—she found that Primrose had somehow fit through the cat flap. Instead of being out in the garden since lunch, she'd been inside with Orien running amuck. By the time Clancy had mopped up muddy paw prints, picked up the shredded gardening magazine she hadn't yet read and cleaned up the knocked over vase of peonies, it was time for a shower.

She chose her outfit with care, settling on a simple denim dress with a fitted waist. Her ankle still gave her the occasional niggle so she decided on flat black shoes instead of heels.

When again in the kitchen, she checked her phone and saw there was a missed call from Heath as well as a text that said good luck followed by a bunch of flower emojis. She went to call him back, but when she saw Brenna's four-wheel drive approaching along the driveway, she sent a quick message that she'd talk to him tonight.

Like Clancy, Brenna had made an effort in choosing what to wear. While her outfit was predictably not a dress, she wore a white linen shirt with her best black jeans and her good cowgirl boots. They exchanged hugs at the front door.

'We've got this,' Brenna said as they walked along the hallway.

Instead of making their way through to the kitchen, Clancy stopped at the dining room door and pushed it open. The last two book clubs she'd held were in the living room and in keeping with tonight being all about staking her claim as a valuable and confident member, she'd changed the venue.

Brenna's fine brows lifted. 'No way. We're in here?'

Clancy followed Brenna into the crimson-walled dining room. The overhead light glinted off her grandmother's silver vases filled with peonies that sat on the dark wood table. Over on the matching antique sideboard, her mother's fine bone china teacups were arranged in rows beside crystal wine glasses.

'This looks amazing,' Brenna said as she turned to take in all of the room.

'I hope so. Mum always made it look so stylish.'

Brenna gave her a smile.

When Clancy's mother had been alive the dining room had always been in use. This was the first time Clancy had since used it.

Keeping an eye on the time, they made the last-minute supper preparations that came with obligatory homemade dip tastings. Brenna also opened a bottle of red wine. Clancy was carrying the final cheese platter into the dining room when the doorbell rang. With there still being ten minutes until the official start time, she knew without seeing the car parked out the front that the first to arrive would be Millicent and Beatrice.

She greeted them both with a kiss on the cheek, hoping the pesto dip hadn't left any green flecks in her teeth. Brenna briefly appeared with a tea towel in one hand and full wine glass in the other, only to disappear and then reappear with empty hands.

When the sisters went to walk along the hallway to the living room, Clancy directed them into the dining room. The sisters' serious expressions didn't change as they stepped through the doorway and then stopped.

Behind them, Clancy swapped a resigned glance with Brenna. Somehow they'd still done something that wasn't quite right.

'I thought it might be a nice change to sit in here this time,' she said in her brightest voice.

To her surprise, Millicent turned with a smile. 'It is.'

The doorbell again rang and it wasn't long until the seats around the table were occupied. Fiona from the gift shop was there, along with Kathy the local librarian. Ruth and Patricia, who'd worn the same dress to the community op shop fundraiser, sat five chairs away from each other. Mabel was the final member to arrive, after having a last-minute article to write.

Once everyone had something to drink and the dips and cheese platters had been enjoyed, Beatrice started the formal part of the evening. After thanking Clancy for her hospitality and tending any member apologies, she opened the discussion about the chosen book.

Clancy was prepared. She deliberately didn't have a cup of tea in front of her. Tonight was all about not needing any props and her and Brenna just being themselves.

Millicent turned to Brenna. 'So Brenna, to start our talk, did any aspect of the book resonate with you?'

'To be honest, I really tried to like it but the book just su—'

'*Sometimes* didn't quite hit the mark,' Clancy interjected.

Brenna threw her a grateful look.

Millicent's eyebrows rose. 'In what way did it not hit the mark for you both?'

Clancy spoke before Brenna could use her next favourite word that was best saved for the stables. 'There were two plot holes—what happened to the elder sister and the artist she met during the war wasn't covered off and the other was that at the start of the book the main antagonist was motivated by revenge but in the end she blamed everything on being an only child.'

Clancy stopped. She'd said too much but when she looked around people were nodding.

'Well said, Clancy,' Ruth said. 'I agree.'

Mabel gave her a smile and a secret thumbs up.

For the next thirty minutes, Brenna and Clancy didn't have to speak again as the book club was divided over who did and didn't enjoy *Banks of the Seine*.

When the conversation lulled, Clancy and Brenna left the dining room to collect the second supper course.

As soon as they reached the kitchen, Brenna gave Clancy a high five. 'You were brilliant. I can't believe I was going to say it sucked again.'

Keeping their laughter quiet, they collected the scones, salted caramel slice and gluten-free carrot cake. Then, making sure they didn't look too pleased with themselves, they delivered everything into the dining room. Clancy made her way to the kitchen for one final dessert, her secret weapon.

When she returned, she placed the plate in front of Millicent and Beatrice. Clancy wasn't sure why but a silence fell over the room.

She hoped it wasn't because the circular, orange-brown dessert looked inedible.

'Is that ... pumpkin pie?' Millicent said, her hand lifting to her chest.

If Clancy didn't know better, she'd have sworn emotion choked the older woman's voice.

'It is. I remember you said it was a favourite of yours and Beatrice's when we once read an American-set book.'

Beatrice beamed Clancy a smile filled with such warmth that she blinked.

Without another word the sisters each cut a large piece.

Conversation again flowed as Mabel volunteered to host the next book club. Clancy didn't immediately eat her own pie. Instead she glanced around the room savouring the hum of chatter and the warmth that came from a collective sense of camaraderie. Between adding her two cents about *Banks of the Seine* and the success of her secret weapon, she no longer felt like a misfit and as though she didn't quite belong.

Usually once their supper was finished and the talk turned to general topics, the sisters left. But tonight they stayed along with Brenna and Mabel. After the dishwasher was loaded and any leftover items handwashed, Clancy offered everyone a cup of tea. Instead of returning to the dining room, they congregated around the kitchen island bench.

Beatrice looked at Millicent before she spoke. 'Clancy, we just wanted to say how touched we were that you made us pumpkin pie.'

'It was very thoughtful of you,' Millicent added, her eyes soft.

'You're very welcome.'

'We don't like to talk too much about ourselves,' Beatrice continued. 'But we want to explain why your gesture meant so much. You see, our father was an American who met our mother in Sydney during the war and our parents always celebrated the traditions of our father's homeland.'

When Beatrice paused, Millicent took over speaking, her tone subdued. 'When we were seven our mother went to hospital to have our baby sister. They never came home.'

Millicent reached for Beatrice's hand. 'The next Thanksgiving, our father promised to make us pumpkin pie. On his way home from work a drunk driver went through a stop sign and he was killed instantly.'

The sisters stared at each other as if lost in another time and place. The grief shadowing their faces kept Clancy, Brenna and Mabel quiet.

Beatrice broke the silence. 'There was no one to take us in so we were adopted out to different people. Both of our sets of parents thought it best that we had no contact, so we would bond with our new families.'

Millicent took over the telling of their story. 'It was only in our late forties that by chance we found each other again. We both frequented the same coffee shop in Sydney. You see, it had an American theme and was the only place around that served pumpkin pie. Thanks to the barista, who thought we were the same person, we were reunited.'

The smile the sisters shared was so full of joy Clancy's throat ached. No wonder the sisters had loved *Banks of the Seine*, which was about siblings finding each other. In her peripheral vision she saw Mabel touch the corner of her eye and Brenna, who often bemoaned having a twin, blink several times.

Clancy spoke for the three of them. 'I'm so glad.'

'We are too,' Beatrice said. 'And that's why, Clancy, you baking us a pumpkin pie means so much.' She paused to look between Clancy and Brenna. 'We know sometimes you both don't feel like you have a place in book club, but you are important members and we would be lost without the way you always listen to others, Clancy, and how you always speak your mind, Brenna.'

'I second that,' said Mabel.

Brenna grinned. 'So does that mean I can say that a book su—'

Millicent cut her off with her usual stern expression. 'No.'

They all laughed.

Beatrice came to her feet. 'It truly was a lovely evening and we're sorry you didn't enjoy the book.'

Everyone else stood, too.

Clancy smiled. 'It wasn't all bad. I did like the descriptions of Paris. I've never wanted to travel but I'm tempted now.'

She didn't add that the artist character reminded her of Heath and that had also kept her turning the pages.

After they'd said their goodbyes, Clancy waited on the veranda steps until the last of the tail-lights faded. Tonight the mountains had merged into the darkness of the night sky and as she gazed at the pinpricks of starlight overhead, the cold wind that rushed past her carried the scent of rain.

She could now understand why the sisters always appeared so reserved and serious. Her mother had been right. Their childhood hadn't given them much to smile about. A part of who they were had been missing for over half their lives. She turned to head inside and to give Ned the all-clear that he was right to come back from the coach house with Primrose and Iris. She'd been watching for lights and Heath wasn't yet home.

At the front door, her hand on the doorknob, she took a last look over her shoulder in the direction the sisters had left.

There was one part of their story they hadn't spoken about which remained a mystery. What had brought them to Bundilla all those years ago and why was Heath so special to them?

'This is it,' Heath said with a grin to Bundy who waited outside the cherry picker. 'The last hurrah.'

He activated the cherry picker controls. Well, it would be unless Murphy's Law wasn't yet done with him and his mechanical problems continued. The platform gave a familiar jolt before it lifted upwards.

Heath watched as Bundy headed for his usual sleeping spot near the shipping container door. He'd grown accustomed to the kelpie's constant presence and was going to miss his companionship. He was sure that once the mural was done Bundy wouldn't want to hang out with him as the majority of his time would be at Hawks Ridge.

The cherry picker reached the height of the mural. It wasn't a coincidence that the only incomplete part of the picture was Clancy's smile. Everything else was finished: her shirt, her hat, Bundy and his collar. It was just the lower half of Clancy's face and her mouth that required the final details. Even now, the knowledge that her beautiful Mona Lisa smile was because she'd been thinking about the two of them being more than friends humbled and moved him.

He touched her cheek. The concrete felt cold beneath his fingers. A part of him didn't want to finish because he'd then be a step closer to leaving. Even with taking things day by day the future still felt uncertain. As much as it kept him awake at night, there didn't yet seem a way to merge their very different lives. The question he had to answer for himself was at which point would he have to make the call that Clancy would only be hurt if their relationship continued.

His hand slowly lowered. In a perfect world he'd never have to make such a decision. But life was far from perfect and long-distance relationships could be hard to sustain, even for the most committed of couples. He'd spoken the truth to Trent. He'd always have Clancy's best interests at heart. He sighed as he slipped on his mask and picked up an aerosol can. Even if by doing so he went against his own interests and everything he'd ever wanted.

For the rest of the morning Heath concentrated on adding the last details to the mural. When he was done, he took a final look, his attention lingering on Clancy's smile. There was just one more thing to do. He lowered the cherry picker to the bottom of the mural and used a brush to sign his signature. He then picked up a stencil he'd made of Bundy's paw print and sprayed Bundy's signature beside his name. The mural was finished.

He lowered the cherry picker for the last time and removed his harness.

Bundy loped over to him and he stroked the kelpie's black coat. 'Thanks, mate, for everything. You do look pretty good up there.'

Bundy gave a doggy grin.

Next on Heath's to-do list was to clean up and pack away the equipment, but right now he had a small window in which he could take a few hours off and see Clancy. Ned had messaged to say she deserved a break. Since book club two days ago, she'd worked both the picking and sorting shifts.

He sent Ned a quick text as he strode towards the Hilux. With any luck the warm weather would hold until at least late afternoon when another spring thunderstorm was supposed to rumble through.

After a few stops in the main street and a brief conversation with Dr Davis about the media conference for the mural opening, he and Bundy headed for Ashcroft. The plan was once at the coach house to change into clean jeans and a shirt and then fill a basket with the items he'd need before going to find Clancy.

Except as he neared Ashcroft's front gate he saw Clancy transferring bunches of peonies from the back of the gator to a flower cart. The white wooden cart, with its small roof and shelves, had been handmade by Rowan as a surprise gift for Clancy to celebrate her first peony season.

Heath parked and left the driver's seat. Clancy walked over with a smile and there was no need for words as he kissed her. She smelled of peonies and fresh mountain air and he never wanted to let her go.

'You're home early,' she said, looping her arms around his waist.

Clancy's use of the word *home* tugged at the loneliness that had filled him ever since he'd left the mountains. 'The mural's done.'

'Really?'

He nodded, examining her face. She didn't appear as thrilled as he thought she'd be. 'I was able to make up for not being able to work Monday.'

'That's so good.'

While excitement now brightened her words, the light in her gaze had dulled.

He plucked a leaf from her hair. 'Which means I can spend more time with you … starting with us having lunch together. Ned says you need to take a break.'

'I wish I could.'

He cupped her jaw, his thumb brushing across the curve of her cheek. Dark smudges underlined her eyes. 'What was on that list you gave me? Counter lunch at the pub, a ride or a sleep.'

She leaned in to his touch. 'You didn't do any of those things.'

'Going out in The Beast counts as doing something relaxing.'

'Since when? Driving with Taite down vertical cliffs doesn't exactly lower blood pressure.'

He smiled as he lowered his arms from around her and they each took a step away. A vehicle approached and would soon drive by. Taking things slow still didn't include having their private lives become public fodder.

'Give me two hours for a long lunch … then I promise I'll have you back.'

'A long lunch?'

Her attention lingered on his mouth before the horn of a four-wheel drive honked. They turned to give Dan a wave.

Clancy then moved to scoop up the last of the peonies from the gator. 'I'll be good to go in fifteen minutes.'

True to her word, when Heath came out of the coach house a short while later, Clancy was waiting by Ned's Hilux. Still dressed in her pink work shirt, jeans and boots, she no longer wore her black cap and her heavy hair fell loose down her back. Both Bundy and Iris had already jumped onto the ute.

'No Primrose?' he asked as he loaded a basket into the back seat.

'Not if we want any minute of our two hours to be peaceful. She's asleep in the packing shed with Ned and that's where she'll stay.'

As they drove along the driveway, Clancy didn't ask any questions about where they were going. Every now and then she'd shoot him a curious glance as they took the road to Hawks Ridge and then turned through the front gate.

When they drew near to the farmhouse, he slowed but didn't stop as they went by where his mother and father sat on the bench overlooking Shadow's paddock. The mare's grey coat gleamed. Every morning he helped his father brush her. Jasper sat in his usual spot beside his father.

His mother paused in her knitting to give them a happy wave. Heath had messaged her to say he was bringing Clancy over for a picnic.

Clancy returned his mother's wave before reaching over to link her fingers with his. Heath knew why she offered him comfort. His frail and too thin father would have been unrecognisable. He'd also seemed oblivious to them as they travelled past. Their hands stayed joined until they reached the first of the gates.

'I've got this,' Clancy said with a squeeze of his fingers.

He drove through the open gate into a paddock that undulated into gentle green slopes to his right. Grey kangaroos rested in the shade of a nearby grey box tree while galahs perched on the water trough, dipping their beaks into the water. He'd never grow tired of painting the mountain landscape in which he'd grown up.

'So, any clues about where we're having this long lunch?' Clancy asked as she slid into her seat.

He pointed towards the ridge that dominated the view in front of them. 'Somewhere up there.'

Clancy bent forward to take a better look. 'Apart from visiting your house, I've never been anywhere on Hawks Ridge before.'

It shouldn't mean as much as it did that he was showing her the home he loved. 'You'll like where we're going.'

It wasn't long until they arrived at a second gate. After they'd driven through, the narrow track climbed and twisted as the bush closed in around them.

Heath soon heard the sound he was listening for.

Clancy heard it too. 'Heath MacBride, do you have a waterfall you've never told me about?'

'I might ... but in my defence it only flows in spring.'

He didn't add that as much as he knew she loved waterfalls, his father would never have given him permission to bring her here. He parked in a clearing and when the noise of the Hilux quietened, the rush of fast-moving water grew louder.

With Bundy and Iris sniffing and exploring as they walked, they made their way through the thick timber to what was usually a dry creek bed. A kookaburra cackled, letting them know they were trespassing on his territory. The trees thinned and then parted to reveal a curtain of white cascading over a wide granite ledge. The crystal-clear water tumbled over strewn rocks and plunged into a deep pool that slowed the downstream flow to a sedate trickle.

The delight on Clancy's face made the late nights painting in the cold and dark to get the mural done worth it. Today was all about carving out time together before life again kept them busy.

'You're right, I do like it.'

He slipped an arm around her waist. 'There's also wildflowers.'

On the grassy verge near the granite ledge the breeze caused the yellow tufts of billy buttons and pink everlasting daisies to sway.

She rested against him as they watched the water surge and fall. The sun warmed their shoulders and the fresh eucalyptus scent of the bush eddied around them.

When Bundy and Iris ran to the pool's edge for a drink, Clancy took out her phone to take a photo. Smiling, she tucked herself beneath his arm and took a selfie of them both with the waterfall behind them.

Conscious they only had limited time, Heath caught her hand and led the way back to the ute. Once there, he laid out a picnic rug and together they unpacked the basket. After sharing the fresh ham and cheese rolls with Bundy and Iris, and then the vanilla slices from the bakery, their lunch soon disappeared.

When Clancy stifled a yawn, Heath moved the basket off the picnic rug so they could lie back and enjoy the sunshine. He stretched out and Clancy lay by his side, resting her head on his arm. Her eyes closed and her breathing became shallow.

As much as fatigue dragged at his eyelids, he resisted the need to rest; he'd be a fool to relax. It would be all too easy to turn and kiss Clancy awake until they forgot why they had to ease their way into being more than friends. So he settled for holding her close and feeling the gentle rise and fall of her breaths.

He knew the moment she woke up. The fingers of the hand resting on his chest curled into his shirt. Wide-eyed, she lifted her head to stare at him and he thought she was going to speak but then she snuggled back against him.

'I can't believe I fell asleep,' she said, voice muffled. 'I've got to get back to work.'

'I know.'

'But I don't want to. I want to stay here.'

He kissed the top of her head. 'That makes two of us.'

She sighed as she eased herself into a sitting position. 'How much time do we have left?'

He stood and offered her his hand to help her up. 'Just enough to say a quick hello to Mum.'

Clancy searched his face. 'Does she know about us?'

'She would, even though we haven't had a chance to have an actual conversation. Clance … now the mural's done I'll be spending more time at home. If you need the coach house back I can move out.'

She stilled and held the picnic blanket that she'd folded against her chest. 'I don't. Though I'm guessing there'll come a time when you'll have to stay to give your mum a break.'

'There will be.'

Clancy moved to place her hand on his arm. 'Heath … this can't be easy. Don't forget I'm here anytime you want to talk about your dad … or your mum.'

'I won't.' He turned away to collect the basket so she wouldn't sense how much her words touched him or his tension that he wasn't yet able to do such a thing.

Revealing his vulnerability from seeing his father decline and their ongoing estrangement would only anchor Clancy to him. Until they knew how their combined lives could work, she had to be free to go her own way if she needed to. As for talking about his worries concerning his mother, the truth as to who his biological father was had to be her secret to tell.

To protect those he loved, he had to continue to say as little as possible.

Clancy sipped her tea and savoured a rare moment of morning peace in the empty kitchen.

She'd been up to hear the dawn birdsong and had been outside by the time the new day's gentle light sneaked over the mountain peaks and the peony paddock. Ned was now out picking with the dogs and she'd come inside to return the warmth to her fingers and toes and to wait for Rowan's call. Before Heath had left for Hawks Ridge he'd come to find her in the packing shed. She could get used to him kissing her good morning every day.

Her contentment faded and she wrapped her hands around the warmth of her mug. If only she could feel more certain that she would have a lifetime of such moments. As much as she hadn't wanted to admit it, these last two weeks of being with Heath had shown her how lonely she'd been. Even though her life had felt complete and she'd been content, a part of her had still yearned for a more intimate connection. And even though things were still progressing at a snail's pace, she had no doubts that Heath was the person she wanted to spend forever with.

She glanced around the too quiet kitchen. She also wanted a house full of noise, children and love. After book club she hadn't packed away her mother's teacups into the china cabinet. Instead she placed them in the kitchen cupboard where her mother had kept them for everyday use. She'd also taken her father's sheepskin coat from off the mudroom rack and hung it in the spare room wardrobe. Her parents' presence still surrounded her but she didn't need as many tangible reminders or have the same need for security. She was ready for whatever the next chapter would bring, even if the way forward with Heath wasn't yet clear.

She stared into her half-drunk tea. At first Heath saying that he'd finished the mural had thrown her. Her fears that he'd again leave without saying goodbye had flickered into life. But now she could see that with the mural being completed they were a step closer to finally being together. He also wouldn't just up and leave when his mother needed him and his father was so unwell. At least his mother knew they were together, even if Heath hadn't actually spoken to her. She only hoped this wasn't a sign that when their relationship did pick up speed Heath would continue to keep his feelings to himself.

A beeping sound broke into her thoughts. She reached for her tablet that sat to her right on the island bench and tapped the screen to accept Rowan's call.

'Hey, sis. Look …' He held up his now plaster-free hand.

'Wonderful. Now can you just stay in one piece?'

'Did I mention we're going to the Chamonix valley for the opening of the ski season?'

Clancy groaned. 'When?'

'Two weeks.'

'Where even is that? No, don't answer. I don't want to have to look up the emergency services for another country.'

Rowan laughed. 'I'll be fine.'

Clancy kinked a brow.

Rowan spoke again. 'You look tired. Are those precious peonies of yours picked yet?'

She smiled. Rowan was always calling her peonies precious or high-maintenance. 'Those precious peonies will hopefully pay some bills this year. Thanks to Ned I'm way ahead of schedule, so we'll be done maybe in another ten days. Which will be perfect timing as my open day is right when you'll be trying not to break a leg on the ski slopes.'

'Have I ever broken a leg skiing?'

'Falling off a horse, yes. But okay, you haven't skiing. But you did get a concussion after you skied over that jump.'

'Blame that on Heath. He went first.' Rowan paused. 'Speaking of a certain street artist that has no fear ...' Rowan's grin couldn't stretch any wider.

'Do I have to remind you we're not sixteen anymore ... your teasing days are over.'

'I was only going to say ...' Rowan's expression turned innocent. 'That as worried as Heath is about his parents, when it comes to you he just sounds happy.'

'I hope so. I saw his dad the other day and you wouldn't recognise him. There's something going on with his mother too, not that Heath has said anything.'

'She'd be just going through a difficult time, which is understandable.'

Clancy didn't voice her belief that whatever was going on was more than that. 'I'd better get back to my precious peonies and you'd better get to sleep. I'll call you tomorrow.'

Rowan gave her a wave before the tablet screen went dark.

Even though she'd already checked the weather online, she did so again. The forecast hadn't changed; mid-afternoon there'd be the usual spring squall. Thankfully it wasn't only Bundilla that'd been getting wet. There'd been big falls out west in the drought-affected areas and heartwarming pictures of people dancing in the rain had flooded social media.

On her way towards the back door she stopped in the living room to pat Orien where he was curled up on the teal-green sofa. The look he shot her was indignant. He no longer was as free to come and go as he once was.

'Yes, I know, the cat flap's still locked. Don't worry, I'm feeding Primrose heaps so her little stomach will soon be too fat to fit through.'

She continued outside where her day again became all about her peonies.

It wasn't until the late-afternoon sunshine waned and the warm breeze turned chilly that she paid any attention to the sky. The predicted storm clouds were gathering on the peaks but there would be time to finish this patch of white peonies before she'd need to go to the packing shed. Over in the yellow peony bed Ned appeared to be having similar thoughts as he looked over her way and gestured towards the mountains. She nodded.

When Bundy dashed past as he raced Iris over to Ned, Clancy straightened to see Heath striding towards her.

He greeted her with a hug and a kiss. 'Thought you might need some help before the storm hits.'

She didn't immediately register his words. When in his arms, it was as though the real world ceased to exist. 'It's just the usual quick thunderstorm, isn't it?'

Heath glanced to where her jacket, which she'd discarded hours ago, lay on the gator seat. 'Your phone's in your pocket, isn't it?'

'Yep … and Ned's in the packing shed.'

Heath took out his mobile and tapped the screen before holding up a picture of a blackened sky. 'Mabel sent this. She's in Tumut. It's heading our way.'

Her stomach lurched. 'Please don't tell me there's hail.'

Ned joined them. When Heath showed him the picture, they exchanged a grave look.

Clancy took a deep breath. 'Okay. The yellow beds can be left as that colour isn't as popular. If we can just get as many of the white and pink peonies picked that will have to do.'

She ran an eye along the bed she was working on. They had maybe one hour to do the work of ten days' picking.

Ned patted her shoulder before he headed for the adjacent pink bed. Heath gave her a reassuring smile as he rolled up his shirtsleeves. Not wasting any time, she busied herself with cutting as many peony stems as she could. Heath drove Ned's Hilux over. No longer would the small trayback of the gator be adequate for the quantities of flowers the three of them were picking.

Hands aching and her lower back protesting, Clancy continued to move along her peony bed. Ned had already reached the end of his row and now worked with Heath on another section of pale pink peonies. The clouds had darkened but the sky above them remained a moderate blue. Hope surged as she allowed herself a brief stretch. Maybe the storm would blow itself out by the time it reached their valley.

But when she next glanced up, she didn't need the wind whipping at her hair and the drop in temperature to tell her that the conditions had deteriorated. The sky was an ominous grey and in the distance sheets of what she hoped was only rain fell over the mountains.

Heath took the Hilux and unloaded it in the packing shed before returning with her oilskin and wide-brimmed hat.

'Ned's taken the dogs inside and gone to put the horses in the stables,' he said as he helped her into the long coat. He then pulled her close for a tight hug. 'Clance ... at the first sign of lightning we stop, okay?'

She slowly nodded against his chest.

When the rain arrived, it didn't issue a polite warning and start with hesitant droplets. Instead it was as though the heavens tore open. A volley of raindrops lashed at her, the force stinging her hands and face.

She bowed her head and kept picking. Every flower was now extra precious. She was vaguely conscious of a rumble of thunder before Heath appeared out of the downpour. By now she'd lost her hat and when she straightened icy water funnelled down her coat collar to soak her shirt. Heath's wet hand clasped hers and when she shook her head, he pointed upwards. A jagged flash of light illuminated the clouds as well as the hard edge to his jaw.

She wasn't sure if it was rain or exhaustion that blurred her vision as Heath guided her into Ned's Hilux. Even though she was now out of the storm it didn't spare her. Water streamed over the windscreen, making it impossible to see, and when Heath opened the driver's side door rain pelted at her. She dragged wet hair out of her eyes so she would be able to see any break in the low and sullen clouds. As heavy as the rain was, as long as there wasn't any hail she'd lose some of the open flowers but not all of what was yet to be picked.

Heath headed the Hilux towards the packing shed where he'd left the double doors open. As they drove inside, the slam of rain on the steel roof was almost deafening. Clancy left her seat and, leaving a trail of water, went over to the table piled high with peonies ready to be sorted. She'd keep working until the rain thinned and she could assess the damage.

Heath had other ideas. He swept off his hat then shook off the water before putting it on her head and gesturing towards the door.

She tipped the brim higher so she could see his face. 'I'll stay,' she shouted above the drum of the rain. 'It will be over soon.'

'You'll freeze.'

She hadn't realised just how soaked she was, or how cold the shed was, until he spoke. A ripple of shivers turned into tremors that would have made her teeth chatter had she not clenched them shut. Even though Heath too had worn an oilskin, his jeans and boots were saturated. She wouldn't be the only one to freeze if they stayed.

She went over to the Hilux where Ned always kept a spare cap behind the driver's seat. A quick cup of tea and a change of clothes and she'd soon be back.

'Your ankle?' she heard Heath say close to her ear as she stood on tiptoes to put his hat back onto his head.

'It's fine.' Even though it was now a case of too little too late, she tugged Ned's cap over her wringing-wet hair.

Heath reached for her hand and, glad of its warmth, she linked her fingers with his. Together they jogged out into the rain. The coach house was closer than the main homestead where Ned and the dogs were, so she went along with Heath when he steered her that way. Her ankle wasn't as healed as she'd said it was.

Their boots clattered as they reached the small porch. Once through the door, they helped each other strip off their oilskins and boots so they could be left in the entryway. She'd thought Heath's chest had stayed dry beneath his coat, but water dripped from the hem of his shirt. The puddle on the floor quickly became a pool. With her feet now bare her chill intensified and she tucked her arms around her waist to stop herself from shaking.

Heath took his phone out of his shirt pocket and as he headed for the kitchen he flicked open his top shirt buttons. In one motion he pulled the shirt over his head before disappearing up the stairs. Discomfort forgotten, Clancy could only stare after him.

From when she'd slid her hands under his hoodie in the studio, she'd known Heath had filled out. But nothing could have prepared her for the honed planes of his bare back and shoulders. The need to feel the heat of his skin beneath her hands caused her fingers to curl into her palms.

Yesterday when she'd slept in his arms on the picnic rug, she'd come so close to abandoning all plans to take things day by day. Somehow she'd stopped herself from doing anything more than clutching at his shirt when she'd woken up. She'd also silenced the words that she loved him. With every day that passed it was becoming more and more difficult to remember why they couldn't rush headlong into being a true couple.

The floorboards overhead creaked as Heath moved around in the upstairs bedroom. He reappeared dressed in a navy T-shirt and faded jeans and carrying two towels along with his old Bundilla Brumbies rugby top.

As he passed them to her she made do with a nod. Her teeth would chatter if she tried to speak.

'Hot chocolate?'

She nodded again.

When he left to go into the kitchen she made use of the privacy of the narrow entryway to peel off her jeans and shirt and put on the ruby top that hit her mid-thigh. She hoped it wasn't her imagination but the rain perhaps wasn't quite as loud on the roof as it had been. She wrapped her hair in a towel and went over to the window that overlooked the garden to check.

But there was no sign of the storm easing. Water streamed from the overflowing gutters and she couldn't see further than the barbeque tucked against the courtyard wall. Bundy's favourite spot to sleep in the usually sheltered space was now obscured by a mini flood.

Heath came over to offer her a sweet-smelling hot chocolate. She wrapped her hands around the mug to return the feeling to her fingertips. Heath moved to stand behind her, his arms enfolding her as his chin rested on her hair. She leaned back against him and took a mouthful of hot chocolate. As warmth filled her, her shaking subsided.

The heavy downpour wasn't ideal but the sun would soon be out and dry the peonies left in the beds. She'd have plenty to pick before the season ended.

At first she thought the bang on the tin roof overhead was a small branch blown onto the roof by the wind. Then another noise sounded, and another. And no longer was she looking at raindrops, but hailstones the size of large marbles.

✕

One minute Heath had been about to dip his head to explore the pale curve of Clancy's nape, the next it was as though a Gatling gun had opened fire.

He tightened his hold on her as hail assaulted the roof. Hard balls of white bounced off the outside pavers while others disintegrated on impact. He winced as the metal cover of the barbeque took multiple hits.

'You're *kidding*.' Clancy's words were barely audible in the loud din.

Whereas seconds before she'd been relaxed, tension now vibrated through her.

She moved out of his arms to put her mug on the table. When the towel on her head unravelled, she hung it over the chair, her attention never leaving the onslaught outside.

He shook his head when she glanced towards the door. 'Don't even think about going out there.'

Mouth set in a tense line, she instead paced the small living room.

'Clance …' He went over to make sure she kept a safe distance between herself and the window in case the hail caused it to shatter. 'Talk to me.'

He was powerless to prevent whatever peonies were left in the beds from being destroyed. All he could do was help Clancy work through her frustration and disappointment and distract her for however long the hail lasted.

She cast him a dark look. 'You first. Tell me something you've stopped yourself from telling me.'

His gaze skimmed over where his red-and-blue rugby top left her slender legs bare. 'That day in the kitchen when you had on that rugby top, and I didn't know it was Rowan's, I was insanely jealous.'

She looked away from where the hail now covered the courtyard like a snowdrift. 'Insanely?'

He nodded.

She gave him a brief smile then stared back at the hail with a sigh. 'I have insurance and I've had a good start to the season so I'm both lucky and really grateful. I know things could be so much worse, except ...' Her shoulders slumped. 'I look forward to my flowers all year. I love what I do but the peonies also remind me of Mum, and of Dad as he helped me plant them, and now they're just ... gone.'

Heath closed the distance between them. Clancy didn't appear to notice his arm around her waist as she stared unseeingly outside. When a large hailstone smashed against the glass, she didn't even flinch.

He turned her away from the window and held her close. The gesture was designed to offer comfort and nothing more. But as Clancy melted against him and her hands skimmed beneath his T-shirt to slide over his back, it was as though they picked right up from where they left off after their kiss in the packing shed. Even before his mouth sought hers, their breaths were unsteady.

The sound of the storm receded. The wet strands of her hair spilled through his fingers and her sweetness filled his soul. He fought for control as Clancy tugged off his T-shirt before running her palms along his chest and over his shoulders.

'Clance ...'

Her hand lowered to grip his as she took a step towards the staircase that led to the bedroom upstairs. But he didn't follow, waiting for a response to his unspoken question.

Her smile answered him even before she pulled on his hand and her husky words sounded. 'Going slow is officially overrated.'

He scooped her into his arms and made short work of the stairs. Once in the loft bedroom there was no more hail, no more loss and no more uncertainty, just sparks so intense they kept the world at bay.

This time when Clancy lay asleep and tucked up by Heath's side, they were under a roof and not a blue sky. While Clancy's hand again rested on his chest, this time his fingers were laced with hers. The emotions that coursed through him made his throat raw and sleep impossible. He'd waited so long for Clancy to be his, he didn't want to let her go or to miss a single second.

The hail had given way to a light rain that would soon stop. When it did, he'd wake her. For now he'd savour the feeling of his world finally being whole. As displaced as he had been from his home and at times his country, in that moment with Clancy warm and soft in his arms, he was at peace. Where his arm curved around her shoulder, his fingertips caressed her satin-smooth skin. There had to be a way to ensure that this was the start of a life together, not just a glimpse of what it could be.

At the thought of losing her, tension coiled around his temples. But it wasn't his own potential anguish that caused his joy to wane but what the effect would be on Clancy should they have no future. There was one last line that he couldn't cross.

While his touch may communicate just how much he loved her, and how he'd done so for so long, he couldn't yet lower his emotional guard by putting his feelings into words. It was the only way to keep protecting her from hurt should the future they both wanted not be achievable.

He hadn't realised Clancy was awake until she spoke. 'What are you thinking about?'

He kept his words light. 'That I should have kissed you at the river all those years ago and not wasted so much time.'

'Mum always said good things come to those who wait.'

'Good things?'

She lifted her head so she could look at him, her smile teasing. 'Well, I think they were good … you'd better remind me.'

After he'd kissed her, her smile resembled the dreamy one he'd painted on the mural.

'As much as I'd like you to keep jogging my memory …' She paused to listen. 'Now the rain's stopped I really need to see how bad things are.'

He'd left his mobile on the bedside table when he'd come up to change and it pinged as a message came in. He showed Clancy his mother's text saying that the storm was hitting Hawks Ridge now and that Heath wasn't to drive over as they'd be fine.

'I can come with you if you're worried,' Clancy said as she gathered the sheet around her and sat up.

His fingers ran though her red-brown hair that fell down her bare back. 'Mum's right. They'll be okay. I'll help clean up here and then head out.'

Clancy studied him for a second before brushing her mouth across his and reaching for the rugby top that lay on the floor beside the bed.

While she went over to the main house for dry clothes, he too took a shower.

Bundy, Iris and Primrose welcomed him as he left the coach house to check for any damage to either the building or garden. It didn't take long for his jeans to sport puppy-sized paw prints. An excited Primrose had already made the most of the puddles and mud.

Most of the hail had melted away apart from the pockets of white banked up in the corners of the dry-stone wall. Where earlier yellow daffodils and pink camellias had bloomed, now a single cluster of jonquils sheltered beneath an old fir tree. Once spring-green branches again appeared winter bare after having had their leaves stripped. His heart ached at the thought of the destruction Clancy would find when she visited her peony beds.

Ned walked over from the stables and through the small wooden gate to join him. Primrose set about imprinting him with her tiny paw prints.

'Remind me next time there's a storm to not be on babysitting duty.' Despite Ned's words, affection warmed his voice as he patted the puppy's dirt-covered head.

'Horses okay?'

'Yes, and Fenella and Fergus are fine, too. They didn't look fazed at all.' Ned gazed around at the decimated garden. 'Poor Clance.'

'At least there's a shed full of peonies.'

'True. Most of which are on the back of my Hilux or the gator.' Ned grinned. 'Which means I will need a vehicle to check the cattle with.'

'Don't even think about taking my car. You like mud as much as Primrose.'

'It's an all-wheel drive.' Ned's eyes twinkled. 'I won't get stuck.'

The back door of the homestead opened. Clancy appeared, her cheeks flushed from the shower and her damp hair pulled into a ponytail. She wore clean jeans, a navy jacket and her peony gumboots but all Heath really noticed was her smile when she caught sight of him.

As she approached her gaze met his before all three dogs crowded around her to say hello. Even just the brief eye contact was enough to make him want to take her back to the coach house and spend the rest of the day inside.

The ringing of his phone had him look away. Hannah's name filled the screen.

'Hi, Hannah.'

'Hi, are you at Clancy's?'

'Yes, everything okay?'

Worry had edged the teenager's voice.

'It's Ruby. Mum doesn't know but she went to meet John at the river near Clancy's and hail's cracked her windscreen.'

'Where is she now?'

'She's still there. She had a fight with John and he left.'

'I'll pick her up. Let me check something with Clancy but I should also be able to get Ruby's car.' He glanced across at Clancy who nodded. She'd known without him asking that he'd wanted to know if Rowan's car trailer was still in the shed. 'All good, Hannah. Tell Ruby I'll be there soon.'

'Thank you so much. She's a bit upset. Mum's going to go ballistic.'

Heath ended the call and explained what had happened.

'As I told my girls,' Ned said, shaking his grey head, 'nothing good ever happens at that spot at the river.'

This time Clancy's gaze met his for longer and he wasn't so sure the pink in her cheeks was from her shower. If so, he shared her thoughts. Good things mightn't always happen at the river but they did in such places as the coach house loft.

A short while later Clancy sat next to him in her dual cab as he towed the car trailer. As soon as she'd heard Ruby was upset, she'd offered to come and help. When they'd walked to her ute she'd held up her phone as if to say she had some calls to make if he was okay to drive. His grip on the steering wheel firmed. Just as well he was driving, as it gave him something to do with his hands other than reach for the woman beside him.

'I'm sorry you didn't have more time to check on your peonies.'

'I saw more than enough.' She sighed. 'There's nothing left even for the bees let alone for my open day. But thanks to you and Ned at least I've peonies for my orders and the markets.'

Her phone whooshed and a quick grin erased her seriousness.

He groaned. 'Don't tell me Ned's sent another picture?'

'Do you want to see it?'

'No.' But even as he said the word he glanced at the photograph of his silver car covered in mud looking like a rally car.

Her phone whooshed again.

'Oops,' she said. 'I won't show you that one until Ned's got himself unbogged.'

Heath briefly closed his eyes.

He soon slowed to take the turn to the notorious hook-up haunt. 'So … have you been here before?'

'Yes.'

He arched a brow. He'd have remembered if Rowan had ever mentioned that someone had taken her there.

She laughed softly. 'I do believe you're jealous, Heath MacBride. This used to be Rowan's and my favourite fishing spot. Well, when it wasn't being used for other purposes. What about you?'

'I was also here with Rowan … and Mandy Wright and another girl who left town, but unlike your brother I just talked. The only girl I ever wanted to bring here was you.'

Clancy smiled her beautiful smile. 'Mandy Wright … there's a name I haven't heard in a while. I think she's married with four kids.'

Heath drove on the far side of the dirt track to avoid a branch that the recent wind had brought down. Ahead he could see a small blue car with green P plates and Ruby sitting on a rock, her arms around her knees. As for the windscreen, it wasn't just cracked, it had holes punched in it and golf ball–sized dents pitted her bonnet and roof.

Ruby walked over to meet them. She'd pulled the sleeves of her short black jacket over her fingers and her ripped jeans were muddy on the cuffs. With her smudged eyeliner and strained expression there was no sign of the sass he'd seen in the café.

Clancy gave her a hug. 'These things happen. Your mum will just be relieved you weren't in the car.'

'I hope so. Her car was only just fixed and she doesn't need any more bills.'

Clancy rubbed Ruby's back. 'I need some help in the packing shed if you were after any extra work.'

'Thanks. I haven't had many shifts at the bakery since uni finished.'

Heath bent to collect the half of the front number plate that lay on the ground. Fresh tyre marks that would have been left by John's ute indented the mud. 'Call me old school but when someone's in trouble they shouldn't be left to deal with it on their own.'

The fire returned to Ruby's blue eyes. 'My car wouldn't have even been left here if John hadn't wanted to go to Genevieve's house. We were supposed to be on a date. When he saw the damage … he just took off. We are *so* over.'

Clancy's lips twitched and Heath hid a grin. He almost pitied John. If Ruby's parting words had been as fierce as her scowl, John's ears would have been burning.

They loaded the damaged car onto the trailer and drove into town. As soon as they arrived at Ruby's house, the front door flew open. Clancy had been right. Cynthia's distressed expression contained no anger, just concern. When she threw her arms around her daughter, as much as the teenager grimaced, Heath also caught the sheen of relief in her eyes. Hannah gave him a thankful smile from the doorway.

He'd just unloaded Ruby's car when his mother called on his mobile. She'd be ringing to say that the storm had passed over Hawks Ridge.

'Hi, Mum, any hail damage?'

His mother didn't reply, then he heard a choked sob.

'Mum?'

His hand tightened on the phone and he sensed Clancy come to his side.

'Your father's not in his room or … anywhere. He went through the bedroom window … the floor's wet from the rain. And … Jasper's not with him.'

CHAPTER

17

The late-afternoon weather was as gloomy as the mood at Hawks Ridge.

Despite the hail having missed the farm and Heath's mother's garden, there were no smiles on the faces of the figures gathered around the horse yards. Heath had kept the initial search party simple and only enlisted the help of neighbours and friends his father would hopefully recognise.

Clancy had heard the calls he'd made on the trip home. In every conversation he'd explained how his mother hadn't wanted Graham's illness to be common knowledge and that was why nobody knew how ill he really was. He'd also mentioned that his father most likely was on horseback as all the farm vehicles were accounted for but Shadow wasn't in her paddock. While no saddle was missing, being an experienced horseman, Graham wouldn't have needed one to ride the old mare.

Oilskins rustled as those who'd come to help prepared for a long night. Dan was there, along with two workmen and another neighbour and his son. Ned had arrived as well as Taite and Brenna. The Beast was parked alongside the yards in which all but one of the saddled horses waited for their riders.

Goliath stood by himself at the low rail near the stables. Thanks to trying to kick Taite's young gelding, the unsociable blood bay had been isolated. But judging by Goliath's satisfied air as his tail swished, she suspected he'd caused a ruckus just so he could receive special treatment.

Brenna came over from where she'd been talking to Millicent. When the sisters had arrived they'd carried what looked like a crockpot containing dinner over to the house. Heath was worried about his mother and the sisters hadn't hesitated to keep her company. Jasper had stayed inside with Lydia while Bundy remained Heath's constant shadow.

Beneath the low brim of her felt hat, Brenna's concerned gaze met Clancy's. 'I can't believe Graham's unwell. He always seemed so invincible.'

'It was a shock when Heath told me.'

'Apparently he's been missing before and Heath found him.'

Clancy swallowed. She knew there'd been so much more to the bad day Heath had said he'd had with his father. 'That's something I didn't know.'

Brenna clasped her shoulder as Heath, carrying a laptop, headed through the garden gate and across to the group. Bundy walked beside him. Gone was the lighthearted man who'd held her in his arms only hours before. His jaw was as set as mountain granite and deep grooves bracketed his mouth. She clenched her hands against the need to smooth the lines away.

His eyes briefly sought hers before he sat the laptop on the back of her dual cab and ran through which sections of the property were allocated to each pair.

When he was done, his grim gaze swept over the group. 'Please check any body of water.'

Clancy saw her own uneasiness reflected back at her in Brenna's expression. Just what had happened when Heath's father had gone missing the first time?

Leather creaked as riders swung into the saddle and left to start their search. Ned held out his hand for Taite's keys, which he dropped into the older man's palm with a pained expression. With Ned's Hilux still in Clancy's packing shed he was using Taite's four-wheel drive instead.

Beside her Brenna laughed quietly. 'It's like Taite's parting with his firstborn child. The Beast is the only car I know to have its own vacuum cleaner.'

As Ned roared away, Taite sighed before going over to his horse. Taite and the young workman were riding together, which left Clancy and Brenna as the final pair. Their assigned area was a strip on the western boundary that stretched into the high country.

Even though Goliath was saddled, Heath hadn't indicated what section he was searching. She assumed he'd stay close to the house to support his mother as well as to keep in contact with everyone.

But when she and Brenna led Ash and Lulu out, he brought Goliath over.

'There's some old mine shafts,' he said as he swung into the saddle, 'as well as a hut in your section so Bundy and I'll tag along. The sisters have offered to coordinate everything from here.'

Clancy examined his shadowed face. Did he really think that was where his father had gone or did he not want to sit around doing nothing? A shiver rippled over her. Or maybe he didn't want them to be the ones to find Graham if he had been intent on doing himself harm.

She tightened her fingers around the reins to stop herself from reaching out to touch him. Now wasn't the time. He had his emotions locked down. But as they rode away she took comfort from the fact that he and Goliath stayed close to her side. As if aware of the serious purpose of their ride, the gelding was unusually cooperative.

Bundy ran ahead while they crossed the home paddock and made their way towards the boundary fence. The earlier downpour hadn't only erased any trace of footprints or hoof prints but it had caused rivulets to flow in the grassy hollows. Clusters of leaves and twigs were strewn across the track and the wind carried the scent of further rain. Wherever Graham was she hoped he'd found shelter. There was only a few more hours of daylight left.

Her heart grew heavy as Heath kept a constant watch on the ground and their surroundings. She couldn't imagine what he was going through, or his mother as she waited at the house in case Graham turned up. Heath glanced across at her and she gave him a small smile. For a moment the tense line of his mouth softened and then he looked back at the track.

Nose down as though following a scent, Bundy dashed into the trees. Clancy shortened her reins, ready to follow, but as a small mob of wallabies bounded away the cause of Bundy's interest became obvious. She sat back in the saddle and made a silent plea that they found Graham soon.

When they came to a dam, Brenna rode around one side while Clancy stayed with Heath as they covered the other. If his father was here, she didn't want him to discover him on his own. But there remained no sign of Graham or Shadow.

They rode away from the dam to where the trees thickened and the hill steepened. At a small grass clearing Heath took a call from Ned and the workman, who were searching on the eastern boundary. Ned had found hoof prints but as the fence was down he believed they were from a brumby mare who, heavy in foal, was looking for somewhere safe to give birth.

As they continued, the trail narrowed and Heath rode ahead. He led them to a gully in which the far side had been cleared of trees. A dark cavernous space to their right had Goliath snort and sidestep before Heath calmed him. He slipped from the saddle, and after securing Goliath's reins to a fallen tree that was now grey with age, he strode over to what had to be a mining tunnel.

Brenna and Clancy also dismounted. Careful with where she walked, Clancy found another overgrown tunnel that once would have given direct access to a seam of gold-rich quartz. When the undergrowth at the tunnel's entrance showed no sign of being disturbed, she climbed to the top of a mullock dump of discarded rock and soil. Through the trees she saw the remnants of the hut Heath had mentioned.

She motioned for Brenna to come over and together they went to check on the derelict building. Whereas the hut on Glenwood Station where they'd camped was intact and functional, the structure in front of them was nothing but a tin and timber shell. Sheets of corrugated iron lay scattered around the base while others hung at precarious angles, only anchored in place by rusted nails.

'He can't be here,' Brenna said, her voice low so Heath, who approached, wouldn't hear. 'Can he?'

Clancy matched her tone. 'If he didn't want to be found he'd know where to hide.'

Heath didn't say anything when he reached them, just walked into the hut to move and lift tin until there was no space left unchecked. Clancy and Brenna went to help while Bundy sniffed around the hut's perimeter. When they'd made certain Graham wasn't there, Heath's shoulders didn't seem quite so braced.

They returned to the horses. After riding up to the top of a rocky ridge they made their way back along the boundary fence. Soon the slopes gentled and the bush opened up into the green pastures of the foothills. By now the afternoon shadows had lengthened and the chill from the wind seeped through Clancy's coat. Her worry had turned into a hard knot within her stomach. Wherever Graham was he had to be getting cold and hungry. As for the man riding beside her, she'd never seen Heath so rigid or subdued.

She glanced to her left to where the cattle grazed. Amongst all the black bodies she thought she saw a glimmer of grey. She pulled Ash to a stop.

Heath also halted Goliath and looked over to where Clancy stared.

'I thought I saw Shadow,' she said as Brenna too stopped.

Brenna frowned. 'I can't see anything.'

Clancy pointed. 'Look, there. I know it doesn't look like a horse but if Shadow's rolled in the mud she'd be more brown than grey.'

'If the storm spooked her,' Heath said, urging Goliath forward, 'she'd also find some cows for company.'

As they cantered over to the Black Angus cattle there was no doubt Shadow was with them. A whinny carried on the breeze before Lulu answered. The two mares had been stable mates.

Shadow galloped over the rise to meet them, her grey coat streaked in mud and her once red head collar now brown.

Heath was off Goliath and looking her over even before Clancy had brought Ash back to a trot.

He finished examining the mare's feet and straightened, his expression drawn. 'Dad didn't have anything to do with Shadow getting out of her paddock.'

Clancy dismounted and went over to him. Ash would stay where he was. 'How do you know?'

'The cuts on Shadow's fetlock. She's jumped a few fences.'

Brenna spoke from where she remained on Lulu. 'You're right … if Graham had ridden her and anything had happened, being an old trekking horse, she would have stayed with him.'

As a muscle worked in Heath's jaw, Clancy closed the distance between them. 'Now we know your father's on foot we can narrow the search area. He can't have gone far.'

She touched his cheek before stretching to give him a kiss. His lips were cold but as he returned her kiss the tension in his muscles seemed to loosen. When they separated, he rested his forehead on hers.

Clancy spoke again. 'The rain or wind must have triggered a memory or something to make your father go out in the storm.'

Heath seemed to still before he lifted his head. He stared at her, his eyes no longer dark but a clear blue before he pressed a kiss to her forehead. Without another word, he swung onto Goliath's back.

When Clancy walked over to Ash, Brenna gave her a look.

'What?' she asked as she mounted.

'When did *that* happen?'

She willed her cheeks not to flush. Thankfully Heath was enough of a distance behind them to not hear their conversation. 'Today.'

Brenna looked skywards. 'You have no idea how many shooting stars I've had to wish on for you and Heath to finally get your act together.'

'Don't celebrate too soon … we're still getting our act together.'

As much as she'd felt loved when in his arms, there'd been no accompanying words to convey his feelings. Heath was still holding a part of himself back.

'From where I was sitting you have your act well and truly together. You know … when I'm your maid of honour I might actually wear a dress.'

Despite the gravity of the situation, Clancy couldn't help but grin. 'You? Wear a dress?'

'I would.' Brenna's expression sobered. 'Clance … you and Heath have to work out because if you don't it will break my heart. You were meant to be together and seeing your connection gives me hope there might be someone out there for me, too.'

Clancy leaned over to squeeze Brenna's arm. 'There will be, and whoever he is he'll be lucky to have you.'

'He'd just better look good on a horse and not call me little lady, that's all I can say.' Brenna dipped her head towards where Shadow grazed nearby. 'How about I take Shadow back so you, Heath and Bundy can keep searching?'

Clancy nodded as she glanced over her shoulder to where Heath had been. When she couldn't see him, she swivelled in her saddle to take a better look.

There was nothing but green grass and an empty paddock. Heath, Goliath and Bundy had gone.

Heath knew where his father was.

Once through the paddock gate, he leaned over Goliath's neck and gave the gelding his head. Mud flicked up from beneath the blood bay's hooves as they galloped towards the farmhouse.

With the light fading and the temperature dropping, he had to get to his father as soon as possible. And he had to do so on his own. If his reasoning was correct, then his father hadn't again tried to end his life. But there was a chance he was wrong and he didn't want either Clancy or Brenna to shoulder any trauma associated with finding him. His heart pounded in time to Goliath's hoof beats. He just hoped he wasn't too late. Whatever had stopped his father from returning home had to be serious. He could have slipped and fallen or simply got lost.

Between knowing that he hadn't left on horseback and Clancy's words, everything had clicked into place. A faded image had returned of his father, his face thunderous, as he came inside during a storm, his oilskin slick with water. He'd stood in the kitchen, water streaming onto the floor, and opened his coat to reveal a wet and frightened Minnie. Even though the Jack Russell was deaf, the storm had terrified her and, disorientated, she'd run out the kitchen door when a young Heath had mistakenly opened it.

Silver glinted ahead where the farmhouse roof could now be seen amongst the tops of the established trees. Instead of continuing on, Heath turned Goliath towards where the house paddock ran down to the creek. He left the corner gate open and stuck to higher ground as he made a beeline for where the creek curved in a bend and had been the home to rabbits for as long as he could remember.

The murmur of running water filled his ears and he slowed Goliath as they entered the dense bush that protected both sides of the creek. He ducked his head as a low branch loomed in front of him. In the corner of his eye he caught the movement of a small grey rabbit and he checked on Bundy to make sure he didn't set off after it. But the kelpie, tongue lolling, trailed beside him.

The noise of the water increased and they emerged out of the undergrowth to see a creek surging over tumbled rocks and pebbles.

Majestic gums with mottled trunks dipped their branches over the grass-covered banks. Even with it not being the height of summer the small clearing with its shade and its beauty was an oasis of calm and tranquillity.

Disappointment filled Heath, causing his hopes to plummet and his shoulders to bow. Apart from a handmade cross that had once held a small pink dog's collar, the glade was empty. He was sure his father would have come to Minnie's resting place amongst the rabbits that she'd liked to chase, to sit with her until the storm passed.

He went to turn Goliath when Bundy dashed forward and disappeared over the creek bank. He thought the kelpie had set off after a rabbit until he gave a sharp bark. Heath swung out of Goliath's saddle to follow on foot.

At first all he saw was a large branch that had fallen on a flat section of the bank close to the water line. Then Bundy bent his head to lick what looked like a hand.

Heath couldn't remember moving but suddenly he was kneeling in the mud beside the man who he still had so much to say to. The solid end of the branch trapped his father's right leg, while the thinner limbs and leaves pressed across his stomach and left leg. Hand unsteady, he checked for a pulse in his father's neck. It seemed like a lifetime before he felt a faint kick against his skin.

He scanned his father's body for any sign of blood loss but there didn't appear to be any. His arms and legs were straight and there was no injury to his head, as far as he could tell. As much as he wanted to move the branch, he knew he couldn't. His father had been pinned for too long. Any movement of the heavy weight without professional assistance and the after-effects of his crush injury could kill him.

Heath stood to peel off his oilskin and to assess their safety. Even when confused his father would have known better than to seek shelter under a gum tree in a storm with strong winds. It appeared as though the branch hadn't fallen straight down but had bounced off another limb to land some distance away.

After a quick check of the tree to their left to make sure there were no more broken branches snagged in the canopy, he placed his coat over his father's chest. Even though he was wet, he at least wore a thick woollen jumper and tracksuit pants with his boots.

Heath sent a text to his mother. The sisters would organise the local emergency and medical help that his father would need.

He settled himself beside his father and clasped his icy hand, willing his warmth to flow into him.

His father's eyelids fluttered. 'Heath.'

Heath's throat thickened. Not only was his father awake but he knew who he was. 'I'm here.'

'Can't feel my legs … don't move the tree.'

'I won't. Are you in pain?'

'Cold.'

Heath rubbed his hand. 'Help will be here soon.'

'I didn't mean to do it. Just wanted to be with Minnie. She hates storms.'

'I know.'

'There's letters … in the drawer in my desk where the keys were … in case I don't get to say goodbye.'

Heath took a moment to reply. He wasn't ready for this. 'Got it.'

A familiar spark fired in his father's eyes. 'Don't forget.'

'I won't.'

'That's a first, you doing what you're told.' But his father's words didn't contain any edge. He coughed. 'Heath ... I need to explain ...'

'No, it's all fine. Save your energy.'

His father gripped his hand. 'There are things you need to know. They're in my letter but I have to tell you ... while I still can.'

Heath nodded. He needed to keep his father talking and conscious.

'Hawks Ridge was always going to be yours. It's in your mother's name and even if it wasn't it would still come to you. It was the only leverage I had to force you to choose.'

'Dad ...'

'Let me finish.' The bite was back in his tone. 'As for Minnie ... you asked how she died. I was getting the truck out of the shed and she mustn't have heard me and I ran over her.' His father's voice weakened. 'She died in my arms.'

Heath squeezed his father's hand to show that he understood why his father had been so gruff when they'd buried Minnie, and why he also could never face having another pet. The raw emotion and guilt on his face said just how much he'd loved the loyal Jack Russell.

His father continued, his words thin. 'Which brings me to the next thing ... what I said to you the night you left was the truth, but not the whole truth. I promised your mother that when the time came we'd tell you together but like the fool I am I allowed my anger to get the better of me. I need to make things right ...'

The grip of his father's hand on his weakened and as his eyes closed Heath again felt for his pulse.

'Dad ...'

His father's eyes fluttered open and for a moment Heath thought he didn't recognise him but then he spoke again, his voice hoarse. 'Heath ... you are not my son ... but my blood runs in your veins. You are my grandson. Andrew was your father.'

Heath had no words. Shock reverberated through him like the echo of a gunshot.

His father coughed, a hollow, almost desperate sound as he fought to speak. 'Everything I love dies. Just like Minnie, it's my fault the boys are gone. I hadn't fixed Kyle's motorbike so he was on an adult bike that was too powerful for him. And Andrew ... that night he'd told me he was quitting his ag degree to do his art, I told him if he walked out the door he wasn't to come back.' His father's throat moved as he swallowed. 'He never even made it out of the mountains.'

Pain for his parents' loss and the need for answers overrode Heath's disbelief and hurt that all his life he'd been lied to. All this time he'd never known his father blamed himself for Kyle and Andrew's deaths. He'd also had no idea that Andrew, his biological father, did more than just draw pictures as a child at school, that he too had wanted to be an artist.

'What happened to my birth mother?'

'Your mother will have to talk to you about that.' His father gripped his hand harder and tried to sit up. Heath moved so he could prop him up in his arms to make him more comfortable.

His father clutched at his arm. 'I thought if I hated you, I'd keep you safe. But I went too far ... you reminded me of what I'd lost and of what I'd done and I took it out on you.' His father's eyes watered. 'I'm so sorry. Even when it didn't feel like it, I loved you.

Your mother showed me a picture of your mural ... I'm proud of you, and what you've achieved, son.'

Heath had no words except for the ones he'd never spoken to the man who'd raised him. 'I love you too, Dad.'

His father seemed to relax against him. When his eyes closed and his chest rose and fell beneath the oilskin in an even rhythm, Heath thought he was asleep.

Then his shaky voice sounded. 'There's one more thing ... I've had a soft spot for Clancy Parker ever since she took me on over the way I treated you. I thought if I told you to stay away from her you'd do the opposite, but you're being slower than a wet week getting together ... hurry up, your mother needs more grandchildren.'

Heath tightened his hold on his father. The strength seemed to be ebbing from his grip on his arm. 'And you ... you need some, too.'

His father didn't answer, then Heath heard his faint, 'It's time.'

Heath shook his head. 'Stay with me, Dad. Help's almost here.'

His father's hand slipped from Heath's sleeve. 'Goodbye, son.'

As if from a long distance away, Heath heard Ned call his name before Bundy burrowed his nose beneath Heath's arm to rest his head on his father's now still chest.

CHAPTER
18

'I'm rather talented, if I do say so myself,' Ruby said as she turned a floral arrangement around on the packing shed table for Clancy to see the full effect.

'It's gorgeous.'

The satisfaction in Ruby's smile was infectious and Clancy found herself smiling. Over the three days since Heath's father had died, Ruby's high spirits had been a welcome distraction.

'It's great, Rubes,' Hannah said from where she was also arranging wildflowers in a vase.

Both Hannah and Ruby had been helping Clancy with the sorting of her peonies as Ned, like Heath, had been busy at Hawks Ridge. This morning they were finishing the flowers for the church hall where everyone would gather after Graham's funeral in less than two hours. Rebecca was taking care of the more formal church displays but Lydia had asked Clancy if she could do some wildflower arrangements with blooms from Hawks Ridge.

Hannah took a step back from her arrangement and frowned. 'Mine just isn't working. The flowers sit too low.' She looked across at Ruby before reaching for a smaller vase. 'See, I told you we should have picked the everlasting daisies with longer stems.'

When Ruby rolled her eyes Clancy masked her amusement. As well as the jovial banter of the past few days there was also bickering. But underneath Clancy sensed the deep connection between the two siblings.

'Any news on your car?' Clancy asked as a distraction. The hail storm had ended up only hitting her side of town but other cars as well as Ruby's had been damaged. Sandra's garden gazebo had also been ruined.

'It's going in to be assessed next Thursday. Dan's certain it'll be written off so he'll help me look for another one that will be better on fuel.'

Not only had Hannah's matchmaking plan worked between her mother and Dan, Dan's kind nature had already endeared himself to the other two girls. It was Dan's spare car that Ruby was driving until she knew what was happening with hers.

Hannah gave Clancy a contented grin.

Clancy returned to arranging the silver eucalyptus and wildflowers that lay in front of her. Her thoughts rushed back to Heath, as they had done ever since Ned had called with the news about Graham.

Her heart broke for both his loss and for the way his father had died. It had been hard enough losing her parents when they'd been a hemisphere away; Heath had been holding his father when he'd taken his last breath. As much as everyone knew that the prognosis of Graham's Lewy Body dementia hadn't been good, and as much as he'd also polarised people, the community deeply mourned his passing. Lydia had been inundated with offers of help, cooked meals and company.

Clancy stared at her half-completed arrangement that she also couldn't seem to get right. Everyone processed grief in different ways; she'd felt powerless and numb and then angry, but with Heath something didn't feel right. There was no doubt he was grieving but sometimes when she'd caught him staring at the mountains he looked just as distracted as he did sad. While their days were spent apart, every night, except for the last, he'd come over to Ashcroft to stay with her.

They'd still not addressed what was going on between them, but when she woke in his arms the tenderness of his kiss told her how glad he was to see in a new day with her. But even though she'd shared about dealing with her own grief to help him, he hadn't spoken about how he was feeling having lost his father.

While Ned had reassured her that even though Heath didn't discuss his emotions, he still cared, his silence left her increasingly uneasy. If there ever was a time they needed each other it was now. If Heath wouldn't let her in when he was hurting and in pain, would he ever lower his guard?

Restless, she forced herself to finish her arrangement. She needed to get changed and into town to deliver the flowers. Heath had insisted that Rowan not fly home for the funeral, so Rowan had been in constant touch with him. Even though Rowan had reassured her that Heath was going as well as could be expected, she still wanted five minutes to check in with him before they buried his father.

As Hannah and Ruby were not heading to the funeral—Cynthia was representing their family—Clancy ran through what was on the day's to-do list. Between filling existing orders and preparing for the weekend markets the girls would have plenty to keep them busy.

As they both seemed to enjoy sorting and preparing the peonies, she had no doubts that they wouldn't take their responsibilities seriously. They also were smitten with Primrose so the high-energy puppy would be in safe hands.

Dressed in her mid-length black woollen coat and little black dress that she hoped she would next wear on a happier occasion, Clancy drove into town. Earlier she'd texted Heath but so far there'd been no reply. He could already be in town with his mother. If he was, he wasn't the only one. Clancy joined a stream of cars heading along the main street and towards the clock tower. The vehicles then all turned right.

The parking spaces outside the stately sandstone church were full so she drove around the corner. Against the muted sky the weathered copper on the pointed steeple gleamed a subdued grey.

Edith was waiting for her at the door of the church hall. As well as being a member of the quilting club, she also belonged to the CWA, which was catering for the mourners who'd later like a cuppa and a sandwich or a scone. 'Need help with the flowers?'

'That would be great.'

They'd finished their final trip to the church hall when Clancy's phone chimed with a message from Heath asking if she could meet him at the water tower.

When she arrived, Heath was already there. Dressed in a dark, well-cut suit, a crisp white shirt, blue tie and brown dress boots, he cast a sombre figure. Hands deep in his pockets, he stood staring at the mural, Bundy by his side.

At the crunch of the gravel beneath her heels, he turned. She walked into his arms and kissed him.

Conscious they didn't have much time until he needed to be at the church, when their kiss ended she pulled slightly away to ask, 'How's your mum?'

'It will be when she stops that everything will hit her. Dad left some letters and we're going through them this afternoon when it's just us at home, so I might not make it to see you tonight.' Heath ran his hand through Clancy's loose hair. 'Everything okay with you?'

Surprised at his question, she nodded. Funerals always made her miss her parents even more but today wasn't about her.

Heath's gaze lingered before he turned to study the water tower. 'Dad saw the mural.'

'He did?'

'Mum showed him a photo … he said he was proud.'

Instead of sounding happy, Heath's voice was as taut as the wire that ran along the nearby fence. A lost expression darkened his eyes.

'That's wonderful.'

Heath didn't reply as he drew her close for a last kiss before they made their way arm in arm over to their vehicles. Clancy waved him and Bundy off before following.

Even though there was still time before the funeral began, the sandstone church was full. Clancy stopped in the doorway to look for Brenna who'd offered to save her a spot. Past the second stained glass window, Clancy caught sight of Brenna's blonde head next to Taite. As Clancy walked down the aisle towards them, Trent gave her a nod from where he sat on an end pew.

Once in her seat beside Brenna, Clancy fixed her attention on Heath where he sat with an arm around his mother in the front row. A hush settled over the church as the service started. Clancy managed to keep herself together until the moment Lydia kissed her fingertips and pressed them to the fine grain wood of her husband's coffin. When Brenna reached for her hand, they both sniffed.

The mourners left the church to the dull light of an overcast day that appeared intent on delivering the forecasted showers. Clancy joined the procession of cars driving to the cemetery where Graham would be buried beside his two sons. Once the last farewells had been said, people drifted away to return to the warmth of the church hall.

'I don't know about you,' Brenna said as she huddled with Clancy under Clancy's oversized umbrella, 'but I'm ready for a cuppa.'

'Me too but I'll stay a little longer … I want to see Mum and Dad.'

Brenna gave her a quick hug before accompanying Taite to his four-wheel drive.

Clancy wove her way through the thinning crowd to where her family headstones were. Light rain splattered her umbrella canopy and splashed on the toes of her thin shoes. After spending a quiet time in reflection and making sure her parents' flowers were tidy, she walked back to where Graham had been buried.

By now the mourners had dwindled to a handful of locals. Ned stood to one side talking to the sisters while Heath and his mother were over near Kyle's headstone. As she watched they moved to Andrew's plot. Heath's mother covered her mouth with her hand while Heath's head bowed.

Not wanting to intrude, she took refuge from the wind beside an old gum. Heath and his mother's pain was so raw it was as though they were grieving anew for Andrew. Heath drew his mother close as they both remained fixed in place. The minutes passed and the rain turned from a drizzle to a shower.

Clancy left the shelter of the tree to walk over. Neither Heath nor his mother had an umbrella and could use hers. As she approached, they were so engrossed in their conversation they appeared oblivious to her footsteps.

Heath's mother lifted her head to look at him. 'We have lots to talk about. There's so much to explain …'

Heath didn't answer, just stared at the gravestone.

Clancy was so close, she was certain Heath and Lydia would notice her. But still they didn't look her way.

His mother spoke again, words teary. 'If he were still here, Andrew would have been so honoured to be your father.'

Clancy froze. She wasn't sure exactly what she'd heard, all she was sure of was that she needed to back away to allow Heath and his mother their privacy. Except then Heath stiffened before he swung around.

She gave what she hoped passed as a serene smile and offered him her umbrella. 'I thought you might need this.'

Heath's dark gaze didn't leave hers as he handed the umbrella to Lydia. He bent towards his mother to say softly, 'Why don't you see Ned and the sisters. I'll be over soon.'

Lydia gave Clancy a small nod before she did as Heath suggested.

Heath's attention stayed on his mother and when she was out of earshot he crossed his arms and looked at Clancy. Her heart sank. He was again the man he'd been when he'd first come home. Emotionless. Guarded. Inaccessible.

Somehow she had to try and reach him. 'Heath … is what your mother said true?'

He gave a single curt nod. 'It's something I can't talk about.'

She touched the damp wool of his coat sleeve. 'When you're ready, I'm here.'

He didn't reply, just went to shrug off his jacket to give to her.

She shook her head. She didn't know what wounded her the most, the fact he couldn't respond or that his expression was still remote. 'Keep your jacket. Heath … I'm here, if you'll just let me help you.'

'I'll give you a call tomorrow.' The hard set of his jaw said more than words that he still wouldn't be talking about what she'd overheard. 'Let's get you out of this rain. I'll walk you to your car.'

'No thanks. I need some more time here.'

As frustrated as she was that he still refused to let her in, Heath had just lost the man who'd raised him. She had to give Heath the benefit of the doubt. The revelation that Andrew was his father was perhaps only recent and apart from the earlier meeting at the water tower she hadn't seen him for two days. Such news was something that would take time to process and deserved more than a phone call or hasty explanation.

He glanced over to where her parents were buried. His fingers clasped hers before he walked over to where his mother waited.

Clancy remained where she was. The rain had soaked through her black coat to wet her skin. Her hair clung to her cheeks. She shivered as the warmth of Heath's brief touch faded. Would he ever talk to her?

Ned came over with her umbrella to hold it over them both. He looked between her and Andrew's headstone.

While Heath was a master at hiding his emotions, she never was. Her anguish and despair had to be all over her face.

'Did Heath tell you?' Ned asked quietly.

Clancy shook her head. 'It was something his mother said … but she can't be his mother, can she?'

'No.'

The chill that had seeped through her coat reached her bones. Ned's voice didn't contain any shock, just sadness. He'd had a chance to digest the news. Heath had talked to someone ... it just hadn't been her. 'He's known for a while, hasn't he?'

'He has about Graham not being his biological father. It's why he left. But he didn't know about Andrew until Graham told him before he died.'

Clancy briefly closed her eyes. As much as she could understand how Heath's life had been thrown into turmoil, the hurt that he'd never confided in her, especially now, rose like a wave. Yes, they were taking things day by day, but they were also working towards a future together. As for the past nights when she'd revealed her deepest vulnerabilities, he'd said nothing.

Ned squeezed her arm. 'Let's go to the church hall and warm up. Heath just needs a few days to get his head straight.'

'You go. I'll be a little while yet.'

Ned studied her before handing her the umbrella. As he walked away, she knew she'd be a long way behind him. In fact, she wouldn't be going to the wake. She was going home. Her hand holding the umbrella shook. Except she wasn't sure if she could.

She stared at the mountains that had always imparted so much peace and strength. They'd weathered every storm Mother Nature had thrown at them. They'd reminded her of who she was and where she'd come from. But now she didn't feel strong at all; she just felt numb. And adrift again. She needed Rowan to anchor her and he was thousands of miles away.

The hope that Heath would one day open up to her shrivelled and withered until it was nothing but the dust that was turning to mud beneath her feet. The pain in her chest made her feel like she was drowning in grief. Except this time it was her dreams she'd lost. As much as Heath kept her at arm's length, she'd let him in. Into her heart, her bed and her life. The home that had been her sanctuary was now filled with memories she couldn't face.

The rugged mountain peaks blurred. She also couldn't pass the water tower every day and see her naive and foolish smile. Real life would never resemble the beauty of the future that she'd hoped for. Heath not turning to her when his world unravelled spoke volumes. The feelings for her he'd never spoken about couldn't run as deep as hers did for him. She couldn't hang in there. She couldn't keep fighting. The risk of Heath never letting her in was too great.

She turned to walk back to her dual cab, her steps slow and leaden. Heath's mother would need his care and attention and he needed time to work through all that had happened. It wouldn't be fair to complicate what was already a stressful situation by her now needing to know where she stood with him. It was as much for his sake as hers that space needed to be put between them.

Her hand hovered on the handle of her car door. She had a small window of opportunity to do such a thing if she was brave enough to take it. Ned and the sisters would look after Heath and Lydia and do far more to help them than she ever could. All of Rowan's cattle had calved and courtesy of the hail storm her peony season had finished. All it would take was a quick call to Brenna, an hour to throw some clothes into a bag and write a list for Hannah and Ruby and she could go somewhere that wouldn't contain memories of Heath.

She'd never wanted to leave the high country that was such an integral part of her but she needed to get her own head straight. No matter how much she loved Heath, she couldn't be with him if he didn't love her in return. She opened the car door. There was only one place she could go.

Never had a day felt so long.

Heath stared unseeingly out the kitchen window as he waited for the kettle to boil to make his mother tea. She hadn't eaten or drunk anything at the church hall. For the first time since his father had died—he still couldn't think of him in any other way—he and his mother had the house to themselves. As much as the Bundilla community's support had been heartwarming and appreciated, he craved silence and solitude and a chance to pull his fragmented life together.

When he'd made it home after being by the creek, he'd told his mother what his father had said. The time for secrets was over. Through her tears she'd promised him that she'd explain the rest but not until they'd buried his father. She needed time. So they'd made the decision to not open his father's letters until they were alone. He had checked and found four letters in the small drawer of his father's desk that had contained his key stash.

When the kettle clicked off, he reached for the teapot. They were going to need more than one cup. The recipients of the other two letters would soon be here.

He checked the time on his phone. He just wished the afternoon was over and he could see Clancy to explain everything. Until he knew the truth, and whether or not he had another family out there, he hadn't wanted to involve her in the rollercoaster that had been his emotions over the past days. The funeral today couldn't but help trigger her own sense of loss and was why it'd been so important to see her at the water tower. He also still felt it wasn't his story to tell until he knew exactly what had happened for him to end up being raised by his grandparents.

Shoulders tight, he spooned tea into the pot. Before he told Clancy anything, and dealt with every emotion he'd ever repressed, he had to get himself in order. His feelings were so raw and unstable that when Clancy had earlier asked him to let her help him, it had taken all of his self-control to not tell her he loved her. When he did say such long overdue words, he didn't want to be standing in a cemetery where they both were weighed down by grief. He hadn't missed how she'd gone to stand by her parents' graves. He wanted to create happy memories with the woman he'd always loved, memories they could tell their kids.

He glanced out the window at the rolling hills as hope shone through the darkness of his grief. The knowledge that Hawks Ridge would be his gave him a sense of certainty and of belonging. He could be a cattleman and an artist. Once his commissioned overseas murals were completed, he'd focus on projects closer to home and on turning Hawks Ridge into the property it once was. His future with Clancy no longer seemed so out of reach.

When a car engine sounded, he moved to take off his tie and unbutton his shirt collar. The day's heavy emotion was far from over. After placing some mugs and the teapot on a tray, he walked along the hallway towards the living room. While the walls were bare, they wouldn't be for long. The pictures he'd been painting of his father's life sat in the kitchen and he and his mother would hang them later that afternoon.

He sat the tray on the coffee table. His mother had gone to open the front door. Voices murmured before his mother and the sisters walked through the doorway. He still wasn't sure why his father had left them each a letter but he hoped things would soon make sense.

Millicent and Beatrice greeted him with a hug before they sat together on the lounge. They wore identical black suits and expressions of sorrow. His mother poured everyone tea before she looked over at Heath with a nod. He took his father's letters from out of his suit jacket pocket.

When he passed them to their owners, no one moved to open the white envelopes. His mother's mouth trembled before she slid her letter between the tapestry cushion and the side of the armchair. She wasn't yet ready to read the contents. Both Beatrice and Millicent sat their unopened letters on their laps, their hands folded.

Heath felt the weight of his letter and as he pressed the envelope he recognised the shape of a key. He cleared his throat. 'I'll open mine.'

'Before you do, Heath,' Millicent said, her voice quiet, 'we need to tell you how we fit in. It might help you to understand why Graham acted like he did.'

Beatrice nodded. 'I'm not sure how much you know so we'll start from the beginning. Millicent and I were separated when we were seven after our mother died in childbirth and our father was killed in a car crash. Our new families thought it for the best that we had no contact ... they also never told us what happened to our younger brother.'

Heath glanced at his mother whose sad but composed expression hadn't altered. She already knew the connection between his father and the sisters.

Millicent took over speaking. 'Your father was only four when our parents died and like us he never got to say goodbye to either of them. Then, when we were taken into care, he was there one day and adopted out the next. We again never got to say goodbye.'

Incapable of words, Heath looked at the letter in his hand that represented how deep his father's scars had been that he'd never said goodbye to those he loved, even before he'd lost his sons and Minnie.

Millicent kept talking. 'When Beatrice and I were reunited, we went looking for your father. It took a long time. While Beatrice and I had loving families, your father didn't. He'd moved around a lot.'

Beatrice nodded. 'So after we found out he was married and living in Hawks Ridge, we travelled to Bundilla for a visit. When we heard about the loss in his life and then met you at the town Christmas party … we made the decision to move here.'

Millicent, after a glance at Heath's mother, spoke again. 'We never knew you weren't Graham's son but what we did know was that you'd inherited our mother's artistic ability. For you, and in memory of her, we couldn't let such a gift be stifled.'

Heath looked around at the three faces all carefully watching him. 'Your letters … Dad knew you were his sisters.'

Sadness touched Beatrice's mouth. 'He did. We met with him when we first arrived to explain who we were. It's no surprise it didn't go well. But we understood why he didn't want anything to do with us. He couldn't remember his birth family, plus he'd had his own battles to fight over the years.'

Heath's chest tightened as he thought back to the anguish in his father's voice when he'd spoken about losing the people he loved. His mother had been right about his father not letting the people he should into his life. It hadn't only been him that his father had closed himself off from to avoid further pain.

Millicent gave a small smile as she ran her hand over her envelope. 'We'd told him it was never too late to reach out, and now he has.'

Silence settled between them before his mother addressed the sisters. 'I'm so sorry for not telling you Graham was sick, and for not returning your calls. Graham didn't want people to see him like that.' She looked across at Heath. 'I'm also sorry for the way you found out Andrew was your father.'

She pushed herself out of her chair and went to the dark wood sideboard. She took out a thick plastic folder from a drawer and handed it to him. 'We were always going to tell you but it never seemed to be the right time … then you left and I needed things to be resolved between you and your father in case the truth drove you further apart.'

Heath glanced at the folder but didn't open it. In the end the truth had been the thing to bring them together. 'Why was everything kept such a secret? Plenty of grandparents raise their grandchildren.'

His mother didn't answer until she'd returned to her chair. 'When I brought you home, no one asked questions and when they assumed you were ours I didn't correct them. It just became easier to keep things simple for all of our sakes … especially for you.'

'For me?'

'Yes. I needed to … spare you.'

'Spare me?'

His mother brushed at the corner of her eye. 'I loved Willow like a daughter but, as hard as this is to say, she wasn't able to love you like you deserved.'

Heath barely registered that one of the sisters gasped.

'Why?'

'Willow had lived a difficult life. Her father left when she was a baby and her mother was in and out of relationships until they lost contact. Andrew met Willow at a Sydney music festival. She was clever, beautiful and an artist. When Andrew came home that weekend to say he was changing from his ag degree to her art course and moving in with her, he never mentioned she was pregnant. But at his funeral I knew.'

His mother stopped to stare into the distance. 'Willow was mentally fragile even before Andrew's death and their unplanned pregnancy, so I moved to Sydney in her second trimester. When I realised how serious she was about not wanting the responsibility of a child and that she planned to travel north indefinitely to paint, I made the decision to stay longer so you'd both have a home and Willow could continue with uni.' His mother's expression grew fierce. 'I'd already lost two sons, I wasn't losing you, too.'

The tick of the old grandfather clock provided the only sound as Heath and the sisters waited for the rest of his birth mother's story.

'I thought once Willow held you, she'd feel more settled. But no sooner had you arrived than Willow returned to her old life. Within weeks she was back with an ex who made it clear he wouldn't raise someone else's child. She'd be gone for days and then one morning she came to pack her bags and say goodbye. She signed the paperwork so we could formally adopt you but made no plans to see you again.' Sorrow clouded his mother's eyes. 'I continued to do all that I could to help her but six months later while up north she overdosed.'

Heath placed his envelope and the folder on the floor and left his seat to kiss his mother's cheek. As she clung to his suit jacket, he held her. His every question had been answered. Sadness flowed through him for his birth mother whose life, like his father's, had ended before it had begun. She'd been young, vulnerable and would have felt lost and overwhelmed and he could understand why she'd made the choices she had. But in the end, she'd made the right one for him. He just wished she could have found peace.

When he was sure his mother was okay, he picked up his father's goodbye letter. He too would read the contents when alone and his emotions weren't quite so volatile. There wouldn't be anything that his father hadn't already said to him down by the creek, but the key was a final question that needed answering.

He opened the envelope and when he held up the old-fashioned key, his mother's eyes widened. 'That's the attic key. It's been missing for so long I can't even remember when I last went up there.'

With the sisters accompanying them, they climbed the stairs to the attic on the top level of the farmhouse. Heath looked around. As a child he'd come here to try to open the locked door but otherwise he'd never ventured to this part of the house. He slid the key into the lock and had to use force to give it a full turn. The wooden door creaked open.

His mother reached past him to turn on the light just inside the doorway. Heath stared. The cluttered and dusty room was full of paintings. Gilded frames surrounded large and small landscapes while unframed painted canvases were stacked in high piles.

'So that's where they all went,' his mother whispered. 'I thought your father had thrown everything onto the bonfire after Andrew died. He couldn't stand to see art anywhere in the house.'

She walked forward to pick up a painting of a mob of cattle and held it to her chest. Heath could see the signature *A. MacBride* in the bottom corner.

She passed it to Beatrice so she could take a look before moving to one of the landscapes with a gilded frame. 'I was with my parents when they bought this at the art show.' She smiled at Heath, the light back in her eyes. 'We're going to be busy hanging these tonight.'

∞

Morning seemed to arrive far too early in Heath's childhood room. He rubbed a hand over his stubbled face as sunlight cast a too bright glow. His mother's prediction had proved true.

It had been late when the sisters left after helping them. By that time, almost every wall on the house displayed a painting. When he'd had time to himself, he'd texted Clancy to say he'd see her tomorrow before reading his father's letter. When Clancy hadn't messaged back, he assumed she'd been asleep.

He reached for his mobile on the bedside table, realising he hadn't turned it off silent. Clancy had since replied to ask him to give her a call as soon as he could. He flipped off the covers to head to the shower. He had no time for breakfast or even a coffee. What he had to say to her wasn't anything that should be said over the phone. Finally, all the words that he'd held inside for so long could be spoken.

When he and Bundy pulled up at Ashcroft, Brenna's car was under the carport but there was no sign of Clancy's dual cab. This wasn't unusual as her ute would be over at the packing shed. Brenna must be here for an early breakfast. But when he tried the normally unlocked front door, he found it locked, so he rang the doorbell.

Primrose's high-pitched puppy yips answered him before she peered at him from beneath the curtains in the dining room. Footsteps sounded and then the door opened to reveal Brenna in a pink jumper and navy tracksuit pants. Hair messy, she looked like she'd slept over. Except her stern expression didn't look like she'd had much sleep.

'MacBride, it's about time. Another fifteen minutes and I was calling you.'

Uneasiness settled deep into his gut. He looked past her but there was no sign of Clancy.

'You'd better come in. Primrose is doing my head in and needs someone else to use her sad puppy eyes on.' Brenna's voice softened. 'You're also not going to like what I have to say.'

Heath already knew Clancy was gone even before he reached the kitchen and saw the tablet, which she never took from off the bench in case Rowan needed her, was missing.

He swung around.

Brenna put her hands on her hips. 'Don't frown at me ... it's not my fault Clancy isn't here, and no, Rowan hasn't done anything stupid.'

As if sensing the tension, Iris and Primrose disappeared into the living room.

Heath speared a hand through his hair. 'When did she go?'

'Last night. I can't tell you where.'

Too busy thinking, Heath didn't reply.

Brenna took her hands off her hips. 'Aren't you going to ask why?'

'I know why.' Even to his own ears his voice was hoarse. 'I was trying to keep distance between us.'

This time Brenna frowned. 'Why? You love her.'

'That's why.'

At Brenna's confused look, he elaborated. 'I want her to be happy and she only will be if she stays in the high country where she belongs. We both know she's a small-town girl. I didn't want to tell her how I felt if I wasn't sure I could give her a life here ... I wanted her to be free to go her own way if she had to.'

Brenna shook her head. 'MacBride ... if I could, I'd spend the next hour giving you a lecture but you don't have that much time. By making sure Clancy never had to leave, you only ended up giving her a reason to.'

Heath looked to where Clancy's tablet had sat before turning to head out the back door to the coach house.

Brenna called out, 'My lips are sealed but you had better be going where I think you are.'

'I am, as soon as I get my passport.' He glanced over his shoulder. 'Look after Bundy for me.'

CHAPTER
19

Leaving everything she'd ever known shouldn't have been so easy.

Clancy pulled her black coat tighter as she strolled down a Cotswolds street so pretty she kept stopping to take photos. Everywhere she looked delighted her senses, from the flowers spilling from baskets hanging on the ornate lampposts to the wisteria covering honeycomb-yellow stone buildings. The scent of something delicious drifted from the bakery where she'd had lunch yesterday after arriving from Heathrow airport. She'd been jet-lagged and feeling out of place, but when the friendly girl behind the counter found out she was from Australia they'd had a long chat.

A brisk mid-morning breeze bustled by, reminding her of home. She refused to again think of Heath. She'd cried enough tears on the long-haul flight over and when she'd stopped in humid Singapore. Today was all about clearing her head so she could untangle her emotions and think of the best way forward for both of them.

A drop of rain hit her cheek and she looked up at the pewter-grey sky. Who knew the autumn weather would be so similar to Bundilla in the spring? Here too seemed to have four seasons in one day. Her attention turned to the sleepy street. There were other similarities. Cars had to stop for ducks waddling across the road and there were numerous bridges, even if they were made out of stone and not wood.

The wide high street also resembled Bundilla's main street with its quaint shopfronts. Just like some of the members of her quilting club, she suspected the lady in the gift shop liked to gossip. When Clancy walked past yesterday afternoon, she'd popped her head out of the door and said that she'd been talking to Sharon in the bakery and they were sure Clancy had to be Rowan's sister.

When she'd asked him about the gift shop owner after he'd arrived home from work last night, he'd groaned and said not to tell her a thing as it would go around the whole village. He'd made the mistake of saying he was single and now received constant invitations to the town's social events.

While Rowan cast her the concerned looks he had when he'd picked her up from the airport early yesterday morning, he hadn't asked any questions. When he hugged her all she'd said was that she needed space to think. The next thing she'd said was that he needed a haircut.

She took a picture of a red postbox before checking her messages. She kept losing track of what time it was back in Bundilla but it would be the night of her second day of being away. Heath knew she was gone. Brenna had said he'd called around the morning after the funeral and even though he'd been worried he hadn't told him where Clancy was. He'd sent her a text saying he understood why she'd needed to go and that, as soon as possible, they needed to talk.

She hadn't been able to text back until she'd reached London but all she'd said in reply was she hoped he and his mother were doing okay and that it would be best if they were face to face when they did talk.

Even the thought of seeing Heath again, let alone telling him that there could be no future together, made her throat ache so she ducked into a nearby shop. Inside she found a handknitted pink scarf that would be a perfect present for Brenna to say thank you for house-sitting. While she still complained about Primrose being high-maintenance, she had sent a photo of the puppy asleep on her lap as though they were the best of buddies. Clancy also found two stylish beanies for Hannah and Ruby, who sounded like they were having the time of their lives delivering peonies and getting ready for the markets on tomorrow.

As she left the shop an older lady with a golden retriever on a lead walked past. When Clancy smiled, the woman stopped. 'It's cold out today.' When Clancy looked at her dog, the woman nodded. 'You can pat her. Her name's Bella and she's very sociable.'

Clancy rubbed the dog's silky neck. 'I have two goldies at home, a mother and daughter.'

The woman's eyes brightened. 'What are their names?'

'Iris and Primrose.'

Clancy showed her a photo on her phone.

'That puppy is adorable.' The woman seemed to take a closer look at her face. 'You're not that nice young Rowan's sister, are you?'

'I am. How did you know? The accent?'

'You have a similar smile. The local book club's at my place tomorrow night if you'd like to come. It's nothing too serious, we just have a giggle and some wine.'

'Thank you so much. I'll keep it in mind.'

'If you can make it, we usually start around seven. I live at the house with the blue door. Rowan will know.'

Clancy walked away, her steps lighter than they had been. Inside she might feel as though a part of her was missing, but on the other side of the world she'd found a community not so different from the one she'd left behind.

She followed the high street until she reached a wooden bench that overlooked a stream babbling beneath a low stone bridge. As she sat to watch the ducks paddle she stifled a yawn. She now knew all about Heath's jet lag.

She wasn't sure what made her aware of someone in her peripheral vision. All she knew was that her senses became hypersensitive. She caught the faint scent of a familiar high-end aftershave. Then she realised the figure coming over to her had to be Heath.

For the first time in a long time, she was speechless.

Heath sat on the bench, his features tense and expression grave. His hands were anchored in the pockets of his fancy navy coat as though he couldn't trust they would do what they were told. His dark hair was ruffled, jaw unshaven and the lines beside his mouth suggested he hadn't slept any of the hours of his flight.

'How did you find me?' Her voice was a mere whisper.

'I guessed. But you weren't at Rowan's.'

She glanced at her phone. She thought she'd turned off her location settings.

'I'm old school, remember. The very helpful lady with the golden retriever said, after I explained why I was here, that you'd come this way.'

Clancy stayed silent. He might have come after her because he knew something was wrong, but if they were going to move forward, she needed all of him to be fully invested. There couldn't be any more walls between them. She'd planned to do the talking when she next saw Heath, but him coming to see her had changed everything. Not only wasn't she sure what to say, she couldn't make any assumptions about why he'd followed her.

Heath slipped out his phone and touched the screen. He passed his mobile to her. 'What do you see?'

She studied the mural Heath had painted of two children on a wheat silo. 'Your work ...'

'Does anything look familiar?'

She frowned. 'The girl has my hair colour.'

Heath leaned in close to swipe to the next photo.

'The model's skin tone is similar to mine,' Clancy said after a moment.

This time she flicked to the next image. She saw her grey eyes staring back at her.

She looked at Heath. She didn't need to see any more. Heath had painted parts of her in almost every mural he'd done.

'Clance ... you've always been with me. You're all I think about. You're the only woman I'll ever want. It would kill me if I didn't make you happy.'

'Why wouldn't you make me happy?'

When his fingers caressed her chin, she didn't move away. 'As soon as I finished a commission, I'd have to go again. We would have been apart for so long. I could never have asked you to come with me and leave your home and the mountains.'

'That's why you thought I'd be happy with Trent?'

He nodded.

'I wouldn't be, even if I was in Bundilla. I'll only ever be happy with you, wherever I might be, but not if you don't talk to me and let me in.'

'It's not that I can't or don't want to. I thought by holding back on telling you how I felt then if things weren't going to work, it wouldn't be so hard for you to walk away.'

Stunned, she could only stare at him. All this time he'd stayed silent to protect her.

He spoke again. 'As for Andrew being my father, I never knew the whole truth until after the funeral. I'm sorry I didn't say anything earlier but it never felt like my story to tell. Now I've got hours' worth of things to tell you.'

'Hours' worth?'

'A lifetime's worth, Clance. I love you.'

The rasp of raw emotion in his words was her undoing. Everything she wanted to hear was in his voice, and everything she needed to see was in the intensity of his eyes. No longer was he keeping any part of himself from her.

She placed a hand on his cheek. 'I love you, too, Heath MacBride. I'm sorry that I left so suddenly and that I doubted your feelings. I've loved you for so long and I couldn't face the thought that you didn't feel the same way.'

His reply was a slow, tender kiss that said more than any words could just how he felt.

When Heath lifted his head, the corners of his mouth curved. He threaded his fingers through her hair. 'So what are we going to do for the next five and a half days?'

At her narrow-eyed look that he knew exactly how long she was there for, his smile grew before his lips brushed her temple. 'After I'd worked out where you were, Rowan might have sent me your ticket details so I could reserve the same return flight as well as know how long to book our Cotswolds cottage for.'

EPILOGUE

The morning of the official mural opening promised sunny skies and a well-behaved wind.

Dr Davis had set up the podium near the water tower even before Clancy had helped Trent arrange the white plastic chairs in neat rows. The day after she'd returned from the Cotswolds she'd bumped into the vet in town. It must have been jet lag but she'd thought there'd been a flash of regret in his eyes when he'd asked her how she was and she'd answered with a smile. Now that there were no more walls between her and Heath, she couldn't seem to stop smiling. But since then, Trent had been his usually easygoing self. She gave him a wave as he headed back to the vet surgery.

From the city cars and fancy clothes it seemed the media were already here, but no longer did being in the spotlight prove daunting. She was the same country girl who loved her simple life, but she now also had stamps in her passport and was a pro at catching the London tube. Though she still wasn't giving an interview to anyone other than Mabel, especially not smooth-talking reporter Mitch Holden who had just arrived. Mabel would be missed today. She'd flown to Perth to bring her sister back to Bundilla to help her through leaving her difficult husband.

Clancy saw the sisters and Lydia walking over and she went to greet them. The sisters had managed to convince Lydia to come to the next book club and they were often seen together in town having a long lunch.

Taite had made a memorial bench out of Graham's tools for both Lydia and Heath. His mother's bench had replaced the garden one that overlooked Shadow's paddock. She was often there knitting when Clancy and Heath visited. Heath and his mother had also sat there when they'd gone through the photographs of his birth mother and the ones the sisters had kept of Graham.

Clancy took the sisters and Lydia over to where Ned was already seated in the front row. He was back running Hawks Ridge and he and Jasper were often in the kitchen having morning smoko. He was still finding any excuse to swap his Hilux for Heath's silver convertible.

She headed over to where Brenna was unrolling a thick pink ribbon she'd been in charge of choosing for the ceremony. Clancy smiled at tomboy Brenna's preference for girly pink. She only hoped that it wouldn't be long until straight-talking Brenna found someone to ease the loneliness she didn't think Clancy saw.

'It will be winter by the time I can cut through that,' she said with a smile as she approached. As the mural model, it was her job to do the official ribbon cutting.

'These will do the trick,' Taite said as he brandished a pair of oversized gold-plated scissors.

Clancy laughed as Taite eyed the ends of his twin's long blonde hair.

As if knowing what he was thinking, Brenna whirled around with a frown before taking the scissors off him. As much as Taite had filled his life with his deer farm and his sculptures and had no time for dating, Clancy also wished he too would find happiness.

She heard Heath's deep voice and turned to see him near the parked cars talking to a journalist. Bundy wagged his tail as she came over. The footloose kelpie had again attached himself to Heath when they returned a fortnight ago. As Heath was now in the main homestead, Bundy and Primrose were always the earliest ones up, wrestling and causing havoc.

But whenever they'd been in town the past week, Bundy had wandered off. His time with them was coming to an end. She knew Heath was going to miss him and while he did adore Iris and Primrose, she'd left a message for Alice at the animal shelter to let her know if any kelpie puppies came in. If they could survive Primrose, they could survive any puppy.

She waited while Heath answered the last of the reporter's questions. In his jeans, brown boots and blue shirt, Heath could have passed for any of the local cattlemen, even if there was paint on his hands. Last night, he'd shown her the picture he'd finished of her in her crimson gown. As it turned out, the dress hadn't represented the end of a chapter in her life, but the beginning of a new one.

Being with Heath was everything she could have dreamed of. It was as though they never stopped talking. For the short term, Heath would complete his commissioned murals and they'd agreed to not go longer than two weeks without seeing each other. As much as she was a homebody, she'd discovered she liked to travel and now looked forward to exploring the world with the man she loved.

For the long term, Heath would run Hawks Ridge and only take commissions that were a domestic flight away. Ashcroft would always be their home. Rowan had volunteered to move into the coach house whenever he returned and one day would build his stone house across the river.

Heath shook the reporter's hand before coming over to give her a kiss. It was Bundilla's worst kept secret that they were together.

He linked his fingers with hers and led her through the parked cars. 'I have a surprise for you.'

'Please tell me it's coffee. I'll need all the help I can get when Dr Davis starts speaking.'

Heath only grinned as he continued over to his silver car.

A figure stood with his back to them before he turned. A figure on crutches. A figure who hadn't been injured when she'd said goodbye to him at Heathrow airport a fortnight ago.

She glanced at Heath who gave her a wink. Shaking her head, she went over to see just what damage Rowan had done while skiing. Despite her concern, she couldn't hide her delight. Rowan's hair had been cut which meant this wasn't a temporary visit. He was home for good.

His grin was sheepish. 'Turns out I needed to know the emergency number for France.'

Clancy hugged him. 'What's the damage?'

'Broken leg.'

'Perfect.'

'Perfect?'

'Yes, guess who won't be able to do anything but be on Primrose-sitting duty.'

Rowan groaned while Heath chuckled behind her. Dr Davis's voice boomed over the microphone asking for everyone to be seated.

When Rowan used his crutches to walk forward, Bundy by his side, Heath caught her hand to hold her still. She turned towards him and he pulled her close.

'Clance … thank you. For being my muse. For waiting for me.'

Dr Davis's voice called out their names. With no time for words, she let her kiss answer how much she loved him and that she would have waited for him forever. Hand in hand they walked towards the crowd assembled beside the water tower.

Against the cloudless blue sky and mountain peaks, the mural was bathed in sunlight. She didn't think she'd ever get used to her face being part of the Bundilla landscape. She squeezed Heath's hand. But for all the people worldwide that would see her, only the two of them knew the truth behind her Mona Lisa smile. And, one day, so too would the next high-country generation of Parkers and MacBrides.

ACKNOWLEDGEMENTS

As hard as it was to leave Woodlea, my previous small town, when I started writing about the mountain community of Bundilla, it soon felt like home. Bundy, the free-spirited kelpie, was the first to appear and then refused to leave. A cast of characters joined him, each determined to have their stories told against the spectacular rugged backdrop of the Snowies. So, while *Snowy Mountains Daughter* is all about Clancy and Heath's journey, there will be more Bundilla books to come.

A huge thank you to HarperCollins and the very lovely Rachael Donovan, Julia Knapman and Chrysoula Aiello for bringing this new series to life. Thank you also to Christine Armstrong who created the most perfect and beautiful cover. Special thanks to my wonderful writing buddies who had iso inboxes full of emails from me. Thank you to my children, Bryana, Callum, Angus and Adeline. Yes, I always put you in a different sequence on purpose but for this book it is finally in birth order. And thank you to Luke; without you there would be no words.

Finally, thank you to my readers. I am so very grateful for your ongoing loyalty, enthusiasm and support. I hope you could smell the mountain wildflowers, hear the thunder of brumby hooves and that Clancy and Heath's story made you smile. Until the next time we meet again in Bundilla, take care and happy reading.

Turn over for a sneak peek.

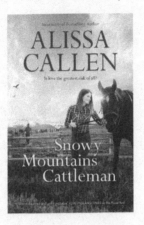

Snowy Mountains Cattleman

by

ALISSA CALLEN

Available February 2022

CHAPTER

1

Grace Davenport had two choices, but she wasn't ready to choose either.

She eased her foot off the accelerator to buy time as the road she'd been on since dawn climbed the sharp incline of a hill. When her car reached the spot where the black bitumen curved over the crest, there could be no turning back.

In her rear-view mirror she caught a last glimpse of the rural town she'd driven through nestled on the edge of the treeless Monaro plain. It didn't matter if her car held some of her most precious possessions, that her Sydney apartment was rented or that a colleague was running her interior stylist business, a single U-turn would send her back through Cooma's wide main street, then on to Canberra and finally home.

Her hand left the steering wheel to hover over the indicator so she could pull over. *Home.* The pitch in her stomach reminded her she no longer had such a place. The parents she'd loved were gone. Her every dream had been blown away by the wind that had scattered their ashes over the pale sand of their favourite beach. First kidney cancer had stolen her mother, and then her father's grief had triggered a heart attack. All it had taken was seven days to dismantle a close-knit family and a lifetime of happiness.

Grace secured her hand back around the steering wheel. She'd driven this road on purpose and the hill crest she'd been waiting for was seconds away. It was time. She had to make a decision: return to the world she knew or drive forwards into the unknown.

Chest tight, she held her breath as her car topped the rise. Everything seemed to still. There was no grief, no loss, just the first look at a distant vista of rugged peaks. Last winter when she'd made this drive with her parents the Snowy Mountains had worn a mantle of pristine snow. Now they were bathed in golden sunlight. Serene, rugged and immovable, they called to her.

Without thought, she pressed her foot on the accelerator and sped down the hill. It was impossible to reclaim what she'd lost, but she could do all that she could to live the life that had been cut short for her parents. As much as her mother and father had enjoyed the beach house she'd bought for them, they'd planned to spend their twilight years in a small town that reminded them of their English village childhoods. She scanned the mountains that now appeared a hazy blue green. On the far-off western slopes, they'd found the perfect place—a little book town called Bundilla.

She settled deeper into her seat and, keeping her eyes on the peaks, readied herself for a long and winding drive. Turning back was no longer an option.

∞

Hours later, with only a brief stop for fuel, Grace passed the WELCOME TO BUNDILLA sign. Despite the ache in her lower back and a non-negotiable need for solitude, her journey wasn't over. She had keys, food and wine to collect, in that order.

A dust-covered white ute approached, the grey-haired male driver lifting a hand in greeting. Grace hesitated and the car passed before she could do the same. On her last visit she'd discovered that the locals waved to everyone, even out-of-towners. While her parents had returned such gestures with enthusiasm, she hadn't been as comfortable. Even when she wasn't preoccupied with work, social skills weren't exactly her forte.

She had no problem conversing about fabric textures and what rugs might suit what hardwood floor, but when it came to casual chitchat, or answering questions about herself, she always felt uneasy. She took the first turn right and banished the schoolyard memories of her English accent being mocked and the taunts about being a whingeing Pom.

A graceful historic building with columns appeared on her left. The old post office was a landmark she remembered along with the red brick clock tower that she could see at the end of the street. Last winter the branches of the Manchurian pears that ran along the footpaths had been bare. Now their summer-green leaves waved in the breeze as if in welcome.

She slowed as she passed the vintage charity shop that she'd spent hours rummaging through. Bundilla also had a regular charity shop with clothes and toys but this one specialised in collectibles and bric-a-brac with all proceeds going to the local hospital. Tucked away in a corner she'd found a perfect duck-egg blue lamp for a living room she'd been styling. Not that she'd been decorating anything of late. It was an effort to even match her socks.

The GPS indicated that she'd soon arrive at the real estate office and she stopped to let two girls cross the road. The younger sister wore a white dress with pink-and-brown cowgirl boots, and she skipped as she pointed towards the park that formed a cool oasis beside the library. The spring in the child's step only magnified Grace's bone-deep weariness. She ignored the uncertainty that would cause her to second-guess her decision to leave the city and instead focused on finding a parking space.

While the street had plenty of empty car spots, the ones directly in front of the real estate office were occupied. A group of three men and one woman chatting outside the building were most likely the owners of the row of utes and four-wheel drives. A tan-and-black kelpie wearing a blue collar with gold lettering sat beside a farmer who wore a wide-brimmed hat. She'd learnt the name of the working dog breed on her previous trip.

Grace parked and left her car to the sound of deep masculine laughter as the local wearing a blue shirt hugged the brunette beside him. While Grace couldn't see their faces, the way the woman embraced him and then kept her arm around his waist spoke of affection and familiarity. Grace looked away, blanking out the long-buried yearning to mean something to someone.

Her lacklustre small talk wasn't the only reason why she was single. Her English parents had sacrificed everything to give her a better life in Australia. She'd worked late nights, weekends and holidays to build her career so she could provide them with everything they'd gone without. Loneliness had been a small price to pay for making the people she loved happy.

She glanced at the man whose easy laughter had made her long to do something spontaneous and out of character like take a day off or dance in the rain. His hair was a sun-streaked tawny brown and his broad shoulders stretched the cotton of his blue shirt that hung loose over faded jeans. He half turned and she caught a glimpse of a tanned, chiselled profile. She again looked away.

Just as well she'd come to Bundilla to rebuild her life and not to socialise. She was far from an expert, but men who looked as good as he did usually had an ego to match. Her best friend, Aubrey, was always telling her she'd catch more bees with honey than vinegar. Not that she was ever rude, but flattery, let alone flirting, wasn't something she'd ever fully understood or seen the point of. She'd once spent two hours of her life that she'd never get back listening to an investment banker run her through his share portfolio over dinner. She didn't have time to waste on shallow conversations, no matter how gorgeous a guy might be.

The local with the felt hat grinned as he slapped the back of the man she'd heard laugh before striding away. The woman and her remaining two companions walked along the street before stopping outside a double-storey pub trimmed in grey wrought iron. The man in the blue shirt held the door open for the others to enter. Instead of following, he waited as if giving the kelpie who had accompanied them time to decide if he would too head inside. As she drew closer, a waft of beer and an air-conditioned breeze washed over her. For a second, she thought the local stared in her direction, but then the dog and the man disappeared into The Bushranger.

Thankful that she now had the footpath to herself, Grace lowered her tight shoulders. *Keys, food, wine*, she reminded herself as her steps dragged. The air pressing against her skin was again warm and she lifted her heavy hair from her nape. If this was a taste of a mountain summer, she'd need a haircut, something that hadn't been a priority for the year she'd been caring for her mother. She'd also need a cooler outfit than the black long-sleeved top and black skinny jeans that had become her go-to clothes.

To her relief, the visit to the real estate office to collect her cottage keys took less than five minutes. The helpful and chatty receptionist didn't expect Grace to reply much in return and she was soon back in the sunshine. She breathed in the aroma of coffee coming from somewhere along the main street and added caffeine to the top of her to-do list. But instead of turning to go in search of the café, she suddenly stopped. Was that a kelpie sitting near her car?

The dog wagged his tail. His blue and gold collar looked familiar and she glanced towards the pub to check whether the locals she'd seen him with earlier were around. But apart from two women strolling towards her with sleek grey bobs wearing similar outfits of black trousers and white shirts, there were no other pedestrians.

Grace stared at the kelpie but didn't move closer. She'd had a sweet chocolate labrador called Cocoa growing up but as an adult her dog-whispering skills were a little rusty.

The kelpie's tail again thumped. The gold letters on his collar spelled out the name Bundy. One thing that had changed in the small town was that the water tower now sported a mural. While she hadn't paid the painting more than a fleeting glance as she'd driven past— she'd been too tired—she had a feeling that a kelpie with a collar like this one had been part of the design.

An impression confirmed when a quiet voice said beside her, 'You might recognise Bundy from the mural.'

Grace turned to the two women who she could now see had to be identical twins. Neither wore a smile but their eyes were clear and kind. As for the seriousness of their stony faces, she wasn't intimidated. She saw a similar expression in the mirror every morning.

She nodded.

The sister whose sleek grey bob was a little longer in length studied her before she spoke. 'Staying in Bundilla long?'

Grace took her time to answer. She wasn't used to strangers being interested in her business, but there was something about the elderly woman's steady stare that reassured her the question had only been asked with the best of intentions. 'How did you know I wasn't passing through?'

A brief smile tilted the other twin's lips. 'Just like how Bundy here knows you're staying at least two nights.' She glanced at the keys Grace held. 'All of the holiday rentals have a minimum two-night stay.'

Grace didn't immediately answer. Her mother had always said nothing much was missed in a small town. It was this sense of community and kinship that her parents had wished to return to.

She glanced at the kelpie who continued to watch her. 'Why would Bundy be interested in how long I'm staying?'

The sisters swapped a quick look before the sibling with the shorter bob replied. 'Bundy's a local legend. He calls the town home and spends his time with whoever he pleases.'

The second sister gestured towards the kelpie. 'By the way he's sitting next to your car, you're the one he wants to tag along with next.'

Grace fought a frown. She had no proper home to take the kelpie to, let alone any food for either of them. Not to mention what would the dog do with her when she wasn't intending to leave her cottage?

The older woman continued. 'I'm Millicent and this is my sister, Beatrice. Bundy's stayed with us many times and we can assure you he's no trouble.'

'He was with a group of locals earlier …'

Beatrice nodded. 'Now he's with you.'

Grace met her gaze. 'He'll be much happier with someone else.'

They all looked across at the kelpie, who had his amber stare fixed on Grace.

Millicent said softly, 'He doesn't want to go with anyone else.'

'If you call into the grocery or rural store,' added Beatrice, her tone gentle, 'they'll give you a bag of the dogfood he likes.'

As if Bundy coming with her was a foregone conclusion, each sister gave her a nod and continued on their way.

Grace narrowed her eyes at the kelpie. 'Really?'

Bundy's doggy grin didn't waver.

'I don't even know if the cottage has power. There's also bound to be rats.'

The kelpie left the footpath to stand beside her passenger-side door.

Grace shook her head at her poor word choice. No doubt Bundy would consider vermin in the roof a good thing.

Surely someone would come over to say what a bad idea this was? But there was no one else in sight.

She rubbed her tight forehead before moving to clear room on the cluttered back seat for the dog to sit. He jumped straight into the car. She slowly closed the door.

That morning, she might have had two choices. Now she had none. In under three minutes she'd become the temporary custodian of Bundilla's living kelpie treasure.

Rowan Parker had been waiting all his life to become a third wheel.

He looked across the pub table in the outdoor beer garden to where his younger sister and best mate sat close together and didn't try to hide his grin. Clancy and Heath might have just come off a long-haul flight from Paris but neither looked jet-lagged.

Clancy, with her red-brown hair and sweet smile, had always drawn stares. But now it was as though she was lit from within. A table to their left filled with tradies in their fluoro work gear had been sneaking frequent glances. He didn't blame them. His sister radiated joy and happiness.

He kept his smile in place even though the contentment within him faded. When they'd lost their parents four years ago after their cruise boat capsized in a flooded Budapest river, Clancy hadn't appeared so radiant. He lifted his beer and took a long swallow. The knowledge that he hadn't been there for her hadn't lost any of its power. He'd been such a fool.

He realised too late that Heath's blue gaze was examining his face. Even before Heath had left to paint a mural on a German skyscraper six weeks ago, he'd been giving him concerned looks.

Rowan forced a smile and made sure his tension didn't show in his voice. 'You have no idea how glad I am you're both home. Every work boot I own is either buried or in pieces.'

Clancy laughed. 'I thought the hug you gave me outside was because you were happy to see me. You just want me to take you shopping.'

Rowan grimaced. He'd rather get bucked off his cantankerous stockhorse than step inside a store.

Clancy patted his arm. 'Monet will soon calm down and stop stealing your shoes. Look at Primrose.'

Rowan raised both brows. There was no hope for Heath's hyperactive kelpie puppy if Primrose was Clancy's measure of a quiet dog. The young golden retriever might technically be out of the puppy phase, but he had no doubt she was the instigator behind the seek-and-destroy mission waged on his wardrobe the second his sister had left.

It wasn't only new boots he needed; his untucked shirt was hiding a rip across the backside of his now only pair of jeans. Just as well Clancy had only been gone three weeks.

Heath chuckled. 'Sorry, Clance, I'm with Rowan on that one.'

Clancy's eyes grew dreamy. 'I can't wait to see all their doggy faces. I loved walking in the Swiss Alps but I've missed them so much.'

Clancy had always been a small-town girl. There was no place she'd rather be than running her peony flower farm and riding in the high country she loved. Now she and Heath were finally together she was discovering a world outside of Bundilla, but their family farm of Ashcroft would always be her, and now Heath's, home. Rowan's grip tightened on his beer. A home he'd left his sister to run alone when she'd been vulnerable, all because he'd allowed a woman's sensual beauty to blind him to who she really was. He avoided Heath's gaze as his best mate again studied him.

The buzzer at the centre of their table beeped and flashed red to indicate that their lunch was ready.

Heath clasped his shoulder as they went to collect their counter meals. 'Let me know when you're heading out on Goliath. I'll come too.'

Rowan nodded. A ride into the granite ridges where the wind carried away all regret sounded pretty good right now. He glanced at the front door as they passed. He wasn't usually so on edge but earlier his testosterone had had a moment that he'd vowed to never have again.

When he'd held the door open for Bundy, a woman on the street dressed in black had caught his attention. All he'd glimpsed was a cloud of long dark hair, pale skin, large eyes and an unsmiling mouth, but that had been enough. The woman had made his blood quicken and his lungs still.

He took his time to reach for his plate of chicken schnitzel that sat on the counter. No longer did he have any appetite. After he'd lost his head over Eloise he'd vowed to never react on a purely physical level to anyone again.

This time when he passed the pub door on the way to his table, he looked straight ahead. Acting on impulse and not taking the time to think through consequences were things he refused to do anymore. He owed it to Clancy, Heath, and all the others he'd let down when consumed with Eloise and then again when he'd fled overseas to get himself together.

Even though he'd dodged a bullet when Eloise had run off with a cashed-up newcomer to town, it had taken time to work though his self-loathing at being so easily fooled. He'd also needed to admit that since his parents had died, chasing an adrenaline rush had been less about the thrill and more about escaping his grief.

He returned to his seat. The only thing he could be grateful for was that the woman he'd seen would be a tourist travelling through town. He wouldn't have forgotten if their paths had crossed before. His reaction and lapse in control was simply a warning that he had more work to do on becoming a new and improved version of himself. He concentrated on listening to Clancy and Heath's travel anecdotes.

When they'd finished their meals, Clancy glanced around the beer garden. 'Where did Bundy go?'

Rowan looked past her shoulder to where he'd last seen the kelpie. 'He was over at the corner table with Ned so he probably followed him out.'

Ned was a family friend who helped Heath's mother run the family property of Hawks Ridge whenever Heath was away painting murals.

Heath's attention didn't leave Rowan. 'Ned said Bundy's spent some time with you?'

'He did but was waiting on the back of my ute this morning to come to town.'

Clancy smiled as she came to her feet. 'He must have known you were coming to meet us.'

Rowan also left his seat. Heath's stare was a little too intent as he finished his beer. Many locals believed that Bundy had a sixth sense. It wasn't unusual for him to turn up wherever he was needed. Over the years he'd kept widows company, sat by the beds of ill children and accompanied a bride who'd lost her father down the aisle. 'No doubt.'

In his case he was sure Bundy only stayed to help him with the cattle work that he'd been doing this past week to get ready for when he'd be working on his next stonemason project. Ashcroft no longer had any working dogs. It had been on Rowan's mind to get a pup to train but after babysitting Monet and Primrose maybe it was an adult dog he needed.

After more hugs were exchanged, Rowan left Clancy and Heath and headed for the grocery store. Now that they were home they'd live in the main farmhouse while he'd move back into the renovated coach house at the end of the garden. He'd left the homestead fridge fully stocked but the fridge over at his place was empty.

The sun warm on his shoulders, Rowan strolled along the main street, his tension ebbing. A white sedan honked its horn as it drove past. He waved at the identical occupants. The sisters were on their way out of town. As he walked by a bright green car his steps quickened.

The colourful vehicle belonged to Cynthia Herbert, the town's equally flamboyant and notorious matchmaker. Except ever since her teenage daughter had turned the tables on her and set her up with the town's longest-serving bachelor, Dan, Cynthia had less time for meddling. But that didn't mean he could relax whenever he came to town.

Conscious of someone watching him through the front window of the nearby gift shop, Rowan crossed the street. He needed to ask Clancy for a list of who was in the quilting club so he'd know who to be wary of. The rumours of the quilting group taking over Cynthia's matchmaking mantle were most likely true. There were only a handful of unattached men in town, and it wasn't his imagination that since he'd returned from overseas, not only did more people smile at him, they were also more interested in his private life. It wouldn't be concerning if almost every person who waylaid him for a chat wasn't female.

He'd almost reached the grocery store when his mobile rang. The name of a local deer farmer who had a talent for turning rusted metal into lifelike sculptures filled the screen. Taite too was single and determined to remain that way.

'Hi,' Rowan said, jogging the last few paces to the grocery store so he could duck inside the sliding door. Mrs Wright had exited the gift shop and now stood on the footpath looking up and down the street.

'You sound out of breath,' Taite said, tone hopeful.

Taite loved his rugby and was always trying to recruit Rowan for a gym session or run even though it was the off-season. Thanks to a stress fracture of his left leg last spring while skiing in France, he had a legitimate excuse to not put his body on the line. No one could keep up with Taite's agility or strength. A *simple* jog would probably lead to heart failure.

'Don't get too excited. Desperate times call for desperate measures.' Rowan rubbed at the dull ache in his leg. 'I'm not out of breath. I'm as fit as a mallee bull.'

'That would be a lame mallee bull.' Taite chuckled. 'The only thing to get you past a walk is either being chased by Mrs Moore's goose or Mrs Moore herself.'

Rowan peered through the glass door. 'It's Mrs Wright.'

'You wonder why I run. It's impossible to ask a moving target to dinner.'

'I might join you.'

'Anytime. I've been going out on Overflow Road.'

Rowan silenced his groan as the doors opened for two teenage girls to walk through. Overflow Road was gravel and all uphill. 'Actually, I'll take my chances with the quilting ladies.'

'You always were a risk-taker.'

When the teenagers shot him flirty looks as they passed, he turned to study the community noticeboard on the back wall that advertised the upcoming Bundilla summer book festival. He was far too old for either of them.

'Trust me, not anymore.'

'I can't tempt you into going mountain biking this weekend at Thredbo?'

Rowan went to say yes and then reconsidered. His leg wasn't up to it plus he was supposed to have retired from thrill-seeking. 'Thanks, but I've got farm work to do before I start on the old Russell mansion next week.'

'Good luck. That place will be a big job. Let me know if you change your mind about the run or mountain biking.'

'Will do.'

Rowan ended the call and, not bothering with a basket, strode along the grocery store aisles. With his arms full of items, he made a beeline for an empty checkout. Heels had clicked on the floor behind him as he'd collected a bottle of milk and he wasn't hanging around to see who it was.

Once outside, he didn't slow his pace as he strode along to where he'd left his dark merlot-red Land Cruiser parked outside the real estate office. That would teach him not to buy a white vehicle so that he blended in with just about every other Bundilla car. Everyone knew when he was in town.

After he'd loaded his grocery bag into the passenger seat he scanned the street for any glimpse of Bundy. As chaotic as it had been having him to stay the past week—the kelpie, Monet and Primrose had wrestled continuously—he now missed having Bundy by his side. Wherever he had moved on to next he hoped it wouldn't be long until he saw him again.

Instead of driving the regular way home, Rowan took the road that carried him over one of the wooden bridges that crisscrossed the flood plain. He'd do a drive by the Russell place. A heavy chain and padlock would secure the front gate shut but he'd be able to see from the driveway if the left-side wall had crumbled any further since his last inspection.

Not that he knew exactly when he'd be starting the restoration. The new owner hadn't replied to his last email, which wasn't out of the ordinary. She'd simply be busy. From the woman's succinct messages he knew nothing more about her except she'd purchased the derelict mansion sight unseen. Her plan was to focus on the stonework first before she brought in a builder. She obviously wasn't in any rush to make the place liveable.

The ute indicator sounded as he took the next turn left to where the valley floor had given way to the gentle undulation of foothills that stretched into granite peaks. A buzz of anticipation filled him. While he was foremost a cattleman, there was no doubt the DNA of a distant Scottish stonemason ran through his veins.

For years the mysterious mansion had fascinated him. Not because it was built of bluestone quarried from a nearby hillside, or because it was said to be both haunted and cursed as none of the last generation had married. His interest had been piqued because whenever he'd been inside something about the layout had felt off and had niggled at him.

Through the trees he made out the angular shapes of chimneys and the rusted planes of a vast roofline. When he reached the usually locked entryway, the gate was open and the chain missing. Without slowing, he continued towards the house to follow the tyre tracks imprinted in the dust. Not only had someone disregarded the large NO TRESPASSING sign that the new owner had organised to be put on the fence, but they'd cut the padlock and stolen the chain. He'd make sure whoever the culprit was, they weren't intent on doing any harm. The old house had already been damaged enough.

When black flashed in his peripheral vison, he didn't think anything of it. Crows liked the abandoned building as much as teenagers did at Halloween or whenever there was a full moon. But no sooner did he register that the shape had legs, he noted an unfamiliar bronze car over near a jacaranda tree to his left.

He parked beside the vehicle. He had no doubt the dog he'd seen was Bundy. He also had no doubt the car beside him wasn't local. The sticker on the back windscreen displayed the name of a Sydney car dealership. He left his driver's seat and walked around to the front of the mansion to meet Bundy as he bounded through the overgrown garden towards him.

'Hi, mate.' Rowan ruffled the kelpie's neck. 'I'm happy to see you too.'

He glanced at the corner of the house where he'd first glimpsed Bundy. He wasn't superstitious but he had a bad feeling about who the kelpie had accompanied here. Bundy turned to look in the same direction, his wagging tail thumping Rowan's leg.

Even before his brain fully catalogued the details of the figure who rounded the house corner, his gut knew it was the woman he'd seen earlier. If Bundy was with her, she also wasn't passing through; she'd have a holiday rental nearby.

He locked his shoulders and his resolve. This time he wasn't reacting to her with anything but mild and curious interest. No matter if every step that brought her closer reinforced how stunning she was.

The stranger wore no makeup and in the full daylight her flawless skin was pale and smooth. In contrast, her windblown hair was a messy and rich brown that spilled over her shoulders. But it was her mouth that he had trouble looking away from. The longer he stared at the sombre curve the more he wanted to make her smile.

The woman stopped a body length away. While her expression was unreadable, just like with the high-country brumbies he sensed an ingrained caution and wariness. But when her chin tilted and her cool hazel gaze met his, any impression of vulnerability vanished.

'Afternoon,' she said, her voice as chilly as the snow that capped the winter mountain peaks.

Rowan grinned. 'Afternoon.' He couldn't have asked for a more perfect reaction. Whatever attraction he felt towards her was one-sided. The reminder he wasn't irresistible would do his male ego good. 'Can I help you?'

She shook her head as she lifted a hand to brush her tousled hair away from her cheek.

When the silence lengthened, he dipped his head towards the mansion, not hiding his reaction to the graffiti or broken windows. He hated seeing the once stately house in such disrepair. 'This is private property. You can understand why the owner isn't keen on people trespassing.'

When his attention returned to the woman, her eyes had widened. But when she turned to study the vandalised front facade all he could view was her profile.

The seconds stretched before she replied. 'It is a shame there's been so much damage.' The subtle lilt of an English accent softened her voice and her tone was now more weary than frosty. 'I know this is private property ... you see, it's my private property.'

Other books by

ALISSA CALLEN

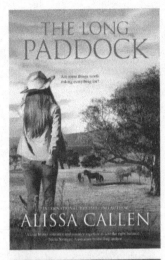

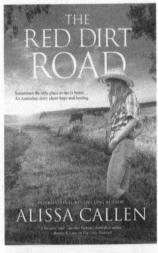

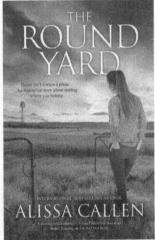

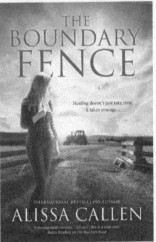

talk about it

Let's talk about books.

Join the conversation:

 facebook.com/romanceanz

 @romanceanz

romance.com.au

If you love reading and want to know about our
authors and titles, then let's talk about it.